Praise for *New York Times* bestselling author Maisey Yates

"Yates's characters are masterfully written with a keen eye for establishing emotional depth… Each book [is] like a mini vacation."
—*RT Book Reviews*

"Fans of Robyn Carr and RaeAnne Thayne will enjoy [Yates's] small-town romance."
—*Booklist*

"Yates's thrilling seventh Copper Ridge contemporary proves that friendship can evolve into scintillating romance…. This is a surefire winner not to be missed."
—*Publishers Weekly*
on *Slow Burn Cowboy* (starred review)

Praise for *USA TODAY* bestselling author Naima Simone

"A passionate romance full of drama, family secrets and ultimately love."
—*Harlequin Junkie* on *The Billionaire's Bargain*

"Passion, heat and deep emotion—Naima Simone is a gem!"
—*New York Times* bestselling author Maisey Yates

New York Times bestselling author **Maisey Yates** lives in rural Oregon with her three children and her husband, whose chiseled jaw and arresting features continue to make her swoon. She feels the epic trek she takes several times a day from her office to her coffee maker is a true example of her pioneer spirit.

USA TODAY bestselling author **Naima Simone**'s love of romance was first stirred by Johanna Lindsey and Nora Roberts years ago. Well, not that many. She is only eighteen…ish. Published since 2009, she spends her days writing sizzling romances with heart, a touch of humor and snark. She is wife to Superman—or his non-Kryptonian equivalent—and mother to the most awesome kids ever. They live in perfect, sometimes domestically challenged bliss in the southern US.

New York Times Bestselling Author

MAISEY YATES

TAKE ME, COWBOY

**HARLEQUIN
BESTSELLING
AUTHOR
COLLECTION**

**HARLEQUIN®
BESTSELLING
AUTHOR
COLLECTION**

Recycling programs
for this product may
not exist in your area.

ISBN-13: 978-1-335-40621-7

Take Me, Cowboy
First published in 2016. This edition published in 2022.
Copyright © 2016 by Maisey Yates

The Billionaire's Bargain
First published in 2019. This edition published in 2022.
Copyright © 2019 by Naima Simone

For questions and comments about the quality of this book, please contact us at CustomerService@Harlequin.com.

Harlequin Enterprises ULC
22 Adelaide St. West, 41st Floor
Toronto, Ontario M5H 4E3, Canada
www.Harlequin.com

Printed in U.S.A.

CONTENTS

TAKE ME, COWBOY

Maisey Yates

To Nicole Helm, for your friendship,
profane texts and love of farm animals in sweaters.
My life would be boring without you.

Chapter 1

When Anna Brown walked into Ace's bar, she was contemplating whether or not she could get away with murdering her older brothers.

That's really nice that the invitation includes a plus one. You know you can't bring your socket wrench.

She wanted to punch Daniel in his smug face for that one. She had been flattered when she'd received her invitation to the community charity event that the West family hosted every year. A lot less so when Daniel and Mark had gotten ahold of it and decided it was the funniest thing in the world to imagine her trying to get a date to the coveted fund-raiser.

Because apparently the idea of her having a date at all was the pinnacle of comedic genius.

I can get a date, jackasses.

You want to make a bet?

Sure. It's your money.

That exchange had seemed both enraging and empowering about an hour ago. Now she was feeling both humiliated and a little bit uncertain. The fact that she had bet on her dating prowess was…well, embarrassing didn't even begin to describe it. But on top of that, she was a little concerned that she had no prowess to speak of.

It had been longer than she wanted to admit since she'd actually had a date. In fact, it was entirely possible that she had never technically been on one. That quick roll in the literal hay with Corbin Martin hadn't exactly been a date per se.

And it hadn't led to anything, either. Since she had done a wonderful job of smashing his ego with a hammer the next day at school when she'd told her best friend, Chase, about Corbin's…limitations.

Yeah, her sexual debut had also been the final curtain.

But if men weren't such whiny babies, maybe that wouldn't have been the case. Also, maybe if Corbin had been able to prove to her that sex was worth the trouble, she would view it differently.

But he hadn't. So she didn't.

And now she needed a date.

She stalked across the room, heading toward the table that she and Chase, and often his brother, Sam, occupied on Friday nights. The lighting was dim, so she knew someone was sitting there but couldn't make out which McCormack brother it was.

She hoped it was Chase. Because as long as she'd known Sam, she still had a hard time making conversation with him.

Talking wasn't really his thing.

She moved closer, and the man at the table tilted his head up. Sam. Dammit. Drinking a beer and looking grumpy, which was pretty much par for the course with him. But Chase was nowhere to be seen.

"Hi," she said, plopping down in the chair beside him. "Bad day?"

"A day."

"Right." At least when it came to Sam, she knew the difficult-conversation thing had nothing to do with her. That was all him.

She tapped the top of her knee, looking around the bar, trying to decide if she was going to get up and order a drink or wait for someone to come to the table. She allowed her gaze to drift across the bar, and her attention was caught by the figure of a man in the corner, black cowboy hat on his head, his face shrouded by the dim light. A woman was standing in front of him looking up at his face like he was her every birthday wish come true.

For a moment the sight of the man standing there struck her completely dumb. Broad shoulders, broad chest, strong-looking hands. The kind of hands that made her wonder if she needed to investigate the potential fuss of sex again.

He leaned up against the wall, his forearm above his head. He said something and the little blonde he was talking to practically shimmered with excitement. Anna wondered what that was like. To be the focus of a man's attention like that. To have him look at you like a sex object instead of a drinking buddy.

For a moment she envied the woman standing there, who could absolutely get a date if she wanted one. Who would know what to wear and how to act if she were invited to a fancy gala whatever.

That woman would know what to do if the guy wanted to take her home after the date and get naked. She wouldn't be awkward and make jokes and laugh when he got naked because there were all these feelings that were so...so weird she didn't know how else to react.

With a man like that one...well, she doubted she would laugh. He would be all lean muscle and wicked smiles. He would look at her and she would... Okay, even in fantasy she didn't know. But she felt hot. Very, very hot.

But in a flash, that hot feeling turned into utter horror. Because the man shifted, pushing his hat back on his head and angling slightly toward Anna, a light from above catching his angular features and illuminating his face. He changed then, from a fantasy to flesh and blood. And she realized exactly who she had just been checking out.

Chase McCormack. Her best friend in the entire world. The man she had spent years training herself to never, ever have feelings below the belt for.

She blinked rapidly, squeezing her hands into fists and trying to calm the fluttering in her stomach. "I'm going to get a drink," she said, looking at Sam. *And talk to Ace about the damn lighting in here.* "Did you want something?"

He lifted his brow, and his bottle of beer. "I'm covered."

Her heart was still pounding a little heavier than usual when she reached the bar and signaled Ace, the establishment's owner, to ask for whatever pale ale he had on tap.

And her heart stopped altogether when she heard a deep voice from behind her.

"Why don't you make that two."

She whisked around and came face-to-chest with Chase. A man whose presence should be commonplace, and usually was. She was just in a weird place, thanks to high-pressure invitations and idiot brothers.

"Pale ale," she said, taking a step back and looking up at his face. A face that should also be commonplace. But it was just so very symmetrical. Square jaw, straight nose, strong brows and dark eyes that were so direct they bordered on obscene. Like they were looking straight through your clothes or something. Not that he would ever want to look through hers. Not that she would want him to. She was too smart for that.

"That's kind of an unusual order for you," she continued, more to remind herself of who he was than to actually make commentary on his beverage choices. To remind herself that she knew him better than she knew herself. To do whatever she could to put that temporary moment of insanity when she'd spotted him in the corner out of her mind.

"I'm feeling adventurous," he said, lifting one corner of his mouth, the lopsided grin disrupting the symmetry she had been admiring earlier and somehow making him look all the more compelling for it.

"Come on, McCormack. Adventurous is bungee jumping from Multnomah Falls. Adventurous is not trying a new beer."

"Says the expert in adventure?"

"I'm an expert in a couple of things. Beer and motor oil being at the top of the list."

"Then I won't challenge you."

"Probably for the best. I'm feeling a little bit blood-thirsty tonight." She pressed her hands onto the bar top and leaned forward, watching as Ace went to get their drinks. "So. Why aren't you still talking to short, blonde and stacked over there?"

He chuckled and it settled oddly inside her chest, rattling around before skittering down her spine. "Not really all that interested."

"You seemed interested to me."

"Well," he said, "I'm not."

"That's inconsistent," she said.

"Okay, I'll bite," he said, regarding her a little more closely than she would like. "Why are you in the mood to cause death and dismemberment?"

"Do I seem that feral?"

"Completely. Why?"

"The same reason I usually am," she said. "Your brothers."

"You're fast, I like that."

Ace returned to their end of the bar and passed two pints toward them. "Do you want to open a tab?"

"Sure," she said. "On him." She gestured to Chase.

Ace smiled in return. "You look nice tonight, Anna."

"I look…the same as I always do," she said, glancing down at her worn gray T-shirt and no-fuss jeans.

He winked. "Exactly."

She looked up at Chase, who was staring at the bartender, his expression unreadable. Then she looked back at Ace.

Ace was pretty hot, really. In that bearded, flannel-wearing way. Lumbersexual, or so she had overheard some college girls saying the other night as they giggled over him. Maybe *he* would want to be her date. Of course, easy compliments and charm aside, he also had his pick of any woman who turned up in his bar. And Anna was never anyone's pick.

She let go of her fleeting Ace fantasy pretty quickly.

Chase grabbed the beer from the counter and handed one to her. She was careful not to let their fingers brush as she took it from him. That type of avoidance was second nature to her. Hazards of spending the years since adolescence feeling electricity when Chase got too close, and pretending she didn't.

"We should go back and sit with Sam," she suggested. "He looks lonely."

Chase laughed. "You and I both know he's no such thing. I think he would rather sit there alone."

"Well, if he wants to be alone, then he can stay at home and drink."

"He probably would if I didn't force him to come out. But if I didn't do that, he would fuse to the furniture and then I would have all of that to deal with."

They walked back over to the table, and gradually, her heart rate returned to normal. She was relieved that the initial weirdness she had felt upon his arrival was receding.

"Hi, Sam," Chase said, taking his seat beside his brother. Sam grunted in response. "We were just talking about the hazards of you turning into a hermit."

"Am I not a convincing hermit already?" he asked. "Do I need to make my disdain for mankind a little less subtle?"

"That might help," Chase said.

"I might just go play a game of darts instead. I'll catch up with you in a minute." Sam took a long drink of his beer and stood, leaving the bottle on the table as he made his way over to the dartboard across the bar.

Silence settled between Chase and herself. Why was this suddenly weird? Why was Anna suddenly conscious of the way his throat moved when he swallowed a sip of beer, of the shift in his forearms as he set the bottle back down on the table? Of just how masculine a sound he made when he cleared his throat?

She was suddenly even conscious of the way he breathed.

She leaned back in her chair, lifting her beer to her lips and surveying the scene around them.

It was Friday night, so most of the town of Copper Ridge, Oregon, was hanging out, drowning the last vestiges of the workweek in booze. It was not the end of the workweek for Anna. Farmers and ranchers didn't take time off, so neither did she. She had to be on hand to make repairs when necessary, especially right now, since she was just getting her own garage off the ground.

She'd just recently quit her job at Jake's in order to open her own shop specializing in heavy equipment, which really was how she found herself in the position she was in right now. Invited to the charity gala thing and embroiled in a bet on whether or not she could get a date.

"So why exactly do you want to kill your brothers today?" Chase asked, startling her out of her thoughts.

"Various reasons." She didn't know why, but something stopped her from wanting to tell him exactly what was going on. Maybe because it was humiliating. Yes, it was definitely humiliating.

"Sure. But that's every day. Why specifically do you want to kill them today?"

She took a deep breath, keeping her eyes fixed on the fishing boat that was mounted to the wall opposite her, and very determinedly not looking at Chase. "Because. They bet that I couldn't get a date to this thing I'm invited to and I bet them that I could." She thought about the woman he'd been talking to a moment ago. A woman so different from herself they might as well be different species. "And right about now I'm afraid they're right."

Chase was doing his best to process his best friend's statement. It was difficult, though. Daniel and Mark had solid asshole tendencies when it came to Anna—that much he knew—but this was pretty low even for them.

He studied Anna's profile, her dark hair pulled back into a braid, her gray T-shirt that was streaked with oil. He watched as she raised her bottle of beer to her lips. She had oil on her hands, too. Beneath her fingernails. Anna wasn't the kind of girl who attracted a lot of male attention. But he kind of figured that was her choice.

She wasn't conventionally beautiful. Mostly because of the motor oil. But that didn't mean that getting a date should be impossible for her.

"Why don't you think you can get a date?"

She snorted, looking over at him, one dark brow raised. "Um." She waved a hand up and down, indicating her body. "Because of all of this."

He took a moment to look at *all of that*. Really look.

Like he was a man and she was a woman. Which they were, but not in a conventional sense. Not to each other. He'd looked at her almost every day for the past fifteen years, so it was difficult to imagine seeing her for the first time. But just then, he tried.

She had a nice nose. And her lips were full, nicely shaped, her top lip a little fuller than her bottom lip, which was unique and sort of…not sexy, because it was Anna. But interesting.

"A little elbow grease and that cleans right off," he said. "Anyway, men are pretty simple."

She frowned. "What does that mean?"

"Exactly what it sounds like. You don't have to do much to get male attention if you want it. Give a guy what he's after…"

"Okay, that's just insulting. You're saying that I can get a guy because men just want to get laid? So it doesn't matter if I'm a wrench-toting troll?"

"You are not a wrench-toting troll. You're a wrench-toting woman who could easily bludgeon me to death, and I am aware of that. Which means I need to choose my next words a little more carefully."

Those full lips thinned into a dangerous line, her green eyes glittering dangerously. "Why don't you do that, Chase."

He cleared his throat. "I'm just saying, if you want a date, you can get one."

"By unzipping my coveralls down to my belly button?"

He tipped his beer bottle back, taking a larger swallow than he intended to, coughing as it went down wrong. He did not need to picture the visual she had just handed to him. But he was a man, so he did.

It was damned unsettling. His best friend, bare beneath a pair of coveralls unfastened so that a very generous wedge of skin was revealed all the way down...

And he was done with that. He didn't think of Anna that way. Not at all. They'd been friends since they were freshmen in high school and he'd navigated teenage boy hormones without lingering too long on thoughts of her breasts.

He was thirty years old, and he could have sex whenever he damn well pleased. Breasts were no longer mysterious to him. He wasn't going to go pondering the mysteries of *her* breasts now.

"It couldn't hurt, Anna," he said, his words containing a little more bite than he would like them to. But he was unsettled.

"Okay, I'll keep that in mind. But barring that, do you have any other suggestions? Because I think I'm going to be expected to wear something fancy, and I don't own anything fancy. And it's obvious that Mark and Daniel think I suck at being a girl."

"That's not true. And anyway, why do you care what they—or anyone else—think?"

"Because. I've got this new business..."

"And anyone who brings their heavy equipment to you for a tune-up won't care whether or not you can walk in high heels."

"But I don't want to show up at these things looking..." She sighed. "Chase, the bottom line is I've spent a long time not fitting in. And people here are nice to me. I mean, now that I'm not in school. People in school sucked. But I get that I don't fit. And I'm tired of it. Honestly, I wouldn't care about my brothers if there wasn't so much...truth to the teasing."

"They do suck. They're awful. So why does it matter what they think?"

"Because," she said. "It just does. I'm that poor Anna Brown with no mom to teach her the right way to do things and I'm just…tired of it. I don't want to be poor Anna Brown. I want to be Anna Brown, heavy equipment mechanic who can wear coveralls and walk in heels."

"Not at the same time, I wouldn't think."

She shot him a deadly glare. "I don't fail," she said, her eyes glinting in the dim bar light. "I won't fail at this."

"You're not in remote danger of failing. Now, what's the mystery event that has you thinking about high heels?" he asked.

Copper Ridge wasn't exactly a societal epicenter. Nestled between the evergreen mountains and a steel-gray sea on the Oregon Coast, there were probably more deer than people in the small town. There were only so many events in existence. And there was a good chance she was making a mountain out of a small-town molehill, and none of it would be that big of a deal.

"That charity thing that the West family has every year," she mumbled. "Gala Under the Stars or whatever."

The West family's annual fund-raising event for schools. It was a weekend event, with the town's top earners coming to a small black-tie get-together on the West property.

The McCormacks had been founding members of the community of Copper Ridge back in the 1800s. Their forge had been used by everyone in town and in the neighboring communities. But as the economy had changed, so had the success of the business.

They'd been hanging on by their fingernails when Chase's parents had been killed in an accident when he was in high school. They'd still gotten an invitation to the gala. But Chase had thrown it on top of the never-ending pile of mail and bills that he couldn't bring himself to look through and forgotten about it.

Until some woman—probably an assistant to the West family—had called him one year when he hadn't bothered to RSVP. He had been...well, he'd been less than polite.

Dealing with a damned crisis here, so sorry I can't go to your party.

Unsurprisingly, he hadn't gotten any invitations after that. And he hadn't really thought much about it since.

Until now.

He and Sam had managed to keep the operation and properties afloat, but he wanted more. He needed it.

The ranch had animals, but that wasn't the source of their income. The forge was the heart of the ranch, where they did premium custom metal-and-leatherwork. On top of that, there were outbuildings on the property they rented out—including the shop they leased to Anna. They had built things back up since their parents had died, but it still wasn't enough, not to Chase.

He had promised his father he would take an interest in the family legacy. That he would build for the McCormacks, not just for himself. Chase had promised he wouldn't let his dad down. He'd had to make those promises at a grave site because before the accident he'd been a hotheaded jackass who'd thought he was too big for the family legacy.

But even if his father never knew, Chase had sworn it. And so he'd see it done.

In order to expand McCormack Iron Works, the heart and soul of their ranch, to bring it back to what it had been, they needed interest. Investments.

Chase had always had a good business mind, and early on he'd imagined he would go to school away from Copper Ridge. Get a degree. Find work in the city. Then everything had changed. Then it hadn't been about Chase McCormack anymore. It had been about the McCormack legacy.

School had become out of the question. Leaving had been out of the question. But now he saw where he and Sam were failing, and he could see how to turn the tide.

He'd spent a lot of late nights figuring out exactly how to expand as the demand for handmade items had gone down. Finding ways to convince people that highly customized iron details for homes and businesses, and handmade leather bridles and saddles, were worth paying more for.

Finding ways to push harder, to innovate and modernize while staying true to the family name. While actively butting up against Sam and his refusal to go out and make that happen. Sam, who was so talented he didn't have to pound horseshoe nails if he didn't want to. Sam, who could forget gates and scrollwork on staircases and be selling his artwork for a small fortune. Sam, who resisted change like it was the black plague.

He would kill for an invitation to the Wests' event. Well, not kill. But possibly engage in nefarious activities or the trading of sexual favors. And Anna had an invitation.

"You get to bring a date?" he asked.

"That's what I've been saying," she said. "Of course, it all depends on whether or not I can actually acquire one."

Anna needed a date; he wanted to have a chance to talk to Nathan West. In the grand tradition of their friendship, they both filled the gaps in each other's lives. This was—in his opinion—perfect.

"I'll be your date," he said.

She snorted. "Yeah, right. Daniel and Mark will never believe that."

She had a point. The two of them had been friends forever. And with a bet on the table her brothers would never believe that he had suddenly decided to go out with her because his feelings had randomly changed.

"Okay. Maybe that's true." That frown was back. "Not because there's something wrong with you," he continued, trying to dig himself out of the pit he'd just thrown himself into, "but because it's a little too convenient."

"Okay, that's better."

"But what if we made it clear that things had changed between us?"

"What do you mean?"

"I mean…what if…we built up the change? Showed people that our relationship was evolving."

She gave him a fierce side-eye. "I'm not your type." He thought back to the blonde he'd been talking to only twenty minutes earlier. Tight dress cut up to the tops of her thighs, long, wavy hair and the kind of smile that invited you right on in. Curves that had probably wrecked more men than windy Highway 101. She was his type.

And she wasn't Anna. Barefaced, scowling with a figure that was slightly more...subtle. He cleared his throat. "You could be. A little less grease, a little more lipstick."

Her top lip curled. "So the ninth circle of hell basically."

"What were you planning on wearing to the fundraiser?"

She shifted uncomfortably in her seat. "I have black jeans. But... I mean, I guess I could go to the mall in Tolowa and get a dress."

"That isn't going to work."

"Why not?"

"What kind of dress would you buy?" he asked.

"Something floral? Kind of...down to the knee?"

He pinched the bridge of his nose. "You're not Scarlett O'Hara," he said, knowing that with her love of old movies, Anna would appreciate the reference. "You aren't going dressed in the drapes."

Anna scowled. "Why the hell do you know so much about women's clothes?"

"Because I spend a lot of time taking them off my dates."

That shut her up. Her pale cheeks flamed and she looked away from him, and that response stirred... well, it stirred something in his gut he wished would go the hell away.

"Why do *you* want to go anyway?" she asked, still not looking at him.

"I want to talk to Nathan West and the other businessmen there about investment opportunities. I want to prove that Sam and I are the kind of people that can move in their circles. The kind of people they want to do business with."

"And you have to put on a suit and hobnob at a gala to do that?"

"The fact is, I don't get chances like this very often, Anna. I didn't get an invitation. And I need one. Plus, if you take me, you'll win your bet."

"Unless Dan and Mark tell me you don't count."

"Loophole. If they never said you couldn't recruit a date, you're fine."

"It violates the spirit of the bet."

"It doesn't have to," he insisted. "Anyway, by the time I'm through with you, you'll be able to get any date you want."

She blinked. "Are you… Are you Henry Higginsing me?"

He had only a vague knowledge of the old movie *My Fair Lady*, but he was pretty sure that was the reference. A man who took a grubby flower girl and turned her into the talk of the town. "Yes," he said thoughtfully. "Yes, I am. Take me up on this, Anna Brown, and I will turn you into a woman."

Chapter 2

Anna just about laughed herself off her chair. "You're going to make me a...a...a woman?"

"Why is that funny?"

"What about it *isn't* funny?"

"I'm offering to help you."

"You're offering to help me be something that I am by birth. I mean, Chase, I get that women are kind of your thing, but that's pretty arrogant. Even with all things considered."

"Okay, obviously I'm not going to make you a woman." Something about the way he said the phrase this time hit her in an entirely different way. Made her think about *other* applications that phrase occasionally had. Things she needed to never, ever, ever think about in connection with Chase.

If she valued her sanity and their friendship.

She cleared her throat, suddenly aware that it was dry and scratchy. "Obviously."

"I just meant that you need help getting a date, and I need to go to this party. And you said that you were concerned about your appearance in the community."

"Right." He wasn't wrong. The thing was, she knew that whether or not she could blend in at an event like this didn't matter at all to how well her business did. Nobody cared if their mechanic knew which shade of lipstick she should wear. But that wasn't the point.

She—her family collectively—was the town charity case. Living on the edge of the community in a run-down house, raised by a single father who was in over his head, who spent his days at the mill. Her older brothers had been in charge of taking care of her, and they had done so. But, of course, they were also older brothers. Which meant they had tormented her while feeding and clothing her. Anyway, she didn't exactly blame them.

It wasn't like the two of them had wanted to raise a sister when they would rather be out raising hell.

Especially a sister who was committed to driving them crazy.

She loved her brothers. But that didn't mean they always had an easy relationship. It didn't mean they didn't hurt her by accident when they teased her about things. She acted invulnerable, so they assumed that she was.

But now, beneath her coveralls and engine grease, she was starting to feel a little bit battered. It was difficult to walk around with a *screw you* attitude barely covering a raw wound. Because eventually that shield started to wear down. Especially when people were used to being able to lob pretty intense rocks at that shield.

That was her life. It was either pity or a kind of merciless camaraderie that had no softness to it. Her dad, her brothers, all the guy friends she had...

And she couldn't really blame them. She had never behaved in a way that would demonstrate she needed any softness. In fact, a few months ago, a few weeks ago even, the idea would have been unthinkable to her.

But there was something about this invitation. Something about imagining herself in yet another situation where she was forced to deflect good-natured comments about her appearance, about the fact that she was more like a guy than the roughest cowboys in town. Yeah, there was something about that thought that had made her want to curl into a ball and never unfurl.

Then, even if it was unintentional, her brothers had piled on. It had hurt her feelings. Which meant she had reacted in anger, naturally. So now she had a bet. A bet, and her best friend looking at her with laser focus after having just promised he would make her a woman.

"Why do you care?" He was pressing, and she wanted to hit him now.

Which kind of summed up why she was in this position in the first place.

She swallowed hard. "Maybe I just want to surprise people. Isn't that enough?"

"You came from nothing. You started your own business with no support from your father. You're a female mechanic. I would say that you're surprising as hell."

"Well, I want to add another dimension to that. Okay?"

"Okay," he said. "Multidimensional Anna. That seems like a good idea to me."

"Where do we start?"

"With you not falling off your chair laughing at me because I've offered to make you a woman."

A giggle rose in her throat again. Hysteria. She was verging on hysteria. Because this was uncomfortable and sincere. She hated both of those things. "I'm sorry. I can't. You can't say that to me and expect me not to choke."

He looked at her again, his dark eyes intense. "Is it a problem, Anna? The idea that I might make you a woman."

He purposefully made his voice deeper. Purposefully added a kind of provocative inflection to the words. She knew he was kidding. Still, it made her chest tighten. Made her heart flutter a little bit.

Wow. How *annoying*. She hadn't had a relapse of Chase Underpants Feelings this bad in a long time.

Apparently she still hadn't recovered from her earlier bit of mistaken identity. She really needed to recover. And he needed to stop being… Chase. If at all possible.

"Is it a problem for *you*?" she asked.

"What?"

"The idea that I might make you a soprano?"

He chuckled. "You probably want to hold off on threats of castration when you're at a fancy party."

"We aren't at one right now."

She was her own worst enemy. Everything that she had just been silently complaining about, she was doing right now. Throwing out barbs the moment she got uncomfortable, because it kept people from seeing what was actually happening inside of her.

Yes, but you really need to keep Chase from seeing that you fluttered internally over something he said.

Yes. Good point.

She noticed that he was looking past her now, and she followed his line of sight. He was looking at that blonde again. "Regrets, Chase?"

He winced, looking back at her. "No."

"So. I assume that to get a guy to come up and hit on me in a bar, I have to put on a dress that is essentially a red ACE bandage sprinkled with glitter?"

He hesitated. "It's more than that."

"What?"

"Well, for a start, there's not looking at a man like you want to dismember him."

She rolled her eyes. "I don't."

"You aren't exactly approachable, Anna."

"That isn't true." She liked to play darts, and hang out, and talk about sports. What wasn't approachable about that?

"I've seen men try to talk to you," Chase continued. "You shut them down pretty quick. For example—" he barreled on before she could interrupt him "—Ace Thompson paid you a compliment back at the bar."

"Ace Thompson compliments everything with boobs."

"And a couple of weeks ago there was a guy in here that tried to buy you a drink. You told him you could buy your own."

"I *can*," she said, "and he was a stranger."

"He was flirting with you."

She thought back on that night, that guy. *Damn.* He had been flirting. "Well, he should get better at it. I'm not going to reward mediocrity. If I can't tell you're flirting, you aren't doing a very good job."

"Part of the problem is you don't think male attention is being directed at you when it actually is."

She looked back over at the shimmery blonde. "Why would any male attention be directed at me when *that's* over there?"

Chase leaned in, his expression taking on a conspiratorial quality that did…things to her insides. "Here's the thing about a girl like that. She knows she looks good. She assumes that men are looking at her. She assumes that if a man talks to her, that means he wants her."

She took a breath, trying to ease the tightness in her chest. "And that's not…a turnoff?"

"No way." He smiled, a sort of lazy half smile. "Confidence is sexy."

He kind of proved that rule. The thought made her bristle.

"All right. So far with our lessons I've learned that I should unzip my coveralls and as long as I'm confident it will be okay."

"You forgot not looking like you want to stab someone."

"Okay. Confident, nonstabby, showing my boobs."

Chase choked on his beer. "That's a good place to start," he said, setting the bottle down. "Do you want to go play darts? I want to go play darts."

"I thought we were having female lessons."

"Rain check," he said. "How about tomorrow I come by the shop and we get started. I think I'm going to need a lesson plan."

* * *

Chase hadn't exactly excelled in school, unless it was at driving his teachers to drink. So why exactly he had decided he needed a lesson plan to teach Anna how to be a woman, he didn't know.

All he knew was that somewhere around the time they started discussing her boobs last night he had become unable to process thoughts normally. He didn't like that. He didn't like it at all. He did not like the fact that he had been forced to consider her breasts more than once in a single hour. He did not like the fact that he was facing down the possibility of thinking about them a few more times over the next few weeks.

But then, that was the game.

Not only was he teaching her how to blend in at a function like this, he was pretending to be her date.

So there was more than one level of hell to deal with. Perfect.

He cleared his throat, walking down the front porch of the farmhouse that he shared with his brother, making his way across the property toward the shop that Anna was renting and using as her business.

It was after five, so she should be knocking off by now. A good time for the two of them to meet.

He looked down at the piece of lined yellow paper in his hand. His lesson plan.

Then he pressed on, his boots crunching on the gravel as he made his way to the rustic wood building. He inhaled deeply, the last gasp of winter riding over the top of the spring air, mixing with the salt from the sea, giving it a crisp bite unique to Copper Ridge.

He relished this. The small moment of clarity before he dived right into the craziness that was his current situation.

Chase McCormack was many things, but he wasn't a coward. He was hardly going to get skittish over giving his best friend some seduction lessons.

He pushed the door open but didn't see Anna anywhere.

He looked around the room, and the dismembered tractors whose various parts weren't in any order that he could possibly define. Though he knew that it must make sense to Anna.

"Hello?"

"Just up here."

He turned, looked up and saw Anna leaning over what used to be a hayloft, looking down at him, a long dark braid hanging down.

"What exactly are you doing up there?"

"I stashed a tool up here, and now I need it. It's good storage. Of course, then I end up climbing the walls a little more often than I would like. Literally. Not figuratively."

"I figured you would be finished for the day by now."

"No. I have to get this tractor fixed for Connor Garrett. And it's been a bigger job than I thought." She disappeared from view for a moment. "But I would like a reputation as someone who makes miracles. So I better make miracles."

She planted her boot hard on the first rung of the ladder and began to climb down. She was covered from head to toe in motor oil and dust. Probably from crawling around in this space, and beneath tractors.

She jumped down past the last three rungs, brushing dirt off her thighs and leaving more behind, since her hands were coated, too. "You don't exactly look like a miracle," he said, looking her over.

She held up her hand, then displayed her middle finger. "Consider it a miracle that I don't punch you."

"Remember what we talked about? Not looking at a guy like you want to stab him? Much less threatening actual bodily harm."

"Hey, I don't think you would tell a woman that you actually wanted to hook up with that she didn't look like a miracle."

"Most women I want to hook up with aren't quite this disheveled. Before we start anyway."

Much to his surprise, color flooded her cheeks.

"Well," she said, her voice betraying nothing, "I'm not most women, Chase McCormack. I thought you would've known that by now."

Then she sauntered past him, wearing those ridiculous baggy coveralls, head held high like she was queen of the dust bowl.

"Oh, I'm well aware of that," he said. "That's part of the problem."

"And now it's your problem to fix."

"That's right. And I have the lesson plan. As promised."

She whipped around to face him, one dark brow lifted. "Oh, really?"

"Yes, really." He held up the lined notepaper.

"That's very professional."

"It's as professional as you're gonna get. Now, the first order of business is to plant the seed that we're more than friends."

She looked as though he had just suggested she eat a handful of bees. "Do we really need to do that?"

"Yeah, we *really* need to do that. You won't just have a date for the charity event. You're going to have a date every so often until then."

She looked skeptical. "That seems…excessive."

"You want people to believe this. You don't want people to think I'm going because of a bet. You don't want your brothers to think for one moment that they might be right."

"Well, they're going to think it for a few moments at least."

"True. I mean, they are going to be suspicious. But we can make this look real. It isn't going to be that hard. We already hang out most weekends."

"Sure," she said, "but you go home with other girls at the end of the night."

Those words struck him down. "Yes, I guess I do."

"You won't be able to do that now," she pointed out.

"Why not?" he asked.

"Because if I were with you and you went home with another woman, I would castrate you with nothing but my car keys and a bottle of whiskey."

He had no doubt about that. "At least you'd give me some whiskey."

"Hell no. The whiskey would be for me."

"But we're not really together," he said.

"Sure, Chase, but the entire town knows that if any man were to cheat on me, I would castrate him with my car keys, because I don't take crap from anyone. So if they're going to believe that we're together, you're going to have to look like you're being faithful to me."

"That's fine." It wasn't all that fine. He didn't do

celibacy. Never had. Not from the moment he'd discovered that women were God's greatest invention.

"No booty calls," she said, her tone stern.

"Wait a second. I can't even call a woman to hook up in private?"

"No. You can't. Because then *she* would know. I have pride. I mean, right now, standing here in this garage taking lessons from you on how to conform to my own gender's beauty standards, it's definitely marginal, but I have it."

"It isn't like you really know any of the girls that I…"

"Neither do you," she said.

"This isn't about me. It's about you. Now, I got you some things. But I left them in the house. And you are going to have to…hose off before you put them on."

She blinked, her expression almost comical. "Did you buy me clothes?"

He'd taken a long lunch and gone down to Main Street, popping into one of the ridiculously expensive shops that—in his mind—were mostly for tourists, and had found her a dress he thought would work.

"Yeah, I bought you clothes. Because we both know you can't actually wear this out tonight."

"We're going out *tonight*?"

"Hell yeah. I'm taking you somewhere fancy."

"My fancy threshold is very low. If I have to go eat tiny food on a stick sometime next month, I'm going to need actual sustenance in every other meal until then."

He chuckled, trying to imagine Anna coping with miniature food. "Beaches. I'm taking you to Beaches."

She screwed up her face slightly. "We don't go there."

"No, we haven't gone there. We go to Ace's. We shoot pool, we order fried crap and we split the tab. Because we're friends. And that's what friends do. Friends don't go out to Beaches, not just the two of them. But lovers do."

She looked at him owlishly. "Right. I suppose they do."

"And when all this is finished, the entire town of Copper Ridge is going to think that we're lovers."

Chapter 3

Anna was reeling slightly by the time she walked up the front porch and into Chase's house. The entire town was going to think that they were...*lovers*. She had never had a lover. At least, she would never characterize the guy she'd slept with as a lover. He was an unfortunate incident. But fortunately, her hymen was the only casualty. Her heart had remained intact, and she was otherwise uninjured. Or pleasured.

Lovers.

That word sounded...well, like it came from some old movie or something. Which under normal circumstances she was a big fan of. In this circumstance, it just made her feel...like her insides were vibrating. She didn't like it.

Chase lived in the old family home on the property. It was a large, log cabin–style house with warm, honey-colored wood and a green metal roof designed to withstand all kinds of weather. Wrought-iron details on the porch and the door were a testament to his and Sam's craftsmanship. There were people who would pay millions for a home like this. But Sam and Chase had made it this beautiful on their own.

Chase always kept the home admirably clean considering he was a bachelor. She imagined that the other house on the property, the smaller one inhabited by Sam, wasn't quite as well kept. But she also imagined that Sam didn't have the same amount of guests over that Chase did. And by *guests*, she meant female companions. Which he would be cut off from for the next few weeks.

Some small, mean part of her took a little bit of joy in that.

Because you don't like the idea of other women touching him. It doesn't matter how long it's been going on, or how many women there are, you still don't like it.

She sniffed, cutting off that line of thinking. She was just a crabby bitch who was enjoying the idea of him being celibate and suffering a bit. That was all.

"Okay, where are my…girlie things?"

"You aren't even going to look at them until you scrub that grease off."

"And how am I supposed to do that? Are you going to hose me off?"

He clenched his jaw. "No. You can use my shower."

She took a deep breath, trying to dispel the slight fluttering in her stomach. She had never used Chase's shower before. She assumed countless women before her had. When he brought them up here, took their clothes off for them. And probably joined them.

She wasn't going to think about that.

"Okay."

She knew where his shower was, of course. Because she had been inside his bedroom casually, countless times. It had never mattered before. Before, she had never been about to get naked.

She banished that thought as she walked up the stairs and down the hall to his room. His room was… well, it was very well-appointed, but then again, obviously designed to house guests of the female variety. The bed was large and full of plush pillows. A soft-looking green throw was folded up at the foot of it. An overstuffed chair was in the corner, another blanket draped over the back.

She doubted the explosion of comfort and cozy was for Chase's benefit.

She tamped that thought down, continuing on through the bathroom door, then locking it for good measure. Not that he would walk in. And he was the only person in the house.

Still, she felt insecure without the lock flipped. She took a deep breath, stripped off her coveralls, then the clothes she had on beneath them, and started the shower. Speaking of things that were designed to be shared…

It was enclosed in glass, and she had a feeling that with the door open it was right in the line of sight from the bed. Inside was red tile, and a bench seat that… She wasn't even going to think what that could be used for.

She turned and looked in the mirror. She was

grubby. More than grubby. She had grease all over her face, all up under her fingernails.

Thankfully, Chase had some orange-and-pumice cleaner right there on his sink. So she was able to start scrubbing at her hands while the water warmed up.

Steam filled the air and she stepped inside the shower, letting the hot spray cascade over her skin.

It was a *massaging* showerhead. A nice one. She did not have a nice massaging showerhead in her little rental house down in town. Next on her list of Ways She Was Changing Her Life would be to get her own house. With one of these.

She rolled her shoulders beneath the spray and sighed. The water droplets almost felt like fingers moving over her tight muscles. And, suddenly, it was all too easy to imagine a man standing behind her, working at her muscles with his strong hands.

She closed her eyes, letting her head fall back, her mouth going slack. She didn't even have the strength to fight the fantasy, God help her. She'd been edgy and aroused for the past twenty-four hours, no denying it. So this little moment to let herself fantasize... she just needed it.

Then she realized exactly whose hands she was picturing.

Chase's. Tall and strong behind her, his hands moving over her skin, down lower to the slight dip in her spine, just above the curve of her behind...

She grabbed hold of the sponge hanging behind her and began to drag it ferociously over her skin, only belatedly realizing that this was probably what he used to wash himself.

"He uses it to wash his balls," she said into the

space. Hoping that that would disgust her. It really should disgust her.

It did not disgust her.

She put the scrubber back, taking a little shower gel and squeezing it into the palm of her hand. Okay, so she would smell like a playboy for a day. It wasn't the end of the world. She started to rub the slick soap over her flesh, ignoring the images of Chase that were trying to intrude.

She was being a crazy person. She had showered at friends' houses before, and never imagined that they were in the shower stall with her.

But ever since last night in the bar, her equilibrium had been off where Chase was concerned. Her control was being sorely tested. She was decidedly unstoked about it.

She shut the water off and got out of the shower, grabbing a towel off the rack and drying her skin with more ferocity than was strictly necessary. Almost as though she was trying to punish her wicked, wicked skin for imagining what it might be like to be touched by her best friend.

But that would be crazy.

Except she felt a little crazy.

She looked around the room. And realized that her stupid friend, who had not wanted her to touch the nice clothing he had bought her, had left her without anything to wear. She couldn't put her sweaty, grease-covered clothes back on. That would negate the entire shower.

She let out an exasperated breath, not entirely certain what she should do.

"Chase?" she called.

She didn't hear anything.

"Chase?" She raised the volume this time.

Still no answer.

"Butthead," she muttered, walking over to the door and tapping the doorknob, trying to decide what her next move was.

She was being ridiculous. Just because she was having an increase of weird, borderline sexual thoughts about him, did not mean he was having them about her. She twisted the knob, undoing the lock as she did, and opened the door a crack. "Chase!"

The door to the bedroom swung open, and Chase walked in, carrying one of those plastic bags fancy dresses were stored in and a pair of shoes.

"I don't have clothes," she hissed through the crack in the door.

"Sorry," he said, looking stricken. At least, she thought he looked stricken.

She opened the door slightly wider, extending her arm outside. "Give them to me."

He crossed the room, walking over to the bathroom door. "You're going to have to open the door wider than that."

She already felt exposed. There was nothing between them. Nothing but some air and the towel she was clutching to her naked body. Well, and most of the door. But she still felt exposed.

Still, he was not going to fit that bag through the crack.

She opened the door slightly wider, then grabbed hold of the bag in his hand and jerked it back through. "I'll get the shoes later," she called through the door.

She dropped the towel and unzipped the bag, staring at the contents with no small amount of horror. There was…underwear inside of it. Underwear that Chase had purchased for her.

Which meant he had somehow managed to look at her breasts and evaluate their size. Not to mention her ass. And ass size.

She grabbed the pair of panties that were attached to a little hanger. Oh, they had no ass. So she supposed the size of hers didn't matter much.

She swallowed hard, taking hold of the soft material and rubbing her thumb over it. He would know exactly what she was wearing beneath the dress. Would know just how little that was.

He isn't going to think about it. Because he doesn't think about you that way.

He never had. He never would. And it was a damn good thing. Because where would they be if either of them acted on an attraction between them?

Up shit creek without a paddle or a friendship.

No, thank you. She was never going to touch him. She'd made that decision a long time ago. For a lot of reasons that were as valid today as they had been the very first time he'd ever made her stomach jump when she looked at him.

She was never going to encourage or act on the attraction that she occasionally felt for Chase. But she would take his expertise in sexual politics and use it to her advantage.

Oh, but those panties.

The bra wasn't really any less unsettling. Though at least it wasn't missing large swathes of fabric.

Still, it was very thin. And she had a feeling that a

cool ocean breeze would reveal the shape of her nipples to all and sundry.

Then again, maybe it was time all and sundry got a look at her nipples. Maybe if they had a better view, men would be a little more interested.

She scowled, wrenching the panties off the hanger and dragging them on as quickly as possible, followed closely by the bra. She was overthinking things. She was overthinking all of this. Had been from the moment Chase had walked into the barn. As evidenced by that lapse in the shower.

She had spent years honing her Chase Control. It was just this change in how they were interacting that was screwing with it. She was not letting this get inside her head, and she was not letting hot, unsettled feelings get inside her pants.

She pulled the garment bag away entirely, revealing a tight red dress slightly too reminiscent of what the woman he had been flirting with last night was wearing.

"Clearly you have a type, Chase McCormack," she muttered, beginning to remove the slinky scrap of material from the hanger.

She tugged it up over her hips, having to do a pretty intense wiggle to get it up all the way before zipping it into place. She took a deep breath, turned around. She faced her reflection in the mirror full-on and felt nothing but deflated.

She looked…well, her hair was wet and straggly, and she looked half-drowned. She didn't look curvy, or shimmery, or delightful.

This was the problem with tight clothes. They only made her more aware of her curve deficit.

Where the blonde last night had filled her dress out admirably, and in all the right places, on Anna this dress kind of looked like a piece of fabric stretched over an ironing board. Not really all that sexy.

She sighed heavily, trying to ignore the sinking feeling in her stomach.

Chase really was going to have to be a miracle worker in order to pull this off.

She didn't really want to show him. Instead, she found the idea of putting the coveralls back on a lot less reprehensible. At least with the coveralls there would still be some mystery. He wouldn't be confronted with just how big a task lay before him.

"Buck up," she said to herself.

So what was one more moment of feeling inadequate? Honestly, in the broad tapestry of her life it would barely register. She was never quite what was expected. She never quite fit. So why'd she expect that she was going to put on a sexy dress and suddenly be transformed into the kind of sex kitten she didn't even want to be?

She gritted her teeth, throwing open the bedroom door and walking out into the room. "I hope you're happy," she said, flinging her arms wide. "You get what you get."

She caught a movement out of the corner of her eye and turned her head, then recoiled in horror. It was even worse out here. Out here, there was a full-length mirror. Out here, she had the chance to see that while her breasts remained stunningly average, her hips and behind had gotten rather wide. Which was easy to ignore when you wore loose attire most days. "I look like the woman symbol on the door of a public restroom."

She looked over at Chase, who had been completely silent upon her entry into the room, and remained so. She glared at him. He wasn't saying anything. He was only staring. "Well?"

"It's nice," he said.

His voice sounded rough, and kind of thin.

"You're a liar."

"I'm not a liar. Put the shoes on."

"Do you even know what size I wear?"

"You're a size ten, which I know because you complain about how your big feet make it impossible for you to find anything in your size. And you're better off buying men's work boots. So yes, I know."

His words made her feel suddenly exposed. Well, his words in combination with the dress, she imagined. They knew each other a little bit too well. That was the problem. How could you impress a guy when you had spent a healthy amount of time bitching to him about your big feet?

"Fine. I will put on the shoes." He held them up, and her jaw dropped. "I thought you were taking me out to dinner."

"I am."

"Do I have to pay for it by working the pole at the Naughty Mermaid?"

"These are *nice* shoes."

"If you're a five-foot-two-inch Barbie like that chick you were talking to last night. I'm like…an Amazon in comparison."

"You're not an Amazon."

"I will be in those."

"Maybe that would bother some men. But you want a man who knows how to handle a woman. Any guy with half a brain is going to lose his mind checking out your legs. He's not going to care if you're a little taller than he is."

She tried her best to ignore the compliment about her legs. And tried even harder to keep from blushing.

"I care," she muttered, snatching the shoes from his hand and pondering whether or not there was any truth to her words as she did.

She didn't really date. So it was hard to say. But now that she was thinking about it, yeah. She was self-conscious about the fact that with pretty low heels she was eye level with half the men in town.

She finished putting the shoes on and straightened. It was like standing on a glittery pair of stilts. "Are you satisfied?" she asked.

"I guess you could say that." He was regarding her closely, his jaw tense, a muscle in his cheek ticking.

She noticed that he was still a couple of inches taller than her. Even with the shoes. "I guess you still meet the height requirement to be my dinner date."

"I didn't have any doubt."

"I don't know how to walk in these," she said.

"All right. Practice."

"Are you out of your mind? I have to *practice* walking?"

"You said yourself, you don't know how to walk in heels. So, go on. Walk the length of the room."

She felt completely awash in humiliation. She doubted there was another woman on the planet that Chase had ever had to instruct on walking.

"This is ridiculous."

"It's not," he said.

"All of women's fashion is ridiculous," she maintained. "Do you have to learn how to walk when you put on dress shoes? No, you do not. And yet, a full-scale lesson is required for me to go out if I want to wear something that's considered *feminine*."

"Yeah, it's sexist. And a real pain in the ass, I'm sure. It's also hot. Now walk."

She scowled at him, then took her first step, wobbling a bit. "I don't understand why women do this."

She took another step, then another, wobbling a little less each time. But the shoes did force her hips to sway, much more than they normally would. "Do you have any pointers?" she asked.

"I date women in heels, Anna. *I've* never walked in them."

"What happened to helping me be a woman?"

"You'll get the hang of it. It's like… I don't know, water-skiing maybe?"

"How is this like water-skiing?"

"You have to learn how to do it and there's a good likelihood you'll fall on your face?"

"Well, I take it all back," she said, deadpan. "These shoes aren't silly at all." She took another step, then another. "I feel like a newborn baby deer."

"You look a little like one, too."

She snorted. "You really need to up your game, Chase. If you use these lines on all the women you take out, you're bound to start striking out sooner or later."

"I haven't struck out yet."

"Well, you're still young and pretty. Just wait. Just wait until time starts to claim your muscular forearms and chiseled jawline."

"I figure by then maybe I'll have gotten the ranch

back to its former glory. At that point women will sleep with me for my money."

She rolled her eyes. "It's nice to have goals."

In her opinion, Chase should have better goals for himself. But then, who was she to talk? Her current goal was to show her brothers that they were idiots and she could too get a date. Hardly a lofty ambition.

"Yes, it is. And right now my goal is for us not to miss our reservation."

"You made a…reservation?"

"I did."

"It's not like it's Valentine's Day or something. The restaurant isn't going to be full."

"Of course it won't be. But I figured if I made a reservation for the two of us, we could start a rumor, too."

"A rumor?"

"Yeah, because Ellie Matthews works at Beaches, and I believe she has been known to *service* your brother Mark."

Anna winced at the terminology. "True."

"I thought the news of our dining experience might make it back to him. Like I said, the more we can make this look organic, the better."

"No one ever need know that our relationship is in fact grown in a lab. And in no way GMO free," she said.

"Exactly."

"I don't have any makeup on." She frowned. "I don't have any makeup. At all."

"Right," he said. "I didn't really think of that."

She reached out and smacked him on the shoulder. "You're supposed to be my coach. You're failing me."

He laughed, dodging her next blow. "You don't need makeup."

She let out an exasperated sigh. "You're just saying that."

"In fairness, you did threaten to castrate me with your car keys earlier."

"I did."

"And you hit me just now," he pointed out.

"It didn't hurt, you baby."

He took a deep breath, and suddenly his expression turned sharp. "Believe me when I tell you you don't need makeup." He reached out, gripping her chin with his thumb and forefinger. His touch was like a branding iron, hot, altering. "As long as you believe it, everyone else will, too. You have to believe in yourself, Anna."

He released his hold on her, straightening. "Now," he said, his tone getting a little bit rougher, "let's go to dinner."

Chase felt like he had been tipped sideways and left walking on the walls from the moment that Anna had emerged from the bathroom at his house wearing that dress. Once she had put on those shoes, the feeling had only gotten worse.

But who knew that underneath those coveralls his best friend looked like that?

She had been eyeing herself critically, and his brain had barely been working at all. Because he didn't see anything to criticize. All he saw was the kind of figure that would make a man willingly submit to car key castration.

She was long and lean, toned from all the physical labor she did. Her breasts were small, but he imagined they would fit in a man's hand nicely. And her hips...well, using the same measurement used for her breasts, they would be about perfect for holding on to while a man…

Holy hell. He was losing his mind.

She was Anna. Anna Brown, his best friend in the entire world. The one woman he had never even considered going there with. He didn't want a relationship with the women he slept with. When your only criteria for being with a woman was orgasm, there were a lot of options available to you. For a little bit of satisfaction he could basically seek out any woman in the room.

Sex was easy. Connections were hard.

And so Anna had been placed firmly off-limits from day one. He'd had a vague awareness of her for most of his life. That was how growing up in a small town worked. You went to the same school from the beginning. But they had separate classes, plus at the time he'd been pretty convinced girls had cooties.

But that had changed their first year of high school. He'd ended up in metal shop with the prickly teen and had liked her right away. There weren't very many girls who cursed as much as the boys and had a more comprehensive understanding of the inner workings of engines than the teachers at the school. But Anna did.

She hadn't fit in with any of the girls, and so Chase and Sam had been quick to bring her into their group. Over the years, people had rotated in and out, moved, gone their separate ways. But Chase and Anna had remained close.

In part because he had kept his dick out of the equation.

As they walked up the path toward Beaches, he considered putting his hand on her lower back. Really, he should. Except it was potentially problematic at the moment. Was he this shallow? Stick her in a tight-fitting dress and suddenly he couldn't control himself? It was a sobering realization, but not really all that surprising.

This was what happened when you spent a lot of time practicing no restraint when it came to sex.

He gritted his teeth, lifting his hand for a moment before placing it gently on her back. Because it was what he would do with any other date, so it was what he needed to do with Anna.

She went stiff beneath his touch. "Relax," he said, keeping his voice low. "This is supposed to look like a date, remember?"

"I should have worn a white tank top and a pair of jeans," she said.

"Why?"

"Because this looks... It looks like I'm trying too hard."

"No, it looks like you put on a nice outfit to please me."

She turned to face him, her brow furrowed. "Which is part of the problem. If I had to do this to please you, we both know that I would tell you to please yourself."

He laughed, the moment so classically Anna, so familiar, it was at odds with the other feelings that were buzzing through his blood. With how soft she felt beneath his touch. With just how much she was affecting him in this figure-hugging dress.

"I have no doubt you would."

They walked up the steps that led into the large white restaurant, and he opened the door, holding it for her. She looked at him like he'd just caught fire. He stared her down, and then she looked away from him, walking through the door.

He moved up next to her once they were inside.

"You're going to have to seem a little more at ease with this change in our relationship."

"You're being weird."

"I'm not being weird. I'm treating you like a lady."

"What have you been treating me like for the past fifteen years?" she asked.

"A...bro."

She snorted, shaking her head and walking toward the front of the house where Ellie Matthews was standing, waiting for guests. "I believe we have a reservation," Anna said.

He let out a long-suffering sigh. "Yes," he confirmed. "Under my name."

Ellie's eyebrow shot upward. "Yes. You do."

"Under Chase McCormack and Anna Brown," Chase clarified.

"I know," she said.

Ellie needed to work on her people skills. "It was difficult for me to tell, since you look so surprised," Chase said.

"Well, I knew you were reserving the table for the two of you, but I didn't realize you were...reserving the table for *the two of you*." She was looking at Anna's dress, her expression meaningful.

"Well, I was," he said. "Did. So, is the table ready?"

She looked around the half-full dining area. "Yeah, I'm pretty sure we can seat you now."

Ellie walked them over to one of the tables by a side window that looked out over the Skokomish River where it fed into the ocean. The sun was dipping low over the water, the rays sparkling off the still surface of the slow-moving river. There were people milling along the wooden boardwalk that was bordered by docks on one side and storefronts on the other, before being split by the highway and starting again, leading down to the beach.

He looked away from the scenery, back at Anna. They had shared countless meals together, but this was different. Normally, they didn't sit across from each other at a tiny table complete with a freaking candle in the middle. Mood lighting.

"Your server will be with you shortly," Ellie said as she walked away, leaving them there with menus and each other.

"I want a burger," Anna said, not looking at the menu at all.

"You could get something fancier."

"I'll get it with a cheese I can't pronounce."

"I'm getting salmon."

"Am I paying?" she asked, an impish smile playing around the corners of her lips. "Because if so, you better be putting out at the end of this."

Her words were like a punch in the gut. And he did his best to ignore them. He swallowed hard. "No, *I'm* paying."

"I'll pay you back after. You're doing me a favor."

"The favor's mutual. I want to go to the fund-raiser. It's important to me."

"You still aren't buying my dinner."

"I'm not taking your money."

"Then I'm going to overpay for rent on the shop next month," she said, her tone uncompromising.

"Half of that goes to Sam."

"Then he gets half of it. But I'm not going to let you buy my dinner."

"You're being stubborn."

She leaned back in her chair, crossing her arms and treating him to that hard glare of hers. "Yep."

A few moments later the waiter came over, and Anna ordered her hamburger, and the cheeses she wanted, by pointing at the menu.

"Which cheese did you get?" he asked, attempting to move on from their earlier standoff.

"I don't know." She shrugged. "I can't pronounce it."

They made about ten minutes of awkward conversation while they waited for their dinner to come. Which was weird, because conversation was never awkward with Anna. It was that dress. And those shoes. And his penis. That was part of the problem. Because, suddenly, it was actually interested in his best friend.

No, it is not. A moment of checking her out does not mean that you want to...do anything with her.

Exactly. It wasn't a big deal. It wasn't anything to get worked up about. Not at all.

When their dinner was placed in front of them, Anna attacked her sweet potato fries, probably using them as a displacement activity.

"Chase?"

Chase looked up and inwardly groaned when he saw Wendy Maxwell headed toward the table. They'd all gone to high school together. And he had, regrettably, slept with Wendy once or twice over the years after drinking too much at Ace's.

She was hot. But what she had in looks had been deducted from her personality. Which didn't matter when you were only having sex, but mattered later when you had to interact in public.

"Hi, Wendy," he said, taking a bite of his salmon.

Anna had gone very still across from him; she wasn't even eating her fries anymore.

"Are you… Are you on a date?" Wendy asked, tilting her head to the side, her expression incredulous.

Wendy wasn't very smart in addition to being not very nice. A really bad combination.

"Yes," he said, "I am."

"With Anna?"

"Yeah," Anna said, looking up. "The person sitting across from him. Like you do on a date."

"I'm just surprised."

He could see color mounting in Anna's cheeks, could see her losing her hold on her temper.

"Are you here by yourself?" Anna asked.

Wendy laughed, the sound like broken crystal being pushed beneath his skin. "No. Of course not. We're having a girls' night out." She eyed Chase. "Of course, that doesn't mean I'm going home with the girls."

Suddenly, Anna was standing, and he was a little bit afraid she was about to deck Wendy. Who deserved it. But he didn't really want to be at the center of a girl fight in the middle of Beaches.

That only worked in fantasies. Less so in real life.

But it wasn't Wendy whom Anna moved toward.

She took two steps, came to a stop in front of Chase and then leaned forward, grabbing hold of the back of his chair and resting her knee next to his thigh. Then she pressed her hand to his cheek and took a deep breath, making determined eye contact with him just before she let her lids flutter closed. Just before she closed the distance between them and kissed him.

Chapter 4

She was kissing Chase McCormack. Beyond that, she had no idea what the flying F-bomb she was doing. If there was another person in the room, she didn't see them. If there was a reason she'd started this, she didn't remember it.

There was nothing. Nothing more than the hot press of Chase's lips against hers. Nothing more than still, leashed power beneath her touch. She could feel his tension, could feel his strength frozen beneath her.

It was…intoxicating. Empowering.

So damn *hot*.

Like she was about to melt the soles of her shoes hot. About to come without his hands ever touching her body hot.

And that was unheard-of for her.

She'd kissed a couple of guys, and slept with one,

and orgasm had never been in the cards. When it came to climaxes, she was her own hero. But damn if Chase wasn't about to be her hero in under thirty seconds, and with nothing more than a little dry lip-to-lip contact.

Except it didn't stay dry.

Suddenly, he reached up, curling his fingers around the back of her head, angling his own and kissing her hard, deep. With tongue.

She whimpered, the leg that was supporting her body melting, only the firm hold he had on her face, and the support of his chair, keeping her from sliding onto the ground.

The slick glide of his tongue against hers was the single sexiest thing she'd ever experienced in her life. And just like that, every little white lie she'd ever told herself about her attraction to Chase was completely and fully revealed.

It wasn't just a momentary response to an attractive man. Not something any red-blooded female would feel. Not just a passing anomaly.

It was real.

It was deep.

She was so screwed.

Way too screwed to care that they were making out in a fancy restaurant in front of people, and that for him it was just a show, but for her it was a whole cataclysmic, near-orgasmic shift happening in the region of her panties.

Seconds had passed, but they felt like minutes. Hours. Whole days' worth of life-changing moments, all crammed into something that probably hadn't actually lasted longer than the blink of an eye.

Then it was over. She was the one who pulled away and she wasn't quite sure how she managed. But she did.

She wasn't breathing right. Her entire body was shaking, and she was sure her face was red. But still, she turned and faced Wendy, or whichever mean girl it was. There were a ton of them in her nonhalcyon high school years and they all blended together. The who wasn't important. Only the what. The *what* being a kiss she'd just given to the hottest guy in town, right in front of someone who didn't think she was good enough. Pretty enough. Girlie enough.

"Yeah," she said, her voice a little less triumphant and a lot more unsteady than she would like, "we're here on a date. And he's going home with me. So I'd suggest you wiggle on over to a different table if you want to score tonight."

Wendy's face was scrunched into a sour expression. "That's okay, honey, if you want my leftovers, you're welcome to them."

Then she flipped her blond hair and walked back to her table, essentially acting out the cliché of every snotty girl in a teen movie.

Which was not so cute when you were thirty and not fifteen.

But, of course, since Wendy was gone, they'd lost the buffer against the aftermath of the kiss, and the terrible awkwardness that was just sitting there, seething, growing.

"Well, I think that started some rumors," Anna said, sitting back down and shoving a fry into her mouth.

"I bet," Chase said, clearing his throat and turning back toward his plate.

"My mouth has never touched your mouth directly

before," she said, then stuffed another fry straight into her mouth, wishing it wasn't too late to stifle those ridiculous words.

He choked on his beer. "Um. No."

"What I mean is, we've shared drinks before. I've taken bites off your sandwiches. Literally sandwiches, not— I mean, whatever. The point is, we've germ-shared before. We just never did it mouth-to-mouth."

"That wasn't CPR, babe."

She made a face, hoping the disgust in her expression would disguise the twist low and deep in her stomach. "Don't call me babe just because I kissed you."

"We're dating, remember?"

"No one is listening to us talk at the table," she insisted.

"You don't know that."

Her heart was thundering hard like a trapped bird in her chest and she didn't know if she could look at him for another minute without either scurrying from the room like a frightened animal or grabbing him and kissing him again.

She didn't like it. She didn't like any of it.

It all felt too real, too raw and too scary. It all came from a place too deep inside her.

So she decided to do what came easiest. Exactly what she did best.

"I expected better," she told him, before taking a bite of her burger.

"What?"

"You're like a legendary stud," she said, after swallowing her food. "The man who every man wants to be and who every woman wants to be with. Blah, blah." She picked up another sweet potato fry.

"It wasn't good for you?" he asked.

"Six point five from the German judge. Who is me, in this scenario." She was a liar. She was a liar and she was a jerk, and she wanted to punch her own face. But the alternative was to show that she was breaking apart inside. That she had been on the verge of the kind of ecstasy she'd only ever imagined, and that she wanted to kiss him forever, not just for thirty seconds. And that was…damaging. It wasn't something she could admit.

"Six point five."

"Sorry." She lifted her shoulder and shoved the fry into her mouth.

They finished the rest of the dinner in awkward silence, which made her mad because things weren't supposed to be awkward between them. They were friends, dammit. She was starting to think this whole thing was a mistake.

She could bring Chase as her plus one to the charity thing without her brothers buying into it. She could lose the bet. The whole town could suspect she'd brought a friend because she was undatable and who even cared?

If playing this game was going to screw with their friendship, it wasn't worth it.

Chase paid the tab—she was going to pay the bastard back whether he wanted her to or not—and then the two of them walked outside. And that was when she realized her truck was back at his place and he was going to have to give her a ride.

That sucked donkey balls. She needed to get some Chase space. And it wasn't going to happen.

She wanted to go home and put on soft pajamas and

watch *Seven Brides for Seven Brothers*. She needed a safe, flannel-lined space and the fuzzy comfort of an old movie. A chance to breathe and be vulnerable for a second where no one would see.

She was afraid Chase might have seen already.

They still didn't talk—all the way back out of town and to the McCormack family ranch, they didn't talk.

"My dirty clothes are in your house," she said at last, when they pulled into the driveway. "You can take me to the house first instead of the shop."

"I can wash them with mine," he said.

Her underwear was in there. That was not happening.

"No, I left them folded in the corner of the bathroom. I'd rather come get them. And put my shoes on before I try to drive home actually. How do people drive in these?" She tapped the precarious shoes against the floor of the pickup.

Chase let out a harsh-sounding breath. "Fine," he said. He sounded aggrieved, but he drove on past the shop to the house. He stopped the truck abruptly, throwing it into Park and killing the engine. "Come on in."

Now he was mad at her. Great. It wasn't like he needed her to stroke his ego. He had countless women to do that. He had just one woman who listened to his bullshit and put up with all his nonsense, and in general stood by him no matter what. That was her. He could have endless praise for his bedroom skills from those other women. He only had friendship from *her*. So he could simmer down a little.

She got out of the truck, then wobbled when her

foot hit a loose gravel patch. She clung tightly to the door, a very wussy-sounding squeak escaping her lips.

"You okay there, *babe*?" he asked, just to piss her off.

"Yeah, fine. Jerk," she retorted.

"What the hell, Anna?" he asked, his tone hard.

"Oh, come on, you're being weird. You can't pretend you aren't just because you're layering passivity over your aggression." She stalked past him as fast as her shoes would let her, walked up the porch and stood by the door, her arms crossed.

"It's not locked," he said, taking the stairs two at a time.

"Well, I wasn't going to go in without your permission. I have manners."

"Do you?" he asked.

"If I didn't, I probably would have punched you by now." She opened the door and stomped up the stairs, until her heel rolled inward slightly and she stumbled. Then she stopped stomping and started taking a little more consideration for her joints.

She was mad at him. She was mad at herself for being mad at him, because the situation was mostly her fault. And she was mad at him for being mad at her for being mad at him.

Mad, mad, *mad*.

She walked into the bathroom and picked up her stack of clothes, careful not to hold the greasy articles against her dress. The dress that was the cause of so many of tonight's problems.

It's not the dress. It's the fact that you kissed him and now you can't deal.

Rationality was starting to creep in and she was

nothing if not completely irritated about that. It was forcing her to confront the fact that she was actually the one being a jerk, not him. That she was the one who was overreacting, and his behavior was all a response to the fact that she'd gone full Anna-pine, with quills out ready to defend herself at all costs.

She took a deep breath and sat down on the edge of his bed, trading the high heels for her sneakers, then collecting her things again and walking back down the stairs, her feet tingling and aching as they got used to resting flat once more.

Chase wasn't inside.

She opened the front door and walked out onto the porch.

He was standing there, the porch light shining on him like a beacon. His broad shoulders, trim waist… oh, Lord, his ass. Wrangler butt was a gift from God in her opinion and Chase's was perfect. Something she'd noticed before, but right now it was physically painful to look at him and not close the space between them. To not touch him.

This was bad. This was why she hadn't ever touched him before. Why it would have been best if she never had.

She had needs. Fuzzy-blanket needs. She needed to get home.

She cleared her throat. "I'm ready," she said. "I just… If you could give me a lift down to the shop, that would be nice. So that I'm not cougar food."

He turned slowly, a strange expression on his face. "Yeah, I wouldn't want you to get eaten by any mangy predators."

"I appreciate that."

He headed down the steps and got back into the truck, and she followed, climbing into the cab beside him. He started the engine and maneuvered the truck onto the gravel road that ran through the property.

She rested her elbow on the armrest, staring outside at the inky black shadows of the pine trees, and the white glitter of stars in the velvet-blue sky. It was a clear night, unusual for their little coastal town.

If only her head was as clear as the sky.

It was full. Full of regret and woe. She didn't like that. As soon as Chase pulled up to the shop, she scrambled out, not waiting for him to put the vehicle in Park. She was heading toward her own vehicle when she heard Chase behind her.

"What are you doing?" she asked, turning to face him.

But her words were cut off by what he did next. He took one step toward her, closing the distance between them as he wrapped his arm around her waist and drew her up against his chest. Then, before she could protest, before she could say anything, he was kissing her again.

This was different than the kiss at the restaurant. This was different than…well, than any kiss in the whole history of the world.

His kiss tasted of the familiarity of Chase and the strangeness of his anger. Of heat and lust and rage all rolled into one.

She knew him better than she knew almost anyone. Knew the shape of his face, knew his scent, knew his voice. But his scent surrounding her like this, the feel of his face beneath her hands, the sound of that voice—transformed into a feral, passionate growl as he continued to ravish her—was an unknown. Was something else entirely.

Then, suddenly—just as suddenly as he had initiated it—the kiss was over. He released his hold on her, pushing her back. There was nothing but air between them now. Air and a whole lot of feelings. He was standing there, his hands planted on his lean hips, his chest rising and falling with each labored breath. "Six point five?" he asked, his tone challenging. "That sure as hell was no six point five, Anna Brown, and if you're honest with yourself, you have to admit that."

She sucked in a harsh, unsteady breath, trying to keep the shock from showing on her face. "I don't have to admit any such thing."

"You're a little liar."

"What does it matter?" she asked, scowling.

"How would you like it if I told you that you were only average compared to other women I've kissed?"

"I'd shut your head in the truck door."

"Exactly." He crossed his arms over his broad chest. "So don't think I'm going to let the same insults stand, honey."

"Don't *babe* me," she spat. "Don't *honey* me."

Triumph glittered in his dark eyes. The smugness so certain it was visible even in the moonlight. "Then don't kiss me again."

"You were the one who kissed me!" she shouted, throwing her arms wide.

"*This* time. But you started it. Don't do it again." He turned around, heading back toward his truck. All she could do was stand there and stare as he drove away.

Something had changed tonight. Something inside of her. She didn't think she liked it at all.

Chapter 5

"Now, I don't want to be insensitive or hurt your feelings, princess, but why are you being such an asshole today?"

Chase looked over at Sam, who was staring at him from his position by the forge. The fire was going hot and they were pounding out iron, doing some repairs on equipment. By hand. Just the way both of them liked to work.

"I'm not," Chase said.

"Right. Look, there's only room for one of us to be a grumpy cuss, and I pretty much have that position filled. So I would appreciate it if you can get your act together."

"Sorry, Sam, are you unable to take what you dish out every day?"

"What's going on with you and Anna?"

Chase bristled at the mention of the woman he'd kissed last night. Then he winced when he remembered the kiss. Well, *remembered* was the wrong word. He'd never forgotten it. But right now he was mentally replaying it, moment by moment. "What did you hear?"

Sam laughed. An honest-to-God laugh. "Do I look like I'm on the gossip chain? I haven't talked to anybody. It's just that I saw her leaving your house last night wearing a red dress and sneakers, and then saw her this morning when she went into the shop. She was pissier than you are."

"Anna is always pissy." Sam treated his statement to a prolonged stare. "It's not a big deal. It's just that her brothers bet her that she couldn't get a date. I figured I would help her out with that."

"How?"

"Well…" he said, hesitating about telling his brother the whole story. Sam wasn't looking to change the business on the ranch. He didn't care about their family legacy. Not like Chase did. But Chase had made promises to tombstones and he wasn't about to break them.

It was one of their main sources of contention. So he wasn't exactly looking forward to having this conversation with his older brother.

But it wasn't like he could hide it forever. He'd just sort of been hoping he could hide it until he'd shown up with investment money.

"That's an awfully long pause," Sam said. "I'm willing to bet that whatever you're about to say, I'm not going to like it."

"You know me well. Anna got invited to go to the big community charity event that the West family hosts every year. Now I want to make sure that we can extend our contract with them. Plus…doing horse-shoes and gates isn't cutting it. We can move into doing details on custom homes. To doing art pieces and selling our work across the country, not just locally. To do that we need investors. And the West fund-raiser's a great place to find them. Plus, if I only have to wear a suit once and can speak to everyone in town that might be interested in a single shot? Well, I can't beat that."

"Dammit, Chase, you know I don't want to commit to something like that."

"Right. You want to continue on the way we always have. You want to shoe horses when we can, pound metal when the opportunity presents itself, build gates, or whatever else might need doing, then go off and work on sculptures and things in your spare time. But that's not going to be enough. Less and less is done by hand, and people aren't willing to pay for hand-crafted materials. Machines can build cheaper stuff than we can.

"But the thing is, you can make it look special. You can turn it into something amazing. Like you did with my house. It's the details that make a house expensive. We can have the sort of clients who don't want work off an assembly line. The kind who will pay for one of a kind pieces. From art on down to the handles on their kitchen cabinets. We could get into some serious custom work. Vacation homes are starting to spring up around here, plus people are renovating to make rentals thanks to the tourism increase. But we need some investors if we're really going to get into this."

"You know I hate this. I don't like the idea of charging a ton of money for a…for a gate with an elk on it."

"You're an artist, Sam," he said, watching his brother wince as he said the words. "I know you hate that. But it's true."

"I hate that, too."

"You're talented."

"I hit metal with a hammer. Sometimes I shape it into something that looks nice. It's not really all that special."

"You do more than that and you know it. It's what people would be willing to pay for. If you would stop being such a nut job about it."

Sam rubbed the back of his neck, his expression shuttered. "You've gotten off topic," he said finally. "I asked you about Anna, not your schemes for exploiting my talents."

"Not really. The two are connected. I want to go to this thing to talk to the Wests. I want to talk about investment opportunities and expanding contracts with other people deemed worthy of an invite. In case you haven't noticed, we weren't on that list."

"Yeah, I get that. But why would the lately not-so-great McCormacks be invited?"

"That's the problem. This place hasn't been what it was for a couple of generations, and when we lost Mom and Dad...well, we were teenagers trying to keep up a whole industry, and now we work *for* these people, not with them. I aim to change that."

"You didn't think about talking to me?" Sam asked.

"Oh, I did. And I decided I didn't want to have to deal with you."

Sam shot him an evil glare. "So you're going as Anna's date. And helping her win her bet."

"Exactly."

"And you took her out last night, and she went back to your place, and now she's mad at you."

Chase held his hands up. "I don't know what you're getting at—"

"Yes, you do." Sam crossed his arms. "Did you bang her?"

Chase recoiled, trying to look horrified at the thought. He didn't *feel* horrified at the thought. Which actually made him feel kind of horrified. "I did not."

"Is that why you're mad? Because you didn't?"

His brother was way too perceptive for a guy who pounded heavy things with other heavy things for a living.

"No," he said. "Anna is my friend. She's just a friend. We had a slight…altercation last night. But it's not that big a deal."

"Big enough that I'm worried with all your stomping around you're eventually going to fling the wrong thing and hit me with molten metal."

"Safety first," Chase said, "always."

"I bet you say that to your dates, too."

"You would, too, if you had any."

Sam flipped Chase the bird in response.

"Just forget about it," Chase said. "Forget about the stuff with the Wests, and let me deal with it. And forget about Anna."

When it came to that last directive, he was going to try to do the same.

Anna was dreading coming face-to-face with Chase again after last night. But she didn't really have a choice. They were still in this thing. Unless she called it off. But that would be tantamount to admitting that what had happened last night *bothered* her. And she didn't want to do that. More, she was almost incapable of doing it. She was pretty sure her pride would wither up and die if she did.

But Chase was coming by her shop again tonight, with some other kind of lesson in mind. Something he'd written down on that stupid legal pad of his. It was ridiculous. All of it was ridiculous.

Herself most of all.

She looked at the clock, gritting her teeth. Chase would be by any moment, and she was no closer to dealing with the feelings, needs and general restlessness that had hit her with the blunt force of a flying wrench than she had been last night.

Then, right on time, the door opened, and in walked Chase. He was still dirty from work today, his face smudged with ash and soot, his shirt sticking to his muscular frame, showing off all those fine muscles underneath. Yeah, that didn't help.

"How was work?" he asked.

"Fine. Just dealing with putting a new cylinder head on a John Deere. You?"

"Working on a gate."

"Sounds…fun," she said, though she didn't really think it sounded like fun at all.

She liked solving the puzzle when it came to working on engines. Liked that she had the ability to get in there and figure things out. To diagnose the situation.

Standing in front of a hot fire forging metal didn't really sound like her kind of thing.

Though she couldn't deny it did pretty fantastic things for Chase's physique.

"Well, you know it would be fine if Sam wasn't such a pain in the ass."

"Sure," she said, feeling slightly cautious. After last night, she felt like dealing with Chase was like approaching a dog who'd bitten you once. Only, in this case he had kissed her, not bitten her, and he wasn't a dog. That was the problem. He was just much too *much* for his own good. Much too much for her own good.

"So," she said, "what's on the lesson plan for tonight?"

"I sort of thought we should talk about…well, talking."

"What do you mean?"

"There are ways that women talk to men they want to date. I thought I might walk you through flirting."

"You're going to show me how to flirt?"

"Somebody has to."

"I can probably figure it out," she said.

"You think?" he asked, crossing his arms over his chest and rocking back on his heels.

His clear skepticism stoked the flames of her temper, which was lurking very close to the surface after last night. That was kind of her default. Don't know how to handle something? Don't know *what* you feel? Get angry at it.

"Come on. Men and women have engaged in horizontal naked kickboxing for millennia. I'm pretty sure flirting is a natural instinct."

"You're a poet, Anna," he said, his tone deadpan.

"No, I'm a tractor mechanic," she said.

"Yeah, and you talk like one, too. If you want to get an actual date, and not just a quick tumble in the back of a guy's truck, you might want to refine your art of conversation a little."

"Who says I'm opposed to a quick rough tumble in the back of some guy's truck?"

"You're not?" he asked, his eyebrows shooting upward.

"Well, in all honesty I would probably prefer my truck, since it's clean. I know where it's been. But why the hell not? I have needs."

He scowled. "Right. Well, keep that kind of talk to yourself."

"Does it make you uncomfortable to hear about my *needs*, Chase?" she asked, not quite sure why she was poking at him. Maybe because she felt so unsettled. She was kind of enjoying the fact that he seemed to be, as well. Really, it wouldn't be fair if after last night he felt nothing at all. If he had been able to one-up her and then walk away as though nothing had happened.

"It doesn't make me uncomfortable. It's just unnecessary information. Now, talking about your needs is probably something you shouldn't do with a guy, either."

"Unless I want him to fulfill those needs."

"You said you wanted to date. You want the kind of date who can go to these functions with you, right?"

"It's moot. You're going with me."

"This time. But be honest, don't you want to be able to go out with guys who belong in places like that?"

"I don't know," she said, feeling uncomfortable.

Truth be told, she wasn't all that comfortable thinking about her needs. Emotional, physical. Frankly, if it went beyond her need for a cheeseburger, she didn't really know how to deal with it. She hadn't dated in years. And she had been fine with that. But the truth of the matter was the only reason Mark and Daniel had managed to get to her when they had made this bet was that she was beginning to feel dissatisfied with her life.

She was starting a new business. She was assuming a new position in the community. She didn't just want to be Anna Brown, the girl from the wrong side of the tracks. She didn't just want to be the tomboy mechanic for the rest of her life. She wanted...more. It had been fine, avoiding relationships all this time, but she was thirty now. She didn't really want to be by herself. She didn't want to be alone forever.

Dear Lord, she was having an existential crisis.

"Fine," she said, "it might be nice to have somebody to date."

Marriage, family—she had no idea how she felt when it came to those things. But a casual relationship... That might be nice. Yes. That might be nice.

Last night, she had gone home and gotten under a blanket and watched an old movie. Sometimes, Chase watched old movies with her, but he did not get under the blankets with her. It would be nice to have a guy to be under the blanket with. Somebody to go home to. Or at least someone to call to come over when she couldn't sleep. Someone she could talk to, make out with. Have sex with.

"Fine," she said. "I will submit to your flirting lessons."

"All the girls submit to me eventually," he said, winking.

Something about that made her stomach twist into a knot. "Talking about too much information..."

"There," he said, "that was almost flirting."

She wrinkled her nose. "Was it?"

"Yes. We had a little bit of back and forth. There was some innuendo."

"I didn't make innuendo on purpose," she said.

"No. That's the best kind. The kind you sort of walk into. It makes you feel a little dangerous. Like you might say the wrong thing. And if you go too far, they might walk away. But if you don't go far enough, they might not know that you want them."

She let out a long, frustrated growl. "Dating is complicated. I hate it. Is it too late for me to become a nun?"

"You would have to convert," he pointed out.

"That sounds like a lot of work, too."

"You can be pleasant, Anna. You're fun to talk to. So that's all you have to do."

"Natural to me is walking up to a hot guy and saying, 'Do you want to bone or what?'" As if she'd ever done that. As if she ever would. It was just…she didn't really know how to go about getting a guy to hook up with her any other way. She was a direct kind of girl. And nothing between men and women seemed direct.

"Fine. Let's try this," he said, grabbing a chair and pulling it up to her workbench before taking a seat.

She took hold of the back of the other folding chair in the space and moved it across from his, positioning herself so that she was across from him.

"What are you drinking?" he asked.

She laughed. "A mai tai." She had never had one of those. She didn't even know what it was.

"Excellent. I'm having whiskey, straight up."

"That sounds like you."

"You don't know what sounds like me. You don't know me."

Suddenly, she got the game. "Right. Stranger," she said, then winced internally, because that sounded a little bit more Mae West in her head, and just kind of silly when it was out of her mouth.

"You here with anyone?"

"I could be?" she said, placing her elbow on the workbench and tilting her head to the side.

"You should try to toss your hair a little bit. I dated this girl Elizabeth who used to do that. It was cute."

"How does touching my hair accomplish anything?" she asked, feeling irritated that he had brought another woman up. Which was silly, because the only reason he was qualified to give her these lessons was that he had dated a metric ton of women.

So getting mad about the thing that was helping her right now was a little ridiculous. But she was pretty sure they had passed ridiculous a couple of days ago.

"I don't know. It's cute. It looks like you're trying to draw my attention to it. Like you want me to notice."

"Which…lets you know that I want you in my pants?"

He frowned. "I guess. I never broke it down like that before. But that stands to reason."

She reached up, sighing as she flicked a strand of her hair as best she could. It was tied up in a loose bun and had fallen partway thanks to the intensity of the day's physical labor. Still, she had a feeling she did not look alluring. She had a feeling she looked like she'd been caught in a wind turbine and spit out the other end.

"Are you new in town?"

"I'm old in town," she said, mentally kicking herself again for being lame on the return volley.

"That works, too," Chase said, not skipping a beat. Yeah, there was a reason the man had never struck out before.

She started to chew on her lip, trying to think of what to say next.

"Don't chew a hole through it," he said, smiling and reaching across the space, brushing his thumb over the place her teeth had just grazed.

And everything in her stopped dead. His touch ignited her nerve endings, sending a brush fire down her veins and all through her body.

She hadn't been this ridiculous over Chase since she was sixteen years old. Since then, she had mostly learned to manage it.

She pulled away slightly, her chair scraping against the floor. She laughed, a stilted, unnatural sound. "I won't," she said, her voice too loud.

"If you're going to chew on your lip," he said, "don't freak out when the guy calls attention to it or touches you. It looks like you're doing it on purpose, so you should expect a comment."

"Duh," she said, "I was. That was…normal."

She wanted to crawl under the chair.

"There was this girl Miranda that I—"

"Okay." She cut him off, growing more and more impatient with the comparisons. "I'm old in town, what about you?"

"I've been around."

"I bet you have been," she said.

"I'm not sure how I'm supposed to take that," he said, flashing her a lopsided grin.

"Right," she said, "because I don't know what I'm doing."

"Maybe this was a bad idea," he said. "I think you actually need to feel some chemistry with somebody if flirting's going to work."

His words were sharp, digging into her chest. *You actually had to feel some chemistry* to be able to flirt.

They had chemistry. She had felt it last night. So had he. This was his revenge for the six-point-five comment. At least, she hoped it was. The alternative was that he had really felt nothing when their lips attached. And that seemed…beyond unfair.

She had all this attraction for Chase that she had spent years tamping down, only to have it come roaring to the surface the moment she had begun to pretend there was more going on between them than just friendship. And then she had kissed him. And far from being a disappointment, he had superseded her every fantasy. The jackass. Then he had kissed her, kissed her because he was angry. Kissed her to get revenge. Kissed her in a way that had kept her awake all night long, aching, burning. And now he was saying he didn't have chemistry with her.

"It's just that usually when I'm with a girl it flows a little easier. The bar to the bedroom is a pretty natural extension. And all those little movements kind of lead into the other. The way they touch their hair, tilt their head, lean in for a kiss…"

Oh, that did it.

"The women that I usually hook up with tend to—"

"Right," she said, her tone hard. "I get it. They flip their hair and scrunch their noses and twitch at all the appropriate times. They're like small woodland creatures who only emerge from their burrows to satisfy your every sexual whim."

"Don't get upset. I'm trying to help you."

She snorted. "I know." Just then, she had no idea what devil possessed her. Only that one most assuredly did. And once it had taken hold, she had no desire to cast it back out again.

She was mad. Mad like Chase had been last night. And she was determined to get her own back.

"Elizabeth was good at flipping her hair. Miranda gave you saucy interplay like so." She stood up, taking a step toward him, meeting his dark gaze with her own. "But how did they do this?" She reached down, placing her hand between his thighs and rubbing her palm over the bulge in his jeans.

Oh, sweet Lord, there was more to Chase McCormack than met the eye.

And she had a whole handful of him.

Her brain was starting to scream. Not words so much as a high-pitched, panicky whine. She had crossed the line. And there was no turning back.

But her brain wasn't running the show. Her body was on fire, her heart pounding so hard she was afraid it was going to rip a hole straight through the wall of her chest and flop out on the ground in front of him. Show him all its contents. Dammit, *she* didn't even want to see that.

But it was her anger that really pushed things forward. Her anger that truly propelled her on.

"And how," she asked, lowering herself slowly, scraping her fingernails across the line of his zipper, before dropping to her knees in front of him, "did they do this?"

Chapter 6

For one blinding second, Chase thought that he was engaged in some sort of high-definition hallucination.

Because there was no way that Anna had just put her hand…there. There was no way that she was kneeling down in front of him, looking at him like she was a sultry-eyed seductress rather than his best friend, still dirty from the workday, clad in motor-oil-smudged coveralls.

He blinked. Then he shook his head. She was still there. And so was he.

But he was so hard he could probably pound iron with his dick right about now.

He knew what he should do. And just now he had enough sense left in his skull to do it. But he didn't want to. He knew he should. He knew that at the end of this road there was nothing good. Nothing good at all. But he shut all that down. He didn't think of the road ahead.

He just let his brain go blank. He just sat back and watched as she trailed her fingers up the line of his zipper, grabbing hold of his belt buckle and undoing it, her movements clumsy, speaking of an inexperience he didn't want to examine too closely.

He didn't want to examine any of this too closely, but he was powerless to do anything else.

Because everything around the moment went fuzzy as the present sharpened. Almost painfully.

His eyes were drawn to her fingers as she pulled his zipper down, to the short, no-nonsense fingernails, the specks of dirt embedded in her skin. That should… well, he had the vague idea it should turn him off. It didn't. Though he had a feeling that getting a bucket of water thrown on him while he sat in the middle of an iceberg naked wouldn't turn him off at this point. He was too far gone.

He was holding his breath. Every muscle in his body frozen. He couldn't believe that she would do what it appeared she might be doing. She would stop. She had to stop. He needed her to stop. He needed her to never stop. To keep going.

She pressed her palm flat against his ab muscles before pushing her hand down inside his jeans, reaching beneath his underwear and curling her fingers around him. His breath hissed through his teeth, a shudder racking his frame.

She looked up at him, green eyes glittering in the dim shop light. She had a smudge of dirt on her face that somehow only highlighted her sharp cheekbones, somehow emphasized her beauty in a way he hadn't truly noticed it before. Yes, last night in the red dress she had been beautiful, there was no doubt about that. But for some reason, her femininity was highlighted wrapped in these traditionally masculine things. By the backdrop of the mechanic shop, the evidence of a day's hard work on her soft skin.

She tilted her chin up, her expression one of absolute challenge. She was waiting for him to call it off. Waiting for him to push her away. But he wasn't going to. He reached out, forking his fingers through her hair and tightening them, grabbing ahold of the loose bun that sat high on her head. Her eyes widened, her lips going slack. He didn't pull her away. He didn't draw her closer. He just held on tight, keeping his gaze firmly focused on hers. Then he released her. And he waited.

She licked her lips slowly, an action that would have been almost comically obvious coming from nearly anyone else. Not Anna.

Then she squeezed him gently before drawing her hand back. He should be relieved. He was not.

But her next move was not one he anticipated. She grabbed hold of the waistband of his jeans and underwear, pulling them down slowly, exposing him. She let out a shaky, shuddering breath before leaning in and flicking her tongue over the head of his arousal.

"Hell." He wasn't sure at first if he had spoken it out loud, not until he heard it echoing around him. It was like cursing in a church somehow, wrong considering the beauty of the gift he was about to receive.

Still, he couldn't think of anything else as she drew the tip of her tongue all the way down to the base of his shaft before retracing her path. She shifted, and that was when he noticed her hands were shaking. Fair enough, since he was shaking, too.

She parted her lips, taking him into her mouth completely, her lips sliding over him, the wet, slick friction almost too much for him to handle. He didn't know what was wrong with him. If it was the shock of the moment, if it was just that he was this base. Or if there was some kind of sick, perverted part of him that took extra pleasure in the fact that this was wrong. That he should not be letting his best friend touch him like this.

Because he'd had more skilled blow jobs. There was no question about that. This didn't feel good because Anna was an expert in the art of fellatio. Far from it.

Still, his head was about to blow off. And he was about to lose all of his control. So there was something.

Maybe it was just her.

She tilted her head to the side as she took him in deep, giving him a good view of just what she was doing. And just who was doing it. He was so aware of the fact that it was Anna, and that most definitely added a kick of the forbidden. Because he knew this was bad. Knew it was wrong.

And not many things were off-limits to him. Not many things had an illicit quality to them. He had kind of allowed himself to take anything and everything that had ever seemed vaguely sexy to him.

Except for her.

He shoved that thought in the background. He didn't like to think of Anna that way, and in general he didn't.

Sure, in high school, there had been moments. But he was a guy. And he had spent a lot of time with Anna. Alone in her room, alone in his. He had a feeling that half the people who had known them had imagined they were getting it on behind the scenes. Friends with benefits, et cetera. In reality, the only benefit to their friendship had been the fact that they'd been there for each other. They had never been there for each other in this way.

Maybe that's what was wrong with him.

Of course, nothing felt wrong with him right now. Right now, pleasure was crackling close to the surface of his skin and it was shorting out his brain. All he could do was sit back and ride the high. Embrace the sensations that were boiling through his blood. The magic of her lips and tongue combined with a shocking scrape of her teeth against his delicate skin made him buck his hips against her even as he tried to rein himself in.

But he was reaching the end of his control, the end of himself. He reached down, cupping her cheek as she continued to pleasure him, as she continued to drive him wild, urging him closer to the edge of control he hadn't realized he possessed.

He felt like he lived life with the shackles off, but she was pushing him so much further than he'd been before that he knew he'd been lying to himself all this time.

He'd been in chains, and hadn't even realized it.

Maybe because of her. Maybe to keep himself from touching her.

She gripped him, squeezing as she tasted him, pushing him straight over the edge. He held on to her hair, harder than he should, as a wave of pleasure rode up inside of him. And when it crashed he didn't ride it into shore. Oh, hell no. When it crashed it drove him straight down to the bottom of the sea, the impact leaving him spinning, gasping for breath, battered on the rocks.

But dammit all, it was worth it. Right now, it was worth it.

He knew that any moment the feeling would fade and he would be faced with the stark horror of what he'd just done, of what he'd just allowed to happen. But for now, he was foggy, floating in the kind of mist that always blanketed the ocean on cold mornings in Copper Ridge.

And he would cling to it as long as possible.

Oh, dear God. What had she done? This had gone so far beyond the kiss to prove they had chemistry. It had gone so far past the challenge that Chase had thrown down last night. It had gone straight into Crazy Town, next stop You Messed Up the Only Friendship You Hadville.

In combination with the swirling panic that was wrapping its claws around her and pulling her into a spiral was the fuzzy-headed lingering arousal. Her lips felt swollen, her body tingling, adrenaline still making her shake.

She regretted everything. She also regretted nothing.

The contradictions inside her were so extreme she felt like she was going to be pulled in two.

One thing her mind and body were united on was the desire to go hide underneath a blanket. This was definitely the kind of situation that necessitated hiding.

The problem was, she was still on her knees in front of Chase. Maybe she could hide under his chair. *What are you doing? Why are you falling apart?*

This isn't a big deal. He has probably literally had a thousand blow jobs.

This one didn't have to be that big a deal. Sure, it was the first one she had ever given. But he didn't have to know that, either.

If she didn't treat it like a big deal, it wouldn't be a big deal. They could forget anything had ever happened. They could forget that in a moment of total insanity she had allowed her anger to push her over the edge, had allowed her inability to back down from a challenge to bring them to this place. And that was all it was—the fact that she was absolutely unable to deal with that blow to her pride. It was nothing else. It couldn't be anything else.

She rocked back on her heels, planting her hands flat on the dusty ground before rising to her feet. She felt dizzy. She would go ahead and blame that on the speed at which she had stood up.

"I think it's safe to say we have a little bit more chemistry than you thought," she said, clearing her throat and brushing at the dirt on her pants.

He didn't say anything. He just kept sitting there, looking rocked. And he was still exposed. She did her very best to look at the wall behind him. "I can still see your..."

He scrambled into action, standing and tugging his pants into place, doing up his belt as quickly as possible. "I think we're done for the day."

She nodded. "Yeah. Well, *you* are."

She could feel the distance widening between them. It was what she needed, what she wanted, ultimately. But for some reason, even as she forced the breach, she regretted it.

"I don't… What just happened?"

She laughed, crossing her arms and cocking her hip out to the side. "If you have to ask, maybe I didn't do a very good job." The bolder she got, the more she retreated inside. She could feel herself tearing in two, the soft vulnerable part of her scrambling to get behind the brash, bold outward version that would spare her from any embarrassment or pain.

"You're…okay?"

"Why wouldn't I be okay?"

"Because you just…"

She laughed. Hysterically. "Sure. But let's not be ridiculous about it. It isn't like you punched me in the face."

Chase looked stricken. "Of course not. I would never do that."

"I know. I'm just saying, don't act like you punched me in the face when all I did was—"

"There's no need to get descriptive. I was here. I remember."

She snorted. "You should remember." She turned away from him, clenching her hands into fists, hoping he didn't notice that they were shaking. "And I hope you remember it next time you go talking about us not having chemistry."

"Do you *want* us to have chemistry?"

She whirled around. "No. But I have some pride. You were comparing me to all these other women. Well, compare that."

"I…can't."

She planted her hands on her hips. "Damn straight."

"We can't… We can't do this again," he said, shaking his head and walking away.

For some reason, that made her feel awful. For some reason, it hurt. Stabbed like a rusty knife deep in her gut.

"I don't want to do it again. I mean, you're welcome, but I didn't exactly get anything out of it."

He stopped, turning to face her, his expression tense. "I didn't ask you to do anything."

"I'm aware." She shook her head. "I think we're done for tonight."

"Yeah. I already said that."

"Well," she said, feeling furious now, "now I'm saying it."

She was mad at herself. For taking it this far. For being upset, and raw, and wounded over something that she had chosen to do. Over his reaction, which was nothing more than the completely predictable response. He didn't want her. Not really.

And she knew that. This evening's events weren't going to change it. An orgasm on the floor of the shop she rented from him was hardly going to alter the course of fifteen years of friendship.

An orgasm. Oh, dear Lord, what had she done? She really had to get out of here. There was no amount of bravado left in her that would save her from the meltdown that was pending.

"I have to go."

She was gone before he had a chance to protest. He should be glad she was gone. If she had stayed, there was no telling what he might have done. What other stupid bit of nonsense he might have committed.

He had limited brainpower at the moment. All of his blood was still somewhere south of his belt.

He turned, surveying the empty shop. Then, in a fit of rage, he kicked something metal that was just to the right of the chair. And hurt his foot. And probably broke the thing. He had no idea if it was important or not. He hoped it wasn't. Or maybe he hoped it was. She deserved to have some of her tractor shit get broken. What had she been thinking?

He hadn't been able to think. But it was a well-known fact that if a man's dick was in a woman's mouth, he was not doing much problem solving. Which meant Chase was completely absolved of any wrongdoing here.

Completely.

He gritted his teeth, closing his eyes and taking in a sharp breath. He was going to have to figure out how to get a handle on himself between now and the next time he saw Anna. Because there was no way things could continue on like this. There weren't a whole lot of people who stuck around in his world. There had never been a special woman. After the death of his and Sam's parents, relatives had passed through, but none of them had put down roots. And, well, their parents, they might not have chosen to leave, but they were gone all the same. He couldn't afford to lose anyone else. Sam and Anna were basically all he had.

Which meant when it came to Sam's moods and general crankiness, Chase just dealt with it. And when it came to Anna…no more touching. No more… No more of any of that.

For one second, he allowed himself to replay the moment when she had unzipped his pants. When she had leaned forward and tasted him. When that white-hot streak of release had undone him completely.

He blinked. Yeah, he knew what he had been thinking. That it felt good. Amazing. Too good to stop her. But physical pleasure was cheap. A friendship like theirs represented years of investment. One simply wasn't worth sacrificing the other for. And now that he was thinking clearly he realized that. So that meant no more. No more. Never.

Next time he saw her, he was going to make sure she knew that.

Chapter 7

Anna was beneath three blankets, and she was starting to swelter. If she hadn't been too lazy to sit up and grab hold of her ice-cream container, she might not be quite so sweaty.

The fact that she was something of a cliché of what it meant to be a woman behind closed doors was not lost on her. Blankets, old movies, Ben & Jerry's. But hey, she spent most of the day up to her elbows in engine grease, so she supposed she was entitled to a few stereotypes.

She reached her spoon out from beneath the blankets and scraped the top of the ice cream in the container, gathering up a modest amount.

"Oklahoma!" she sang, humming the rest of the line while taking the bite of marshmallow and chocolate ice cream and sighing as the sugar did its good work.

Full-fat dairy products were the way to happiness. Or at least the best way she knew to stop from obsessing.

Her phone buzzed and she looked down, cringing when she saw Chase's name. She swiped open the lock screen and read the message.

In your driveway. Didn't want to give you a heart attack.

Why are you in my dr—

She didn't get a chance to finish the message before there was a knock on her front door.

She closed her eyes, groaning. She really didn't want to deal with him right now. In fact, he was the last person on earth she wanted to deal with. He was the reason she was currently baking beneath a stack of blankets, seeking solace in the bosom of old movies.

Still, she couldn't ignore him. That would make things weirder. He was still her best friend, even if she had— Well, she wasn't going to think about what she had. If she ignored him, it would only cater to the weirdness. It would make events from earlier today seem more important than they needed to be. They did not need to be treated as though they were important.

Sure, she had never exactly done *that* with a man. Sure, she hadn't even had sexual contact of any kind with a man for the past several years. And sure, she had never had that kind of contact with Chase. But that was no reason to go assigning meaning. People got ribbons and stickers for their first trips to the dentist. They did not get them for giving their first blow job.

She groaned. Then she rolled off the couch, pushing herself into a standing position before she padded through the small living area to the entryway. She jerked the door open, pushing her hair out of her face and trying to look casual.

Too late, she realized that she was wearing her pajamas. Which were perfectly decent, in that they covered every inch of her body. But they were also baggy, fuzzy and covered in porcupines.

All things considered, it just wasn't the most glorious of moments.

"Hello," she said, keeping her body firmly planted in the center of the doorway.

"Hi," he returned. Then he proceeded to study her pajamas.

"Porcupines," she informed him, just for something to say.

"Good choice. Not an obvious one."

"I guess not. Considering they aren't all that cuddly. But neither am I. So maybe it's a more obvious choice than it originally appears."

"Maybe. We'll have to debate animal-patterned pajama philosophy another time."

"I guess. What exactly did you come here to debate if not that?"

He stuffed his hands in his pockets. "Nothing. I just came to…check on you."

"Sound of body and mind."

"I see that. Except you're in your pajamas at seven o'clock."

"I'm preparing for an evening in," she said, planting her hand on her hip. "So pajamas are logical."

"Okay."

She frowned. "I'm fine."

"Can I come in?"

She was frozen for a moment, not quite sure what to say. If she let him come in…well, she didn't feel entirely comfortable with the idea of letting him in. But if she didn't let him in, then she would be admitting that she was uncomfortable letting him in. Which would betray the fact that she actually wasn't really all that okay. She didn't want to do that, either.

No wonder she had avoided sexual contact for so long. It introduced all manner of things that she really didn't want to deal with.

"Sure," she said finally, stepping to the side and allowing him entry.

He just stood there, filling up the entry. She had never really noticed that before. How large he was in the small space of her home. Because he was Chase, and his presence here shouldn't really be remarkable. It was now.

Because things had changed. She had changed them. She had kissed him the other day, and then… well, she had changed things.

"There. You are in," she said, moving away from him and heading back into the living room. She took a seat on the couch, picking up the remote control and muting the TV.

"Movie night?"

"Every night is movie night with enough popcorn and a can-do attitude."

"I admire your dedication. What's on?"

"Oklahoma!"

He raised his brows. "You haven't seen that enough times?"

"There is no such thing as seeing a musical too

many times, Chase. Multiple viewings only enhance the experience."

"Do they?"

"Sing-alongs, of course."

"I should have known."

She smiled, putting a blanket back over her lap, thinking of it as a sort of flannel shield. "You should know these things about me. Really, you should know everything about me."

He cleared his throat, and the sudden awkwardness made her think of all the things he didn't know about her. And the things that he did know. It hit her then—of course, right then, as he was standing in front of her—just how revealing what had happened earlier was.

Giving a guy pleasure like that...well, a woman didn't do that unless she wanted him. It said a lot about how she felt. About how she had felt for an awfully long time. No matter that she had tried to quash it, the fact remained that she did feel attraction for him. Which he was obviously now completely aware of.

Silence fell like a boulder between them. Crushing, deadly.

"Anyway," she said, the transition as subtle as a landslide. "Why exactly are you here?"

"I told you."

"Right. Checking on me. I'm just not really sure why."

"You know why," he said, his tone muted.

"You check on every woman you have...encounters with?"

"You know I don't. But you're not every woman I have encounters with."

"Still. I'm an adult woman. I'm neither shocked nor injured."

She was probably both. Yes, she was definitely perilously close to being both.

He shifted, clearly uncomfortable. Which she hated, because they weren't uncomfortable with each other. Ever. Or they hadn't been before. "It would be rude of me not to make sure we aren't...okay."

She patted herself down. "Yes. Okay. Okay?"

"No," he said.

"No? What the hell, man? I said I'm fine. Do we have to stand around talking about it?"

"I think we might. Because I don't think you're fine."

"That's bullshit, McCormack," she said, rising from the couch and clutching her blanket to her chest. "Straight-up bullshit. Like you stepped in a big-ass pile somewhere out there and now you went and dragged it into my house."

"If you were fine, you wouldn't be acting like this."

"I'm sorry, how did you want me to act?"

"Like an adult, maybe?" he said, his dark brows locking together.

"Um, I am acting like an adult, Chase. I'm pretending that a really embarrassing mistake didn't happen, while I crush my regret and uncertainty beneath the weight of my caloric intake for the evening. What part of that isn't acting like an adult?"

"We're friends. This wasn't some random, forgettable hookup."

"It is so forgettable," she said, her voice taking on that brash, loud quality that hurt her own ears. That she was starting to despise. "I've already forgotten it."

"How?"

"It's a penis, Chase, not the Sistine Chapel. My life was hardly going to be changed by the sight of it."

He reached forward, grabbing hold of her arm and drawing her toward him. "Stop," he bit out, his words hard, his expression focused.

"What are you doing?" she asked, some of her bravado slipping.

"Calling you on *your* bullshit, Anna." He lowered his voice, his tone no less deadly. She'd never seen Chase like this. He didn't get like this. Chase was fun, and light. Well, except for last night when he'd kissed her. But even then, he hadn't been quite this serious. "I've known you for fifteen years. I know when your smile is hiding tears, little girl. I know when you're a whole mess of feelings behind that brick wall you put up to keep yourself separate from the world. And I sure as hell know when you aren't fine. So don't stand there and tell me that it didn't change anything, that it didn't mean anything. Even if you gave out BJs every day with lunch—and I know you don't—that would have still mattered because it's *us*. And we don't do that. It changed something, Anna, and don't you dare pretend it didn't."

No. *No.* Her brain was screaming again, but this time she knew for sure what it was saying. It was all denial. She didn't want him to look at her as if he was searching for something, didn't want him to touch her as if it was only the beginning of something more. Didn't want him to see her. To see how scared she was. To see how unnerved and affected she was. To see how very, very not brave she was beneath the shield she held up to keep the world out.

He already knows it's a shield. And you're already screwed ten ways, because you can't hide from him and you never could.

He'd let her believe she could. And now he'd changed his mind. For some reason it was all over now. Well, she knew why. It had started with a dress and high heels and ended with an orgasm in her shop. He was right. It had changed things.

And she had a terrible, horrible feeling more was going to change before they could go back to normal.

If they ever could.

"Well," she said, hearing her voice falter. Pretending she didn't. "I don't think anything needs to change."

"Enough," he said, his tone fierce.

Then, before she knew what was happening, he'd claimed her lips again in a kiss that ground every other kiss that had come before it into dust, before letting them blow away on the wind.

This was angry. Intense. Hot and hard. And it was happening in her house, in spite of the fact that she was holding a blanket and *Oklahoma!* was on mute in the background. It was her safe space, with her safe friend, and it was being wholly, utterly invaded.

By him.

It was confronting and uncomfortable and scary as hell. So she responded the only way she could. She got mad, too.

She grabbed hold of the front of his shirt, clinging to him tightly as she kissed him back. As she forced her tongue between his lips, claiming him before he could stake his claim on her.

She shifted, scraping her teeth lightly over his bottom lip before biting down. Hard.

He growled, wrapping his arms around her waist. She never felt small. Ever. She was a tall girl with a broad frame, but she was engulfed by Chase right now. His scent, his strength. He was all hard muscle against her, his heart thundering beneath her hands, which were pinned between their bodies.

She didn't know what was happening, except that right now, kissing him might be safer than trying to talk to him.

It certainly felt better.

It let her be angry. Let her push back without saying anything. And more than that…he was an amazing kisser. He had taken her from zero to almost-there with one touch of his lips against hers.

He slid his hand down her back, cupping her butt and bringing her up even harder against him so she could feel him. All of him. And just how aroused he was.

He wanted her. Chase wanted her. Yes, he was pissed. Yes, he was…trying to prove a point with his tongue or whatever. But he couldn't fake a hard-on like that.

She was angry, but it was fading. Being blotted out by the arousal that was crackling in her veins like fireworks.

Suddenly, she found herself being lifted off the ground, before she was set down on the couch, Chase coming down over her, his expression hard, his eyes sharp as he looked down at her.

He pressed his hand over her stomach, pushing the hem of her shirt upward.

She should stop him. She didn't.

She watched as his strong, masculine hand pushed

her shirt out of the way, revealing a wedge of skin. The contrast alone was enough to drive her crazy. Man, woman. Innocuous porcupine pajamas and sex.

Above all else, above anything else, there was Chase. Everything he made her feel. All of the things she had spent years trying *not* to feel. Years running from.

She couldn't run. Not now. Not only did she lack the strength, she lacked the desire. Because more than safety, more than sanity, she wanted him. Wanted him naked, over her, under her, *in* her.

He gripped the hem of her top and wrenched it over her head, the movement sudden, swift. As though he had reached the end of his patience and had no reserve to draw upon. That left her in nothing more than those ridiculous baggy pajama pants, resting low on her hips. She didn't have anything sexier underneath them, either.

But Chase didn't look at all disappointed. He didn't look away, either. Didn't have a faraway expression on his face. She wasn't sure why, but she had half expected to look up at him and be able to clearly identify that he was somewhere else in his mind, with someone else. But he was looking at her with a sharp focus, a kind of single-mindedness that no man, no *one*, had ever looked at her with before.

He knew. He knew who she was. And he was still hot for her. Still hard for her.

"You are so hot," he said, pressing his hand flat to her stomach and drawing it down slowly, his fingertips teasing the sensitive skin beneath the waistband. "And you don't even know it, do you?"

Part of her wanted to protest, wanted to fight back,

because that was what she did. Instead, everything inside of her just kind of went limp. Melted into a puddle. "N-no."

"You should know," he said, his voice low, husky. A shot of whiskey that skated along her nerves, warming her, sending a kick of heat and adrenaline firing through her blood. "You should know how damn sexy you are. You're the kind of woman who could make a man lose his mind."

"I could?"

He laughed, but it wasn't full of humor. It sounded tortured. "I'm exhibit A."

He shifted his hips forward, his hard length pressing up against that very aroused part of her that wanted more of him. Needed more of him. She gasped. "Soon," he said, the promise in his words settling a heavy weight in her stomach. Anticipation, terror. Need.

He continued to tease her, his fingertips resting just above the line of her panties, before he began to trail his hand back upward. He rested his palm over her chest, reaching up and tracing her lower lip with his thumb.

She darted her tongue out, sliding the tip of it over his skin, tasting salt, tasting Chase. A flavor that was becoming familiar.

Then she angled her head, taking his thumb into her mouth and sucking hard. His hips arched forward hard, his cock making firm contact, sending a shower of sparks through her body as he did.

"You're going to be the death of me," he said, every word raw, frayed.

"I might say the same about you," she said, her

voice thick, unrecognizable. She didn't know who she was right now. This creature who was a complete and total slave to sexual sensation. Who was so lost in it, she could feel nothing else. No sense of self-preservation, no fear kicking into gear and letting her know that she needed to put her walls up. That she needed to go on the defense.

She was reduced. She had none of that. And she didn't even care.

"You're a miracle," he said, tracing the line of her collarbone with the tip of his tongue. "A damn *miracle*, do you know that?"

"What?"

"The other day I told you you didn't look like a miracle. I was a fool. And I was wrong. Every inch of you is a miracle, Anna Brown."

Those words were like being submerged in warm water, feeling it flow over every inch of her, a kind of deep, soul-satisfying comfort that she really, really didn't want. Or rather, she didn't *want* to want it. But she did, bad enough that she couldn't resist.

But it was all a little too heavy. All a little too much. Still, she didn't have the strength to turn him away.

"Kiss me."

She said that instead of *get the hell out of my house*, and instead of *we can't do this*, because it was all she had strength for. Because she needed that kiss. And maybe, just maybe, if they didn't talk, she could make it through.

Chase—gentleman that he was—obliged her.

He angled his head, reaching up to cup her breast as he did, his mouth crashing down on hers just as his palm skimmed her nipple. She gasped, arching up against him, the combination of sensations almost too much to handle.

Yeah, she did not remember sex being like this. Granted, it had been a million years, but she would have remembered if it had come anywhere close to this. And her conclusion most certainly wouldn't have been that it was vaguely boring and a little bit gross. Not if it had even been in the same ballpark as what she was feeling now.

There was no point in comparing. There was just flat out no comparison.

He kissed her, long, deep and hard; he kissed her until she couldn't breathe. Until she thought she was going to die for wanting more. He kissed her until she was dizzy. And when he abandoned her mouth, she nearly wept. Until he lowered his head and skimmed his tongue over one hardened bud, until he drew it between his lips and sucked hard, before scraping her sensitized flesh with his teeth.

She arched against him, desperate for more. Desperate for satisfaction. Satisfaction he seemed intent on withholding.

"I'm so close," she said, panting. "Just do it now." Then it would be over. Then she would have what she needed, and the howling, yawning ache inside of her would be satisfied.

"No," he said, his tone authoritative.

"What do you mean no?"

"Not yet. You're not allowed to come yet, Anna. I'm not done."

His words, the calm, quiet command, made everything inside of her go still. She wanted to fight him.

Wanted to rail against that cruel denial of her needs, but she couldn't.

Not when this part of him was so compelling. Not when she wanted so badly to see where complying would lead.

"We're not done," he said, tracing her nipple with the tip of his tongue, "until I say we are." He lifted his head so that their eyes met, the prolonged contact touching something deep inside of her. Something that surpassed the physical.

He kissed her again, and as he did, he pulled his T-shirt over his head, exposing his incredible body to her.

Her mouth dried, and other parts of her got wet. Very, very wet.

"Oh, sweet Lord," she said, pressing her hand to his chest and drawing her fingertips down over his muscles, his chest hair tickling her skin as she did.

It was a surreal moment. So strange and fascinating. To touch her best friend like this. To see his body this way, to know that—right now—it wasn't off-limits to her. To know that she could lean forward and kiss that beautiful, perfect dip just next to his hip bone. Suddenly, she was seized with the desire to do just that. And she didn't have to fight it.

She pushed against him, bringing herself into a sitting position, lowering her head and pressing her lips to his heated skin.

"Oh, no, you don't," he said, his voice rough. He took hold of her wrist, drawing her up so that she was on her knees, eye to eye with him on the couch. "We're not finishing it like that," he said.

"Damn straight we aren't," she said. "But that doesn't mean I didn't want to get a little taste."

"You give way too much credit to my self-control, honey."

"You give too much credit to mine. I've never..." She stared at his chest instead of finishing her sentence. "It's like walking into a candy store and being told I can have whatever I want. Restraint is not on the menu."

"Good," he said, leaning in, kissing her, nipping her lower lip. "Restraint isn't what I want."

He wrapped his arm around her, drawing her up against him, her bare breasts pressing against his hard chest, the hair there abrading her nipples in the most fantastic, delicious way.

And then he was kissing her again, slow and deep as his hand trailed down beneath the waistband of her pants, cupping her ass, squeezing her tight. He pushed her pants down over her hips, taking her panties with them, leaving her completely naked in front of him.

He stood up, taking his time looking at her as he put his hands on his belt buckle.

Nerves, excitement, spread through her. She didn't know where to look. At the harsh, hungry look on his face, at the beautiful lines of muscle on his perfectly sculpted torso. At the clear and aggressive arousal visible through his jeans.

So she looked at all of him. Every last bit. And she didn't have time to feel embarrassed that she was sitting there naked as the day she was born, totally exposed to him for the first time.

She was too fascinated by him in this moment. Too fascinated to do anything but stare at him.

This was Chase McCormack. The man that women lost their minds—and their dignity—over on a regular basis. This was Chase McCormack, the sex god who could—and often did—have any woman he pleased.

She had known Chase McCormack, loyal friend and confidant, for a very long time. But she realized that up until now, she had never met *this* Chase McCormack. It was a strange, dizzying realization. Exhilarating.

And she was suddenly seized by the feeling that right now, he was hers. All hers. Because who else knew both sides of him? Did anyone?

She was about to.

"Get your pants off, McCormack," she said, impatience overriding common sense.

"You don't get to make demands here, Anna," he said.

"I just did."

"You want to try giving orders? You have to show me you can follow them." His eyes darkened, and her heart hammered harder, faster. "Spread your legs," he said, his words hard and uncompromising.

She swallowed. There was that embarrassment that she had just been so proud she had bypassed. But this was suddenly way outside her realm of experience. It was one thing to sit there in front of him naked. It was quite another to deliberately expose herself the way he was asking her to. She didn't move. She sat there, frozen.

"Spread your legs for me," he repeated, his voice heavy with that soft, commanding tone. "Or I put my clothes on and leave."

"You wouldn't," she said.

"You don't know what I'm capable of."

That was true. In this scenario, she really didn't know him. He was a stranger, except he wasn't.

Actually, if he had been a stranger, all of this would've been a lot easier. She could have spread her legs and she wouldn't have worried about how she looked. Wouldn't have worried about the consequences. If a stranger saw her do something like that, was somehow unsatisfied and then walked away, well, what did it matter? But this was Chase. And it mattered. It mattered so very much.

His hands paused on his belt buckle. "I'm warning you, Anna. You better do as you're told."

For some reason, that did not make her want to punch him. For some reason, she found herself sitting back on the couch, obeying his command, opening herself to him, as adrenaline skittered through her system.

"Good girl," he said, continuing his movements, pushing his jeans and underwear down his legs and exposing his entire body to her for the first time. And then, it didn't matter so much that she was sitting there with her thighs open for him. Because now she had all of him to look at.

The light in his eyes was intense, hungry, and he kept them trained on her as he reached down and squeezed himself hard. His jaw was tense, the only real sign of just how frayed his control was.

"Beautiful," he said, stroking himself slowly, leisurely, as he continued to gaze at her.

"Are you just going to look? Or are you going to touch?" She wasn't entirely comfortable with this. With him just staring. With this aching silence between them, and this deep, overwhelming connection that she felt.

There were no barriers left. There was no way to

hide. She was vulnerable, in every way. And normally she hated it. She kind of hated it now. But that vulnerability was wrapped in arousal, in a sharp, desperate need unlike anything she had ever known. And so it was impossible to try to put distance between them, impossible to try to run away.

"I'm going to do a lot more than look," he said, dropping down to his knees, "and I'm going to do a hell of a lot more than touch." He reached out, sliding his hands around to her ass, drawing her forward, bringing her up toward his mouth.

"Chase," she said, the short, shocked protest about the only thing she managed before the slick heat of his tongue assaulted that sensitive bundle of nerves at the apex of her thighs. "You don't have to…"

He lifted his head, his dark eyes meeting her. "Oh, I know I don't have to. But you got to taste me, and I think turnabout is fair play."

"But that wasn't…"

"What?"

"It's just that men…"

"Expect a lot more than they give. At least some of them. Anyway, as much as I liked what you did for me—and don't get me wrong, I liked it a lot—you have no idea how much pleasure this gives me."

"How?"

He leaned in, resting his cheek on her thigh. "The smell of you." He leaned closer, drawing his tongue through her slick folds. "The taste of you," he said. "You."

And then she couldn't talk anymore. He buried his face between her legs, his tongue and fingers working black magic on her body, pushing her harder, higher, faster than she had imagined possible. Yeah, making out with Chase had been enough to nearly give her an orgasm. This was pushing her somewhere else entirely.

In her world, orgasm had always been a solo project. Surrendering the power to someone else, having her own pleasure not only in someone else's hands but in his complete and utter control, was something she had never even thought possible for her. But Chase was proving her wrong.

He slipped a finger deep inside of her as he continued to torture her with his wicked mouth, then a second, working them in and out of her slick channel while he teased her with the tip of his tongue.

A ball of tension grew in her stomach, expanded until she couldn't breathe. "It's too much," she gasped.

"Obviously it's not enough yet," he said, pushing her harder, higher.

And when the wave broke over her, she thought she was done for. Thought it was going to drag her straight out to sea and leave her to die. She couldn't catch her breath as pleasure assaulted her, going on and on, pounding through her like a merciless tide, battering her against the rocks, leaving her bruised, breathless.

And when it was over, Chase was looming over her, a condom in his hand.

She felt like a creature without its shell. Sensitive, completely unprotected. She wanted to hide from him, hide from this. But she couldn't. How could she? The simple truth was, they still weren't done. They had gone only part of the way. And if they didn't finish this, she would always wonder. He would, too.

She imagined that—whether or not he admitted it— was why he had come here tonight in the first place.

They had opened the lid on Pandora's box. And they couldn't close it until they had examined every last dirty, filthy sin inside of it.

Even though she thought it might kill her, she knew that they couldn't stop now.

He tore open the condom, positioning the protection over the blunt head of his arousal, rolling it down slowly.

She was transfixed. The sight of his own hand on his shaft so erotic she could hardly stand it.

She would pay good money to watch him shower, to watch his hands slide over all those gorgeous muscles. To watch him take himself in hand and lead himself to completion.

Oh, yeah. That was now her number-one fantasy. Which was a problem, because it was a fantasy that would never be fulfilled.

Don't think about that now. Don't think about it ever.

He leaned in, kissing her, guiding her so that she was lying down on the couch, then he positioned himself between her legs, testing the entrance to her body before thrusting forward and filling her completely.

She closed her eyes tight, unable to handle the feeling of being invaded by him, both in body and in her soul.

"Look at me," he said.

And once more, she was completely helpless to do anything other than obey.

She opened her eyes, her gaze meeting his, touching her down deep, where his hands never could.

And then he kissed her, soft, gentle. That kind of tenderness that had been missing from her life for so long. The kind that she had always been too embarrassed to ask for from anyone. Too embarrassed to show that she needed. That she desperately craved.

But Chase knew. Because he was Chase. He just knew.

He flexed his hips again, his pelvis butting up against her, sending a shower of sparks through her body. There was no way she was ready to come again. Except he kept moving, creating new sensations inside of her, deeper than what had come before.

It shouldn't be possible for her to have another orgasm now. Not after the first one had stripped her so completely. But apparently tonight, nothing was impossible.

There was something different about this. About the two of them, working toward pleasure together. This wasn't just her giving it out to him, or him reciprocating. This was something they were sharing.

She focused on pieces of him. The intensity in his eyes. The way the tendons in his neck stood out, evidence of the control he was exerting. She looked at his hand, up by her head, grabbing hold of one of the blankets she had been using, clinging tightly to it, as though it were his lifeline.

She looked down at his throat, at the pulse beating there.

All these close, intimate snapshots of this man that she knew better than anyone else.

Her chest felt heavy, swollen, and then it began to expand. She was convinced that she was going to break apart. All of these feelings, all of this pleasure. It was just too much. She couldn't handle it.

"Please," she begged. "Please."

He released his grip on the blanket to grasp her hips, holding her steady as he pounded harder into her, as he pounded them both toward release. Toward salvation. It was too much. It needed to end. It was all she could think. She was begging him inside. *End it, Chase. Please, end it.*

Orgasm latched on to her throat like a wild beast, gripping her hard, violently, shaking her, pleasure exploding over her. Ugly. Completely and totally beyond control.

And then Chase let out a hoarse cry, freezing above her as he thrust inside her one last time, shivering, shaking as his own release took hold.

They were captive to it together. Powerless to do anything but wait until the savage beast was finished having its way. Until it was ready to move on.

And when it was over, only the two of them were left.

Just the two of them. Chase and Anna. No clothes, no shields.

She remembered the real reason she hadn't had sex since that first time. It had nothing to do with how good or bad it had felt. Nothing to do with what a jerk she'd been after.

It had been this. This feeling of being unable to hide. But with the other guy, it had been easy to regroup. Easy to pretend she felt nothing.

She couldn't do that with Chase. She was defenseless.

And for the first time in longer than she could remember, a tear slid down her cheek.

Chapter 8

He couldn't swear creatively enough. He had just screwed his best friend's brains out on a couch in her living room. On top of what might be the world's friendliest, most nonsexual-looking blanket. With a Rodgers and Hammerstein musical on the TV in the background.

And then she had started crying. She had started crying, and she had wiggled out from beneath him and gone into the bathroom. Leaving him alone.

He had been sitting there by himself for a full thirty seconds attempting to reconcile all of these things.

And then he sprang into action.

He got up—still bare-ass naked—and walked down the hall. "Anna!" He didn't hear anything. And so he pounded on the bathroom door. "Anna!"

"I'm in the bathroom, dumbass!" came the terse, watery reply.

"I know. That's why I'm knocking on the bathroom door."

"Go away."

"No. I'm not going to go away. You need to talk to me."

"I don't want to talk."

"Anna, dammit, did I hurt you?"

He got nothing in return but silence. Then he heard the lock rattle, and the door opened a crack. One green eye looked up at him, accusing. "No."

"Why are you hiding?" He studied the eye more closely. It was red-rimmed. Definitely still weeping a little bit.

"I don't know," she said.

"Well…you had me convinced that I… Anna, it happened really fast."

"Not *that* fast. Believe me, I've had faster."

"You wanted all of that…? I mean…"

She laughed. Actually laughed, pushing the door open a little bit wider. "After my emphatic… After all the *yes-ing*… You can honestly ask whether or not I wanted it?"

"I have a lot of sex," he said. "I don't see any point in beating around the bush there. And women have had a lot of reactions to the sex. But I can honestly say none of them have ever run away crying. So, yeah, I'm feeling a little bit shaky right now."

"You're shaky? I'm the one that's crying."

"And if I was alone in this…if I pushed you further than you wanted to go… I'm going to have to ask Sam to fire up the forge and prepare you a red-hot poker so you can have your way with me in an entirely different manner."

"I wanted it, Chase." Her tone was muted.

"Then why are you crying?"

"I'm not very experienced," she said.

"Well, I mean, I know you don't really hook up."

"I've had sex once. One other time."

He was stunned. Stunned enough that he was pretty sure Anna could have put her index finger on his chest, given a light push and knocked him flat on his ass. "Once."

"Sure. You remember Corbin. And that whole fiasco. Where I kind of made fun of his...lack of...attributes and staying power in the hall at school. And... basically ensured that no guy would ever touch me ever again."

"Right." He remembered that.

"Well, I didn't really get what the fuss was about."

"But you... I mean, you've had..."

"Orgasms? Yes. Almost every day of my life. Because I am industrious, and red-blooded, and self-sufficient."

He cleared his throat, trying to ignore the shot of heat that image sent straight through his blood. Anna. Touching herself.

What the hell was happening to him? Well, there was nothing happening. It had damn well *happened*. On the couch in Anna's living room.

He could never look at her again without seeing her there, obeying his orders. Spreading her thighs for him so that he could get a good look at her. Yeah, he could never unsee that. Wasn't sure if he wanted to. But where the hell did he go from here? Where did they go?

There were a lot of women he could have sex with, worry-free. Anna wasn't one of them. She was a rare, precious thing in his life. Someone who knew him. Who knew all about how affected he and Sam had been by the loss of their parents.

Someone he never had to explain it to because she'd been there.

He didn't like explaining all that. So the solution was keep the friends that were there when it happened, and make sure everyone else was temporary.

Which meant Anna couldn't be temporary. She was part of him. Part of his life. A load-bearing wall on the structure that was Chase McCormack. Remove her, and he would crumble.

That was why she had always stayed a friend. Why he had never done anything like this with her before. It wasn't because of her coveralls, or her don't-step-on-the-grass demeanor. Or even because she'd neatly neutered the reputation of the guy she'd slept with in high school.

It was because he needed her friendship, not her body.

But the problem was now he knew what she looked like naked.

He couldn't get that image out of his head. And he didn't even want to.

Same with the image of all her self-administered, industrious climaxes.

Damn his dirty mind.

"Okay," he said, taking a step away from the door. "Why don't you come out?"

"I'm naked."

"So am I."

She looked down. "So you are."

"We need to talk."

"Isn't it women who are supposed to require conversation after basic things like sex?"

"I don't know. Because I never stick around long enough to find out. But this is different. This is you and me, Anna, and I will be damned if I let things get messed up over a couple of orgasms."

She chewed her lower lip. She looked...well, she looked young. And she didn't look too tough. It made him ache. "They were pretty good ones."

"Are you all right?"

"I'm fine. It's just that all of this is a little bit weird. And I'm not really experienced enough to pretend that it isn't."

"Right." The whole thing about her having been with only one guy kind of freaked him out. Made him feel like he was responsible for some things. Big things, like what she would think of sex from this day forward. And then there was the bone-deep possessiveness. That he was the first one in all this time... He should hate it. It should scare him. It should not make him feel...triumph.

He was triumphant, dammit. "Why haven't you slept with anyone else?"

She lifted a shoulder. "I told you. I didn't really think my first experience was that great."

"So you just never..."

"I'm also emotionally dysfunctional, in case you hadn't noticed."

A shocked laugh escaped his lips. "Right. Same goes."

"I don't know. Sex kind of weirds me out. It's a lot of closeness."

"It doesn't have to be," he pointed out. It felt like a weird thing to say, though, because what they'd done just now had been the epitome of closeness.

"It just all feels…raw. And…it was good. But I think that's kind of why it bothered me."

"I don't want it to bother you."

"Well, the other thing is it was *you*. You and me, like you said. We don't do things like this. We hang out, we drink beer. We don't screw."

"Turns out we're pretty compatible when it comes to the screwing." He wasn't entirely sure this was the time to make light of what had just happened. But he was at sea here. So he had to figure out some way to talk to her. He figured he would make his best effort to treat her like he always did.

"Yeah," she said, finally pushing her way out of the bathroom. "But I'm not really sure there's much we can do with that."

He felt like he was losing his grip on something, something essential, important. Like he was on a rope precariously strung across the canyon, trying to hang on and not fall to his doom. Not fall to *their* doom, since she was right there with him.

What she was saying should feel like safety. It didn't. It felt like the bottom of the damn canyon.

"I don't know if that's the way to handle it."

"You don't?" she asked, blinking.

Apparently. He hadn't thought that statement through before it had come out of his mouth. "Yeah. Look, you kissed me yesterday. You gave me…oral pleasure earlier. And now we've had sex. Obviously, this isn't going away. Obviously, there's some attraction between us that we've never really acknowledged before."

"Or," she said, "someone cast a spell on us. Yeah, we drank some kind of sex potion. Makes you horny for twenty-four hours and then goes away."

"Sex potion?"

"It's either that or years of repressed lust, Chase. Pick whichever one makes you most comfortable."

"I would go with sex potion if I thought such a thing existed." He took a deep breath. "You know there's a lot of people that think men and women can't just be friends. And I've always thought that was stupid. Maybe this is why. Maybe it's because eventually, something happens. Eventually, the connection can't just be platonic. Not when you've spent so long in each other's company. Not when you're both reasonably attractive and single."

She snorted. "*Reasonably* attractive. What happened to me being a *damn miracle*?"

"I was referring to myself when I said reasonably. I'd hate to sound egotistical."

"Honestly, Chase, after thirty years of accomplished egotism, why worry about it now?"

He looked down at her. She was stark naked, standing in front of him, and he felt like he was in front of the pastry display case at Pie in the Sky. He wanted to sample everything, and he didn't know where to start.

But he couldn't do anything about that now. He was trying to make amends. Dropping to his knees in front of her and burying his face between her legs probably wouldn't help with that.

He could feel his dick starting to wake up again. And since he was naked he might as well just go ahead and shout his intentions at her, because he wouldn't be able to hide them.

He couldn't look at her and not get hard, though. A new development in their relationship. But then, so was standing in front of each other without clothes.

"You're beautiful," he said, unable to help himself.

She wasn't as curvy as the women he usually gravitated toward. Her curves were restrained, her waist slim, with no dramatic sweep inward, just a slow build down to those wide, gorgeous hips that he now had fantasies about grabbing hold of while he pumped into her from behind. Her breasts were small but perfection in his mind. More would just be more.

He couldn't really imagine how he had ever looked at her face and found it plain. He had to kick his own ass mentally for that. He had been blind. Someone with unrefined, cheap taste. Who thought that if you stuck rhinestones and glitter on something, that meant it was prettier. But that wasn't Anna. She was simple, refined beauty. Something that only a connoisseur might appreciate. She was like a sunset over the ocean in comparison to a gaudy ballroom chandelier. Both had their strong points. But one was real, deep. Priceless instead of expensive.

That was Anna.

Something about those thoughts made a tightening sensation start in his gut and work its way up to his chest.

"Maybe what happened was just inevitable," he said, looking at her again.

"I can't really disprove that," she said, shifting uncomfortably. "You know, since it happened. I really need to put my clothes on."

"Do you have to?"

She frowned. "Yes. And you do, too. Because if we don't..."

"We'll have sex again."

The words stood between them, stark and far too true for either of their liking.

"Probably not," she said, sounding wholly unconvinced.

"Definitely yes."

She sighed heavily. "Chase, you can have sex with anyone you want. I'm definitely hard up. If you keep walking around flashing that thing, I'm probably going to hop on for a ride, I'll just be honest with you. But I understand if I'm not half as irresistible to you as you are to me."

Anger roared through him, suddenly, swiftly. And just like earlier, when she'd thrown her walls up and tried to drive a wedge between them, he found himself moving toward her. Moving to break through. He growled, backing her up against the wall, almost sighing in relief when his hardening cock met up with her soft skin, when her small breasts pressed against his chest. He grabbed hold of her hands, drawing them together and lifting them up over her head. "Let's get one thing straight, Anna," he said. "You are irresistible to me. If you weren't irresistible to me, I would still be at home. I never would have come here. I never would have kissed you. I never would have touched you. Don't you dare put yourself down. If this is because of your brothers, because of your dad..."

She closed her eyes, looking away from him. "Don't. It's not that."

"Then what is it? Why don't you think you can have this?"

"There's nothing to have. It's just sex. You mean the world to me. And just because I'm…suddenly unable to handle my hormones, I'm not going to compromise our friendship."

"It doesn't have to compromise it," he said, lowering his voice.

"What are you suggesting? We can't have a relationship with each other. We don't have those kinds of feelings for each other. A relationship is more than sex. It's romance and all kinds of stuff that I'm not even sure I want."

"I don't want it, either," he said. "But we're going to see each other. Pretty much every day. Not just because of the stupid bet. Not just because of the charity event. I'd call all that off right now if I thought it was going to ruin our friendship. But the horse has left the stable, Anna, well and truly. It's not going back in." He rolled his hips forward, and she gasped. "See what I mean? And if you were resistible? Then sure, I would tell you that we could just be done. We could pretend it didn't happen. But you're not. So I can't."

She opened her eyes again, looking up at him. "Then what are we doing?"

"You've heard of friends with benefits. Why can't we do that? I mean, I would never have set out to have that relationship. Because I don't think it's very smart. But…it's a little bit late for smart."

"Friends with benefits. As in…we stay friends by day and we screw each other senseless by night?"

Gah. That about sent him over the edge. "Yeah."

"Until what? Until…"

"Until you get that other date. Until the charity thing. As long as we're both single, why not? You're working toward the relationship stuff. You said you didn't want to be alone anymore. So, maybe this is good in the meantime. I know you're both industrious and red-blooded, and can get those orgasms all by yourself." He rolled his hips again and, much to his satisfaction, a small moan of pleasure escaped her lips. "But are they this good?"

"No," she said, her tone hushed.

"This is possibly the worst idea in the history of the world. But hell, you wanted to get some more experience… I'm offering to give it to you." The moment he said the words he wanted to bite his tongue off. The idea of giving Anna more experience just so she could go and do things with other men? That made him see red. Made him feel violent. Jealous. Things he never felt.

But what other option was there? He couldn't keep her. Not like this. But he couldn't let her go now.

He was messed up. *This* was messed up.

"I guess… I guess that makes sense. You know, until earlier today I'd never even given a guy a blow job."

"You're killing me," he said, closing his eyes.

"Well, I don't want you to die. You just offered me your penis for carnal usage. I want you alive."

"So that's it? My penis has now become the star of the show. Wow, how quickly our friendship has eroded."

"Our friendship is still solid. I think it just goes to prove how solid your dick is."

"With romantic praise like that, how are you still single?"

"I have no idea. I spout sonnets effortlessly."

He leaned forward, kissing her, a strange, warm sensation washing over him. He was kissing Anna. And it didn't feel quite as rushed and desperate as all the other times before it. A decision had been made. This wasn't a hasty race against sanity. This wasn't trying to get as much satisfaction as possible squeezed into a moment before reality kicked in. This was… well, in the new world order, it was sanctioned.

Instantly, he was rock hard again, ready to go, even though it'd been only a few minutes since his last orgasm. But there was one problem. "I don't have a condom," he said, cursing and pushing himself away from her. "I don't suppose the woman who has been celibate for the past thirteen years has one?"

"No," she said, sagging against the wall. "You only carry one on you?"

"Yeah. I'm not superhuman. I don't usually expect to get it on more than once in a couple of hours."

"But you were going to with me?"

He looked down at his very erect cock. "Does this answer your question?"

"Yeah."

"Well, then." He let out a heavy sigh.

"You could stay and watch… *Oklahoma!* with me."

He nodded slowly. He should stay and watch *Oklahoma!* with her. If he didn't, it kind of made a mockery of the whole friends-with-benefits thing. Because, before the sex, he would have stayed with her to watch a movie, of course. To hang out, because she was one of his favorite people on earth to spend time with. Even if her taste in movies was deeply suspect.

Of course, he didn't particularly want to stay now, because she presented the temptation that he could not give in to.

"Unless you have to work early tomorrow."

"I really do," he said.

"Thank God."

His eyebrows shot up. "You want to get rid of me?"

"I don't really want to hang out with you when I know I can't have you."

"I felt the same way, but I didn't want to say it. I thought it seemed kind of offensive."

Strangely, she smiled. "I'm not offended. I'm not offended at all. I kind of like being irresistible."

Instead of leaving, he knew that he could drive down to the store and buy a box of condoms. And he seriously considered it. The problem with that was there had to be some boundaries. Some limits. He was pretty sure being so horny and desperate that you needed to buy condoms right away instead of just waiting until you had protection on hand probably didn't fit within the boundaries of friends with benefits.

"I'll see you tomorrow, then."

She nodded. "See you tomorrow."

Chapter 9

By the time Anna swung by the grocery store in the afternoon, she was feeling very mature, and very proud of herself. She was having a no-strings sexual relationship with her friend. And she was going to buy milk, cheese and condoms. Because she was mature and adult and completely fine with the whole situation. Also, mature.

She grabbed a cart and began to slowly walk up and down the aisles. She was not making sure that no one she knew was around. Because, of course, she wasn't at all embarrassed to be in the store looking for milk, cheese and—incidentally—prophylactics. She was *thirty*. She was entitled to a little bit of sexual release. Anyway, no one was actually watching her.

She swallowed hard, trying to remember exactly

which aisle the condoms were in. She had never bought any. Ever. In her entire life.

She had been extremely tempted to make a dash to the store last night when Chase had discovered he didn't have any more protection, but she had imagined that was just a little bit too desperate. She was going to be nondesperate about this. Very chill. And not like a woman who was a near virgin. Or like someone who was so desperate to jump her best friend's bones it might seem like there were deeper emotions at play. There were not.

The strong feelings she had were just…in her pants. Pants feelings. That's it.

Last night's breakdown had been purely because she was unaccustomed to sex. Just a little post-orgasmic release. That's all it was. The whole thing was a release. Post-orgasmic tears weren't really all that strange.

She felt bolstered by that thought.

She turned down the aisle labeled Family Planning and made her way toward the condoms. Lubricated. Extra-thin. Ribbed. There were options. She had to stand there and seriously ponder ribbed. She should have asked Chase what he had used last night. Because whatever that had been had been perfect.

"Anna." The masculine voice coming from her left startled her.

She turned and—to her utter horror—saw her brother Mark standing there.

"Hi," she said, taking two steps away from the condom shelf, as though that would make it less obvious why she was in the aisle. Whatever. They were adults. Neither of them were virgins and they were both aware of that.

Still, she needed some distance between herself and anything that said "ribbed for her pleasure" when she was standing there talking to her brother.

"Haven't seen you in a couple days."

"Well, you pissed me off last time I saw you."

He lifted a shoulder. "Sorry."

He probably was, too.

"Hey, whatever. I win your bet."

His brows shot up. "I heard a rumor about you and Chase McCormack kissing at Beaches, but I was pretty sure that…" His eyes drifted toward the condoms. *"Really?"*

Dying of embarrassment was a serious risk at the moment, but she was caught. Completely and totally caught. And as long as she was drowning in a sea of horror…well, she might as well ride the tide.

If he needed proof her date with Chase was real, she imagined proof of sex was about the best there was.

She took a fortifying breath. "Really," she said, crossing her arms beneath her breasts. "It's happening. I have a date. I have more than a date. I have a whole future full of dates because I have a relationship. With Chase. You lose."

"I'm supposed to believe that you and McCormack are suddenly—" his eyes drifted back to the condoms again *"—that."*

"You don't have to believe it. It's true. He's also going to be my date to the charity gala that I'm invited to. I will take my payment in small or large bills. Thank you."

"I'm not convinced."

"You're not convinced?" She moved closer to the shelf and grabbed a box of condoms. "I am caught in the act."

"Convenient," he said, grabbing his own box.

She made a face. "It's not convenient. It happened."

"You're in love with him?"

The question felt like a punch to the stomach. She did not like it. She didn't like it at all. More than that, she had no idea what to say. *No* seemed…wrong. *Yes* seemed worse. And she wasn't really sure either answer was true.

You can't love Chase.

She couldn't not love him, either. He was her friend, after all. Of course she wasn't in love with him.

Her stomach twisted tight. No. She did not love him. She didn't do love. At all. Especially not with him. Because he would never…

"You look like you just got slapped with a fish," Mark said, and, to his credit, he looked somewhat concerned.

"I… Of course I love him," she said. That was a safe answer. It was also true. She did love him. As a friend. And…she loved his body. And everything about him as a human being. Except for the fact that he was a man slut who would never settle down with any woman, much less her.

Why not you?

No. She was not thinking about this. She wasn't thinking about any of this.

"Tell you what. If you're still together at the gala, you get your money."

"That isn't fair. That isn't what we agreed on."

He lifted a shoulder. "I know. But I also didn't expect you to grab your best friend and have him be your date. That still seems suspicious to me, regardless of…purchases."

"You didn't put any specifications on the bet, Mark. You can't change the rules now."

"We didn't put any specifications on it saying I couldn't."

"Why do you care?"

He snorted. "Why do you care?"

"I have pride, jackass."

"And I don't trust Chase McCormack. If you're still together at the gala, you get your money. And if he hurts you in any way, I will break his neck. After I pull his balls off and feed them to the sharks."

It wasn't very often that Mark's protective side was on display. Usually, he was too busy tormenting her. Their childhood had been rough. Their father didn't have any idea how to show affection to them, and as a result none of them were very good at it, either. Still, she never doubted that—even when he was a jerk— Mark cared about her.

"That's not necessary. Chase is my best friend. And now…he's more. He isn't going to hurt me."

"Sounds to me like he has the potential to hurt you worse than just about anybody."

His words settled heavily in the pit of her stomach. She should be able to brush them off. Because she and Chase were in a relationship. She and Chase were friends with benefits. And nothing about that would hurt at all.

"I'll be fine."

"If you need anything, just let me know."

"I will."

He lifted the condom box. "We'll pretend this didn't happen." Then he turned and started to walk away.

"Pretend what didn't happen?" She pulled her own box of condoms up against her chest and held it tightly. "See? I've already forgotten. Mostly because I can't afford therapy. At least not until you pay me the big bucks at the gala."

"We'll see," he said, walking out of sight.

She turned, chucking the box into her cart and making her way quickly down to the milk aisle. Chase wasn't going to hurt her, because Mark was wrong. They were only friends, and she quashed the traitorous flame in her stomach that tried to grow, tried to convince her otherwise.

She wasn't going to get hurt. She was just going to have a few orgasms and then move on.

That was her story, and she was sticking to it.

"I'm taking you dancing tonight," Chase said as soon as Anna picked up the phone.

"Did you bump your head on an anvil today?"

He supposed he shouldn't be that surprised to hear Anna's sarcasm. After last night—vulnerability, tears—he'd had a feeling that she wasn't going to be overly friendly today. In fact, he'd guessed that she would have transformed into one of the little porcupines that were on her pajamas. He had been right.

"No," he said. "I'm just following the lesson plan. I said I was taking you out, and so I am."

"You know," she said, her voice getting husky, "I'm curious about whether or not making me scream was anywhere on the lesson plan."

His body jolted, heat rushing through his veins. He

looked over his shoulder at Sam, who was working steadily on something in the back of the shop. It was Anna's day off, so she wasn't on the property. But he and Sam were in the middle of a big custom job. A gate with a lot of intricate detail, with matching work for the deck and interior staircase of the home. Which meant they didn't get real time off right now.

"No," he returned, satisfied his brother wasn't paying attention, "that wasn't on the lesson plan. But I'm a big believer in improvisation."

"That was improvisation? In that case, it seems to be your strength."

The sarcasm he had expected. This innuendo, he had not. They'd both pulled away hard last night, no denying it. It would have been simple to go out and get more protection and neither of them had.

But damn, this new dynamic between them was a lot to get used to. Still, for all that it was kind of crazy, he knew what he wanted. "I'd like to show you more of my strengths tonight."

"You're welcome to improvise your way on over to my bed anytime." There was a pause. "Was that flirting? Was that *good* flirting?"

He laughed, tension exiting his body in a big gust. He should have known. He wasn't sure how he felt about this being part of the lesson. Not when he had been on the verge of initiating phone sex in the middle of a workday with his brother looming in the background. But keeping it part of the lesson was for the best. He didn't need to lose his head. This was Anna, after all. He was walking a very fine line here.

On the one hand, he knew keeping a clear line drawn in the sand was the right thing to do. They weren't just going to be able to slide right back into their normal relationship. Not after what had happened. On the other hand, Anna was… Anna. She was essential to him. And she wasn't jaded when it came to sexual relationships. Wasn't experienced. That meant he needed to handle her with care. And it would benefit him to remember that he couldn't play with her the way he did women with a little more experience. Women who understood that this was sex and nothing more.

It could never be meaningless sex with Anna. He couldn't have a meaningless conversation with her. That meant that whatever happened between them physically would change things, build things, tear things down. That was a fact. A scary one. Taking control, trying to harness it, label it, was the only solution he had. Otherwise, things would keep happening when they weren't prepared. That would be worse.

Maybe.

He cleared his throat. "Very good flirting. You got me all excited."

"Excellent," she said, sounding cheerful. "Also, I bought condoms."

He choked. "Did you?"

"They aren't ribbed. I wasn't sure if the one you used last night was."

"No," he said, rubbing the back of his neck and casting a side eye at his brother. "It wasn't."

"Good. I was looking for a repeat performance. I didn't want to get the wrong thing. Though maybe sometime we should try ribbed."

Sometime. Because there would be more than once.

More than last night. More than tonight. "We can try it if you want."

"I feel like we might as well try everything. I have a lot of catching up to do."

"Dancing," he said, trying to wage a battle with the heat that was threatening to take over his skull. "Do you want to go dancing tonight?"

"Not really. But I can see the benefit. Seeing as there will be dancing at the fund-raiser. And I bet I'm terrible at dancing."

"Great. I'm going to pick you up at seven. We're going to Ace's."

"Then I'll be ready."

He hung up the phone and suddenly realized he was at the center of Sam's keen focus. That bastard had been listening in the entire time. "Hot date tonight?" he asked.

"Dancing. With Anna," he said meaningfully. The meaning being *with Anna and not with you*.

"Well, then, you wouldn't mind if I tagged along." Jerkface was ignoring his meaning.

"I would mind."

"I thought this was just about some bet."

"It is," he lied.

"Uh-huh."

"You don't want to go out. You want to stay home and eat a TV dinner. You're just harassing me."

Sam shrugged. "I have to get my kicks somewhere."

"Get your own. Get laid."

"Nope."

"You're a weirdo."

"I'm selective."

Maybe Sam was, maybe he wasn't. Chase could

honestly say that his brother's sex life was a mystery to him. Which was fine. Really, more than fine. Chase had a reputation, Sam…did not. Well, unless that reputation centered around being grumpy and antisocial.

"Right. Well, you enjoy that. I'm going to go out."

"Chase," Sam said, his tone taking on a note of steel. "Don't hurt her."

Those words poked him right in the temper. "Really?"

"She's the best thing you have," Sam said, his voice serious. "You find a woman like that, you keep her. In whatever capacity you can."

"She's my best friend. I'm not going to hurt her."

"Not on purpose."

"I don't think you're in any position to stand there and lecture me on interpersonal relationships, since you pretty much don't have any."

"I have you," Sam said.

"Right. I'm not sure that counts."

"I have Anna. But if you messed things up with her, I won't have her, either."

Chase frowned. "You don't have feelings for her, do you?" He would really hate to have to punch his brother in the face. But he would.

"No. Not like you mean. But I know her, and I care about her. And I know you."

"What does that mean?"

Sam pondered that for a second. "You're not her speed."

"I'm not trying to be." He was getting ready to punch his brother in the face anyway.

"I'm just saying."

"You're just saying," he muttered. "Go *just say*

somewhere else. A guy whose only friends are his younger brother and that brother's friend maybe shouldn't stand there and make commentary on relationships."

"I'm quiet. I'm perceptive. As you mentioned, I am an artist."

"You can't pull that out when it suits you and put it away when it doesn't."

"Sure I can. Artists are temperamental."

"Stop beating around the bush. Say what you want to say."

Sam sighed. "If she offers you more than friendship, take it, dumbass."

"Why would you think that she would ever offer that? Why would you think that I want it?"

He felt defensive. And more than a little bit annoyed. "She will. I'm not blind. Actually, being antisocial has its benefits. It means that I get to sit back and watch other people interact. She likes you. She always has. And she's the kind of good… Chase, we don't get good like that. We don't deserve it."

"Gee. Thanks, Sam."

"I'm not trying to insult you. I'm just saying that she's better than either of us. Figure out how to make it work if she wants to."

Everything in Chase recoiled. "She doesn't want to. And neither do I." He turned away from Sam, heading toward the door.

"Are you sleeping with her yet?"

Chase froze. "That isn't any of your business."

"Right. You are."

"Still not your business."

"Chase, we both have a lot of crap to wade through.

Which is pretty obvious. But if she's standing there willing to pull you out, I'm just saying you need to take her up on her offer."

"She has enough crap of her own that she's hip deep in, Sam. I don't need her taking on mine."

Sam rubbed his hand over his forehead. "Yeah, that's always the thing."

"Anyway, she doesn't want me. Not like that. I mean, not forever. This is just a…physical thing." Which was way more information than his brother deserved.

"Keep telling yourself that if it helps you sleep at night."

"I sleep like a baby, Sam." He continued out the door, heading toward his truck. He had to get back to the house and get showered and dressed so that he could pick up Anna. And he was not going to think about anything his brother had said.

Anna didn't want forever with him.

That thought immobilized him, forced him to imagine a future with Anna, stretching on and on into the distance. Holding her, kissing her. Sleeping beside her every night and waking up with her every morning.

Seeing her grow round with his child.

He shut it down immediately. That was a fantasy. One he didn't want. One he couldn't have.

He would have Anna as a friend forever, but the "benefits" portion of their relationship was finite.

So, he would just enjoy this while it lasted.

Chapter 10

She looked like a cliché. A really slutty one. She wasn't sure she cared. But in her very short denim skirt and plaid shirt knotted above the waistline she painted quite the picture.

One of a woman looking to get lucky.

"Well," she said to her reflection—her made-up reflection, compliments of her trip to the store in Tolowa today, as was everything else. "You *are* looking to get lucky."

Fair. That was fair.

She heard the sound of a truck engine and tires on the gravel in her short little driveway. She was renting a house in an older neighborhood in town—not right in the armpit of town where she'd grown up, but still sort of on the fringe—and the yard was a little bit…rustic.

She wondered if Chase would honk. Or if he would come to the door.

Him coming to the door would feel much more like a date. A real date.

A *date* date.

Oh, Lord, what were they doing?

She had flirted with him on the phone, and she'd enjoyed it. Had wanted—very much—to push him even harder. Trading innuendo with him was…well, it was a lot more fun than she'd imagined.

There was a heavy knock on the door and she squeaked, hopping a little bit before catching her breath. Then she grabbed her purse and started to walk to the entry, trying to calm her nerves. He'd come to the door. That felt like A Thing.

You're being crazy. Friends with benefits. Not boyfriend.

The word *boyfriend* made her stomach lurch, and she did her best to ignore it. She jerked the door open, watching his face intently for his response to her new look. And she was not disappointed.

"Damn," he said, leaning forward, resting his forearm on the doorjamb. "I didn't realize you would be showing up dressed as Country Girl from My Dirtiest Dreams."

She shouldn't feel flattered by that. But she positively glowed. "It seemed fair, since you're basically the centerfold of *Blacksmith Magazine*."

He laughed. "Really? How would that photo shoot go?"

"You posing strategically in front of the forge with a bellows over your junk."

"I am not getting my *junk* near the forge. The

last thing I need is sensitive body parts going up in flames."

"I know I don't want them going up in flames." She cleared her throat, suddenly aware of a thick blanket of awkwardness settling over them. She didn't know what to do with him now. Did she...not touch him unless they were going to have sex? Did she kiss him if she wanted to or did she need permission?

She needed a friends-with-benefits handbook.

"Um," she began, rather unsuccessfully. "What exactly are my benefits?"

"Meaning?"

"My benefits additional to this friendship. Do I... kiss you when I see you? Or..."

"Do you want to kiss me?"

She looked up at him, all sexy and delicious looking in his tight black T-shirt, cowboy hat and late-in-the-day stubble. "Is that a trick question? Because the only answer to 'Do I want to kiss a very hot guy?' is yes. But not if you don't want to kiss me."

He wrapped his arm around her waist, drawing her up against him before bending down to kiss her slowly, thoroughly. "Does that help?"

She let out a long, slow breath, the tension that had been strangling her since he'd arrived at her house leaving her body slowly. "Yes," she said, sighing. "It does."

"All right," he said, extending his hand. "Let's go."

She took hold of his hand, the warmth of his touch flooding her, making her stomach flip. She let him lead her to the truck, open her door for her. All manner of date-type stuff. The additional benefits were getting bound up in the dating lessons and at the moment she wasn't sure what was for her and what was for the Making Her Datable mission.

Then she decided it didn't matter.

She just clung to the good feelings the whole drive to Ace's.

When they got there, she felt the true weight of the spectacle they were creating in the community. Beaches was one thing. Them being together there had certainly caused a ripple. But everyone in Copper Ridge hung out at Ace's.

Sierra West, whose family was a client of both her and Chase, was in the corner with some other friends who were involved with local rodeo events. Sheriff Eli Garrett was over by the bar, along with his brother, Connor, and their wives, Sadie and Liss.

She looked the other direction and saw Holly and Ryan Masters sitting in the corner, looking ridiculously happy. Holly and Ryan had both grown up in foster care in Copper Ridge and so had been part of the town-charity-case section at school. Though Holly was younger and Ryan a little older, so she'd never been close friends with them. Behind them was Jonathan Bear, looking broody and unapproachable as usual.

She officially knew too many damn people.

"This town is the size of a postage stamp," she muttered as she followed Chase to a table where they could deposit their coats and her purse.

"That's good," he said. "Men are seeing you attached. It's all part of changing your reputation. That's what you want."

She grunted. "I guess." It didn't feel like what she wanted. She mostly just wanted to be alone with Chase now. No performance art required.

But she was currently a dancing monkey for all of Copper Ridge, so performance art was the order of the evening.

She also suddenly felt self-conscious about her wardrobe choice. Wearing this outfit for Chase hadn't seemed bad at all. Wearing it in front of everyone was a little much.

The jukebox was blaring, and Luke Bryan was demanding all the country girls shake it for him, so Anna figured—regardless of how comfortable she was feeling—it was as good a time as any for them to get out on the dance floor.

The music was fast, so people weren't touching. They were just sort of, well, *shaking it* near each other.

She was just standing there, looking at him and not shaking it, because she didn't know what to do next. It felt weird to be here in front of everyone in a skirt. It felt weird to be dancing with Chase. It felt weird to not touch him. But it would be weirder to touch him.

Hell if she knew what she was doing here.

Then he reached out, brushing his fingers down her arm. That touch, that connection, rooted her to the earth. To the moment. To him. Suddenly, it didn't matter so much what other people around them were doing. She moved in slightly, and he put his hand on her hip.

Then, before she was ready, the song ended, slowing things down. And now she really didn't know what to do. It seemed that Chase did, though. He wrapped his arm around her waist, drawing her in close, taking hold of her hand with his free one.

Her heart was pounding hard. And she was pretty sure her face was bright red. She looked up at Chase, his expression unreadable. He was not bright red. Of course he wasn't. Because even if this relationship was new for him, this kind of situation was not. He knew how to handle women. He knew how to handle sex feelings. Meanwhile, she was completely unsure of what to do. Like a buoy floating out in the middle of the ocean, just bobbing there on her own.

Her breathing got shorter, harder. Matching her heartbeat. She couldn't just dance with him like this. She needed to not be in front of people when she felt these things. She felt like her arousal was written all over her skin. Well, it was. She was blushing like a beacon. She could probably guide ships in from the sea.

She looked at Chase's face again. There was no way to tell what he was thinking. His dark gaze was shielded by the dim lighting, his jaw set, hard, his mouth in a firm line. That brief moment of connection that she'd felt was gone now. He was touching her still, but she had no idea what he was feeling.

She looked over to her left and noticed that people were staring. Of course they were. She and Chase were dancing and that was different. And, of course, a great many of the stares were coming from women. Women who probably felt like they should be in her position. Like she didn't belong there.

And they could all see how much she wanted it. That she wanted him more than he wanted her. That she was the one who was completely and totally out of control. Needing him so much she couldn't even hide it.

And they all knew she didn't deserve it.

She pulled away from him, looking around, breathing hard. "I think... I just need a break."

She crossed the room and went back to their table, grabbing her purse and making her way over to the bar.

Chase joined her only a few moments later. "What's up?"

She shook her head. "Nothing."

"We were dancing, and then you freaked out."

"I don't like everybody watching us."

"That's the point, though."

That simple statement stabbed her straight through the heart. "Yeah. I know." That was the problem. He was so conscious of why they were doing this. This whole thing. And she could so easily forget. Could so easily let down all the walls and shields that she had put in place to protect her heart. And just let herself want.

She hated that. Hated craving things she couldn't have. Affection she could never hope to earn.

Her mother had left. And no amount of wishing that she would come back, no amount of crying over that lost love, would do anything to fix it. No amount of hoping her father would drop that crusty exterior and give her a hug when she needed it would make it happen. So she just didn't want. Or at least, she never let people see how much she wanted.

"I know," she said, her tone a little bit stiffer than she would like.

She was bombing out here. Failing completely at remaining cool, calm and unaffected. She was standing here in public, hemorrhaging needs all over the place.

"What's wrong?"

"I need a drink."

"Why don't we leave?"

She blinked. "Just...leave?"

"If you aren't having fun, then there's no point. Let's go."

"Where are we going?"

He grabbed her hand and started to lead her through the bar. "Somewhere fun."

She followed him out into the night, laughing helplessly when they climbed into the truck. "People are going to talk. That was all a little weird."

"Let them talk. They need something to do."

He started the engine and backed out of the parking lot, turning sharply and heading down the road, out of town.

"Where are we going?"

"Somewhere I bet you've never been."

"You don't know my life, Chase McCormack. You don't know where I've been."

"I do know your life, Anna Brown."

She gritted her teeth, because, of course, he did. She said nothing as they continued to drive up the road. And still said nothing when he turned onto a dirt road that forked into a narrower dirt road as it went up the mountain.

"What are we doing?" she asked again.

Just then, they came to a flat, clear area. She couldn't see anything; there were no lights except for the headlights on the truck, illuminating nothing but the side of another mountain, thick with evergreens.

"I want to make out with you. This is where you go do that."

"We're adults," she said, ignoring the giddy fluttering in her stomach. "We have our own bedrooms. And beds. We don't need to go make out in a car."

"*Need* is not the operative word here. We're expanding experiences and stuff." He flicked the radio on, country music filling the cab of the truck. "Actually, I think before we make out—" he opened the driver's-side door "—we should dance."

Now there was nobody here. Which meant there was no excuse. Actually, this made her a lot more emotional. She did not like that. She didn't like the superpower that Chase seemed to have of reaching down inside of her, past all the defenses, and grabbing hold of tender, emotional things.

But she wasn't going to refuse, either.

It was dark out here. At least there was that.

Before she had a chance to move, Chase was at her side of the truck, opening her door. He extended his hand. "Dance with me?"

She was having a strange out-of-body experience. She wasn't sure who this woman was, up in the woods with only a gorgeous man for company. A man who wanted to dance with her. A man who wanted to make out with her.

She unbuckled, accepting his offered hand and popping out of the truck. He spun her over to the front of the vehicle, the headlights serving as spotlights as the music played over the radio. "I'm kind of a crappy dancer," he said, pulling her in close.

"You don't seem like a crappy dancer to me."

"How many men have you danced with?"

She laughed. "Um, counting now?"

"Yeah."

"One."

He chuckled, his breath fanning over her cheek-bone. So intimate to share the air with him like this. Shocking. "Well, then, you don't have much to compare it to."

"I guess not. But I don't think I would compare either way."

"Oh, yeah? Why is that?"

"You're in a league of your own, Chase McCormack, don't you know?"

"Hmm. I have heard that a time or two. When teachers told me I was a unique sort of devil, sent there to make their lives miserable. Or all the times I used to get into it with my old man."

"Well, you did raise a lot of hell."

"Yeah. I did. I continue to raise hell, in some fashion. But I need people to see a different side of me," he said, drawing her even tighter up against him. "I need for them to see that Sam and I can handle our business. That we can make the McCormack name big again."

"Can you?" she asked, tilting her head up, her lips brushing his chin. The stubble there was prickly, masculine. Irresistible. So she bit him. Just lightly. Scraping her teeth over his skin.

He gripped her hair, pulling her head back. The sudden rush of danger in the movements sending a shot of adrenaline through her blood. This was so strange. Being in his arms and feeling like she was home. Like he was everything comforting and familiar. A warm blanket, a hot chocolate and a musical she'd seen a hundred times.

Then things would shift, and he would become something else entirely. A stranger. Sex, sin and all the things she'd never taken the time to explore. She liked that, too.

She was starting to get addicted to both.

"Oh, I can handle myself just fine," he said, his tone hard.

"Can you handle me?" she asked.

He slid his hand down to cup her ass, his eyes never leaving hers as they swayed to the music. "I can handle you. However you want it."

"Hard," she said, her throat going dry, her words slightly unsteady. She wasn't sure what had possessed her to say that.

"You want it hard?" he asked, his words sounding strangled.

"Yes," she said.

"How else do you want it?" he asked, holding her against him, moving in time with the beat. She could feel his cock getting hard against her hip.

"Aren't you the one with the lesson plan?"

"You're the one in need of the education," he said.

"I don't want tonight to be about that," she said, and she was as sure about that as she'd been about wanting it hard and equally unsure about how she knew it.

"What do you want it to be about?"

"You," she said, tracing the sharp line of his jaw. "Me. That's about it."

"What do you want from me?" he asked.

Only everything. She shied away from that thought. "Show me what the fuss is about."

"I did that already."

Something hot and possessive spiked in her blood. Something she never could have anticipated, because she hadn't even realized that it lived inside of her. "No.

Something you don't give other women, Chase. You're my friend. You're…more to me than one night and an orgasm. You're right. I could have gotten that from a lot of guys. Well, maybe not the orgasm. But sex for sure. My coveralls aren't that much of a turnoff. And you could have any woman. So give me you. And I'll give you me. Don't hold back."

"You're…not very experienced."

She stretched up on tiptoes, pressing her lips to his. "Did I ask for a gentleman? Or did I ask for hard?"

He tightened his grip on her hair, and this time when she looked up at his face, she didn't see a stranger. She saw Chase. The man. The whole man. Not divided up into parts. Not Her Friend Chase or Her Lover Chase, but just… Chase.

He was all of these things. Fun and laid-back, intense and deeply sexual. She wanted it all. She craved it all. As hard as he could. As much as he could. And still, it would never, ever be enough.

"Go ahead," she said, "take me, cowboy."

She didn't have to ask twice.

He propelled them both backward, pressing her up against the truck, kissing her deeply, a no-holds-barred possession of her mouth. She hadn't even realized kissing like this existed. She wasn't entirely sure what she had thought kissing was for. Affection. A prelude to sex. This was something else entirely. This was a language all its own. Words that didn't exist in English. Words that she knew Chase would never be able to say.

And her body knew that. Understood it. Responded. As surely as it would have if he had spoken.

She was drowning. In this, in him. She hadn't expected emotion to be this…fierce. She hadn't really expected emotion at all. She hadn't understood. She really had not understood.

But then she didn't have the time to think about it. Or the brainpower. He tugged on her hair, drawing her head to the side before he pressed his lips to her tender neck, his teeth scraping along the sensitive skin before he closed his lips around her and sucked hard.

"You want it hard?" he asked, his voice rough. "Then we're going to do it my way."

He grabbed hold of her hips, turning her so that she was facing the truck. "Scoot just a little bit." He guided her down to where the cab of the truck ended and the bed began. "Grab on." She curved her fingers around the cold metal, a shiver running down her spine. "You ever do it like this?" he asked.

She laughed, more because she was nervous than because she thought the question was funny. "Chase, before you I had never even given a guy a blow job. Do you think I've ever done this before?"

"Good," he said, his tone hard, very definitely him. "I like that. I'm a sick bastard. I like the fact that no other man has ever done this to you before. I should feel guilty." He reached around and undid the top button on her top. "But I'm just enjoying corrupting you."

He undid another button, then another. She wasn't wearing a bra underneath the top. Because, frankly, when you were as underendowed as she was, there really wasn't any point. Also, it made things a little bit more easy access. Though that wasn't something she had thought about until just now. Until Chase undid the last button and left her completely bare to the cool night air.

"I'm kind of enjoying being corrupted."

"I didn't tell you you could talk."

She shut her mouth, surprised at the commanding tone he was taking. Not entirely displeased about it. He cupped her breasts, squeezing them gently before moving his hands down her stomach, bringing them around her hips. Then he tugged her skirt down, leaving her in nothing but her boots and her underwear.

"We'll leave the boots on. I wouldn't want you to step on anything sharp."

She didn't say anything. She bit her lip, eagerly anticipating what he might do next. He slipped his hand down between her thighs, his fingertips edging beneath her panties. He stroked his fingers through her folds, a harsh growl escaping his lips. "You're wet for me," he said—not a question.

She nodded, closing her eyes, trying to keep from hurtling over the edge as soon as his fingertips brushed over her. But it was a pretty difficult battle she was waging. Just the thought of being with Chase again was enough to take her to the precipice. His touch nearly pushed her over immediately.

He gripped her tightly with his other hand, drawing her ass back up against his cock as he teased her between her legs with his clever fingers. He slipped one deep inside of her, continuing to toy with her with the edge of his thumb while he thrust in and out of her slowly. He added a second finger, then another. And she was shaking. Trembling with the effort of holding back her climax.

But she didn't want it to end like this. Didn't want it to end so quickly. Mostly, she just didn't want him to know that with one flick of his fingertip over her sensitized flesh he could make her come so hard she wouldn't be able to see straight. Because at the end of the day it didn't matter how much she wanted him; she still had her pride. She still rebelled against the idea of revealing herself quite so easily.

She probably already had. Here she was, mostly naked, out underneath the stars. Here she was, telling him she wanted just the two of them, that she wanted it hard. Probably there were no secrets left. Not really. There were all sorts of unspoken truths filling in the silences between them, but she felt like they were easy enough to read, if he wanted to look at them.

He might not. She didn't really want to. Yet it didn't make them go away.

But she could ignore them. She could focus on this. On his touch. On the dark magic he was working on her body, the spell that was taking her over completely.

He swept her hair to the side, pressing a hot kiss to the back of her neck. And then there was no holding back. Climax washed over her like a wave as she shuddered out her release.

"Good girl," he whispered, kissing her again before moving away for a moment. He pushed her panties down her legs, helping her step out of them, then he kissed her thigh before straightening.

She heard him moving behind her. But she didn't change her position. She stood there, gripping the back of the truck. Dimly, she was aware the radio was still on. That they had a sound track to this illicit encounter in the woods. It added to the surreal, out-of-body quality.

But then he was back with her, touching her, kissing her, and it didn't feel so surreal anymore. It was too raw. Too real. His voice, his scent, his touch. He was there. There was no denying it. This wasn't fantasy. Fantasy was gauzy, distant. This was sharp, so sharp she was afraid it would cut right into her. Dangerous. She wanted it. All of it. And she was afraid that in the end there would be nothing of her left. At least nothing that she recognized. That his friendship wouldn't be something that she recognized. But they'd gone too far to turn back, and she didn't even want to anymore. She wanted to see what was on the other side of this. Needed to see what was on the other side.

He reached up, bracing his hand on the back of her neck, holding her hip with the other as he positioned himself at the entrance to her body. He pressed the blunt head of his erection against her, sliding in easily, thrusting hard up inside her. She gasped as he went deeper than he had before. This was almost overwhelming. But she needed it. Embraced it.

His hold was possessive, all-encompassing. She felt like she was being consumed by him completely. By her desire for him. Warmth bloomed from where he held her, bled down beneath the surface of her skin, hemorrhaged in her chest.

"I fantasized about this," he said, the words seeming to scrape along his throat. Rough, raw. "Holding you like this. Holding on to your hips as I did this to you."

She couldn't respond. She couldn't say anything. His words had grabbed ahold of her, squeezing her throat tight, making it impossible for her to speak. He had fantasized about her. About this.

This position should feel less personal. More distant. But it didn't. That made it… It made it exactly what she had asked for. This was for her. And this was him. What he wanted, not just the next item on a list of things she needed to learn. Not just a set routine that he had with women he slept with.

He slid his hand down along the line of her spine, pressing firmly, the impression of his possession lingering on her skin. Then he held both of her hips tight, his blunt fingertips digging into her skin. He thrust harder into her, his skin slapping against hers, the sound echoing in the darkness. She gripped the truck hard, lowering her head, a moan escaping her lips.

"You wanted hard, baby," he ground out. "I'll give it to you hard."

"Yes," she whispered.

"Who are you saying yes to?" There was an edge to his words, a desperation she hadn't imagined he would feel, not with her. Not over this.

"Chase," she said, closing her eyes tight. "Yes, Chase. Please. I need this. I need you."

She needed all of him. And she suddenly realized why those thoughts about having someone to spend her nights with had seemed wrong. Because at the end of the day when she thought of sharing evenings with someone, when she thought of curling up under a blanket with someone, of watching *Oklahoma!* with someone for the hundredth time, it was Chase. It was always Chase. And that meant no other man had ever been able to get close enough to her. Because he was the fantasy. And as long as he was the fantasy, no one else had a place.

And now, now after this, she was ruined forever. Because she would never be able to do this with another man. Ever. It would always be Chase's hand she imagined on her skin. That firm grip of his that she craved.

He flexed his hips, going harder into her, then slipped his fingers around between her thighs again, stroking her as he continued to fill her. Then he leaned forward, biting her neck as he slammed into her one last time, sending them both over the edge. He growled, pulsing inside of her as he found his release. The pain from his teeth mingled with the all-consuming pleasure rolling through her in never-ending waves, pounding over her so hard she didn't think it would ever end. She didn't think she could survive it.

And when it passed, it was Chase who held her in his arms.

There was no denying it. No escaping it. And she was scraped raw. As stripped as she'd been after their first encounter, she was even more exposed now. Because she had read into all those empty, unspoken things. Because she had finally realized what everything meant.

Her asking him for help. Her kissing him. Her going down on him.

Her not having another man in her life in any capacity.

It was because she wanted Chase. All of Chase. It was why everything had come together for her tonight. Why she'd realized she couldn't compartmentalize him.

She wasn't ready to think the words yet, though. She couldn't. She did her very best to hold them at bay. To stop herself from thinking the things that would crumble her defenses once and for all.

Instead, she released her hold on the truck and turned to face him, looping her arms around his neck, pressing her bare body against his, luxuriating in him.

"That was quite the dance lesson," she said finally.

"A lot more fun than it would have been in Ace's." He slid his hand down to her butt, holding her casually. She loved that. So much more than she should.

"Yeah, we would have gotten thrown out for that."

"But can you imagine the rumors?"

"Are they really rumors if everyone has actually seen you screw?"

"Good question," he said, leaning forward and nipping her lower lip.

"You're bitey," she said.

"And you like to be bitten."

She couldn't deny it. "I guess I should… I mean, I have to work tomorrow."

"Me, too," he said, sounding regretful.

She wanted so badly to ask him to stay with her. But he wasn't bringing it up. And she didn't know if the almighty Chase McCormack actually *slept* with the women he was sleeping with.

So she didn't ask.

And when he dropped her off at her house, leaving her at her doorstep, she tried very, very hard not to regret that.

She didn't succeed.

Chapter 11

The best thing about having her own shop was working alone. Some people might find it lonely; Anna found it a great opportunity to run through every musical number she knew. She had already gone through the entirety of *Oklahoma!* and was working her way through *Seven Brides for Seven Brothers*.

Admittedly, she wasn't the best singer in the world, but in her own shop she was the best singer around.

And if the music helped drown out all of the neuroses that were scampering around inside of her, asking her to deal with her Chase feelings, then so much the better. She didn't want to deal with Chase feelings.

"When you're in love, when you're in love, there is no way on earth to hide it," she sang operatically, the words echoing off the walls.

She snapped her mouth shut. That was a bad song.

A very bad song for this moment. She was not... She just wasn't going to think about it.

She turned her focus back to the tractor engine she currently had in a million little pieces. At least an engine was concrete. A puzzle she could solve. It was tactile, and most of the time, if she could just get the right parts, find the source of the problem, she could fix it. That wasn't true with much of anything else in life. That was one reason she found a certain sort of calm in the garage.

Plus, it was something her father knew how to do. He was his own mechanic, and weekends were often spent laboring over his pickup truck, getting it in working order so that he could drive it to work Monday. So she had watched, she had helped. It was about the only way she had been able to connect with her gruff old man. It was still about the only way she could connect with him.

It certainly wasn't through musicals. It could never have been a desire to be seen differently by other kids at school. A need to look prettier for a boy that she liked.

So she had chosen carburetors.

"But it can't be carburetors forever." Well, it could be. In that she imagined she would do this sort of work for the rest of her life. She loved it. She was successful at it. She filled a niche in the community that needed to be filled. But...it couldn't be the only thing she was. She needed to do more than fill. She needed to...be filled.

And right now everything was all kind of turned on its head. Or bent over the back of a pickup truck. Her cheeks heated at the memory.

Yeah, Chase had definitely come by his reputation honestly. It wasn't difficult to see why women lost their ever-loving minds over him.

That made her frown. Because she didn't like to think that she was just one of the many women losing their minds over him because he had a hot ass and skilled hands. She had known about the hot ass for years. It hadn't made her lose her mind. In fact, she didn't really think she had lost her mind now. She knew exactly what she was doing. She frowned even more deeply.

Did she know what she was doing? They had stopped and had discussions, made conscious decisions to do this friends-with-benefits thing. Tricked themselves into thinking that they were in control of this. Or at least that's what she had been doing. But as she had been carried away on a wave of emotion last night, she had known for an absolute fact that she wasn't in control of any of this.

"Doesn't mean I'm going to stop."

That, at least, was the absolute truth. He would have to be the one to call it off.

Just the thought made her heart crumple up into a little ball.

"Quitting time yet?"

She turned to see Chase standing in the doorway. This was a routine she could get used to. She wanted to cross the space between them and kiss him. And why not? She wasn't hiding her attraction to him. They weren't hiding their association.

She dropped her ratchet, wiped her hands on her coveralls and took two quick steps, flinging herself into his arms and kissing him on the lips. She wasn't embarrassed until about midway through the kiss, when she realized she had been completely and totally enthusiastic and hadn't hidden any of it. But he was holding on to her, and he was kissing her back, so maybe it didn't matter. Maybe it was okay.

When they parted, he was smiling.

Her heart felt tender, exposed. But warm, like it was being bathed in sunlight. Something to do with that smile of his. With that easy acceptance of what she had offered. "I think it's about time to quit," she said.

"I like your look," he said, gesturing to her white tank top, completely smeared with grease and dirt, and her coveralls, which were unbuttoned and tied around her waist.

"Really?"

"Last night you were my dirty country girl fantasy and today you're a sexy mechanic fantasy. Do you take requests? Around Christmas you could go for Naughty Mrs. Claus."

She rolled her eyes, grabbing the end of her tank top and knotting it up just under her breasts. "Maybe more like this? Though I think I'm missing the breast implants."

His smile turned wicked. "Baby, you aren't missing a damn thing."

Her heart thundered harder, a rush of adrenaline flowing through her. "I didn't think this was your type. Remember? You had to give me a makeover."

"Yeah, that was stupid. I actually think I just needed to get knocked upside the head."

"Did I…knock you upside the head?"

"Yeah." He wrapped his arms around her bare waist, his fingertips playing over her skin. "You're

pretty perfect the way you are. You never needed a
dress or high heels. I mean, you're welcome to wear
them if you want. I'm not going to complain about that
outfit you wore last night. But all that stuff we talked
about in the beginning, about you needing to change
so that people would believe we were together... I
guess everyone is just going to have to believe that I
changed a little bit."

"Have you changed?" she asked, brushing her
thumb over his lower lip. A little thrill skittered down
her spine. That she could touch him like this. Be so
close to him. Share this kind of intimacy with a man
she had had a certain level of emotional intimacy with
for years and years.

It was wonderful. It also made her ache. Made her
feel like her insides were being broken apart with a
chisel. And she was willingly submitting to it. She
didn't know quite what was happening to her.

Are you sure you don't?

"Something did," he said, his dark eyes boring into
hers.

"You know," she said, trying to tamp down the fluttering that was happening in her chest, "I think it's
only fair that I give you a few lessons."

"What kind of lessons?" he asked, his gaze sharp-
ening.

"I'm not sure you know your way around an engine quite the way you should," she said, smiling as
she wiggled out of his hold.

"Oh, really?"

She nodded, grabbing hold of a rag and slinging it
over her shoulder before picking up her ratchet again.
"Really."

"Is this euphemistic engine talk?"

"Do you think I'm expressing dissatisfaction with the way you work under my hood?"

He chuckled. "You're really getting good at this flirting thing."

"I am. That was good. And dirty."

"I noticed." He moved behind her, sweeping her hair to the side and kissing her neck. "But if you're implying that I didn't do a very good job… I would have to clear my good name."

"I was talking about literal engines, Chase. But if you really want to try to up your game, I'm not going to stop you."

"What's that?" he asked, reaching past her and pointing to one of the parts that were spread out on the worktable in front of her.

"A cylinder head. I'm replacing that and the head gasket on the engine. And I had to take a lot of things apart to get to it."

"When do you need to have it done?"

"Not until tomorrow."

"So you don't need me to play the part of lovely assistant while you finish up tonight?"

"I would like you to assist me with a few things," she said, planting her hand at the center of his chest and pushing him lightly. The backs of his knees butted up against the chair that was behind him and he sat down, looking up at her, a predatory smile curving his lips.

"Is this going to be a part of my lesson?"

"Yeah," she said, "I thought it might be."

Last night had been incredible. Last night, he had given her something that felt special. Personal. Now she wanted to give him something. To show him what was happening inside of her, because she could hardly bring herself to think it. She wanted... She just wanted. In ways that she hadn't allowed herself to want in a long time. More. Everything.

"What exactly are you going to teach me?"

"Well, I could teach you all the parts of the tractor engine. But we would be here all night. And it would just slow me down. Someday, we can trade. You can give me some welding secrets. Teach me how to pound steel."

"That sounds dirty, too."

"Lucky me," she said, stretching her arms up over her head, her shirt riding up a little higher. She knew what she wanted to do. But she also felt almost petrified. This was...well, this was the opposite of protecting herself. This was putting herself out there. Risking humiliation. Risking doing something wrong while revealing how desperately she wanted to get it right.

But she wanted to give him something. And honestly, there was no bigger gift she could give him than vulnerability. To show him just how much she wanted him.

She swayed her hips to the right, then moved them back toward the left in a slow circle. She watched his face, watched the tension in his jaw increase, the sharpness in his eyes get positively lethal. And that was all the encouragement she needed. She'd seen enough movies with lap dances that she had a vague idea of how this should go. Maybe her idea was the PG-13-rated version, but she could improvise.

He moved his hand over the outline of his erection, squeezing himself through the denim as she contin-

ued to move. Maybe it wasn't rhinestones and a mini-
skirt, but he didn't seem to mind her white tank top
and coveralls. He was still watching her with avid interest as she untied the sleeves from around her waist
and let the garment drop down around her feet. She
kicked it off to the side, revealing her denim cutoff
shorts underneath it.

"Come here," he said, his voice hard.

"I'm not taking orders from you. You have to be
patient."

"I'm not feeling very patient, honey."

"What's my name?"

"Anna," he ground out. "Anna, I'm not feeling very
patient."

"Not enough women have made you wait. You're
getting spoiled."

She slid her hand up her midsection, her own fingertips combined with the electric look on Chase's
face sending heat skittering along her veins. She let
her fingers skim over her breast, gratified when his
breath hissed through his teeth.

"Anna…"

"You know me pretty well, don't you? But you
didn't know all this." She moved her hand back down,
over her stomach, her belly button, sliding her fingers
down beneath the waistband of her shorts, stroking
herself where she was wet and aching for him. His fingers curled around the edge of the chair, his knuckles
white, the cords on his neck standing out, the strength
it was taking him to remain seated clear and incredibly compelling.

"Take them off," he said.

"Didn't I just tell you that you're not in charge?"

"Don't play games with me."

"Maybe patience is the lesson you need to learn."

"I damn well don't," he growled.

She turned around, facing away from him, taking a deep breath as she unsnapped her shorts and pushed them down her hips, revealing the other purchase she had made at the store yesterday. A black, lacy thong, quite unlike any other pair of underwear she had ever owned. And she had slipped it on this morning hoping that this would be the end of her day.

"Holy hell," he said.

She knew that she was not the first woman to take her clothes off for him. Much less the first woman to reveal sexy underwear. But that only made his appreciation for hers that much sweeter. She swayed her hips back and forth before dropping down low, and sweeping back up. It felt so cheesy, and at the same time she was pretty proud of herself for pulling it off.

When she turned to face him, his expression was positively feral.

Her shirt was still knotted beneath her breasts, and now she was wearing work boots, a thong and the top. If Chase thought the outfit was a little bit silly, he certainly didn't show it.

She moved over to the chair, straddling him, leaning in and kissing him on the lips. "I want you," she said.

She had said it before. But this was more. Deeper. This was the truth. Her truth, the truest thing inside of her. She wanted Chase. In every way. Forever. She swallowed hard, grabbing hold of his T-shirt and tugging it up over his head. She licked her lips, looking at his body, at his chest, speckled with just the right amount of dark hair, at his abs, so perfectly defined and tempting.

She reached between them, undoing his belt and jerking it through the loops, before tugging his pants and underwear down low on his hips. He put his hand on her backside, holding her steady as she maneuvered herself so that she was over him, rubbing up against his arousal. "I would never have considered doing something like this before last week. Not with anyone. It's just you," she said, leaning in and kissing his lips lightly. "You do this to me."

He shuddered beneath her, her words having the exact effect she hoped they would. He liked feeling special, too.

He took hold of her hand, drawing it between them, curving her fingers around him. "And you do this to me. You make me so hard, it hurts. I've never wanted a woman like this before. Ever."

She flexed her hips, squeezed him tighter, trapping him between her palm and the apex of her thighs. "Why? Why do you want me like this?"

It was important to know. Essential.

"Because it's you, Anna. There's this idea that having sex with a stranger is supposed to be exciting. Because it's dirty. Because it's wrong. Maybe because it's unknown? But I've done that. And this is... You're right. I know you. Knowing you like this... Your face is so familiar to me, your voice. Knowing what it looks like when I make you come, how you sound when I push you over the edge, baby, there's nothing hotter than that."

His words washed over her, everything she had never known she needed. This full, complete acceptance of who she was. Right here in her garage. The mechanic, the woman. The friend, the lover. He wanted her. And everything that meant.

She didn't even try to keep herself from feeling it now. Didn't try to keep herself from thinking it.

She loved him. So much. Every part of him, with every part of her. Her friend. The only man she really wanted. The only person she could imagine sharing her days and nights and blankets and musicals with.

And that realization didn't even make her want to pull away from him. Didn't make her want to hide. Instead, she wanted to finish this. She wanted to feel connected to him. Now that she was in, she was in all the way. Ready to expose herself completely, scrape herself raw, all for him.

She rose up so that she was on her knees, tugged her panties down her hips and maneuvered herself so that she was able to dispense with them completely before settling over him, grabbing hold of his broad shoulders as she sank down onto his hardened length.

He swore, the harsh word echoing in the empty space. "Anna, I need to get a condom."

She pulled away from him quickly, hovering over him as he lifted his hips, grabbing his wallet and pulling out a condom with shaking hands, taking care of the practicalities quickly. She was trembling, both with the adrenaline rush that accompanied the stupidity of her mistake and with need. With regret because she wished that he was still inside of her even though it wouldn't be responsible at all.

Soon, he was guiding her back onto him, having protected them both. Thankfully, he was a little more with it than she was.

He gripped her tightly, guiding her movements at first, helping her establish a rhythm that worked for them both.

He moved his hands around, brushing his fingertips along the seam of her ass before teasing her right where their bodies were joined. She gasped, grabbing hold of the back of the chair, flexing her hips, chasing her own release as he continued to touch her. To push her higher.

She slid her hands up, cupping his face, holding him steady. She met his gaze, a thrill shooting down her spine. "Anna," he rasped, the words skating over her skin like a caress, touching her everywhere.

Pleasure gripped her, low and tight, sending her over the edge. She held his face as she shuddered out her orgasm and chanted his name, endlessly. Over and over again. And when it was over, he held her to him, kissing her lips, whispering words against her mouth that she could barely understand. She didn't need to. The only words she understood were the ones she most needed to hear.

"Stay with me tonight."

Chapter 12

They dressed and drove across the property in Chase's truck. His heart was still hammering like crazy, and he had no idea what the hell he was doing. But then, it was Anna. She wasn't some random hookup. He wanted her again, and having her spend the night seemed like the best way to accomplish that.

He ignored the little terror claws that wrapped themselves around his heart and squeezed, and focused instead on the heavy sensation in his gut. In his dick. He wanted her, and dammit, he was going to have her.

The image of her dancing in front of him in the shop...that would haunt him forever. And it was his goal to collect a few more images that would make his life miserable when their physical relationship ended.

That was normal.

He parked the truck, then got out, following Anna

mutely up the steps. When they got to the door, Anna paused.

"I don't…have anything with me. No porcupine pajamas."

Some of the tension in his chest eased. "You won't need pajamas in my bed," he said, his voice low, almost unrecognizable even to himself.

Which was fair enough, since this whole damn situation was unrecognizable. Saying this kind of stuff to Anna. Seeing her like this. Wanting her like this.

She was a constant. She was stability. And he felt shaky as hell right now.

"I've never spent the night with anyone," she blurted.

The words hit him hard in the chest. Along with the realization that this was a first for him, too. He knew it, logically. But for some reason it hadn't seemed momentous when he'd issued the invitation. Because it was Anna and sleeping with her had seemed like the most natural thing on earth. He liked talking to her, liked kissing her, liked having sex with her, and he didn't want her to leave. So the obvious choice was to ask her to stay the night.

Now it was hitting him, though. What that usually meant. Why he didn't do it.

But it was too late to take the invitation back, and anyway, he didn't know if he wanted to.

"I haven't, either," he said.

She blinked. "You…haven't? I mean, I had a ten-minute roll in the hay—literally—with a loser in high school, so I know why I've never spent the night with anyone. But you…you do this a lot."

"Are you calling me a slut?"

"Yes," she said, deadpan. "No judgment, but yeah, you're kind of slutty."

"Well, you don't have to spend the night with someone when you're done with them. I guess that's why I haven't. Because I am kind of slutty, and it has nothing to do with liking the person I'm with. Just…"

Oblivion. The easiest, most painless connection on earth with no risk involved whatsoever.

But he wasn't going to say that.

Anna wasn't oblivion. Being with her was like… being inside his own skin, really in it, and feeling it, for the first time since he was sixteen.

Like driving eighty miles per hour on the same winding road that had killed his parents, daring it to come for him, too. He'd felt alive then. Alive and pushing up against the edge of mortality as hard as he could.

Then he'd backed way off the gas. And he'd backed way off ever since.

This was the closest thing to tasting that surge of adrenaline, that rush he'd felt since the day he'd basically begged the road to take him, too.

You're a head case.

Yes, he was. But he'd always known that. Anna hadn't, though.

"Just?" she asked, eyebrows shooting up. She wasn't going to let that go, apparently.

"It's just sex."

"And what is this?" she asked, gesturing between the two of them.

"Friendship," he said honestly. "With some more to it."

"Those benefits."

"Yeah," he said. "Those."

He shoved his hands in his pockets, feeling like he'd just failed at something, and he couldn't quite figure out what. But his words were flat in the evening air. Just sort of dull and resting between them, wrong and weird, but he didn't know what to do about it.

Because he didn't know what else to say, either.

"Want to come inside?" he asked finally.

"That is where your bed is," she said.

"It is."

They made their way to the bedroom, and somehow it all felt different. He could easily remember when she'd been up here just last week, walking in those heels and that dress. When he'd been overwhelmed with the need to touch her, but wouldn't allow himself to do so.

He could also remember being in here with her plenty of times before. Innocuous as sharing the space with any friend.

How? How had they ever existed in silences that weren't loaded? In moments that weren't wrapped in tension. In isolation that didn't present the very tempting possibility of chasing pleasure together. Again and again.

This wasn't friendship plus benefits. That implied the friendship remained untouched and the benefits were an add-on. Easy to stick there, easy to remove. But that wasn't the case.

Everything was different. The air around them had changed. How the hell could he pretend the friendship was the same?

"I'm just—" She smiled sheepishly and pulled her shirt up over her head. "Sorry." Then she unhooked her bra, tossing it onto the floor. He hadn't had a chance to look at her breasts the last time they'd had sex. She'd kept them covered. Something that had added nicely to the tease back in the shop. But he was ready to drop to his knees and give thanks for their perfection now.

"Why are you apologizing for flashing me?"

"Because. In the absence of pajamas I need to get comfortable now." She stripped her shorts off, and her underwear—those shocking black panties that he simply hadn't seen coming, much like the rest of her—and then she flopped down onto his bed. He didn't often bring women back here.

Sometimes, depending on the circumstances, but if they had a hotel room, or their own place available, that was his preference. So it was a pretty unusual sight in general. A naked woman in his room. Anna, in this familiar place—naked and warm and about as inviting as anything had ever been—was enough to make his head explode.

His head, and other places.

"You never have to apologize for being naked." He stripped his shirt off, then continued to follow her lead, until he was wearing nothing.

He lay down beside her, not touching her, just looking at her. This was hella weird. If a woman was naked, he was usually having sex with her, bottom line. He didn't lie next to one, simply looking at her. Right now, Anna was something like art and he just wanted to admire her. Well, that wasn't *all* he wanted. But it was what he wanted right now. To watch the soft lamplight cast a warm glow over her curves, to examine every dip and hollow on the map of her figure. To memorize the rosy color of her nipples, the dark hair at the apex of her thighs. The sweet flare of her hips and the slight roundness of her stomach. She was incredible. She was Anna. Right now, she was his.

That thought made his stomach tighten. How long had it been since something was his?

This place would always be McCormack, through and through. The foundation of the forge and the business…it was built on his great-grandfather's back, carried down by his grandfather, handed to their father.

And he and Sam carried it now.

This ranch would always be something they were bound to by blood, not by choice. Even if given the choice, he could probably never leave. Their family… It didn't feel like their family anymore. It hadn't for a lot of years.

It was two of them, him and Sam. Two of them trying so damn hard to push this legacy back to where it had been. To make their family extend beyond these walls, beyond these borders. To fulfill all of the promises he'd made to his dad, even though the old man had never actually heard them.

Even though Chase had made them too late.

And so there was something about that. Anna, this moment, being for him. Something that he chose, instead of something that he'd inherited.

"I like when you look at me like that," she said, her voice hushed.

"I like when you take control like you did back in the shop. I like seeing you realize how beautiful you are," he said. It was true. He was glad that she knew now. And pissed that she was going to take that knowledge and work her magic on some other man with her newfound power. He wanted to kill that man.

But he could never hope to take his place, so he wouldn't.

"You're the first person who has made me feel like it all fit. And maybe it's because you're my friend. Maybe it's because you know me," she said.

"I don't follow."

"I had to be tough," she said, her tone demonstrating just that. "All my life I've had to be tough. My brothers raised me, and they did a damn good job, and I know you think they're jerks, and honestly a lot of the time they are. But they were young boys who were put in charge of taking care of their kid sister. So they took care of me, but they tortured me in that way only brothers can. Probably because I tortured them in ways that most little sisters could never dream. They didn't go out in high school. They had to make sure I was taken care of. They didn't trust my dad to do it. He wasn't stable enough. He would go out to the bar and get drunk, and he would call needing a ride home. They handled things so that I didn't have to. And I never felt like I could make their lives more difficult by showing how hard it was for me."

She shifted, sighing heavily before she continued. "And then there was my dad. He didn't know what to do with a daughter. As pissed as he was that his wife left, I think in some ways he was relieved, because he didn't have to figure out how to fit a woman into his life anymore. But then I kind of started becoming a woman. And he really didn't know what to do. So I learned how to work on cars. I learned how to talk about sports. I learned how to fit. Even though it pushed me right out of fitting when it came to school. When it came to making friends."

He knew these things about Anna. Knew them because he'd absorbed them by being in her house, being near her, for fifteen years. But he'd never heard her say them. There was something different about that.

"You've always fit with me, Anna," he said, his voice rough.

"I know. And even though we've never talked about this, I'm pretty sure somehow you knew all of it. You always have. Because you know me. And you accept me. Not very many people know about the musicals. Because it always embarrassed me. Kind of a girlie thing."

"I guess so," he said, the words feeling inadequate.

"Also, it was my thing. And… I never like anyone to know how much I care about things. I… My mom loved old musicals," she said, her voice soft. "Sometimes I wonder what it would be like to watch them with her."

"Anna…"

"I remember sneaking out of my room at night, seeing the TV flickering in the living room. She would be watching *The Sound of Music* or *Cinderella*. *Oklahoma!* of course. And I would just hang there in the hall. But I didn't want to interrupt. Because by the end of the day she was always out of patience, and I knew she didn't want any of the kids to talk to her. But it was kind of like watching them with her." Anna's eyes filled with tears. "But now I just wish I had. I wish I had gone in and sat next to her. I wish I had risked her being upset with me. I never got the chance. She left, and that was it. So, maybe she would've been mad at me, or maybe she wouldn't have let me watch them with her. But at least I would've had the answer. Now

I just wonder. I just remember that space between us. Me hiding in the hall, and her sitting on the couch. She never knew I was there. Maybe if I'd done a better job of connecting with her, she wouldn't have left."

"That's not true, Anna."

"She didn't have anyone to watch the movies with, Chase. And my dad was so… I doubt he ever gave her a damn scrap of tenderness. But maybe I could have. I think… I think that's what I was always trying to do with my dad. To make up for that. It was too late to make her stay, but I thought maybe I could hang on to him."

Chase tried to breathe past the tightness in his chest, but it was nearly impossible. "Anna," he said, "any parent that chooses to leave their child…the issue is with them. It was your parents' marriage. It was your mom. I don't know. But it was never you. It wasn't you not watching a movie with her, or irritating her, or making her angry. There was never anything you could do."

She nodded, a tear tracking down her pale cheek. "I do know that."

"But you still beat yourself up for it."

"Of course I do."

He didn't have a response to that. She said it so matter-of-factly, as though there was nothing else but to blame herself, even if it made no sense. He had no response because he understood. Because he knew what it was like to twist a tragedy in a thousand different ways to figure out how you could take it on yourself. He knew what it was like to live your life with a gaping hole where someone you loved should be. To try to figure out how you could have stopped the loss from happening.

In the years since his parents' accident he had moved beyond blame. Not because he was stronger than Anna, just because you could only twist death in so many different directions. It was final. And it didn't ask you. It just was. Blaming himself would have been a step too far into martyrdom.

Still, he knew about lingering scars and responses to those scars that didn't make much sense.

But he didn't know what it was like to have a parent choose to leave you. God knew his parents never would have chosen to abandon their sons.

As if she'd read his mind, Anna continued. "She's still out there. I mean, as far as I know. She could have come back. Anytime. I just feel like if I had given her even a small thing…well, then, maybe she would have missed me enough at some point. If she'd had anything back here waiting for her, she could have called. Just once."

"You were you," he said. "If that wasn't enough for her…fuck her."

She laughed and wiped another tear from her face. Then she shifted, moving closer to him. "I appreciate that." She paused for a moment, kissing his shoulder, then she continued. "It's amazing. I've never told you that before. I've never told anyone that before. It's just kind of crazy that we could know each other for so long and…there's still more we don't know."

He wanted to tell her then. About the day his parents died. About the complete and total hole it had torn in his life. She knew to a degree. They had been friends when it happened. He had been sixteen, and Sam had been eighteen, and the loss of everything they knew had hit so hard and fast that it had taken them out at the knees.

He wanted to tell her about his nightmares. Wanted to tell her about the last conversation he'd had with his dad.

But he didn't.

"Amazing" was all he said instead.

Then he leaned over and kissed her, because he couldn't think of anything else to do, couldn't think of anything else to say.

Liar.

A thousand things he wanted to tell her swirled around inside of him. A thousand different things she didn't know. That he had never told anybody. But he didn't want to open himself up like that. He just… He just couldn't.

So instead, he kissed her, because that he could do. Because of all the changes that existed between them, that was the one he was most comfortable with. Holding her, touching her. Everything else was too big, too unknown to unpack. He couldn't do it. Didn't want to do it.

But he wanted to kiss her. Wanted to run his hands over her bare curves. So he did.

He touched her, tasted her, made her scream. Because of all the things that were happening in his life, that felt right.

This was…well, it was a detour. The best one he'd ever taken, but a detour all the same. He was building the family business, like he had promised his dad he would do. Or like he should have promised him when he'd had the chance. He might never have been able to tell the old man to his face, but he'd promised it to his grave. A hundred times, a thousand times since he'd died.

That was what he had to do. That was on the other side of making love with Anna. Going to that benefit with her all dressed up, trying to help her get the kind of reputation she wanted. To send her off with all her newfound skills so that she could be with another man after.

To knuckle down and take the McCormack family ranch back to where it had been. Beyond. To make sure that Sam used his talents, to make sure that the forge and all the work their father had done to build the business didn't go to waste.

To prove that the fight he'd had with his father right before he died was all angry words and teenage bluster. That what he'd said to his old man wasn't real.

He didn't hate the ranch. He didn't hate the business. He didn't hate their name. He was their name, and damn him for being too young and stupid to see it then.

He was proving it now by pouring all of his blood, all of his sweat, all of his tears into it. By taking the little bit of business acumen he had once imagined might get him out of Copper Ridge and applying it to this place. To try to make it something bigger, something better. To honor all the work their parents had invested all those years.

To finish what they started.

He might not have ever made a commitment to a woman, but this ranch, McCormack Iron Works…was his life. That was forever.

It was the only forever he would ever have.

He closed those thoughts out, shut them down com-

pletely and focused on Anna. On the sweet scent of
her as he lowered his head between her thighs and
lapped at her, on the feel of her tight channel pulsing around his fingers as he stroked them in and out.
And finally, on the tight, wet clasp of her around him
as he slid home.

Home. That's really what it was.

In a way that nowhere else had ever been. The ranch
was a memorial to people long dead. A monument that
he would spend the rest of his life building.

But she was home. She was his.

If he let her, she could become everything.

No.

That denial echoed in his mind, pushed against him
as he continued to pound into her, hard, deep, seeking the oblivion that he had always associated with
sex before her. But it wasn't there. Instead, it was like
a veil had been torn away and he could see all of his
life, spreading out before him. Like he was standing
on a ridge high in the mountains, able to survey everything. The past, the present, the future. So clear,
so sharp it almost didn't seem real.

Anna was in all of it. A part of everything.

And if she was ever taken away...

He closed his eyes, shutting out that thought, a wave
of pleasure rolling over him, drowning out everything.
He threw himself in. Harder than he ever had. Grateful as hell that Anna had found her own release, because he'd been too wrapped up in himself to consider
her first.

Then he wrapped his arms around her, wrapped
her up against him. Wrapped himself up in her. And
he pushed every thought out of his mind and focused

on the feeling of her body against his, the scent of her skin. Feminine and sweet with a faint trace of hay and engine grease.

No other woman smelled like Anna.

He pressed his face against her breasts and she sighed, a sound he didn't think he'd ever get tired of. He let everything go blank. Because there was nothing in his past, or his future, that was as good as this.

Chapter 13

Chase woke in a cold sweat, his heart pounding so heavily he thought it would burst through his bone and flesh and straight out into the open. His bed was empty. He sat up, rubbing his hand over his face, then forking his fingers through his hair.

It felt wrong to have the bed empty. After spending only one night wrapped around Anna, it already felt wrong. Not having her… Waking up in the morning to find that she wasn't there was… He hated it. It was unsettling. It reminded him of the holes that people left behind, of how devastating it was when you lost someone unexpectedly.

He banished the thought. She might still be here. But then, she didn't have any clean clothes or anything, so if she had gone home, he couldn't necessarily blame her. He went straight into the bathroom, took a shower, took care of all other morning practicalities. He resisted the urge to look at his phone, to call Anna's phone or to go downstairs and see if maybe she was still around. He was going to get through all this, dammit, and he was not going to behave as though he were affected.

As though the past night had changed something fundamental, not just between them, but in him.

He scowled, throwing open the bedroom door and heading down the stairs.

He stopped dead when he saw her standing there in the kitchen. She was wearing his T-shirt, her long, slim legs bare. And he wondered if she was bare all the way up. His mouth dried, his heart squeezing tight.

She wasn't missing. She wasn't gone. She was cooking him breakfast. Like she belonged here. Like she belonged in his life. In his house. In his bed.

For one second it made him feel like he belonged. Like she'd been the missing piece to making this his, to making it more than McCormack.

He felt like he was standing in the middle of a dream. Standing there looking at somebody else's life. At some wild, potential scenario that in reality he would never get to have.

Right in front of him was everything. And in the same moment he saw that, he imagined the hole that would be left behind if it was ever taken away. If he ever believed in this, fully, completely. If he reached out and embraced her now, there would be no words for how empty his arms would feel if he ever lost her.

"Don't you have work?" he asked, leaning against the doorjamb.

She turned around and smiled, the kind of smile

that lit him up inside, from his head, down his toes. He did his very best not to return the gesture. Did his best not to encourage it in any way.

And he cursed himself when the glow leached out of her face. "Good morning to you, too," she said.

"You didn't need to make breakfast."

"*Au contraire.* I was hungry. So breakfast was needed."

"You could've gone home."

"Yes, Grumpy-Pants, I could have. But I decided to stay here and make you food. Which seemed like an adequate thank-you for the multiple orgasms I received yesterday."

"Bacon? You're trying to pay for your orgasms with bacon?"

"It seemed like a good idea at the time." She crossed her arms beneath her breasts and revealed that she did not, in fact, have anything on beneath the shirt. "Bacon is a borderline orgasmic experience."

"I have work. I don't have time to eat breakfast."

"Maybe if you had gotten up at a decent hour."

"I don't need you to lecture me on my sleeping habits," he bit out. "Is there coffee?"

"It's like you don't know me at all." She crossed the room and lifted a thermos off the counter. "I didn't want to leave it sitting on the burner. That makes it taste gross."

"I don't really care how it tastes. That's not the point."

She rested her hand on the counter, then rapped her knuckles against the surface. "What's going on?"

"Nothing."

"Stop it, Chase. Maybe you can BS the other bimbos that you sleep with, but you can't do it to me. I know you too well. This has nothing to do with waking up late."

"This is a bad idea," he said.

"What's a bad idea? Eating bacon and drinking coffee with one of your oldest friends?"

"Sleeping with one of my oldest friends. It was stupid. We never should've done it."

She just stood there, her expression growing waxen, and as the color drained from her face, he felt something even more critical being scraped from his chest, like he was being hollowed out.

"It's a little late for that," she pointed out.

"Well, it isn't too late to start over."

"Chase…"

"It was fun. But, honestly, we accomplished everything we needed to. There's no reason to get dramatic about it. We agreed that we weren't going to let it affect our friendship. And it…it just isn't working for me."

"It was working fine for you last night."

"Well, that was last night, Anna. Don't be so needy."

She drew back as though she had been slapped and he wanted to punch his own face for saying such a thing. For hitting her where he knew it would hurt. And he waited. Waited for her to grow prickly. For her to retreat behind the walls. For her to get angry and start insulting him. For her to end all of this in fire and brimstone as she scorched the earth in an attempt to disguise the naked pain that was radiating from her right now.

He knew she would. Because that was how it went. If he pushed far enough, then she would retreat.

She closed the distance between them, cupping his

face, meeting his eyes directly. And he waited for the blow. "But I feel needy. So what am I going to do about that?"

He couldn't have been more shocked than if she had reached up and slapped him. "What?"

"I'm needy. Or maybe…wanty? I'm both." She took a deep breath. "Yes, I'm both. I want more. Not less. And this is… This is the moment where we make decisions, right? Well, I've decided that I want to move forward with this. I don't want to go back. I can't go back."

"Anna," he said, her name scraping his throat raw.

"Chase," she said, her own voice a whisper in response.

"We can't do this," he said.

He needed the Anna he knew to come to his rescue now. To laugh it all off. To break this tension. To say that it didn't matter. To wave her hand and say it was all whatever and they could forget it. But she wasn't doing that. She was looking at him, her green eyes completely earnest, vulnerability radiating from her face. "We need to do this. Because I love you."

Anna could tell that her words had completely stunned Chase. Fair enough, they had shocked her just as much. She didn't know where all of this was coming from. This strength. This bravery.

Except that last night's conversation kept echoing in her mind. When she had told him about her mother. When she had told him about how she always regretted not closing the distance between them. Always regretted not taking the chance.

That was the story of her entire life. She had, from

the time she was a child, refused to make herself vulnerable. Refused to open herself up to injury. To pain. So she pretended she didn't care. She pretended nothing mattered. She did that every time her father ignored her, every time he forgot an important milestone in her life. She had done it the first time she'd ever had sex with a guy and it had made her feel something. Rather than copping to that, rather than dealing with it, she had mocked him.

All of her inner workings were a series of walls and shields, carefully designed to keep the world from hitting the terrible, needy things inside of her. Designed to keep herself from realizing they were there. But she couldn't do it anymore. She didn't want to do it anymore. Not with Chase. She didn't want to look back and wonder what could have been.

She wanted more. She needed more. Pride be damned.

"I do," she said, nodding. "I love you."

"You can't."

"I'm pretty sure I can. Since I do."

"No," he said, the word almost desperate.

"No, Chase, I really do. I mean, I have loved you since I was fifteen years old. And intermittently thought you were hot. But mostly, I just loved you. You've been my friend, my best friend. I needed you. You've been my emotional support for a long time. We do that for each other. But things changed in the past few days. You're my...everything." Her voice broke on that last word. "This isn't sex and friendship, it isn't two different things, this is all the things, combined together to make something so big that it fills me completely. And I don't have room inside my chest for shields and protection anymore. Not when all that I am just loves you."

"I can't do this," he bit out, stepping away from her.

"I didn't ask if you could do this. This isn't about you, not right now. Yes, I would like you to love me, too, but right now this is just about me saying that I love you. Telling you. Because I don't ever want to look back and think that maybe you didn't know. That maybe if I had said something, it could have been different." She swallowed hard, battling tears. "I don't know what's wrong with me. Unless it's a movie, I almost never cry, but you're making me cry a lot lately."

"I'm only going to make you cry more," he said. "Because I don't know how to do this. I don't know how to love somebody."

"Bull. You've loved me perfectly, just the way I needed you to for fifteen years. The way that you take care of this place, the way that you care for Sam… Don't tell me that you can't love."

"Not this kind. Not this… Not this."

"I'm closing the gap," she said, pressing on, even though she could see that this was a losing battle. She was charging in anyway, sword held high, chest exposed. She was giving it her all, fighting even though she knew she wasn't going to walk away unscathed. "I'm not going to wonder what would've happened if I'd just been brave enough to do it. I would rather cut myself open and bleed out. I would rather risk my heart than wonder. So I'm just going to say it. Stop being such a coward and love me."

He took another step back from her and she felt that gap she was so desperate to close widening. Watched as her greatest fear started to play out right before her eyes. "I just… I don't."

"You don't or you won't?"

"At the end of the day, the distinction doesn't really matter. The result is the same."

She felt like she was having an out-of-body experience. Like she was floating up above, watching herself get rejected. There was nothing she could do. She couldn't stop it. Couldn't change it. Couldn't shield herself.

It was…horrible. Gut-wrenching. Destructive. Freeing.

Like watching a tsunami racing to shore and deciding to surrender to the wave rather than fight it. Yeah, it would hurt like hell. But it was a strange, quiet space. Past fear, past hope. All she could hear was the sound of her heart beating.

"I'm going to go," she said, turning away from him. "You can have the bacon."

She had been willing to risk herself, but she wouldn't stand there and fall apart in front of him. She would fall apart, but dammit, it would be on her own time.

"Stay and eat," he said.

She shook her head. "No. I can't stay."

"Are we going to… Are we going to go to the gala together still?"

"No!" She nearly shouted the word. "We are not going to go together. I need to… I need to think. I need to figure this out. But I don't think things can be the same anymore."

It was his turn to close the distance between them. He grabbed hold of her arms, drawing her toward him, his expression fierce. "That was not part of the deal. It was friends plus benefits, remember? And then in the end we could just stop with the benefits and go back to the friendship."

"We can't," she said, tears falling down her cheeks. "I'm sorry. But we can't."

"What the hell?" he ground out.

"We can't because I'm all in. I'm not going to sit back and pretend that it didn't really matter. I'm not going to go and hide these feelings. I'm not going to shrug and say it doesn't really matter if you love me or not. Because it does. It's everything. I have spent so many years not wanting. Not trying. Hiding how much I wanted to be accepted, hiding how desperately I wanted to try to look beautiful, how badly I wanted to be able to be both a mechanic and a woman. Hiding how afraid I was of ending up alone. Hiding under a blanket and watching old movies. Well, I'm done. I'm not hiding any of it anymore. And you know what? Nothing's going to hurt after this." She jerked out of his hold and started to walk toward the front door.

"You're not leaving in that."

She'd forgotten she wasn't exactly dressed. "Sure I am. I'm just going to drive straight home. Anyway, it's not your concern. Because I'm not your concern anymore."

The terror that she felt screaming through her chest was reflected on his face. Good. He should be afraid. This was the most terrifying experience of her life. She knew how horrible it was to lose a person you cared for. Knew what kind of void that left. And she knew that after years it didn't heal. She knew, too, you always felt the absence. She knew that she would always

feel his. But she needed more. And she wasn't afraid
to put it all on the line. Not now. Not after everything
they had been through. Not after everything she had
learned about herself. Chase was the one who had told
her she needed more confidence.

Well, she had found it. But there was a cost.

Or maybe this was just the cost of loving. Of caring, deeply and with everything she had, for the first
time in so many years.

She strode across the property, not caring that she
was wearing nothing more than his T-shirt, rage pouring through her. And when she arrived back at the shop
she grabbed her purse and her keys, making her way
to the truck. When she got there, Chase was standing
against the driver's-side door. "Don't leave like this."

"Do you love me yet?"

He looked stricken. "What do you want me to say?"

"You know what I want you to say."

"You want me to lie?"

She felt like he had taken a knife and stabbed her
directly through the heart. She could barely breathe.
Could barely stand straight. This was... This was her
worst fear come true. To open herself up so completely,
to make herself so entirely vulnerable and to have it
all thrown back in her face.

But in that moment, she recognized that she was un-
touchable from here on out. Because there was nothing
that could ever, ever come close to this pain. Nothing
that could ever come close to this risk.

How had she missed this before? How had she
missed that failure could be such a beautiful, terrible,
freeing experience?

It was the worst. Absolutely the worst. But it also

broke chains that had been binding her for years. Because if someone had asked her what she was so afraid of, this would have been the answer. And she was in it. Living it. Surviving it.

"I love you," she repeated. "This is your chance. Listen to me, Chase McCormack, I am giving you a chance. I'm giving you a chance to stop being so afraid. A chance to walk out of the darkness. We've walked through it together for a long time. So I'm asking you now to walk out of it with me. Please."

He backed away from the truck, his jaw tense, a muscle there twitching.

"Coward," she spat as he turned and walked away from her. Walked away from them. Walked back into the damned darkness.

And she got in her truck and started the engine, driving away from him, driving away from the things she wanted most in the entire world.

She didn't cry until she got home. But then, once she did, she was afraid she wouldn't stop.

Chapter 14

She was going to lose the bet. That was the safest thought in Anna's head as she stood in her bedroom the night of the charity event staring at the dress that was laid across her bed.

She was going to have to go there by herself. And thanks to the elaborate community theater production of their relationship everyone would know that they had broken up, since Chase wouldn't be with her. She almost laughed.

She was facing her fears all over the place, whether she wanted to or not.

Facing fears and making choices.

She wasn't going to be with Chase at the gala tonight. Wasn't going to win her money. But she had bought an incredibly slinky dress, and some more makeup. Including red lipstick. She had done all of that for him. Though in many ways it was for her, too.

She had wanted that experience. To go, to prove that she was grown-up. To prove that she had transcended her upbringing and all of that.

She frowned. Was she really considering dressing differently just because she wasn't going to be with Chase?

Screw that. He might have filleted her heart and cooked it like those hideous charred Brussels sprouts cafés tries to pass off as a fancy appetizer, but he *wasn't* going to take his lessons from her. She had learned confidence. She had learned that she was stronger than she thought. She had learned that she was beautiful. And how to care. Like everything inside her had been opened up, for better or for worse. But she would never go back. No matter how bad it hurt, she wouldn't go back.

So she wouldn't go back now, either.

As she slipped the black dress over her curves, laboring over the makeup on her face and experimenting with the hairstyle she had seen online, she could only think how much harder it was to care about things. All of these things. It had been so much easier to embrace little pieces of herself. To play the part of another son for her father and throw herself into activities that made him proud, ignoring her femininity so that she never made him uncomfortable.

All of these moments of effort came at a cost. Each minute invested revealing more and more of her needs. To be seen. To be approved of.

But there were so many other reasons she had avoided this. Because this—she couldn't help but think as she looked in the mirror—looked a lot like trying. It looked a lot like caring. That was scary. It was hard.

Being rejected when you had given your best effort was so much worse than being rejected when you hadn't tried at all.

This whole being-a-woman thing—a whole woman who wanted to be with a man, who loved a man—it was hard. And it hurt.

She looked at her reflection, her eyes widening. Thanks to the smoky eye shadow her green eyes glowed, her lips looking extra pouty with the dark red color on them. She looked like one of the old screen legends she loved so much. Very Elizabeth Taylor, really.

This was her best effort. And yes, it was only a dress, and this was just looks, but it was symbolic.

She was going to lay it all on the line, and maybe people would laugh. Because the tractor mechanic in a ball gown was too ridiculous for words. But she would take the risk. And she would take it alone.

She picked up the little clutch purse that was sitting on her table. The kind of purse she'd always thought was impractical, because who wanted a bag you had to hold in your hand all night? But the salesperson at the department store had told her it went with her dress, and that altogether she looked flawless, and Anna had been in desperate need of flattery. So here she was with a clutch.

It *was* impractical. But she *did* look great.

Of course, Chase wouldn't be there to see it. She felt her eyes starting to fill with tears and she blinked, doing her best to hold it all back. She was not going to smear her makeup. She had already put it all out there for him. She would be damned if she undid all this hard work for him, too.

With that in mind, Anna got into her truck and drove herself to the ball.

* * *

"Hey, jackass," Sam shouted from across the shop. "Are you going to finish with work anytime today?"

Okay, so maybe Chase had thrown himself into work with a little more vehemence than was strictly necessary since Anna had walked out of his life.

Anna. Anna had walked out of his life. Over something as stupid as love.

If love was so stupid, it wouldn't make your insides tremble like you were staring down a black bear.

He ignored his snarky internal monologue. He had been doing a lot of that lately. So many arguments with himself as he pounded iron at the forge. That was, when he wasn't arguing with Sam. Who was getting a little bit tired of him, all things considered.

"Do I look like I'm finished?" he shouted back.

"It's nine o'clock at night."

"That's amazing. When did you learn to tell time?"

"I counted on my fingers," Sam said, wandering deeper into the room. "So, are we just going to pretend that Anna didn't run out of your house wearing only a T-shirt the other morning?"

"I'm going to pretend that my older brother doesn't Peeping Tom everything that happens in my house."

"We live on the same property. It's bound to happen. I was on my way here when I saw her leaving. And you chasing after her. So I'm assuming you did the stupid thing."

"I told her that I couldn't be in a relationship with her." That was a lie. He had done so much more than that. He had torn both of their hearts out and stomped them into the ground. Because Sam was right, he was an idiot. But he had made a concerted effort to be a safe idiot.

How's that working for you?

"Right. Why exactly?"

"Look, the sage hermit thing is a little bit tired. You don't have a social life, I don't see you with a wife and children, so maybe you don't hang out and lecture me."

"Isn't tonight that thing?" Sam seemed undeterred by Chase's rudeness.

"What thing?"

"The charity thing that you were so intent on using to get investors. Because the two of us growing our family business and restoring the former glory of our hallowed ancestors is so important to you. And exploiting my artistic ability for your financial gain."

"Change of plans." He grunted, moving a big slab of iron that would eventually be a gate to the side. "I'm just going to keep working. We'll figure this out without schmoozing."

"Who are you and what have you done with my brother?"

"Just shut up. If you can't do anything other than stand there looking vaguely amused at the fact that I'm going through a personal crisis, then you can go straight to hell without passing Go or collecting two hundred dollars."

"I'm not going to be able to afford Park Place anyway, because you aren't out there getting new investors."

"I'm serious, Sam," Chase shouted, throwing his hammer down on the ground. "It's all fine for you because you hold everyone at a distance."

Sam laughed. The bastard. "*I* hold everyone at a distance. What do you think you do? What do you think your endless string of one-night stands is?"

"You think I don't know? You think I don't know that it's an easy way to get some without ever having to have a conversation? I'm well aware. But I don't need you standing over there so entertained by the fact that…"

"That you actually got your heart broken?"

Chase didn't have anything to say to that. Every single word in his head evaporated like water against molten metal. He had nothing to say to that because his heart was broken. But Anna wasn't responsible. It was his own fault.

And the only reason his heart was broken was because he…

"Do you know what I said to Dad the day that he died?"

Sam froze. "No."

No, he didn't. Because they had never talked about it. "The last thing I ever said to him was that I couldn't wait to get away from here. I told him I wasn't going to pound iron for the rest of my life. I was going to get away and go to college. Make something real out of myself. Like this wasn't real."

"I didn't realize."

"No. Because I didn't tell you. Because I never told anybody. But that's why I needed to fix this. It's why I wanted to expand this place."

"So it isn't really to harness my incredible talent?"

"I don't even know what it's for anymore. To what? To make up for what I said to a dead man. And for promises that I made at his grave… He can't hear me. That's the worst thing."

Sam stuffed his hands in his pockets. "Is that the only reason you're still here?"

"No. I love it here. I really do. I had to get older. I had to put some of my own sweat into this place. But now... I get it. I do. And I care about it because I care about it, not just because they cared about it. Not just because it's a legacy, but because it's worth saving. But..."

"I still remember that day. I mean, I don't just remember it," Sam said, "it's like it just happened yesterday. That feeling... The whole world changing. Everything falling right down around us. That's as strong in my head now as it was then."

"How many times can you lose everything?" Chase asked, making eye contact with his brother. "Anna is everything. Or she could be. It was easy when she was just a friend. But... I saw her in my house the other morning cooking me breakfast, wearing my T-shirt. For a second she made me feel like...like that house was our house, and she could be my...my everything."

"I wouldn't even know what that looked like for me, Chase. If you find that...grab it."

"And if I lose it?"

"You'll have no one to blame but yourself."

Chase thought back to the day his parents died. That was a kind of pain he hadn't even known existed. But, as guilty as he had felt, as many promises as he had made at his father's grave site, he couldn't blame himself for their death. It had been an accident. That was the simple truth.

But if he lost Anna now... Pushing her away hadn't been an accident. It was in his control. Fully and absolutely. And if he lost her, then it was on him.

He thought of her face as she had turned away from him, as she had gotten into her truck.

She had trusted him. His prickly Anna had trusted him with her feelings. Her vulnerability. A gift that he had never known her to give to anybody. And he had rejected it. He was no better than he had been as an angry sixteen-year-old, hurtling around the curves of the road that had destroyed his family, daring it to take him, too.

Anna, who had already endured the rejection of a mother, the silent rejection of who she was from her father, had dared to look him in the face and risk his rejection, too.

"I'll do it," Sam said, his voice rough.

"What?"

"I'm going to start...pursuing the art thing to a greater degree. I want to help. You missed this party tonight and I know it mattered to you..."

"But you hate change," Chase reminded him.

"Yeah," Sam said. "But I hate a lot of things. I have to do them anyway."

"We're still going to have to meet with investors."

"Yeah," Sam replied, stuffing his hands in his pockets. "I can help with that. You're right. This is why you're the brains and I'm the talent."

"You're a glorified blacksmith, Sam," Chase said, trying to keep the tone light because if he went too deep now he might just fall apart.

"With talent. Beyond measure," Sam said. "At least my brother has been telling me that for years."

"Your brother is smart." Though he currently felt anything but.

Sam shrugged. "Eh. Sometimes." He cleared his

throat. "You discovered you cared about this place too late to ever let Dad know. That's sad. But at least Dad knew you cared about him. You know he never doubted that," Sam said. "But, damn, bro, don't leave it too late to let Anna know you care about her."

Chase looked at his brother, who was usually more cynical than he was wise, and couldn't ignore the truth ringing in his words.

Anna was the best he'd ever had. And had been for the past fifteen years of his life. Losing her...well, that was just a stupid thing to allow.

But the thing that scared him most right now was that it might already be too late. That he might have broken things beyond repair.

"And if it is too late?" he asked.

"Chase, you of all people know that when something is forged in fire it comes out the other side that much stronger." His brother's expression was hard, his dark eyes dead serious. "This is your fire. You're in it now. If you let it cool, you lose your chance. So I suggest you get your ass to wherever Anna is right now and you work at fixing this. It's either that or spend your life as a cold, useless hunk of metal that never became a damn thing."

It had not gone as badly as she'd feared. It hadn't gone perfectly, of course, but she had survived. The lowest point had been when Wendy Maxwell, who was still angry with Anna over the whole Chase thing, had wandered over to her and made disparaging comments about last season's colors and cuts, all the while implying that Anna's dress was somehow below the height of fashion. Which, whatever. She had gotten the dress on clearance, so it probably was. Anna might care about looking nice, but she didn't give a rat's ass about fashion.

She gave a couple of rat's asses about what had happened next.

Where's Chase?

Her newfound commitment to honesty and emotions had compelled her to answer honestly.

We broke up. I'm pretty upset about it.

The other woman had been in no way sympathetic and had in fact proceeded to smug all over the rest of the conversation. But she wasn't going to focus on the low.

The highs had included talking to several people whom she was going to be working with in the future. And getting two different phone numbers. She had made conversation. She had felt…like she belonged. And she didn't really think it had anything to do with the dress. Just with her. When you had already put everything out there and had it rejected, what was there to fear beyond that?

She sighed as she pulled into her driveway, straightening when she saw that there was a truck already there.

Chase's truck.

She put her own into Park, killing the engine and getting out. "What are you doing here, McCormack?" She was furious now. She was all dressed up, wearing her gorgeous dress, and she had just weathered that party on her own, and now he was here. She was going to punch his face.

Chase was sitting on her porch, wearing well-worn jeans and a tight black T-shirt, his cowboy hat firmly in place. He stood up, and as he began to walk toward her, Anna felt a raindrop fall from the sky. Because of course. He was here to kick her while she was down, almost certainly, and it was going to rain.

Thanks, Oregon.

"I came to see you." He stopped, looking her over, his jaw slightly slack. "I'm really glad that I did."

"Stop checking me out. You don't get to look at me like that. I did not put this dress on for you."

"I know."

"No, you don't know. I put this dress on for me. Because I wanted to look beautiful. Because I didn't care if anybody thought I was pretty enough, or if I'm not fashionable enough for Wendy the mule-faced ex-cheerleader. I did it because I cared. I do that now. I care. For me. Not for you."

She started to storm past him, the raindrops beginning to fall harder, thicker. He grabbed her arm and stopped her, twirling her toward him. "Don't walk away. Please."

"Give me a reason to stop walking."

"I've been doing a lot of thinking. And hammering."

"Real hammering, or is this some kind of a euphemism to let me know you're lonely?"

"Actual hammering. I didn't feel like I deserved anything else. Not after what happened."

"You don't. You don't deserve to masturbate ever again."

"Anna…"

"No," she said. "I can't do this. I can't just have a little taste of you. Not when I know what we can have. We can be everything. At first it was like you were my friend, but also we were sleeping together. And I looked at you as two different men. Chase, my friend. And Chase, the guy who was really good with his hands. And his mouth, and his tongue. You get the idea." She swallowed hard, her throat getting tight. "But at some point…it all blended together. And I can't separate it anymore. I just can't. I can't pull the love that I feel for you out of my chest and keep the friendship. Because they're all wrapped up in each other. And they've become the same thing."

"It's all or nothing," he said, his voice rough.

"Exactly."

He sighed heavily. "That's what I was afraid of."

"I'm sorry if you came over for a musical and a look at my porcupine pajamas. But I can't do it."

He tightened his hold on her, pulling her closer. "I knew it was going to be all or nothing."

"I can even understand why you think that might not be fair—"

"No. When you told me you loved me, I knew it was everything. Or nothing. That was what scared me so much. I have known… For a lot of years, I've realized that you were one of the main supports of my entire life. I knew you were one of the things that kept me together after my parents died. One of the only things. And I knew that if I ever lost you…it might finish me off completely."

"I'm sorry. But I can't live my life as your support."

"I know. I'm not suggesting that you do. It's just… when we started sleeping together, I had the same realization. That we weren't going to be able to separate the physical from the emotional, from our friendship. That it wasn't as simple as we pretended it could be.

When I came downstairs and saw you in my kitchen…
I saw the potential for something I never thought I
could have."

"Why didn't you think you could have that?"

"I was too afraid. Tragedy happens to other people,
Anna. Until it happens to you. And then it's like…the
safety net is just gone. And everything you never thought
you could be touched by is suddenly around every corner.
You realize you aren't special. You aren't safe. If I could
lose both my parents like that… I could lose anybody."

"You can't live that way," she said, her heart crum-
pling. "How in the world can you live that way?"

"You live halfway," he said. "You let yourself have
a little bit of things, and not all of them. You pour your
commitment into a place. Your passion into a job, into
a goal of restoring a family name when your family
is already gone. So you can't disappoint them even
if you do fail." He took a deep breath. "You keep the
best woman you know as a friend, because if she ever
became more, your feelings for her could consume
you. Anna… If I lost you… I would lose everything."

She could only stand there, looking at him, feeling
like the earth was breaking to pieces beneath her feet.
"Why did you—"

"I wanted to at least see it coming." He lowered his
head, shaking it slowly. "I was such an idiot. For a long
time. And afraid. I think it's impossible to go through
tragedy like I did, like we did, and not have it change
you. I'm not sure it's even possible to escape it doing
so much as defining you. But you can choose how. It
was so easy for me to see how you protected yourself.
How you shielded yourself. But I didn't see that I was
doing the same thing."

"I didn't know," she said, feeling stupid. Feeling blind.

"Because I didn't tell you." He reached up, drawing his thumb over her cheekbone, his expression so empty, so sad. Another side of Chase she hadn't seen very often. But it was there. It had always been there, she realized that now. "But I'm telling you now. I'm scared. I've been scared for a long time. And I've made a lot of promises to ghosts to try to atone for stupid things I said when my parents were alive. But I've been too afraid to make promises to the people that are actually still in my life. Too afraid to love the people that are still here. It's easier to make promises to ghosts, Anna. I'm done with that.

"You are here," he said, cupping her face now, holding her steady. "You're with me. And I can have you as long as I'm not too big an idiot. As long as you still want to have me. You put yourself out there for me, and I rejected you. I'm so sorry. I know what that cost you, Anna, because I know you. And please understand I didn't reject you because it wasn't enough. Because you weren't enough. It's because you were too much, and I wasn't enough. But I'm going to do my best to be enough for you now. Now and forever."

She could hardly believe what she was hearing, could hardly believe that Chase was standing there making declarations to her. The kind that sounded an awful lot like love. The kind that sounded an awful lot like exactly what she wanted to hear. "Is this because I'm wearing a dress?"

"No." He chuckled. "You could be wearing coveralls. You could be wearing nothing. Actually, I think I like you best in nothing. But whatever you're wearing, it wouldn't change this. It wouldn't change how I feel. Because I love you in every possible way. As my friend, as my lover. I love you in whatever you wear, a ball gown or engine grease. I love you working on tractors and trying to explain to me how an engine works and watching musicals."

"But do you love my porcupine pajamas?" she asked, her voice breaking.

"I'm pretty ambivalent about your porcupine pajamas, I'm not going to lie. But if they're a nonnegotiable part of the deal, then I can adjust."

She shook her head. "They aren't nonnegotiable. But I probably will irritate you with them." Then she sobbed, unable to hold her emotions back any longer. She wrapped her arms around his neck, burying her face in his skin, breathing his scent in. "Chase, I love you so much. Look what we were protecting ourselves from."

He laughed. "When you put it that way, it seems like we were being pretty stupid."

"Fear is stupid. And it's strong."

He tightened his hold on her. "It isn't stronger than this."

Not stronger than fifteen years of friendship, than holding each other through grief and pleasure, laughter and pain.

When she had pulled up and seen his truck here, Anna Brown had murder on her mind. And now, everything was different.

"Remember when you promised you were going to make me a woman?" she asked.

"Right. I do. You laughed at me."

"Yes, I did." She stretched up on her toes and kissed his lips. "Chase McCormack, I'm pretty sure you did make me a woman. Maybe not in the way you meant. But you made me feel…like a whole person. Like I could finally put together all the parts of me and just be me. Not hide any of it anymore."

He closed his eyes, pressing his forehead against hers. "I'm glad, Anna. Because you sure as hell made me a man. The man that I want to be, the man that I need to be. I can't change the past, and I can't live in it anymore, either."

"Good. Then I think we should go ahead and make ourselves a future."

"Works for me." He smiled. "I love you. You're everything."

"I love you, too." It felt so good to say that. To say it and not be afraid. To show her whole heart and not hold anything back.

"I bet that I can make you say you love me at least a hundred more times tonight. I bet I can get you to say it every day for the rest of our lives."

She smiled, taking his hand and walking toward the house, not caring about the rain. "I bet you can."

He led her inside, leaving a trail of clothes in the hall behind them, leaving her beautiful dress on the floor. She didn't care at all.

"And I bet—" he wrapped his arm around her waist, then laid her down on the bed "—tonight I can make you scream."

"I'll take that bet," she said, wrapping her legs around his hips.

And that was a bet they both won.

* * * * *

THE BILLIONAIRE'S BARGAIN

Naima Simone

To Gary. 143.

Chapter 1

Delilah. Jezebel. Yoko. Monica.

According to past and recent history, they were all women who'd supposedly brought down a powerful man. Isobel Hughes silently snorted. Many of the people inside this North Shore mansion would include her name on that tarnished list.

Swallowing a sigh, she started up the stairs of the pillared mansion that wouldn't be out of place in the French countryside. Sitting on acres of meticulously landscaped grounds, the structure screamed decadence and obscene wealth. And though only a couple of hours' travel separated it from her tiny South Deering apartment, those minutes and miles might as well be years and states.

I can do this. I have no choice *but to do this.*

Quietly dragging in another deep breath, she paused

as the tall, wide stained-glass doors opened to reveal an imposing gentleman dressed in black formal wear. His tuxedo might fit him perfectly, but Isobel didn't mistake him for who, or what, he was: security.

Security to protect the rarefied elite of Chicago high society and keep the riffraff out of the Du Sable City Gala.

Nerves tumbled and jostled inside her stomach like exes battling it out. Because she was a member of the riffraff who would be booted out on her common ass if she were discovered.

Fixing a polite but aloof mask on her face, she placed the expected invitation into the guard's outstretched hand as if it were a Golden Ticket. As he inspected the thick ivory paper with its gold engraved wording, she held her breath and resisted the urge to swipe her damp palms down the floor-length black gown she'd found at a consignment shop. Once upon a time, that invitation would've been authentic. But that had been when she'd been married to Gage Wells, golden child of the Wells family, one of Chicago's oldest and wealthiest lineages. When she'd believed Gage had been her handsome prince, the man who loved her as much as she'd adored him. Before she'd realized her prince was worse than a frog—he was a snake with a forked tongue.

She briefly closed her eyes. The present needed all of her focus. And with Gage dead these past two years and her exiled from the social circle she'd never belonged in, the present required that she resort to deception. Her brother's highly illegal skills were usually employed for forged IDs such as driver's licenses, birth certificates and passports for the city's more criminal element, not counterfeit invites to Chicago's balls. But he'd come through, and as the security guard scanned the invitation and waved a hand in front of him, she whispered a thanks to her brother.

The music that had sounded subdued outside seemed to fill the space here. Whimsical notes of flutes and powerful, bright chords of violins reverberated off the white marble walls. Gold tiles graced the floor, ebbing out in the shape of a flowering lotus, and a huge crystal-and-gold chandelier suspended from the glass ceiling seemed to be a delicate waterfall over that bloom. Two sets of staircases with gilded, intricate railings curved away from the walls and ascended to the next level of the home.

And she was stalling. Ogling her surroundings only delayed the inevitable.

And the inevitable awaited her down the hall, where music and chatter and laughter drifted. All too soon, she approached the wide entrance to the ballroom, and the glass doors opened wide in invitation.

But instead of feeling welcomed, nausea roiled and shuddered in her belly.

You can still turn around and leave. It's not too late.

The tiny whisper inside her head offered a lifeline she desperately wanted to grasp.

But then an image of her son wavered across her mind's eye, invoking an overwhelming swell of love. The thought of Aiden never failed to grasp her heart and squeeze it. He was a gift—*her* gift. And she would do anything—suffer anything—for him.

Including seeking out her dead husband's family and throwing her pride at the feet of the people who despised her. She'd committed the cardinal sins of being poor and falling for their golden child.

Well, she'd paid for that transgression. In spades.

Over the last couple of years, she'd reached out to her husband's family through email and old-fashioned snail mail, sending them pictures of Aiden, offering updates. But every email bounced back, and every letter was returned to the sender. They hadn't wanted anything to do with her or with the beautiful boy they considered her bastard.

She wanted nothing more than to forget their existence, just as they'd wiped hers out of their minds. But to keep a roof over Aiden's head, to ensure he didn't have to shiver in the increasingly chilly October nights or go to sleep hungry as she debated which overdue bill to pay, she would risk the wrath and derision of the Wells family.

The mental picture of her baby when she'd left him tonight—safe and happy with her mom—extinguished her flare of panic. Because it wouldn't do to enter these doors scared. The guests in this home would sense that weakness. And like sharks with bloody chum, they would circle and attack. Devour.

Inhaling yet another deep breath, she moved forward. Armored herself with pride. Ready to do battle.

Because she could never forget. This was indeed a battle.

One she couldn't afford to lose.

Hell no. It can't be.

Darius King tightened his fingers on the champagne flute in his hand, the fragile stem in danger of snapping.

Shock and disbelief blasted him like the frigid winds of a Chicago winter storm, freezing him in place. Motionless, he stared at the petite brunette across the ballroom as she smiled at a waiter and accepted her own glass of wine. Though he'd only met her a couple of times, he recognized that smile. Remembered the shyness in it. Remembered the lush, sensual curve of the mouth that belied that hint of coy innocence.

Isobel fucking Hughes.

Not Wells. He refused to honor her with the last name she'd schemed and lied to win, then defiled for the two years she'd been married to his best friend. She didn't deserve to wear that name. Never had.

Rage roared through him, incinerating the astonishment that had paralyzed him. Only fury remained. Fury at her gall. Fury at the bold audacity it required to walk into this mansion as if she belonged here. As if she hadn't destroyed a man and dragged his grieving, ravaged family to the very brink of destruction.

"Oh, my God." Beside him, Gabriella Wells gasped, her fingers curling around his biceps and digging deep. "Is that…"

"Yes," Darius growled, unable to soften his tone for Gage's sister, whom he cared for as if she were his own sibling. "It's her."

"What is she doing here?" Gabriella snarled, the same anger that had gripped him darkening her lovely features. "How did she even manage to get in?"

"I have no idea."

But he'd find out. And asses would be kicked when he did. The security here was supposed to be tighter than that of the goddamn royal family's, considering the people in attendance: politicians, philanthropists, celebrities, the country's wealthiest business people. Yet evidence that the security team wasn't worth shit stood in this very room, sipping champagne.

"How could she dare show her face here? Hell, *in Chicago*?" Gabriella snapped. "I thought we were rid of her when she left for California. No doubt whatever sucker she attached herself to finally got tired of her and kicked the gold-digging bitch out. And she's probably here to suck Dad and Mother dry. I swear to God..." She didn't finish the thought, but charged forward, her intentions clear.

"No." He encircled her arm, his hold gentle but firm. Gabriella halted, shooting him a let-me-go-now-dammit glance over her shoulder. Fire lit the emerald gaze that reminded him so much of Gage's. At twenty-four, she was six years younger than her older brother, and had adored him. And though she'd been in college, studying abroad for most of her brother's marriage, tales of her sister-in-law had reached her all the way in England, and Gabriella despised the woman who'd hurt Gage so badly.

Darius shook his head in reply to her unspoken demand of freedom. "No," he repeated. "We're not causing a scene. And running over there and confronting her will do just that. Think of your parents, Gabriella," he murmured.

The anger didn't bleed from her expression at the reminder, but concern banked the flames in her eyes to a simmer, and the thin, grim line of her mouth softened. Neither of them needed to voice the worry that Darius harbored. Gabriella and Gage's father, Baron Wells, had suffered a heart attack the previous year.

Nothing could convince Darius that it hadn't been grief over his son's death in a sudden car accident that had precipitated the attack, added to long work hours, poor eating habits and a lax exercise regimen.

The last several months had finally seen the return of the imposing, dignified man Darius had known and admired all of his life. Still, a sense of fragility stubbornly clung to Baron. A fragility Darius feared could escalate into something more threatening if Baron glimpsed his dead son's widow.

"I'll go and find security so they can escort her out," he said, the calm in his voice a mockery of the rage damn near consuming him. "You can locate your parents to make sure they don't realize what's going on."

Yes, he'd have Isobel Hughes thrown out, but not before he had a few words with her. The deceitful, traitorous woman should've counted herself lucky that he hadn't come after her when she'd skipped town two years ago. But with the Wells family shattered over their son and brother's death, they'd been his first priority. And as long as Isobel had remained gone, they didn't have to suffer a daily reminder of the woman who'd destroyed Gage with her manipulations and faithlessness. In spite of the need to mete out his own brand of justice, Darius had allowed her to disappear with the baby the Wells family doubted was their grandson and nephew. But now…

Now she'd reappeared, and all bets were off.

She'd thrown down the gauntlet, and fuck if he wouldn't enjoy snatching it up.

"Okay," Gabriella agreed, enclosing his hand in hers and squeezing. "Darius," she whispered. He tore his attention away from Isobel and transferred it to Gabriella. "Thank you for…" She swallowed. "Thank you," she breathed.

"No need for any of that," he replied, brushing a kiss over the top of her black curls. "Family. We always take care of one another."

She nodded, then turned and disappeared into the throng of people.

Anticipation hummed beneath his skin as he moved forward. Several people slowed his progress for meaningless chatter, but he didn't deter from his path. He tracked her, noting that she'd moved from just inside the entrance to one of the floor-to-ceiling glass doors that led to a balcony. Good. The only exit led out onto that balcony, and the temperature of the October night had probably dropped even more since he'd arrived. She wouldn't venture through those doors and into the cold. He had a location to give security.

It was unfair that a woman who possessed zero morals and conscience should exhibit none of it on her face or her body. But then, if her smooth, golden skin or slender-but-curvaceous body did reveal any of her true self, she wouldn't be able to snare men in her silken web.

Long, thick, dark brown hair that gleamed with hints of auburn fire under the chandelier's light flowed over one slim shoulder and a just-less-than-a-handful breast. Dispassionately, he scanned her petite frame. The strapless, floor-length black gown clung to her, lifting her full curves so a hint of shadowed cleavage teased, promised. A waist that a man—not him—could span with his hands flowed into rounded hips and a tight, worship-worthy ass that he didn't need to see to remember. Even when he'd first met her—as the only witness and friend at her and Gage's quickie courthouse marriage—it'd amazed him how such a small woman could possess curves so dangerous they should come with a blaring warning sign. Back then he'd appreciated her curves. Now he despised them for what they truly were—an enticing lure to trap un-suspecting game.

Dragging his inspection up the siren call of her body, he took in the delicate bones that provided the structure for an almost elfin face. One of his guilty pleasures was fantasy novels and movies. Tolkien, Martin, Rowling, King. And he could easily imagine Arwen, half-Elven daughter of King Elrond in *The Lord of the Rings*, resembling Isobel. Beautiful. Ethe-real. Though he couldn't catch the color of her eyes from this distance, he clearly recalled their striking color. A vivid and startling blue-gray that only en-hanced the impression of otherworldly fragility. But then there was her mouth. It splintered her air of inno-cence. The shade-too-wide lips with their full, plump curves called to mind ragged, hoarse groans in the darkest part of night. Yeah, those lips could cause a man's cock to throb.

He ground his teeth together, the minute flare of pain along his jaw grounding him. It didn't ease the stab of guilt over the sudden, unexpected clench of lust in his gut. He could hate himself for that gut-punch of desire. Didn't he, more than anyone, know that a pretty face could hide the black, empty hole where a heart should be? Could conceal the blackest of souls? His own ex-wife had taught him that lesson, and he'd received straight fucking A's. Yeah, his dick might be slow on the uptake, but his head—the one that ruled him, contrary to popular opinion about men—possessed full disclosure and was fully aware.

Isobel Hughes was one of those pretty faces.

As if she'd overheard her name in his head, Isobel lifted her chin and surveyed the crowded ballroom. Probably searching for Baron and Helena. If she thought he'd allow her within breathing space of Gage's parents, she'd obviously been smoking too much of that legalized California weed. He'd do anything to protect them; he'd failed to protect Gage, and that knowledge gnawed at him, an open wound that hadn't healed in two years. No way in hell would this woman have another shot at the people he loved. At his family.

The thought propelled him forward. Time to end this and escort her back to whatever hole she'd crawled out of.

Clenching his jaw, he worked his way to the ballroom entrance. Several minutes later, he waited in one of the side hallways for the head of security. Glancing down at his watch, he frowned. The man should've arrived already...

Darkness.

Utter darkness.

Dimly, Darius caught the sound of startled cries and shouts, but the deafening pounding of his heart muted most of the fearful noise.

He stumbled backward, and his spine smacked the wall behind him. Barely able to draw a breath into his constricted lungs, he frantically patted his jacket and then his pants pockets for his cell phone. Nothing. *Damn.* He must've left it in the car. He never left his phone. Never...

The thick blackness surrounded him. Squeezed him so that he jerked at his bow tie, clawing at material that seconds ago had been perfectly comfortable.

Air.

He needed air.

But all he inhaled, all he swallowed, was more of the obsidian viscosity that clogged his nostrils, throat and chest.

In the space of seconds, his worst, most brutal nightmare had come to life.

He was trapped in the dark.

Alone.

And he was drowning in it.

Chapter 2

*B*lackout.
  Malfunction. Doors locked.
  Remain calm.
  The words shouted in anything but calm voices outside the bathroom door bombarded Isobel. Perched on the settee in the outer room of the ladies' restroom, she hunched over her cell phone, which had only 2 percent battery life left.

  "C'mon," she ordered her fingers to cooperate as she fumbled over the text keyboard. In her nerves, she kept misspelling words, and *damn autocorrect*, it kept "fixing" the words that were actually right. Finally she finished her message and hit send.

Mom, is everything okay? How is Aiden?

Fingers clutching the little burner phone, she—not for the first time—wished she could afford a regular cell. But with her other responsibilities, that bill had been one of the first things she'd cut. Constantly buying minutes and battling a battery that didn't hold a charge presented a hassle, but the prepaid phone did the job. After seconds that seemed like hours, a message popped up on the screen.

He's fine, honey. Sleeping. We're all good. Stay put. It's a blackout and we've been advised to remain inside. I love you and take care of yourself.

Relief washed over Isobel in a deluge. If she hadn't already been sitting down, she would've sunk to the floor. For the first time since the world had plunged into darkness, she could breathe.

After several moments, she located the flashlight app and aimed it in the direction of where she believed the door to be. The deep blackness seemed to swallow up the light, but she spied the handle and sighed. Without ventilation, the area was growing stuffy. The hallway had to be better. At the very least, she wouldn't feel like the walls were closing in on her. Claustrophobia had never been a problem for her, but this was enough to have anyone on edge.

She grabbed the handle and pulled the door open, the weak beam illuminating the floor only feet in front of her. As soon as she stepped out into the hall, the light winked, then disappeared.

"No, not yet," she muttered, flipping the phone over. But, nope, the cell had died. "Dammit."

Frustration and not-a-little fear scrabbled up her

chest, lodging there. Inhaling a deep breath and holding it, she forced herself to calm down. Okay. One thing her two years in Los Angeles had granted her was a sense of direction. The ballroom lay to the left. Follow the wall until it gave way to the small alcove and the side entrance she'd exited.

No problem. She could do this.

Probably.

Maybe.

Releasing that same gulp of air, she shuffled forward, hands groping until they knocked against the wall. Step one down.

With halting steps, she slid along, palms flattened, skimming. The adjacent corridor shouldn't be too far…

Her chest bumped into a solid object seconds after her hands collided with it. A person. A big person, if the width of the shoulders and chest under her fingers were anything to go by.

"Oh, God. I'm sorry." She snatched her arms back. Heat soared up her neck and poured into her face. She'd just felt up a man in the dark.

Horrified, she shifted backward, but her heel caught on the hem of her dress, and she pitched forward. Slamming against that same hard expanse of muscles she'd just molested. "*Dammit.* I—"

The second apology drifted away as a hoarse, ragged sound penetrated the darkness and reached her ears. For a long moment, she froze, her hands splayed wide over the stranger's chest. It rapidly rose and fell, the pace unnatural. She jerked her head up, staring into the space where his face should've been. But she didn't need to glimpse his features to understand this man suffered some kind of distress. Because those rough, serrated, *wounded* sounds originated from him.

The urge to comfort, to stop those god-awful moans overrode all embarrassment at having touched him without his permission. At this moment, she needed to touch him. To ease his pain.

As she slid one palm over his jackhammering heart, she swept the other over his shoulder and down his arm until she enclosed his long fingers in hers. Then she murmured, "Hi. Talk about an awkward meet cute, right? Citywide blackout. Get felt up in the hallway. Sounds like the beginning of a rom-com starring Ryan Reynolds."

The man didn't reply, and his breathing continued to sough out of his lungs, but his fingers curled around hers, clutching them tight. As if she were his lifeline.

Relief and determination to tow him away from whatever tormented him swelled within her. It didn't require a PhD in psychology to figure out that this man was in the throes of a panic attack. But she had zero experience with how to handle that situation. Still, he'd responded to her voice, her presence. So she'd continue talking.

"Do you know who Ryan Reynolds is?" She didn't wait for his answer but kept babbling. "*The Green Lantern*? *Deadpool*? I'm leading with those movies, because if you're anything like my brother, if I'd have said *The Proposal*, you would've stared at me like I'd suddenly started speaking Mandarin. Well...that is, if you *could* stare at me right now." She snickered. "What I wouldn't give for Riddick's eyes right now. To be able to see in the dark? Although you could keep Slam City and, ya know, the murder. Have you ever seen *Pitch Black* or *The Chronicles of Riddick*?"

This time she received a squeeze of her fingers and a slight change in the coarseness of his breathing. A grin curved her lips. Good. That had to be a positive sign, right?

"*The Chronicles of Riddick*? I enjoyed watching Vin Diesel for two hours, but the movie? Meh. *Pitch Black*, though, was amazing. One of the best sci-fi movies ever. Only beat out by *Aliens* and *The Matrix*. Although I still maintain that *The Matrix Revolutions* never happened, just as *Dirty Dancing 2* is a dirty rumor. They're like Voldemort. Those Movies That Shall Not Be Named."

A soft, shaky chuckle drifted above her, but seemed to echo in the dark, empty hallway like a sonic boom. Probably because she'd been aching to hear it. Not that she'd been aware of that need until this moment.

An answering laugh bubbled up inside her, but she shoved it back down, opting to continue with what had been working so far. Talking. The irony that this was the longest conversation she'd indulged in with a person outside of her family in two years wasn't lost on her. Cruel experience had taught her to be wary of strangers, especially those with pretty faces wielding charm like a Highlander's claymore. The last time she'd trusted a beautiful appearance, she'd ended up in a loveless, controlling, soul-stealing sham of a marriage.

But in the dark…

In the dark lived a kind of freedom where she could lose her usual restrictions, step out of the protective box she'd created for her life. Because here, she couldn't see this man, and he couldn't see her. There was no judgment. If he were attending the Du Sable City Gala, then that meant he most likely came from wealth—the kind of wealth that had once trapped her in a gilded prison. Yet in this corridor in the middle of a blackout, money, status, lineage traced back to the Mayflower—none of that mattered. Here, they were only two people holding on to each other to make it through.

"My next favorite sci-fi is *Avatar*. Which is kind of funny, considering the famous line from the movie is 'I see you.'" She couldn't smother her laughter. And didn't regret the display of amusement when it garnered another squeeze of her hand. "Do you have a favorite?"

She held her breath, waiting. Part of her waited to see if his panic attack had finally passed. But the other part of her wanted—no, *needed*—to hear his voice. That part wondered if it would match his build.

Being tucked away in a mansion's dark hallway in a blackout...the insane circumstances had to be the cause of her desire. Because it'd been years since she'd been curious about anything regarding a man.

"The Terminator."

Oh. Wow. That voice. Darker than the obsidian blanket that draped the city. Deeper than the depths of the ocean she sorely missed. Sin wrapped in the velvet embrace of sweet promise.

A dangerous voice.

One that invited a person to commit acts that might shame them in the light of day, acts a person would revel in during the secretive, shadowed hours of night.

Her eyes fluttered closed, and her lips parted, as if

she could breathe in that slightly abraded yet smooth tone. As if she could taste it.

As if she could taste him.

What the hell?

The inane thought rebounded against the walls of her skull, and she couldn't evict it. Her eyes flew open, and she stared wide into nothing. For the second time that evening, she thanked God. At this moment, she offered her gratitude because she couldn't be seen. That no one had witnessed her unprecedented, humiliating reaction to a man's *voice*.

"A classic." She struggled to recapture and keep hold of the light, teasing note she'd employed with him BTV. Before The Voice. "But I take your *Terminator* and one-up you with *Predator*."

A scoff. "That wasn't sci-fi."

Isobel frowned even though he couldn't see her disapproval. "Are you kidding me?" She dropped her hand from his chest and jammed it on her hip. "Hello? There was a big-ass alien in it. How is that not sci-fi?"

A snort this time. "It's horror. Using your logic would mean *Avatar* was a romance."

Okay, so this guy might have the voice of a fallen angel tempting her to sin, but his movie knowledge sucked.

"I think I liked you better when you weren't talking," she grumbled.

She was rewarded with a loud bark of laughter that did the impossible. Made his voice even sexier. Desire slid through her veins in a slow, heady glide.

She stiffened. No. Impossible. It'd been years since she'd felt even the slightest flicker of this thing that heated her from the inside out.

If she harbored even the tiniest shred of common sense, she'd back away from this man now and blind-man's bluff it until she placed some much needed distance between them. Desire had once fooled her into falling in love. And falling in love had led to a heart-breaking betrayal she was still recovering from.

No, she should make sure he was okay, then leave. With moving back to Chicago, raising her son as a single mother and working a full-time job, she didn't have the time or inclination for something as mercurial as desire.

You're sitting here in the dark with him, not dating him.

One night. Just one night.

She sighed.

And stayed.

"Is something wrong?" A large hand settled on her shoulder and cupped it. She gritted her teeth, refusing to lean into that gentle but firm hold.

"Nothing. Just these shoes," she lied, bending and slipping off one and then the other to validate the fib. "They're beautiful, but hell on the feet."

He released another of those soft chuckles that sent her belly into a series of tumbles.

"What's your name?" His thumb stroked a lazy back-and-forth caress over her bare skin, and she sank her teeth into her bottom lip. Heat radiated from his touch. Until this moment, she hadn't known her shoulder was an erogenous zone. Funny the things she was finding out in the dark.

What had he asked? Right. Her name.

Alarm and dread filtered into her pleasure, tainting it. Gage had done a damn good job of demonizing her to his family, and then his family had made sure everyone with a willing ear and flapping gums knew Isobel as a lying, greedy whore. It'd been two years since she'd left Chicago, but the insular ranks of high society never forgot names when it came to scandals.

Again, she squeezed her eyes shut as if she could block out the scorn and derision that had once flayed her soul. She still yearned to be known as more than the cheap little gold digger people believed her to be.

"Why do you want my name?" she finally replied.

A short, but weighty pause. "Because I need to know who to thank," he murmured. "And considering we've known each other all of ten minutes, 'sweetheart' seems a little forward."

"I don't mind 'sweetheart,'" she blurted out. His grasp on her shoulder tightened, and a swirl of need pooled low in her belly. "What I mean is we don't need names here. In the dark, we can be other people, different people, and I like the idea of that."

The bit of deception plucked at her conscience. Because she had no doubt that if he was familiar with her name, he would want nothing to do with her. And selfish though it might be, she'd rather him believe she was some coy debutante than the notorious Widow Wells.

That large hand slid over her shoulder, up her neck and cradled the back of her head. A sigh escaped her before she could contain it.

"Are you hiding, sweetheart?" he rumbled.

The question could have sounded inane since it seemed like the whole city was hunkered down, cloaked in darkness. But she understood what he asked. And the lack of light made it easier to be honest. At least in this.

"Yes," she breathed, and braced herself for his possible rejection.

"You're stiffening again." The hand surrounding hers squeezed lightly, a gesture of comfort. "Don't worry, your secrets are as safe with me as you are." He paused, his fingertips pressing into her scalp. "Just as I am with you."

Oh, God. That…vulnerable admission had no business burrowing beneath skin and bone to her heart. But it did.

"Keep your name, but, sweetheart—" he heaved a heavy sigh, and for an all-too-brief moment he pressed his forehead to hers "—thank you."

"I…" She swallowed, a shiver dancing down her spine. Whether in delight or warning, she couldn't tell. Probably both. "You're welcome. Anyone would've done the same," she whispered.

Something sharp edged through his low chuckle. "That's where you're wrong. Most people would've kept going, only concerned with themselves. Or they would've taken advantage."

She didn't answer; she wanted to refute him but couldn't. Because the sad fact was, he'd spoken the truth. Once she'd been a naïve twenty-year-old who'd believed in the good in people, in the happily-ever-after peddled by fairy tales. Gage had been her drug. And the withdrawal from him had nearly crushed her into the piece of nothing he'd constantly told her she was without him.

Shaking her head to get him out of her mind, she bent down and swept her hands along the floor, seeking the purse she'd dropped. Her fingertips bumped the beaded clutch, and with a small sound of victory, she popped it open and withdrew the snack bar she'd stashed there before leaving her apartment. With a two-year-old, keeping snacks on hand was a case of survival. And though her son hadn't joined her at the gala, she'd tossed the snack in out of habit. Now she patted herself on the back for her foresight.

Unbidden, a smile curved her lips. If Aiden could see her, he would be holding out his chubby little hand, demanding his "eats."

She pinched the bridge of her nose, battling back the sting in her eyes. Obtaining help for her son had driven her to this mansion, and she'd failed. It would be easy to blame the blackout for her not locating and approaching the Wellses. But she couldn't deny the truth. She'd left the ballroom and headed to the restroom to convince herself not to leave. The plunge of the city into darkness had snatched the decision out of her hands, granting her a convenient reprieve from facing down the people who'd made it their lives' purpose to ensure she understood just how unworthy and hated she was.

But it was only that—a reprieve. Because when it came down to a choice between her pride and providing a stable environment for her son, there wasn't a choice.

When the blackout ended, she still had to face the Wellses.

"Did I lose you?" His softly rumbled question drew her from her desperate thoughts.

Clearing her throat, she settled on the floor, tucking her legs under her. She tugged on the hem of his pants, and he accepted her silent invitation, sinking down beside her. When the thick muscles of his leg brushed her knee, she reached out and skated a palm down his arm until she located his hand. She pressed half the cereal bar into it.

"What is this?" His low roll of rich laughter slid over her skin, and she involuntarily tightened her grip on her half.

"Dinner." Isobel bit into the snack and hummed. The oats, almonds and chocolate weren't caviar and toast points, but they did the job in a pinch. And this situation definitely qualified as a pinch.

"I have to say this is a first," he murmured, amusement still warming his voice.

God, she liked it. A lot. No matter how foolish that feeling might be.

"So, you don't want to share your name," he continued. "And I'll respect that. But since I'm sharing a cereal bar with you, I feel like I should know more about you besides your predilection for sci-fi movies. Tell me something about you."

She didn't immediately reply, instead nibbling on her snack while she figured out how to dodge his request. She didn't want to give him any details that might assist him in figuring out her identity. But another nebulous reason, one that she felt silly for even thinking, flitted through her head.

Giving him details about herself…pieces of herself…meant she couldn't get them back.

And she feared that. Had been taught to fear that. Yet…

She bowed her head, silently cursing herself. What was it about this man? She'd never seen his face, didn't know his name. And still, he called to her in a way that electrified her. If she'd learned anything from the past, she would shield herself.

"I'm a grudge-holder," she said, the words escaping. *Damn it.* "I'll never let my brother off the hook for burning my Christmas Barbie's hair to the scalp when I was seven. I still give Elaine Lanier side-eye, whenever I see her, for making out with my boyfriend in the eleventh grade. And I will never, ever forgive Will Smith for *Wild, Wild West.*"

A loud bark of laughter echoed between them, and she grinned. The sound warmed her like the sun's beams.

She tapped his leg. A mistake on her part. As she settled her hand back in her lap, she could still feel the strength of his muscle against her fingertips. Good God. The man was *hard.* She rubbed her fingertips against her leg as if she could erase the sensation. "Now your turn," she said, forcing a teasing note into her voice. "Tell me something about yourself."

He hesitated, and for a moment, she didn't think he would answer, but then he shifted beside her, and his thigh pressed closer, harder against her knee. Her breath snagged in her throat. Heat pulsed through her from that point of contact, and she savored it. For the first time in years, she...embraced it.

"I love to fish," he finally murmured. "Not deep sea or competitive fishing. Just sitting on a dock with a rod, barefoot, sun beating down on you, surrounded by quiet. Interrupted only by the gently lapping water. We would vacation at our summer home in Hilton Head, and my father and I would spend hours at the lake and dock behind the house. We'd talk or just enjoy the silence and each other. We even caught fish sometimes."

His low chuckle contained humor, but also a hint of sadness. Her heart clenched at the possible reason why.

"Those were some of my best memories, and I still try to visit Hilton Head at least once a year, although I haven't been in the last two…"

His voice trailed off, and unable to resist, she reached out, found his hand and wrapped her fingers around his, squeezing. Her heart thumped against her chest when his fingers tightened in response.

"I have the hugest crush on Dr. Phil. He's so sexy."

He snorted. "I cook the best eggplant parmesan you'll ever taste in your life. It's an existential experience."

Isobel snickered. "I can write with my toes. I can also eat, brush my teeth and play 'Heart and Soul' on the piano with them."

A beat of silence passed between them. "You do know I recognize that's from *The Breakfast Club*, right?"

Laughter burst from her, and she fell back against the wall, clutching her stomach. Wow. She hadn't laughed this hard or this much in so long. It was… freeing. And felt so damn good. Until this moment, she hadn't realized how much she'd missed it.

At twenty, she'd met Gage, and within months, they'd married. She'd gone from being a college student who worked part-time to help pay her tuition to the wife of one of Chicago's wealthiest men. His family had disapproved of their marriage and threatened to cut him off. Initially, Gage hadn't seemed to care. They'd lived in a small one-bedroom apartment in the Ukrainian Village neighborhood of Chicago, and they'd been happy. Or at least she'd believed they had been.

Months into their marriage, the charming, affectionate man she'd wed had morphed into a spoiled, emotionally abusive man-child. Not until it'd been too late had she discovered that his fear of being without his family's money and acceptance had trumped any love he'd harbored for Isobel. Her life had become a living hell.

So the last time she'd laughed like this had been those first four months of her marriage.

A failed relationship, tarnished dreams, battered self-confidence and single motherhood had stolen the carefree from her life, but here, stuck in a mansion with a faceless man, she'd found it again. Even if only for an instant.

"Hey." Masculine fingers glanced over her knee. "You still with me?"

"Yes," she said, shaking her head. "I'm still here."

"Good." His hand dropped away, and she missed it. Insane, she knew. But she did. "It's your turn. Because you phoned it in with the last one."

"So, we're *really* not going to talk about how you know the dialogue to *The Breakfast Club*?" she drawled.

"Yes, we're going to ignore it. Your turn."

After chuckling at the emphatic reply, she continued, "Fine. Okay, I…"

Seconds, minutes or hours had passed—she couldn't tell in this slice of time that seemed to exist outside of reality. They could've been on another plane, where his delicious scent provided air, and his deep, melodic voice wrapped around her, a phantom embrace.

And his touch? His touch was gravity, anchoring him to her, and her to him. In some manner—fingers enclosing hers, a thigh pressed to hers, a palm cupping the nape of her neck—he never ceased touching her. Logic reasoned that he needed that lodestone in the blackness so he didn't surrender to another panic attack.

Yet the heated sweetness that slid through her veins belied reason. No, he wanted to touch her…and, God, did she want to be touched.

She'd convinced herself that she didn't need desire anymore. Didn't need the melting pleasure, the hot press of skin to skin, of limbs tangling, bodies straining together toward that perfect tumble over the edge into the abyss.

Yes, she missed all of it.

But in the end, those moments weren't worth the disillusionment and loneliness that inevitably followed.

Here, though, with this man she didn't know, she basked in the return of the need, of the sweet ache that sensitized and pebbled her skin, and teased places that had lain dormant for too long. Her nipples furled into tight points, pressing against her strapless bra and gown. Sinuous flames licked at her belly…and lower.

God, she was hungry.

"You've gone quiet on me again, sweetheart," he murmured, sweeping a caress over the back of her hand that he clasped in his. "Talk to me. I need to hear your beautiful voice."

Did he touch all women this easily? Was he always

this affectionate? Or was it the darkness? Did he feel freer, too? Without the accountability of propriety?

Or is it me?

As soon as the traitorous and utterly foolish thought whispered through her head, she banished it. Yes, these were extraordinary circumstances, and she was grabbing this slice in time for herself, but never could she forget who she was. Because this man might not know her identity, but he still believed her to be someone she absolutely wasn't—wealthy, a socialite…a woman who belonged.

"Sweetheart?"

That endearment. She shivered. It ignited a curl of heat in her chest. It loosed a razor-tipped arrow at the same target. No one had ever called her "sweetheart." Or "baby" or any of those personal endearments. Gage used to call her Belle, shortening her name and because he'd met her in her regular haunt, the University of Illinois's library, like a modern-day version of the heroine from *Beauty and the Beast*. Later, the affectionate nickname had become a taunt, a criticism of her unsophisticated and naïve nature.

She hated that name now.

But every time this man called her sweetheart, she felt cherished, wanted. Even though it was also a stark reminder that he didn't know her name. That she was lying to him by omission.

"Can I ask you a question?" she blurted out.

"Isn't that kind of our MO?" he drawled. "Ask."

Now that she could satisfy the curiosity that had been gnawing at her since she'd first encountered him, she hesitated. She had no right—never mind it not being her business—to probe into his history and private pain. But as hypocritical as it made her, she sought a piece of him she sensed he wouldn't willingly offer someone else.

"Earlier, when I first bumped into you...you were having a panic attack," she began. He stiffened, tension turning his body into a replica of the marble statue adorning the fountain outside the mansion. Sitting so close to him, she swore she could feel icy waves emanate from him. Unease trickled through her. *Damn it.* She should've left it alone. "I'm sorry..." she rasped, tugging on her hand, trying to withdraw it from his hold. "I shouldn't have pried."

But he didn't release her. Her heart stuttered as his grip on her strengthened.

"Don't," he ordered.

Don't what? Ask him any more questions? Pull away? How pathetic did it make her that she hoped it was the latter?

"You're the only thing keeping me sane," he admitted in a voice so low that, even in the blackness that magnified every sound, she barely caught the admission.

A thread of pain throbbed through his confession, and she couldn't resist the draw of it. Scooting closer until her thigh pressed against his, she lifted the hand not clasped in his to his hard chest. The drum of his heart vibrated against her palm, running up her arm and echoing in her own chest.

She felt and heard his heavy inhale. And she parted her lips, ready to tell him to forget it. To apologize again for intruding, but his big hand covered hers, halting her words.

"My parents died when I was sixteen."

"God," she breathed. That hint of sadness she'd detected earlier when he'd talked about fishing with his father... She'd suspected, and now he'd confirmed it. "I'm so sorry."

"Plane crash on their way back from a business meeting in Paris. Ordinarily my mother wouldn't have been with my father, but they decided to treat it as an anniversary trip. They were my foundation. And I..." He paused, and Isobel waited.

She couldn't imagine... Her father had been a non-factor in her life for most of her childhood, but her mom... Her mother had been her support system, her rock, even through the years with Isobel and Aiden's move to California and back. Losing her...she closed her eyes and leaned her head against his shoulder, offering whatever comfort he needed as he relayed the details of the tragedy that had scarred him.

"My best friend and his family took me in. I don't know what would've happened to me, where I would be now, without them. But at the time, I was lost. Adrift. In the months afterward, I'd skip school or leave my friend's house in the middle of the night to go to the building where we'd lived. The penthouse had been sold, so I no longer had access to my home, but I would sneak into the basement through a window. It had a loosened bar that I would remove and squeeze through. I'd sit there for hours, just content to be in the building, if not in the place where I'd lived with them. My best friend—he followed me one night when I sneaked out, so he knew about it. But he never told."

Another pause, and again she didn't disturb him. She wanted to hug that best friend for standing by the boy-now-man. She'd had girlfriends in the past, but none that would've—or could've, given their own family situations—taken her in as if she were family. This friend of his, he must've been special.

"About four months after my parents' death, I'd left school again and went to the basement. I'd had a rough night. Nightmares and no sleep. That's the only reason I can think of for me falling asleep in the basement that day. I don't know what woke me up. The noise? The heat?" His shoulder rose and fell in a shrug under her cheek. "Like I said, I don't know. But when I did, the room was pitch-black. I couldn't even see my hands in front of my face. I heard what sounded like twigs snapping. But underneath that, distant but growing louder, was this dull roar. Like engines revving in a closed garage. I'd never been in one before, but somehow I knew. The building was on fire, and I was trapped."

"No," she whispered, fingers curling against his chest.

"I couldn't move. Thick black smoke filled the basement, and I choked on it, couldn't breathe. I can't tell you how long I laid there, paralyzed by fear or weak from inhaling smoke, but I thought I was going to die. That room—it became my tomb. A dark, burning tomb. But then I heard someone shouting my name and saw the high beam of a flashlight. It was my friend. I found out later that he'd heard about the fire on the news, and when I hadn't shown up at his house after school, he'd guessed where I'd gone. The firemen had believed they'd cleared the entire building, but he'd forced them to go back in and search the basement. He should've stayed outside and let them come find me, but he'd barreled past them and entered with only his shirt over his face to battle the smoke, putting his life in danger. But if he hadn't... He saved my life that day."

"Oh, thank God." Sliding her hand from under his, she wrapped her arm around his waist, curving her body into his. She'd known him for mere hours, and yet the thought of him dying, of being consumed by flames? It bothered her in a way that made no sense. "He was a hero."

"Yes, he was," he said softly. "He was a good man."

Was a good man. No. It couldn't be... Horror and disbelief crowded up her throat. "He's gone, too?"

"A couple of years now, but sometimes it seems like yesterday."

"I'm so sorry." Isobel shifted until she knelt beside him. She stroked her hand up his torso, searching out his face. Once she brushed over his hard, faintly stubbled jaw, she cupped it and lowered her head, until her forehead met his temple.

His fingers drifted over her cheek, and after a moment's hesitation, tunneled into her hair. Her lungs seized, shock infiltrating every vein, organ and limb. Only her heart seemed capable of movement, and it threw itself against her sternum, like an animal desperate for freedom from its cage.

Blunt fingertips dragged over her scalp. A moan clawed its way up her throat at the scratch and tug of her hair, but she trapped the sound behind clenched teeth. She couldn't prevent the shudder that worked its way through her. Not when it'd been *so long* since she'd been touched. Since pleasure had even been a factor. So. Long.

"I need to hear that lovely voice, sweetheart," he rumbled, turning and bowing his head so his lips grazed the column of her throat as he spoke. Sparks snapped under her skin as if her nerve endings had transformed into firecrackers, and his mouth was the lighter. "There are things I want to do to your mouth that require your permission."

"Like what?" Had she really just asked that question? And in that breathy tone? What was he doing to her?

Giving you what you're craving. Be brave and find out, her subconscious replied.

"Find out if it's as sweet as you are. Taste you. Savor you. Learn you," he murmured, answering her question. He untangled their clasped fingers and with unerring accuracy, located her chin and pinched it. Cool but soft strands of hair tickled her jaw, and then her cheek, as he lifted his head. Then warm gusts of air bathed her lips. She could taste him, his breath. Something potent with faint hints of lemon, like the champagne from earlier. But also, underneath, lay a darker, enigmatic flavor. Him. She didn't need to pinpoint its origin to know it was all him. "Then I want to take your mouth. Want you to take mine."

"I…" Desperate, aching need robbed her of words. Of thought.

"Give me the words, sweetheart." He didn't breach that scant inch of space between them, waiting on her consent, her permission.

When so much had been ripped from her in the past, choices not even offered, that seeking of her agreement squeezed her heart even as his words caused a spasm to roll through her sex.

"Yes," she said. Then, as if confirming to herself that she was indeed breaking her self-imposed rules about caution and recklessness, she whispered again, "Yes."

With a growl, he claimed that distance.

She expected him to crush his mouth to hers, to conquer her like a wild storm leveling everything in its path. And she would've thrown herself into the whirlwind, been willingly swept up. But his tenderness was as thorough in its destruction as any tornado.

His lips, full, firm yet somehow soft, brushed over hers. Pressed, then withdrew. Rubbed, cajoled, gave her enough of him, but waited until she granted him more. On the tail end of a sigh she couldn't contain, she parted for him. Welcomed the penetration of his tongue. Slid into a sensual dance with him. It was she who sucked him, licking the roof of his mouth, sampling the dark, heady flavor of his groan. She who first brought teeth into play, nipping at the corner of his mouth, raking them down his chin, only to return to take just as he'd invited her to do.

She who crawled onto his lap, jerking her skirt up and straddling his powerful thighs.

But it was he who threw oil onto their fire, ratcheting their desire from a blaze into a consuming inferno.

With a snarl that vibrated through his chest and over her nipples, he tugged her head back and opened his mouth over her neck. She arched into the hot, wet caress of tongue and teeth, her hands shifting from his shoulders to his hair and holding on. Every flick and suck echoed low in her belly, between her thighs. Fleetingly, the thought that she should be embarrassed at how drenched her panties were flitted through her head. But the clamp of his hand on her hip and the roll of his hips, stroking the hard, thick length of his cock over her sex, obliterated every rationalization.

Think? All she could do was *feel*.

Pleasure, its claws tipped with greed, tore at her. She whimpered, clung to him.

"Again," she ordered. Begged. Didn't matter. As long as he did it *again*.

"That's it," he praised against her throat, licking a path to her ear, where he nipped the outer curve. Hell, when had *that* become an erogenous zone? "Tell me what you want, what you need from me. I'll give it to you, sweetheart. You just have to ask."

Keep turning me inside out. Keep holding me like I'm wanted, cherished. Keep making me forget who I am.

But those pleas veered too close to exposing that part of her she'd learned to protect with the zeal of a dragon guarding a treasure.

So instead she gave him what she could. What she'd be too embarrassed to admit in the light of day. "Here." With trembling, jerky movements, she yanked down the top of her dress, drew him to her bared breasts. "Kiss me. Mark me."

He followed through on his promise, giving her what she'd requested. His tongue circled her nipple, lapped at it, swirled before sucking so hard the corresponding ache twinged deep and high inside her. She tried to hold in her cry but couldn't. Not when lust arrowed through her, striking at the heart of her. He murmured against her flesh, switching breasts, and treating her other peak to the same erotic torture. Skillful fingers plucked and pinched the tip that was damp from his mouth.

"More," she gasped. "Oh, God, more."

"Tell me." The hand on her hip tightened, and he delivered another slow, luxurious stroke to her empty, wet sex. "Tell me once more. I want your voice, your words."

Frustration, the last stubborn remnants of shyness and passion warred within her. Her lips moved, but the demand *make me come* that howled inside her head refused to emerge. Finally she grabbed the hand at her waist and slid it over her hiked-up dress, down her inner thigh and between her legs. She pressed his palm to her, moaning at the temporary relief of him cupping her.

"You're cheating," he teased, but the almost guttural tone had her hips bucking against him. As did his, "You're soaked. For me."

"Yes," she rasped. "For you. Only for you." Truth. That piece of herself, she offered him. She'd never been this hungry, this desperate before. Not even for—*no!*

She flung herself away from the intrusive thought. Not here. In this hall, there was only room for her and this nameless, faceless man, who nonetheless handled her like the most desirable, beautiful creature he'd ever held. Or at least that's what she was convincing herself of for these stolen moments.

"Touch me," she whispered, grinding down against his hand. "Please touch me."

The fingers still sweeping caresses over her nipple abandoned her flesh to cradle her face. He tipped her head down until their mouths met. "Don't beg me to touch you," he said, his lips grazing hers with each word. "You'll never have to beg me to do that."

He sealed the vow with a plunge of his finger inside her.

She cried out, tossing her head back on her shoulders as pleasure rocked through her like an earthquake, cracking her open, exposing her.

"Damn," he swore. "So damn tight. So damn…" He bit off the rest of his litany, slowly pulling free of her, then just as slowly, just as tenderly thrusting back inside. But she didn't want slow, didn't want tender. And she told him so with a hard, swift twist of her hips, taking him deeper. "Sweetheart," he growled, warned.

"No," she panted. "I need to… Please." He'd said she didn't need to plead with him, but if it would get her what she craved—release, oblivion—she wasn't above it.

With a snarl, he crushed his mouth to hers, tongue driving between her lips as he buried himself inside her. She moaned into his kiss, even as she spread her legs wider, granting him deeper access to her body. And he took it. He withdrew one finger and returned to her with two, working them into her flesh, working *her*.

Something snapped within her, and she rode his hand, rode the exquisite storm he whipped to a frenzy with every stroke, every brush of his thumb over her clit, every curl of his fingertips on that place high and deep in her sex. He played her, demanding her body sing for him. And God, did it.

With one last rub over that, before now, untouched place, she splintered, screaming into his mouth. And he swallowed it, clutching her to him, holding her tight as she crashed headlong into the abyss, a willing sacrifice to pleasure.

Isobel snuggled under her warm blanket, grabbing ahold of those last few moments of lazy sleepiness be-

fore Aiden cried out, demanding she come free him
from his crib and feed him. She sighed, curling into
her pillow...

Wait. Her pillow wasn't this firm. Frowning, she
rolled over...or tried to roll over. Something prevented
the movement...

Oh, hell.

Not something. Some*one.*

She stiffened as reality shoved the misty dredges
of sleep away and dragged in all the memories of the
night before. Gala. Blackout. Finding a mysterious
man. Calming him. Laughing with him. Kissing him...

She jerked away, her lashes lifting.

Weak, hazy pink-and-orange light poured in
through the large window at the end of the hall. Morning, but just barely. So maybe about six o'clock. Still,
the dawn-tinged sky provided enough light to realize
the warm blanket was really a suit jacket. Instead of
a mattress, she perched on a strong pair of muscular
thighs. And her pillow was a wide, solid chest covered
in a snow-white dress shirt.

Heart pounding like a heavy metal-drum solo, she
inched her gaze up to the patch of smooth golden skin
exposed by the buttons undone at a powerful throat.
Her belly clenched, knots twisting and pulling tight
as she continued her wary, slow perusal.

A carved-from-a-slab-of-stone jaw dusted with dark
stubble.

An equally hard chin with just the faintest hint of
a cleft.

A beautiful, sensual mouth that promised all kinds
of decadent, corrupting pleasures. Pleasures she had
firsthand knowledge that he could deliver. She clearly

remembered sinking her teeth into the bottom, slightly fuller curve.

Suppressing a shiver that he would surely feel, as they were pressed so closely together, she continued skimming her gaze upward past a regal, patrician nose and sharp, almost harsh cheekbones.

As she raised her scrutiny that last scant inch to his eyes, his dense, black, ridiculously long lashes lifted.

She sucked in a painful breath. And froze. Except for her frantic pulse, which reverberated in her head like crashing waves relentlessly striking the shore. Deafening her.

Not because of the striking, piercing amber eyes that could've belonged to a majestic eagle.

No. Because she recognized those eyes.

It'd been two years since they'd coldly stared at her over a yawning, freshly dug grave with a flower-strewn mahogany casket suspended above it. But she'd never forget them.

Darius King.

Gage's best friend.

The man who blamed her for Gage's death.

The man who hated her.

Hated her... Hated her... As the words—and the throbbing pain of them—sank into her brain, her paralysis shattered. She scrambled off him, uncaring of how clumsy her backward crab-walk appeared. She just needed to be away from him. From the shock that quickly bled from his gaze and blazed into rage and disgust.

God, no. How could she have kissed...touched... Let him...

You're fucking him, aren't you? Admit it, god-

damn you. Admit it! You're fucking my best friend! You whore!

The memory of Gage's scream ricocheted off the walls of her skull, gaining volume and power by the second. Darius hadn't been the first man he'd thought she'd been cheating with—not even the third or fifth. But she'd never seen him as enraged, as out-of-control at the thought of her being with this man. Gage had never physically abused her during their marriage, but that night... That night she'd truly been afraid he would hit her.

Afterward she'd made a conscious effort to not look at Darius, not be alone in the same room with him if she couldn't avoid him altogether. Even after he'd married an iceberg of a woman, she'd maintained her distance.

And now, not only had she laughed and talked with him, but she had allowed him inside her body. She'd allowed him to bring her the most soul-shattering pleasure.

Meeting his stare, she could read the condemnation there. The confirmation that she was indeed the whore Gage had called her.

Humiliation, hurt and fury—at him and herself—barreled through her, propelling her to her feet. Snatching up her purse and shoes, she clutched them to her chest.

"Isobel." The voice that had caressed her ears with its deep, melodious tone, that had stirred desire with explicit words, now caused ice to coat her veins. Gage used to take great delight in telling her how much his friend disliked her. Though she now knew when her husband's lips were moving, he was lying, hearing Darius's frigid disdain directed at her, meeting his derisive gaze... She believed it now, just as she had then.

"I-I..." She dragged in a breath, shaking her head as she backpedaled. "I need to go. I'm sorry," she rasped.

Hating that she'd apologized, that she sounded scared and...broken, she whirled around and damn near sprinted down the thankfully empty hallway, not feeling the cold marble under her feet. Or the stone as she escaped the mansion. None of the valets from the night before appeared, but she'd glimpsed the direction in which they'd driven off and followed that path.

Twenty minutes later, with keys snatched from the valet stand and car successfully located, she exited onto the freeway. Though with every mile she steadily placed between her and the mansion—and Darius—she couldn't shake the feeling of being pursued.

Couldn't shake the sense that she could run, but couldn't hide.

But that damn sure wouldn't stop her from trying.

Chapter 3

Darius stood outside the weathered brick apartment building, the chill of the October morning not having evaporated yet.

At eight thirty, the overcast sky didn't add any cheer to this South Deering neighborhood. The four rows of identical windows facing the front sported different types of shades, and someone had set potted plants with fake flowers by the front entrance, but nothing could erase the air of poverty that clung to this poor, crime-stricken section of the city. Foam cups, paper and other bits of trash littered the patch of green on the left side of the apartment complex. Graffiti and gang tags desecrated the side of the neighboring building. It sickened him that only thirty minutes away, people lived in almost obscene wealth, a good many of them willingly choosing to pretend this kind of poverty didn't exist. He'd been born into those rarefied circles, but he wasn't blind to the problems of classism, prejudice and ignorance that Chicago faced.

Still… Gage's son was growing up here, in this place that hovered only steps above a tenement. And that ate at Darius like the most caustic acid.

Stalking up the sidewalk, he approached the front entrance. A lock sat above the handle, but on a whim, he tugged on it, and the door easily opened.

"You have to be kidding me," he growled. Anyone off the street could walk into the building, leaving all the residents here vulnerable where they should feel safest. Aiden being one of the most vulnerable.

Darius stepped into the dimly lit foyer, the door shutting behind him. Rectangular mailboxes mounted the wall to his right, and to his left, the steel doors to an elevator. In front of him, a flight of stairs stretched to the upper floors. With one last glance at the elevator doors, he headed for the stairs. He wasn't trusting the elevator in a building this damn old.

According to the information his investigator had provided, Isobel lived on the third floor. He climbed several flights of stairs and entered the door that led to her level. Like the lobby, the hallway was clean, even if the carpet was threadbare. Bulbs lit the area, and the paint, while not fresh, wasn't as desperately in need of a new coat as the downstairs. The broken lock on the front door notwithstanding, it appeared as if the landlord, or at least the residents, cared about their home.

Seconds later, he arrived in front of Isobel's apartment door, standing on a colorful welcome mat depicting a sleeping puppy. It should've seemed out of place, but oddly it didn't strike him that way. But it did serve to remind him that a young boy lived behind the closed door. A boy who deserved to live in a home where he and the puppy could run free and play. A place with a yard, a swing set.

A safe place.

Anger rekindled in his chest, and raising his fist, he knocked on the door. Moments passed, and it remained shut. He rapped on the door again. And still no one answered.

Suppressing a growl, he tucked his hands into the pockets of his coat and narrowed his gaze on the floor.

"Isobel, I know you're home. I can see the shadow of your feet. So open the door," he ordered.

Several more seconds passed before the sound of locks twisting and disengaging reached him, and then she stood in the entrance.

He deliberately inhaled a calming breath. For the entire drive from his Lake Forest home, he'd tried to prepare himself for seeing her again. It'd been a week since the night of the blackout. A week since he'd suffered a panic attack, and she'd held his hand and dragged him back from the edge with her teasing, silly conversation and lilting laughter. A week since he'd feasted on her mouth, experienced the tight-as-hell grip of her body spasming around his fingers, and her greedy cries of pleasure splintering around his ears.

A week since he woke and the piercing anticipation of finally glimpsing the face of the mysterious woman he'd embraced faded into a bright, hot anger as he realized her true identity.

Yes, he'd tried to ready himself for the moment they'd face each other again. And staring down at her now, with all that long, thick hair tumbling over her shoulders, framing a beautiful face with fey eyes that should have existed only within the pages of a fantasy novel, his attempt at preparation had been for shit. Even in a faded pink tank top and cotton pajama pants, with what appeared to be fat leprechauns and rainbows, she knocked him on his ass.

And he resented her for it. Hated himself more.

Because no matter how he tried, he couldn't forget how she'd burned in his arms that night. Exploded. Never had a woman been that uninhibited and hot for him. She'd scorched him so that even now—even a week later—he still felt the marks on his fingers, his chest, his cock. He had an inkling why his best friend had been driven crazy because of her infidelities.

Because imagining Isobel aflame like that with another man had a green-tinted anger churning his own gut.

Which was completely ridiculous. Gage had tortured himself over this woman. It would be a breezy spring day in hell before Darius allowed himself to be her next victim.

"What do you want?" Isobel asked, crossing her arms under her breasts. Her obviously braless breasts.

"To talk," he said, trying and failing to completely keep the snap out of his voice. "And I'd rather not do it out in the hallway."

Her delicate chin kicked up, and even though she stood almost a foot shorter than his own six feet three inches, she continued defiantly standing there, a female Napoleon guarding her empire. "We don't have anything to talk about, so whatever you came here to say should be a very short conversation. The hallway is as good a place as any."

"Fine." He smiled, and it must have appeared as false as it felt because her eyes narrowed on him. "But the private investigator I hired to find you also spoke with your neighbors. Including a Mrs. Gregory, who lives across the hall. A lovely woman, from what he tells me. Seventy-three, lives alone, never misses an episode of the *Young and the Restless* and is a terrible gossip. At this very moment, she probably has her ear against the door, trying to eavesdrop on our conversation. So if you don't mind her finding out where you spent the night of the blackout—and *how* you spent it—I don't either."

Her head remained tilted at that stubborn angle, and the flat line of her mouth didn't soften. But she did slant a glance around him to peek at the closed door across the hall. Whatever she saw made her lips flatten even more.

"Come in." She stepped back, allowing him to pass by her. When he moved into the tiny foyer, she called out, "Good morning, Mrs. Gregory," and shut the door. "I swear that woman could tell the cops where Jimmy Hoffa is buried," she muttered under her breath.

Humor, unexpected and unwelcome, rippled through his chest. He remembered this about her from the night of the blackout. Funny, self-deprecating, charming. Given everything he knew of Isobel's character, the side she'd shown him in the darkness must've been a charade.

Her shock and horror the following morning had been real, though.

He gave his head a mental shake. He wasn't here to rehash the colossal mistake he'd committed in the dark. He had a purpose, an agenda. And before he left this morning, it would be accomplished.

Making resolve a clear, hard wall in his chest, he moved into the living room. Well, *moved* was generous. The change in location from foyer to the main room only required two steps.

Jesus, the whole apartment could fit into his great room—three times. The living room and dining room melded into one space, only broken up by a small counter that separated it from the equally small kitchen. A cramped tunnel of a hallway shot off to the left and led to what he knew from floorplans of the building to be a miniscule bedroom, bathroom and closet.

At least it was clean. The obviously secondhand couch, coffee table and round dining table wore signs of life—scratches, scuff marks and ragged edges in the upholstery. But everything was neat and shined, the scent of pine and lemon a pleasant fragrance under the aroma of brewing coffee. Even the colorful toys—blocks, a plastic easel, a colorful construction set and books—were stacked in chaotic order in one corner.

A hard tug wrenched his gut to the point of pain at the sight of those symbols of childhood. A tug that resonated with yearning. Aiden had been only six months old the last time Darius had seen him. That'd been at Gage's funeral. How much had the boy changed in the two years since? Had his light brown hair darkened to the nearly black of Gage's own color? As he'd matured, had he grown to resemble his mother, or had he inherited more of his father's features?

That had been the seed of Gage's and the family's doubts regarding the baby's parentage. The boy had possessed neither Gage's nor Isobel's features, except for her eyes. So they'd assumed he must look like his father—his true father. That Isobel had refused a paternity test had further solidified their suspicions that Gage hadn't been Aiden's father. And then, out of spite, she'd made Gage choose—his family or her. Of course, out of love and loyalty, and foolish blindness, he'd chosen her, isolating himself from his parents and friends. Till the end.

Selfish. Conniving. Cold.

Except maybe not so cold. Darius had a firsthand example of how hot she could burn...

Shit.

Focus.

Unbuttoning his jacket, he turned and watched Isobel stride toward him. She did another of those chin lifts as she entered the living room. Jesus, even with suspicion heavy in those blue-gray eyes, they were striking. Haunting. Beautiful.

Deceitful.

"You're not going to ask me to have a seat?" he drawled, the dark, twisted mix of bitterness and lust grinding relentlessly within him.

"Since you won't be staying long, no," she replied, crossing her arms over her chest again. "What do you want?"

"That's my question, Isobel." Without her invite, he lowered to the dark blue, worn armchair across from the couch. "What do you want? Why were you at the gala last week?"

"None of your business."

"See, that's where you're wrong. If you came there to pump the Wellses for money, then it is most definitely my business," he said. Studying her, he caught the flash of emotion in her eyes. Emotion, hell. Guilt. That flash had been guilt. Satisfaction, thick and bright, flared within him. "What happened, Isobel? Did whatever fool you sank your claws into out there in Los Angeles come to his senses and kick you out before you sucked him dry?"

She stared at him, slowly uncoiling her arms and sinking to a perch on her sofa. "The *poor fool* you're so concerned about was my Aunt Lila, who I stayed with to help her recover from a stroke," she continued, derision heavy in her voice. "She died a couple of months ago from another massive stroke, which is why I'm back here in Chicago. Any more insults or assumptions you want to throw out there before finally telling me why you're here?"

"I'm sorry for your loss," he murmured. And he was sorry. He, more than anyone, understood the pain of losing a loved one. But that's all he would apologize for. Protecting and defending his family from someone who sought to use them? No, he'd never regret that. "Now... What do you want with the Wells family? Although—" he deliberately turned his head and scanned the tight quarters of her apartment, lingering on the pile of envelopes on the breakfast bar before returning his attention to her "—I can probably guess if you don't want to admit it."

Her shoulders rolled back, her spine stiffening. Even with her just-rolled-out-of-bed hair and clothes, she appeared...regal. Pride. It was the pride that clung to her as closely as the tank top molding to her breasts.

"What. Do. You. Want. With. Them?" he ground out, when she didn't answer.

"Help," she snapped, leaning forward, a matching

anger lighting her arctic eyes. "I need their help. Not for me. I'd rather hang pictures and lay a welcome mat out in a freshly dug hole than go to them for anything. But for the grandson they've rejected and refused to acknowledge, I need them."

"You would have the nerve to ask them for help— no, let's call it what it is—for *money* and use your son to do it? The son you've kept from them for two years? That's low even for you, Isobel." The agony and help-lessness over Gage's death, the rage toward the woman who was supposed to have loved him, but who had instead mercilessly and callously broken him, surged within him. Tearing through him like a sword, damn near slicing him in half. But he submerged the roiling emotions beneath a thick sheet of ice. "The answer is no. You don't get to decide when they can and can't have a relationship with the grandson who is the only part they have left of the son they loved and lost. You might be his *mother*, and I use that term loosely—"

"Get out." The quiet, sharp words cut him off. She stood, the fine tremor shivering through her body vis-ible in the finger she pointed toward the door. "Get the hell out and don't come back."

"Not until we discuss—"

"You're just like them," she snarled, continuing as if he hadn't even spoken. "Cut from the same golden but filthy cloth. You don't know shit about me as a mother, because you haven't been there. You, Baron or Helena. So you have zero right to have an opinion on how I'm raising my son. And for the record, I didn't try to keep them from Aiden. They didn't want him. Didn't want to know him. Didn't even believe he was their grandson. So don't you dare walk in here, look at this apartment and judge me—"

"Oh, no, Isobel," he contradicted her, slowly rising to his feet as well, tired of her lies. Especially about the people, the *family*, who'd taken him in when he'd lost his own. Who'd accepted him as their own. "I judged you long before this. Your actions as a wife—" he spat the word out, distasteful on his tongue "—condemned you."

"Right." She nodded, a sneer matching his own, curling her mouth. "I was the money-grabbing, social-climbing whore who tricked Gage into marriage by getting knocked up. And he was the sacrificial lamb who cherished and adored me, who remained foolishly loyal to me right up until the moment of his death."

"Don't," he growled, the warning low, rough. He'd never called her a whore; he detested that word. Even when he'd discovered his ex-wife was fucking one of his vice presidents, Darius had never thrown that ugly name at her. Yet to hear Isobel talk about Gage in that dismissive manner when his biggest sin had been loving her... "You don't get to talk about him like that."

"Yes." Her harsh crack of laughter echoed in the room. "That's right, another rule I forgot from my time in my loving marriage. I don't get to speak until I'm spoken to. And even then, keep it short before I embarrass him and myself. Well, sorry to break it to you, but this isn't your home. It's mine, and I want you out—"

"Mommy." The small, childish voice dropped in the room like a hand grenade, cutting Isobel off. Both of them turned toward it. A toddler with dark, nearly black curls and round cheeks, and clad in Hulk pajamas, hovered in the entrance to the living room. Shuffling back and forth on his bare feet, he stuck his thumb into his mouth and glanced from Isobel to Darius before returning his attention to her.

Aiden.

An invisible fist bearing brass knuckles landed a haymaker against Darius's chest. The air in his lungs ejected on a hard, almost painful *whoosh*. He couldn't breathe, couldn't move. Not when his best friend's son dashed across the floor and threw his tiny but sturdy body at his mother, the action full of confidence that she would catch him. Which she did. Kneeling, Isobel gathered him in her arms, standing up and holding him close.

Over his mother's shoulder, Aiden stared at Darius with a gaze identical to Isobel's. A hand roughly the size of a toddler's reached into his chest and squeezed Darius's heart. Hard.

Christ.

He'd expected to be happy or satisfied at finally seeing Aiden. But he hadn't been prepared for this… this overwhelming joy or fierce protectiveness that swamped him, weakened his knees. Gage's son—and there was no mistaking he was indeed Gage's son. He might have Isobel's eyes, but the hair, the shape of his face, his brow, nose, the wide, smiling mouth… They were all his best friend.

The need to protect the boy intensified, swelled. Darius would do anything in his power to provide for him…raise him the way Gage didn't have the opportunity to do. Resolve shifting and solidifying in his chest, his paralysis broke, and he moved across the room, toward mother and son.

"Hello," he greeted Aiden, the gravel-roughened tone evidence of the emotional storm still whirling inside him.

Aiden grinned, and the tightening around Darius's ribcage increased.

"Aiden, this is Mr. King. Can you tell him hi?" Isobel shifted so she and Aiden faced Darius. Her voice might've been light and cheerful, but her eyes revealed that none of the anger from their interrupted conversation had abated. "Tell Mr. King, hi, baby," she encouraged.

"Hi, Mr. King," he mimicked. Though it actually sounded more like, *Hi, Mih Key.*

"Hi, Aiden," he returned, smiling. And unable to help himself, he rubbed the back of a finger down the boy's warm, chubby cheek.

A soft catch of breath reluctantly tugged his attention away from the child. He glanced at Isobel, and she stared at him, barely blinking. After a moment, she shook her head, turning her focus back to her son.

What had that been about? He studied her, trying to decipher the enigma that was Isobel Hughes.

There's no enigma, no big mystery. Only what she allows you to see.

As the reminder boomed in his head, he frowned. His ex-wife had been an expert at hiding her true self until she'd wanted him to glimpse it. And that had only happened toward the end of the relationship, when both of them had stopped pretending they shared anything resembling a marriage. Not with her screwing other men, and Darius refusing to play the fool or pay for the black American Express card any longer.

"Want milk," Aiden demanded as Isobel settled him on the floor again. "And 'nana."

She brushed a hand over his curls, but the hair just fell back into his face. "You want cereal with your milk and banana?" she asked. Aiden nodded, smiling, as if congratulating her for understanding him. "Okay, but can you go play in the room while I fix it?"

Aiden nodded again, agreeing. "Go play."

She took his hand in hers and led him back down the hall, talking to him the entire time until they disappeared. Several minutes later, she returned alone, the adoring, gentle expression she gave her son gone.

"I have things to do, so..." She waved toward the front door, but Darius didn't move. "Seriously, this is ridiculous," she snapped.

"He's Gage's son," he murmured.

Fire flared in her eyes as they narrowed. "Are you sure? You can tell that from just a glance at him? After all, I've been with so many men. Any of them could be his real father."

"Don't play the victim, Isobel. It doesn't fit," he snapped. "And I'm not leaving until we talk."

"I repeat," she ground out. "We have nothing to—"

"We're getting married."

She rocked back on her bare heels as if struck. Shock rounded her fairy eyes, parted her lips. She gaped at him, her fingers fluttering to circle her neck. He should feel regret at so bluntly announcing his intentions. Should. But he didn't.

He'd had a week to consider this idea. Yes, it seemed crazy, over-the-top, and he'd rejected it as soon as the thought had popped into his head. But it'd nagged at him, and the reasons why it would work eventually outweighed the ones why it wouldn't. Of all the words used to describe him, *impetuous* or *rash* weren't among them. He valued discipline and control, in business and in his personal life. His past had taught him both were important. It'd been an impromptu decision that had robbed him of both his parents, and an impulsive one that had led him to marry a woman he'd known for a matter of months. The same mistake Gage had made.

But this…proposition was neither. He'd carefully measured it, and though just the thought of tying himself to another manipulative woman sickened him, he was willing to make the sacrifice.

Whatever doubts might've lingered upon walking up to her building, they had disintegrated as soon as he'd laid eyes on Aiden.

"You're crazy," she finally breathed.

He smiled, and the tug to the corner of his mouth felt cynical, hard. "No. Just realistic." He slid his hands into the front pockets of his pants, cocking his head and studying her pale, damnably lovely features. "Regardless of what you believe, I'm not judging you on the neighborhood you live in or your home. But the fact is you aren't in the safest area of Chicago, and this building isn't a shining example of security. The lock on the front door doesn't work. Anyone could walk in here. The locks on your apartment door are for shit. There isn't an alarm system. What if someone followed you home and busted in here? You would have no protection—you or Aiden."

"So I have a security system installed and call the

landlord about the locks on the building entrance and my door. Easy fixes, and none of them require marriage to a man I barely know who despises me."

"If they were easy fixes," he said, choosing to ignore her comment about his feelings toward her, "why haven't you done them?" He paused, because something flickered in her gaze, and a surge of both anger and satisfaction glimmered in his chest. "You have contacted your landlord," he stated, taking her silence as confirmation. "And he hasn't done a damn thing about it." He stepped forward, shrinking the space between them. "Pride, Isobel. You're going to let pride prevent you from protecting your son."

Lightning flashed in her gaze, and for a moment he found himself mesmerized by the display. Like a bolt of electricity across a morning sky.

"Let me enlighten you. Pride became a commodity I couldn't afford a long time ago. But in the last two years, I've managed to scrape mine back together again. And neither you nor the Wellses can have it. I'm not afraid to ask for help. That's why I was at the gala. Why I was willing to approach Baron and Helena again. *For my son.* But you're not here to offer me help. You're demanding I sell my soul to another devil, just with a different face and name. Well, sorry. I'm not going to play your game. Not when it won't only be me losing this time, but Aiden, as well."

"Selling your soul to the devil? Not playing the game?" he drawled. "Come now, Isobel. A poor college student nabbing herself the heir to a fortune? Trapping him with a pregnancy, then isolating him from his family? Cry me a river, sweetheart. I was there, so don't try to revise history to suit your narrative."

"You're just like him," she whispered.

Darius stifled a flinch. Then cursed himself for recoiling in the first place. Gage had been a good man—good to her.

"You have two choices," he stated. "One, agree to marry me and we both raise Aiden. Or two, disagree, and I'll place the full weight of my name and finances behind Baron and Helena to help them gain custody of Aiden."

She gasped and wavered on her feet. On instinct, he shifted forward, lifting his arms to steady her. But she backpedaled away from him, pressing a hand against the wall and holding up the other in a gesture that screamed *stop right there*.

"You," she rasped, shaking her head. "You wouldn't do that."

"I would," he assured her. "And I will."

"Why?" She straightened, lowering both arms, but the shadows darkening her eyes gathered. "Why would you do that? Why would they? Baron and Helena…they don't even believe Aiden is Gage's. They've wanted nothing to do with him since he was born. Why would they seek custody now?"

"Because he *is* their grandson. I'll convince them of that. And he deserves to know them, love them. Deserves to learn about his father and come to know him through his parents. Aiden is all Baron and Helena have left of Gage. And you would deprive them of that relationship. I won't let you." The unfairness of Isobel's actions, of her selfishness, gnawed at him. She hadn't witnessed the devastation Gage's death had left behind, the wreckage. Baron had suffered a heart attack not long after, and yes, most of it could be attributed to lifestyle choices. But the loss of his only son, that had definitely been a contributing factor.

Yet if they'd had Aiden in their lives during these last two difficult years…he could've been a joy to them. But Isobel had skipped town, not even granting them the opportunity to bond. If she'd stayed long enough, Baron and Helena would've done just what Darius had—taken one look at the child and *known* he belonged to Gage.

"And I won't let you make Aiden a pawn. Or worse, a substitute for Gage. *He won't become Gage.* I refuse to allow you and the Wellses to turn him into his father. I'll fight that with every breath in my body."

"He would be lucky to become like the man his father was," Darius growled. "To be loved by his parents. They welcomed me into their home, raised me when I had no one."

She didn't get to smear the family that had become his own. Gage had been his best friend, his confidante, his brother. Helena had stepped in as his mother. And Baron had been his friend, his mentor, his guiding hand in the multimillion-dollar financial-investment company Darius's father had left behind for his young, inexperienced son.

So no, she didn't get to malign them.

"I'm his mother," she said.

As if that settled everything.

When it didn't.

"And they're his grandparents," he countered. "Grandparents who can afford to provide a stable, safe, secure and loving home for him to thrive and grow in. He'll never want for anything, will have the best education and opportunities. Aiden should have all of his family in his life. You, me, his grandparents and aunt. He should enjoy a fulfilled, happy childhood, with the security of two parents and without the weight of struggle. With you marrying me, he will."

And the Wellses would avoid a prolonged custody battle that could further tax Baron's health and possibly endanger his life. His recovery from the heart attack was going well, but Darius refused to add stress if he could avoid it.

Besides, as CEO and president of King Industries Unlimited, the conglomerate he'd inherited from his father, not only would Aiden be taken care of, but so would Isobel. She would want for nothing, have all the money available to satisfy her every materialistic need. He had experience with bearing the albatross of a greedy woman with Faith, his ex-wife, and though it galled him to have to repeat history, he'd rather take the financial hit than allow Isobel to extort more money from the Wellses. They'd protected him once, and he would gladly, willingly do the same for them.

"No." Isobel stared up at him, shoulders drawn back, hands curled into fists at her side. Though she still wore the evidence of her worry, she faced him like one general standing off against another. A glimmer of admiration slipped through his steely resolve. She'd reminded him of Napoleon earlier, and she did so again. But like that emperor, she would fail and eventually surrender. "I don't care how pretty you wrap it up, blackmail is still blackmail. And I'm not giving in to it. Now, for the last time, get out of my house."

"Call it what you want to help you sleep at night," he murmured. He reached inside his suit jacket and removed a silver business card holder. He withdrew one as he strode to the breakfast bar, and then set it on the counter. "Think carefully before you make a rash decision you'll regret. Here's where you can reach me."

She didn't reply, just stalked to the front door and yanked it open.

"This isn't anywhere near over, Isobel," he warned, exiting her apartment.

"Maybe it isn't for you. But for me, I'm going to forget all about you as soon as you get out." And with that parting shot, she closed the door shut behind him. Or more accurately, in his face.

He didn't immediately head down the hallway, instead pausing a moment to stare at the door. And smile.

He'd meant what he'd told her. This wasn't over.

And damn if he wasn't looking forward to the next skirmish.

Chapter 4

A week later, Isobel drove through the winding, tidy streets of Lake Forest. During the hour and fifteen minutes' drive from South Deering, the inner-city landscape gave way to the steel-and-glass metropolis of downtown, to the affluent suburb that made a person believe she'd stepped into a pretty New England town. The quaint ice cream shop, bookstore, gift shop and boutiques in the center of the town emanated charm and wealth. All of it practically shouted history, affluence and *keep the hell out, riffraff!*

She would be the aforementioned riffraff. Discomfort crawled down her neck. Her decade-old Honda Civic stuck out like a sore thumb among the Aston Martins, Bugattis and Mercedes Benzes like a poor American relation among its luxurious, foreign cousins. Her GPS announced her upcoming turn, and she returned her focus to locating Darius's home.

Minutes later, Siri informed her that she'd reached her destination.

Good. God.

She didn't know much about architecture other than what she retained from the shows on HGTV, but even she recognized the style of the three-story home as Georgian. Beautiful golden bricks—not the weathered, dull color of her own apartment building—formed the outside of the huge structure, with its sloped roof and attached garage. It curved in an arc, claiming the land not already seized by the towering maple trees surrounding the property. Black shutters framed the many windows that faced the front and bracketed the wide wine-red door.

"You are not in South Deering anymore," she murmured to herself.

No wonder Darius had scrutinized her tiny apartment with a slight curl to his lips. He called this beautiful, imposing mansion home. Her place must've appeared like a Hobbit hole to him. A Hobbit hole from the wrong side of the Shire tracks.

Sighing, she dragged her attention back to the reason she'd driven out here.

She had a marriage bargain to seal.

After climbing the three shallow steps that led to the front door, she rang the bell. Only seconds passed before it opened and—instead of a housekeeper or butler—Darius stood in the entryway.

It wasn't fair.

His masculine beauty. His affect on her.

She was well versed in the danger of handsome

men. They used their appearance as a lure—a bright, sensual lure that entranced a woman, distracted her from the darkness behind the shiny exterior. And by the time a woman noticed, it was way too late…

Even though she was aware of the threat he presented, she still stared at him, fighting the carnal thrall he exuded like a pheromone. His dark brown hair waved away from his strong brow, emphasizing the slashing cheekbones, patrician nose, full lips and rock-hard jaw with the faint dent in the chin. And his eyes… vivid, golden and piercing. They unleashed a warm slide of heat in her veins, even as she fought the urge to duck her head and avoid that scalpel-sharp gaze.

With a quick glance, she took in the black turtleneck and slacks that draped over his powerful shoulders, wide chest and muscular thighs. It didn't require much effort to once again feel those thighs under hers or recall the solid strength of his chest under her hands. Her body tingled with the memory, as if he'd imprinted himself in her skin, in her senses, that night. And no matter how she tried, she couldn't evict him.

"Isobel." The way that low, cultured drawl wrapped around her name was indecent. "Come in."

She dipped her chin in acknowledgment and moved forward. Doing her best not to touch him, she still couldn't avoid breathing in his delicious scent—cedar and sun-warmed air, with a hint of musk that was all male. All him. She'd tried her best to forget the flavor of him from that night, too. Epic fail.

The heels of her boots clacked against the hardwood floor of the foyer, and she almost bent to remove them, not wanting to make scuff marks. She studied the house, not even attempting to hide her curiosity. Yes, the inside lived up to the splendor of the exterior. A wide staircase swept to an upper level, and two airy rooms extended from each side of the entryway. Huge fireplaces, furniture that belonged in magazines and rugs that could've taken up space in museums. And windows. So many windows, which offered views of acres of land.

But she examined her surroundings for hints into the man who owned the home. Framed photos lined the mantel in one of the living rooms, but she couldn't glimpse the images from this distance. Were they of the parents he'd told her about during the blackout? Were they of Gage, when they were teens? Around the time he'd saved Darius's life? Did the photographs contain images of the Wellses?

Her survey swept over the expected but beautiful portraits of landscapes and zeroed in on a glass-and-weathered-wood box. A step closer revealed a collection of antique pocket watches. She shifted her inspection to Darius, who watched her, his expression shuttered. Oh, there had to be a story there.

But she wasn't here to find it out.

"You know why I'm here," she said. "I'd like to get this over with."

"We can talk in the study." He turned, and after a moment of hesitation, she followed.

They entered the massive room, where two walls were floor-to-ceiling windows and the other two were filled with books. A large, glossy black desk dominated one end, and couches, armchairs and an immense fireplace claimed the rest. It invited a person to grab a book and settle in for a long read. She couldn't say how she knew, but she'd bet her last chocolate bar that Darius spent most of his time here.

"So, you've come to a decision." He perched on the edge of his desk and waved toward one of the armchairs. "Please, have a seat."

"No, thank you," Isobel murmured. "I—" She swallowed, for an instant unable to force the words past her suddenly constricted throat. A wave of doubt assailed her, but she broke through it. This was the right decision. "I'll agree to marry you."

She expected a gloating smile or a smirk. Something that boasted, *I win*.

Instead his amber gaze studied her, unwavering and intense. Once more she had the inane impression that he could see past her carefully guarded shields to the vulnerable, confused and scared woman beneath. Her head argued it was impossible, but her heart pounded in warning. His figuring out her fears and insecurities when it came to the situation and *him* would be disastrous.

"What made you change your mind?" he asked.

No way was she telling him about arriving home with Aiden after work one night last week to find the police staked out in front of her building because of a burglary and assault. It'd only nailed home Darius's warning about the unsafety of her environment—for her and for Aiden.

Instead she shrugged. "Does it matter?"

"This was a hard decision for you, wasn't it?" he murmured.

Anger flared inside her like a struck match. "Why would you say that? Maybe I just held out longer so you wouldn't guess how giddy I am to have a chance at all your money? Or maybe I was hoping you would just offer more. I'm a mercenary, after all, always searching for the next opportunity to fill my pockets." His mouth hardened into a firm line, but she didn't care. She was only stating what they both knew he thought of her character. Straightening from the chair, she crossed her arms over her chest and hiked her chin up. "Like I said, I'll agree to marry you, but I have a few conditions first. And they're deal breakers."

He nodded, but the slight narrowing of his eyes relayed his irritation. Over her sarcasm or her stipulations, she couldn't tell, but in the end, neither mattered. Just as long as he conceded.

"First, you must promise to place Aiden, his welfare and protection above anything else. Including the Wellses' needs and agenda."

Another nod, but this one was tighter. And the curves of his mouth remained flattened, grim. As if he forced himself to contain words he wanted to say. If that were the case, he controlled it, and she continued.

"Second, I'm Aiden's mother, and since he's never known a father, you'll fill that role for him. If you don't, I won't go through with this. If you can't love and accept him as if he's your own blood, your son, then we're done. I won't have him hurt or rejected. Or worse, feel like he doesn't belong." Like she had. The soul-deep pain of being unworthy had wounded her, and she still bore the scars. She wouldn't subject Aiden to that kind of hurt. Even if it meant going to court.

"He *is* my blood," Darius said, and she blinked, momentarily stunned by his fierceness. "Gage and I might not have shared the same parents, but in all other ways we were brothers. And his son will be mine, and I'll love Aiden how his father would have if he'd lived and had the chance."

Satisfaction rolled in, flooding her and sweeping

away the last of her doubts surrounding that worry. Even if Darius knew next to nothing about the man he called his brother. She believed him when he said he'd love Aiden how Gage *should have*.

"Which brings me to my next concern. I'm Aiden's mother and have been making all decisions regarding him since he was born. I'm not going to lie and claim including you will be an easy adjustment, but I promise to try. But that said, we're his parents, and we will make those decisions together. Us. Without interference from the Wellses."

"Isobel," he growled, pushing off the desk. He stalked a step closer to her, but then drew to an abrupt halt. Shoving a hand through his hair, he turned his head to stare out the window, a tic pulsing along his clenched jaw.

Cursing herself for doing it, she regarded the rigid line. That night when they'd been two nameless, faceless people in the dark, she hadn't needed sight to tell how strong and hard his jaw had been. Her fingers and lips had relayed the information.

God, she needed to stop dwelling on that night. It was gone, and for all intents and purposes, it didn't happen. It'd disappeared as soon as the morning light had dawned.

"Isobel." He returned his attention to her, and she braced herself for both the impact of his gaze and his words. "I agree with your conditions, but they are his grandparents. And you need to understand that I won't keep him away from them."

Like you have. The accusation remained unsaid, but it screamed silently in the room.

"I emailed Baron and Helena pictures of Aiden after

I left for California. And when every one of those messages bounced back as if I'd been blocked, I mailed them, along with letters telling them how he was doing and growing. But they came back unopened, marked 'return to sender.' So I didn't keep him from them. They kept themselves out of his life."

Darius frowned. "Why would they lie about that?"

"Yes. Why would they lie about that?" She shook her head, holding up a hand when his lips parted to what would, no doubt, be another defense of his friend's family. "I have one last condition."

She paused, this one more difficult than the previous ones. Demanding things on Aiden's behalf proved easy for her. But this one… This one involved her and Darius. And it acknowledged that something had happened between them. That "something" being he'd made her body sing like an opera diva hitting notes high enough to shatter glass.

"What is it?" Darius asked when she didn't immediately state the added rule.

"No sex," she blurted out. Mentally rolling her eyes at herself, she inhaled a deep breath and tried it again. "This arrangement is in name only. No sex."

He stilled, his powerful body going motionless. Shadows gathered in his gaze, broiling like a storm building on a dark horizon.

"I guess I need to applaud your honesty," he drawled. "This time around, you're being up front about your plans to betray your husband with another man."

Fury scalded her, and as unwise as it was, she stalked forward, until only inches separated them. "You're so damn sure of yourself. It must be nice to know everything and have all the answers. To be so sure you have all the facts, when in truth you don't. Know. A. Damn. Thing," she bit out.

He lowered his head until their noses nearly bumped, and his breath coasted across her mouth. She could taste his kiss, the sinful, addictive flavor of it.

Memories bombarded her. Memories of his lips owning hers, taking, giving. Of his hands cupping her breasts, tweaking the tips that even now ached and taunted beneath her bra. Of his fingers burying themselves inside her over and over, stroking places inside her that had never been touched before.

Of his cock, so hard and demanding beneath her...

"So you don't care if I take another woman?" he pressed, shifting so another inch disappeared.

An image of him covering someone else, moving over her, straining against her...driving into her, filled her head. A hot wave of anger swamped her, green-tipped claws raking her chest. Her fingers curled into her palms, but she shook her head. Whether it was to rid herself of the mental pictures or in denial of the emotion that smacked of jealousy—a jealousy she had no business, no right, to feel—she didn't know.

"No," she lied, retreating. "Just respect my son and me."

The corner of his mouth tipped into a scornful half smile. "Of course," he said, the words containing more than a hint of a sneer. "Now I have a couple of conditions. The first, we marry in three months. That should give you plenty of time to become accustomed to the arrangement, me and condition number two. You and Aiden are going to move in with me."

Oh, hell no. "No, not happening."

He nodded. "Yes, you are," he contradicted, the

flint in his voice echoed in his eyes. "That's my deal breaker. One of my reasons for this whole arrangement is for Aiden to be raised in a safe, secure environment. He'll have both here."

"Okay, fine. I understand that. But why do we need to live with you. We could find an apartment or home in Edison Park or Beverly—"

"No," he stated flatly, cutting her protest off at the knees. "You'll both live here, and Aiden will know a home with two parents. This isn't a point for discussion, Isobel."

Shit. Living under the same roof as Darius? That would be like Eve sleeping under the damn apple tree. Temptation. Trouble. But what option did she have? Sighing, she pinched the bridge of her nose. Okay, she could do it. Besides, this house was huge. She didn't even have to occupy the same side as Darius.

"Fine," she breathed. "Is there anything else?" She had the sudden need to get out of the house. Away from him. At least until she had no choice but to share his space.

"One last thing," he said, his tone deepening, sending an ominous tremor skipping up her spine. "Say my name."

She stared at him, not comprehending his request. No, his order.

"What?"

"Say my name, Isobel," he repeated.

Tilting her head to the side, she conceded warily. "Darius."

Heat flashed in his eyes, there and gone so fast, she questioned whether she imagined it. "That's the first time you've said my name since that morning."

He didn't need to specify to which morning he referred. But the first time... That couldn't be true. They'd had several conversations, or confrontations, since then... Then again, if it were true...

"Why does it matter?" she asked, something dark, complicated and hot twisting her stomach, pooling lower. "Why do you want to hear me say your name?"

He stared at her, the silence growing and pulsing until its deafening heartbeat filled the room. Her own heart thudded against her sternum, adding to the rhythm.

"Because I've wanted to know what it sounds like on your tongue," he said, his voice quiet.

But so loud it rang in her ears. *On your tongue.* The words, so charged with a velvet, sensual promise, or threat—she couldn't decide which—ricocheted against the walls of her head.

She shivered before she could check her telltale reaction. And those eagle eyes didn't miss it. They turned molten, and his nostrils flared, his lips somehow appearing fuller, more carnal.

Danger.

Every survival instinct she possessed blared the warning in bright, blinking red. And in spite of the warmth between her legs transforming to an aching pulse, she heeded it.

Without a goodbye, she whirled around and got the hell out of there.

Maybe one day she could discover the trick to outrunning herself.

But for now, escaping Darius would have to do.

Chapter 5

Darius passed through the iron gate surrounding the Wellses' Gold Coast mansion and climbed the steps to the front door. The limestone masterpiece had been in their family for 120 years, harkening back to a time when more than the small immediate family lived under its sloped-and-turreted slate roof. As he twisted his key in the lock and pushed the heavy front door open, he considered himself blessed to be counted among that family. Not by blood, but by choice and love.

After entering the home, he bypassed the formal living and dining areas, and moved toward the rear of the home, the multihued glow from the stained-glass skylight guiding his way. This time of day, a little after five o'clock, Baron should have arrived home from the office. Since his heart attack, he'd cut his work days shorter. Helena and Gabriella should also be home, since they served dinner at six o'clock sharp every evening. In the chaotic turns Darius's life had suffered, this routine and the surety of family tradition had been—and still was—a reassurance, one strong, steady stone in a battered foundation.

But tonight, with the news he had to deliver, he hated potentially being the one taking a hammer to them.

"Darius," Helena greeted, rising from the feminine couch that had been her domain as long as he could remember. The other members of the family could occupy the armchairs or the other sofa, but the small, antique couch was all hers, like a queen with her throne. "There you are."

She crossed the room, clasping his hands in hers and rising on her toes. Obediently, he lowered his head so she could press her lips to one cheek and then the other. Her floral perfume drifted to his nose and wrapped him in the familiarity of home. "I have to admit we've all been discussing you, wondering what it is you have to talk to us about. You're being so mysterious."

She smiled at him, and her expression only increased the unease sitting in his gut. He'd called to give them a heads-up without relaying the reason. This kind of information—about his impending marriage—required a face-to-face conversation.

"Hi, son." Baron came forward and patted him on the shoulder, enfolding Darius's hand in his. Warmth swirled in his chest, as it did every time the man he admired claimed him. "Sit and please tell us your news. Helena and Gabriella have been driving me crazy with their guessing. Do us all a favor and put them out of their gossipy misery."

"Oh, it's just been us, hmm?" Gabriella teased, arching an eyebrow at her father. She turned to Darius and handed him a glass of the Remy Martin cognac he preferred. "He wasn't exactly tuning out over the gossip about the blackout. It seems several people have leveled suits against Richard Dent, the tech billionaire who owns the mansion, for emotional distress. Apparently his apology for trapping people in overnight wasn't enough." She shook her head. "I didn't see him, but I even hear Gideon Knight was there. Can you imagine being caught in the dark with *him*?"

"I've met the man," Darius said, referring to the financial genius who'd launched a wildly successful start-up a couple of years ago. "He's reserved, but not as formidable as people claim."

He accepted the drink, bending to brush a kiss across Gabriella's cheek. She clasped his other hand in hers, squeezing it before releasing him to sit on a chair adjacent to her mother. He sank onto one across from her, while, with a sigh, Baron lowered to the largest armchair in the small circle.

Darius shot him a glance. "How're you feeling, Baron?"

"Fine, fine." He waved off the concerned question. "I'm just old," he grumbled.

After studying him for another few seconds, Darius finally nodded, but his worry over causing Baron more stress with his announcement doubled. Even so, he had to tell them, rather than have them discover the truth from another source.

"You already know Isobel Hughes has returned to Chicago."

All warmth disappeared from Helena's face, her gaze freezing into emerald chips of ice, her lips thinning. Gabriella wore a similar expression, but Baron's differed from the women in his family. Instead of furious, he appeared...tired.

"Yes," Helena hissed. "Gabriella told us Isobel showed up at the gala. How dare she?" she continued. "I would've had her arrested immediately."

"Attending a social event isn't a punishable offense, honey," Baron said, his tone weary.

His wife aimed a narrow-eyed glare in his direction, while Gabriella shook her head. "She's lucky the blackout occurred. Criminal or not, I would've had her escorted from the premises."

Leaning forward and propping his elbows on his spread knees, Darius sighed. "I have an announcement, and it concerns Isobel...and her son. I've asked her to marry me, and I'll become Aiden's stepfather."

A heavy silence plummeted into the room. They gaped at him, or at least Helena and Gabriella did. Again, Baron's reaction didn't coincide with his wife's or daughter's. He didn't glare at Darius, just studied him with a measured contemplation, his fingers templed beneath his chin.

"Are you insane?" Gabriella rasped. She jolted from the chair as if propelled from a cannon. Fury snapped in her eyes. But underneath, Darius caught the shivering note of hurt and betrayal. "Darius, what are you thinking?"

"You saw for yourself what she did to Gage, how she destroyed him. How could you even contemplate tying yourself to that woman?" Helena demanded, her voice trembling.

Pain radiated from his chest, pulsing and hot, with the knowledge that he was hurting the two women he loved most in the world. "I—"

"He's doing it for us," Baron declared, his low baritone quieting Helena's and Gabriella's agonized tirades. "He's marrying her so we can have a relationship with the boy."

"Is this true?" Helena demanded. Darius nodded, and she spread her bejeweled hands wide, shaking her head. "But why? He's not even our grandson."

"He is," Darius stated, his tone brooking no argument. "I've seen him," he added, softening his tone. "He's definitely Gage's son."

Gabriella snorted, crossing her arms over her chest. "You'll forgive us if we don't trust her lying, cheating words."

"Then trust mine."

He and Gabriella engaged in a visual standoff for several seconds before she spun on her heel and stalked across the room, toward the small bar.

"Gabriella's right," Helena said. "Sentimentality could be coloring your opinion, have you seeing a resemblance to Gage because you want there to be one." She paused, her pale fingers fluttering to her throat. "That she refused to have a DNA test done after his birth solidified that he wasn't Gage's son, for me. If he was, she wouldn't have been afraid to have one performed. No." She shook her head. "She's caused too much harm to this family," Helena continued. "I can't forget how she isolated Gage from us, so he had to sneak away just to see us. She destroyed him. I'll never forgive her. Ever."

"And no one asked you to be our sacrificial lamb," Gabriella interjected. "What about your life, marrying someone you love?" she rasped. Clearing her throat, she crossed the room and handed her mother a glass of wine before returning to the chair she'd vacated. "There's a very reasonable solution, and it doesn't require you shackling yourself to a woman who's proven she can't be trusted. If by some miracle the child is really Gage's, then we can fight for custody. We would probably be more fit guardians than *her* anyway."

"Take a small boy away from the only parent he's ever known? Regardless of our opinion concerning her moral values, I've seen her with him. She adores him, and she's his world. It would devastate Aiden to be removed from her." And it would kill Isobel. Of that, Darius had zero doubt. "Isobel wouldn't give up custody without a hard battle, which would be taxing on all of you, too. No, this is the best solution for everyone." He met each of their eyes. "And it's done."

Several minutes passed, and Darius didn't try to fill the silence, allowing them the time to accept what he understood was hard news. But they didn't have a choice. None of them did.

"Thank you, Darius," Baron murmured. "I know this wasn't an easy decision, and we appreciate it, support you in it. Bringing the boy into his family—it's what Gage would've wanted. And we will respect Isobel as his mother…and your wife."

Helena emitted a strangled sound, but she didn't contradict her husband. Gabriella didn't either. But she stood once more and rushed from the room.

"Just be careful, Darius. I've lost one son to Isobel Hughes. I don't think I could bear it if I lost another," Helena pleaded, the pain in her softly spoken words like jagged spikes stabbing his heart. Rising, she cradled his cheek before following Gabriella.

"They'll be fine, son," Baron assured him.

Darius nodded, but apprehension settled in his chest, an albatross he couldn't shake off. His intentions were to unite this family, return some of Helena and Baron's joy by reconciling them with their son's child.

But staring at the entrance where Helena and Gabriella had disappeared, he prayed all his efforts wouldn't end up destroying what he desired to build.

Chapter 6

Isobel leaned over Aiden, gently sweeping her hand down his dark curls. After the excitement of moving into a new home and new room jammed with new toys and a race car bed he adored, Aiden had finally exhausted himself. She'd managed to get him fed, bathed and settled in for the night, and all while avoiding Darius.

It'd been a week since she'd agreed to the devil's bargain, and now, fully ensconced in his house, she could no longer use Aiden as an excuse to hide away. With a sigh, she ensured the night-light was on and exited the bedroom, leaving the door cracked behind her. She quietly descended the staircase and headed toward the back of the home, where the kitchen was. She would've preferred not to come downstairs at all, but her stomach rumbled.

The room followed what appeared to be the theme of the home—huge, with windows. Top-of-the-line appliances gleamed under the bright light of a crystal chandelier, and a butcher block and marble island dominated the middle of the vast space. A breakfast nook with a round table and four chairs added a sense of warmth and intimacy to the room. Isobel shook her head as she approached one of the two double-door refrigerators.

She should be grateful. But even now, standing in a kitchen her mother would surrender one of her beloved children to have, she couldn't escape the phantom noose slowly tugging tighter, strangling her. Powerlessness. Purposelessness. Futile anger. The emotions eddied and churned within her like a storm-tossed sea, pitching her, drowning her.

She'd promised herself two years ago that she'd never be at the mercy of another man. Yet if she didn't find some way to protect herself, maintain the identity of the woman she'd come to be, she would end up in a prison worthy of *Architectural Digest*.

Minutes later, she had the makings of a ham-and-cheese sandwich on the island. Real ham—none of that convenience-store deli ham for Darius King—and some kind of gourmet cheese that she could barely pronounce but that tasted like heaven.

"Isobel."

She glanced up from layering lettuce and tomatoes onto her bread to find Darius in the entrance. Her fingers froze, as did the rest of her body. Would this deep, acute awareness occur every time she saw him? It zipped through her body like an electrical current, lighting every nerve ending.

"Darius," she replied, bowing her head back over her dinner.

Though she'd removed her gaze from him, the image of his powerful body seemed emblazoned on her mind's eye. Broad shoulders encased in a thin but soft wool sweater, the V-neck offering her a view of his strong, golden throat, collarbone and the barest hint of his upper chest. Jeans draped low on his hips and clung to the thick strength of his thighs. And his feet…bare.

This was the most relaxed she'd ever seen him, and that he'd allow her to glimpse him this way…it created an intimacy between them she resented and, God, foolishly craved. Because as silly as the presumption might be, she had a feeling he didn't unarm himself like this around many people.

Remember why you're here, her subconscious sniped. *Blackmail and coercion, not because you belong.*

"Did you want a sandwich?" she offered, the reminder shoring up any chinks in her guard.

"Thank you. It looks good." He moved farther into the room and withdrew one of the stools lining the island. Sitting down across from her, he nabbed the bread bin—because what else would one store freshly baked bread in?—and cut two thick slices while she returned to the refrigerator for more meat and cheese. "I'm sorry I had to leave earlier. I didn't want to miss Aiden's first night in the house. There was a bit of an emergency at the office."

"On a Saturday?" she asked, glancing at him.

He shook his head, the corner of his mouth quirking in a rueful smile. "When you're the CEO and president of the company, there's no such thing as a Saturday. Every day is a workday."

"If you let it be," she said. But then again, she understood the need to work when it called. As a single mom with more bills than funds, she hadn't been able to turn down a shift at the supermarket or tell her mom she would skip helping her clean a house.

"True," he agreed, accepting the ham she handed him. "But then I've never had a reason to dial back on the work. I do now," he murmured.

Aiden. He meant Aiden and being a stepfather. She silently repeated the words to herself. But they didn't prevent the warm fluttering in her belly or the hitch in her breath.

"How old are you?" she blurted out, desperate to distract herself from the completely inappropriate and stupid heat that pooled south of her belly button. "I don't mean to be rude, but you don't seem old enough to run a company."

"Thirty," he replied. She could feel his weighty gaze on her face like a physical touch as she finished preparing his meal. "My grandfather started the business as one corporation, and my father grew it into several corporations, eventually folding them all under one parent company. When he died, my father left King Industries Unlimited to me, and I started working there when I was seventeen, in the mail room. I went from there to retail sales associate to account manager and through the ranks, learning the business. By the time I stepped in as CEO and president at twenty-five, and with the guidance of Baron, I had been an employee for seven years."

"Wow," she breathed. "Many men would've just as-

sumed that position as their due and wouldn't bother
with starting from the bottom." She hesitated, but then
whispered, "I can only imagine your father would've
been proud of your work ethic."

With his amber eyes gleaming, Darius nodded. "I
hope so. It's how he did it, and I followed in his footsteps."

Their gazes connected, and the breath stuttered in
her lungs. Her pulse jammed out an erratic beat at her
neck and in her head.

Clearing her throat, she dropped her attention to
her sandwich, and with more effort than it required,
sliced it in half and did the same to his. "Tell me more
about your work?" she requested, cursing the slight
waver in her voice. Her biggest mistake would be letting Darius know he affected her in any manner. *Get
it together, woman*, she scolded herself. "Was it hard
suddenly running such a huge company?"

Over ham-and-cheese sandwiches, they spoke about
his job and all it required. Eventually the conversation
curved into more personal topics. He shared that his
home had been his parents', one they'd purchased only
months before they'd died. And the pocket watch collection had been his father's, and like the family company, Darius had taken it over and continued to add to
it. She told him about her family, leaving out the part
about her brother's lucrative but illegal side business.
Even her mother pretended it didn't exist and refused
to accept any money earned from it. Isobel also added
amusing stories about Aiden from the last two years.

"He took one look at Santa and let out the loudest,
most terrified scream. I think the old guy damn near
had a heart attack." She chuckled, remembering her

baby's reaction to the mall Santa. "He started squirming and kicking his legs. His foot caught good ol' Saint Nick right in the boys, and they had to shut down Winter Wonderland for a half hour while, I'm sure, Santa iced himself in his workshop."

Darius laughed, the loud bark echoing in the room. He shook his head, shoulders shaking. His eyes, bright with humor, crinkled at the corners, and his smile lit up his normally serious expression.

An unsmiling Darius was devastatingly handsome.

A smiling Darius? Beyond description.

Slowly, as they continued to meet each other's gazes, the lightness in the room dimmed, converting into something weightier, darker. A thickness—congested with memories, things better left unspoken and desire—gathered between them. Even though her mind screamed caution, she didn't—couldn't—glance away. And if she were brutally honest? She didn't want to.

"You're different from how I remember you," he said, his gaze roaming over her face. Her lips prickled when that intense regard fell on her mouth and hovered for several heated moments. "Even though it was only a couple of times, you were quieter then, maybe even a little timid and withdrawn. At least around me. Gage said you were different around your family."

"I trusted them." She knew they wouldn't mock her just because she didn't use the proper fork or couldn't discuss politics. They accepted her, loved her. She'd never feared them.

Darius frowned, leaning forward on the crossed arms he'd propped on the marble island. "You didn't trust your husband?"

She paused, indecision about how much to share temporarily muting her. But, in the end, she refused to lie. "No," she admitted, the ghostly remnants of hurt from that time in her life rasping her voice. "I didn't."

How could she? Gage had been a liar, and he'd betrayed their short marriage. He'd promised her Harry and Meghan and had given her Henry VIII and wives one, two and five.

To gain his family's sympathy after marrying Isobel, he'd thrown her under the proverbial bus, accusing her of tricking him into marrying her by claiming she'd been pregnant. She hadn't been, though it'd happened shortly after their marriage. At first, they'd been happy—or at least she'd believed they'd been. True, they'd lived in a tiny apartment, living off her small paycheck from the grocery store while he looked for work since his family had cut him off, but they'd loved one another. After she'd refused to take a paternity test at the demand of his parents, things had changed. Subtly, at first, he'd isolated her from family and friends. He'd claimed that since his family had disowned him, it was just the two of them—soon to be the three of them—against the world. But that world had become smaller, darker, lonelier...scarier.

Gage had been a master gaslighter. Unknown to her, he'd thrown himself on his parents' mercies, spewing lies—that she'd demanded he abandon his family, that she was cheating on him. All to remain in the family fold as their golden child and maintain their compassion and empathy by making Isobel out to be a treacherous bitch he couldn't divorce and turn back out on the street. In truth, he'd been a spoiled, out-of-control child who hadn't wanted her but didn't want anyone else to have her either.

"He was your husband," Darius said, his tone as low as the shadows already accumulating in his eyes.

"He was my jailor," she snapped.

"Just like this is a prison?" he growled, sweeping a hand to encompass the kitchen, the beautiful home. "He gave you everything, while giving up his own family, his friends—hell, his world—for you. What more could he have possibly done to make you happy?"

Pain and anger clashed inside her, eating away any trace of the calm and enjoyment she'd found with Darius during the past hour. "Kindness. Compassion. Loyalty. Fidelity."

"It's convenient that he isn't here to defend himself, isn't it? Still, it's hard to play the victim now when we all know how you betrayed him, made a fool of him. In spite of all that, he wouldn't walk away from you." Fire flared in his eyes. The same fierce emotion incinerating her, hardened his full lips into a grim line. "I saw him just before he died. I begged him to walk away, to leave you. But he wouldn't. Even as it broke him that he couldn't even claim his son because of the men you'd fucked behind his back."

Trembling, Isobel stood, the scratch of the stool's legs across the tiled floor a discordant screech. Flattening her palms on the counter, she glared at him, in this moment, hating him.

"I broke him? He broke me! And destroyed whatever love I still had for him when he looked at our baby and called him a bastard. So don't you dare talk to me about being ungrateful. You don't know what the hell you're talking about."

Refusing to remain and accept any more accusations, she whipped around the island and stalked toward the kitchen entrance. Screw him. He didn't know her, had no clue—

"Damn it, Isobel," he snapped, seconds before his fingers wrapped around her upper arm.

"Don't touch—" She whirled back around and, misjudging how close he stood behind her, slammed into the solid wall of his chest. Her hands shot up in an instinctive attempt to prevent the tumble backward, but the hard band of his arms wrapped around her saved her from falling onto her ass.

The moment her body collided with his, the protest died on her tongue. Desire—unwanted, uncontrollable and greedy—swamped her. Her fingers curled into his sweater in an instinctive attempt to hold on to the only solid thing in a world that had constricted then yawned endlessly wide, leaving her dangling over a crumbling edge.

"Isobel." Her name, uttered in that sin-on-the-rocks voice, rumbled through her, and she shook her head, refusing to acknowledge it—or the eruption of electrical pulses that raced up and down her spine. "Look at me."

His long fingers slid up her back, over her nape and tunneled into her hair. She groaned, unable to trap the betraying sound. Not when his hand tangled in the strands, tugging her head backward, sending tiny prickles along her scalp. She sank her teeth into her bottom lip, locking down on another embarrassing sound of pleasure.

"No," he growled, pressing his thumb to the center of her abused lip and freeing it. With a low, carnal hum, he rubbed a caress over the flesh. "Don't hold back from me. Let me hear what I do to you."

Oh, God. If she could ease her grip on his shirt, she'd clap her palms over her ears to block out his words. She hadn't forgotten how his voice had aided and abetted his touch in unraveling every one of her inhibitions the night of the blackout. It was a velvet weapon, one that slipped beneath her skin, her steel-encased guards, to wreak sensual havoc.

"Look at me, sweetheart," he ordered again. This time she complied, lifting her lashes to meet his golden gaze. "Good," he murmured, giving her bottom lip one last sweep with his fingers before burying them in her hair so both hands cupped her head. "Keep those fairy eyes on me."

Fairy eyes.

The description, so unlike him and so reminiscent of the man in the dark hallway weeks ago, swept over her like a soft spring rain. And then she ceased to think.

Because he proceeded to devastate her.

If their first kiss in the dark weeks ago started as a gentle exploration, this one was fierce. His mouth claimed and conquered, his tongue demanding an entrance she willingly surrendered. Wild and raw, he devoured her like a starving man intent on satisfying a bottomless craving. Again and again, he sucked, lapped, dueled, demanding she enter into carnal battle with him.

Submit to him. Take him. Dominate him.

With a needy whimper that should probably have mortified her, she fisted his shirt harder and rose on her toes, granting him even more access and commanding more of him. Angling her head, she opened her mouth wider, savoring his unique flavor, getting drunk on it.

But it wasn't enough. Never enough.

"Jesus Christ," he swore against her lips, nipping the lower curve, then pressing stinging kisses along her jaw and down her throat.

Kisses that echoed in her breasts, sensitizing them, tightening the tips. Kisses that eddied and swirled low in her belly. Kisses that had her thighs squeezing to contain the ache between her legs. Already a nagging emptiness stretched wide in her sex, begging to be filled by his fingers, his cock. Didn't matter. Just as long as some part of him was inside her, branding her.

The thought snuck under the desire, and once it infiltrated, she couldn't eject it. Instead it rebounded against her skull, loud and aggressive. *Branding me. Branding me.*

And Darius would do it; he would imprint himself into her skin, her body until she couldn't erase him from her thoughts...her heart. Until he slowly took over, and she ceased to exist except for the sole purpose of pleasing him...of loving him.

No. No, damn it.

Never again would she allow that to happen.

With a muted cry, she shoved her palms against his chest, lunging out of his embrace, away from his kiss, his touch.

Their harsh, jagged breaths reverberated in the kitchen. His broad chest rose and fell, his piercing gaze narrowed on her like that of a bird of prey's, waiting for her to make the slightest move so he could swoop in and capture her.

Even as her brain yelled at her to get the hell out of there, her body urged her to let herself be caught and devoured.

"No," she whispered, but not to him, to her traitorous libido.

"Then you better go," Darius ground out as if she'd spoken to him. *"Now."*

Not waiting for another warning, she whipped around, raced down the hall and bounded up the stairs. Once she closed the bedroom door behind her, she stumbled across the floor and sank to the mattress.

Oh, God, what had she done?

The no-sex rule had been hers. And yet the first time he'd touched her, she'd burned faster than kindling in a campfire.

Desire and passion were the gateways to losing reason, control and, eventually, independence.

Those who forget the past are condemned to repeat it.

She'd heard the quote many times throughout her life. But never had it been so true as this moment.

She'd made this one mistake.

She couldn't afford another.

Chapter 7

An ugly sense of déjà vu settled over Isobel as she stared at the ornate front door of the Wellses' home. It'd been a slightly brisk October evening just like this one four years ago when she'd arrived on this doorstep, arm tucked in Gage's, excited and nervous to meet his family. She'd been so painfully naïve then, at twenty, never imaging the disdain she would experience once she crossed the threshold.

The differences between then and now could fill a hoarder's house. One, she was no longer that young girl so innocently in love. Second, she fully expected to be scorned and derided. And perhaps the most glaring change.

She stood next to Darius, but with Gage's son riding her hip.

Her stomach clenched, pulling into knots so snarled

and tight, they would need Houdini himself to un-ravel them.

"There's no need to be nervous," Darius murmured beside her, settling a hand at the small of her back. The warmth of his hand penetrated the layers of her coat and dress, and she steeled herself against it, wishing he'd remove it. When about to enter the lion's den, she couldn't allow her focus and wits to be compromised by his touch. "I've already talked to them about us, and I'll be right here with you."

Was that supposed to be a reassurance? A pep talk? Well, both were epic fails. She wore no blinders when it came to Gage's family. Nothing—no talk or his pres-ence—would ever convince them to accept her. She'd robbed them of their most precious gift. There was no forgiveness for that.

"This night is about Aiden," she said more to her-self than him. "All I care about is how they treat him."

The weight of his stare stroked her face like the last rays of the rapidly sinking sun. She kept her attention trained on the door. It'd been almost a week since she'd moved into his home—since the night they'd kissed. And in that time, she'd become a master of avoidance. With a house the size of a museum, it hadn't proven to be difficult. When he spent time with Aiden, she withdrew to her room. And when she couldn't evade him, she ensured Aiden remained a buffer between them. A little cowardly? Yes. But when engaged in a battle for her dignity and emotional sanity, the say-ing "by any means necessary" had become her motto.

"They'll love him," he replied, with certainty and determination ringing in his voice.

Before she could respond, the door opened and Gabriella, Gage's sister, stood in the entranceway. The beautiful, willowy brunette, who was a feminine version of her brother, smiled, stepping forward to press a kiss to Darius's cheek.

An unfamiliar and nasty emotion coiled and rattled in Isobel's chest. Her grip on Aiden tightened, while her vision sharpened on the other woman.

Whoa.

Isobel blinked. Sucked in a breath. What the hell was going on? No way could she actually be…*jealous.* Not by any stretch of the imagination did Darius belong to her. And even if in some realm with unicorns and rainbows where he was hers to claim, Gabriella was like a sister to him.

Get a grip.

If this overreaction heralded the evening's future, it promised to be a long one. Long and painful.

"It's about time you arrived," Gabriella said, laying a hand on his chest. "Mother and Dad are climbing the walls."

"Now, that I'd pay money to see," he drawled.

So would Isobel.

"Gabriella, you remember Isobel." Darius's hand slid higher, to the middle of her back, and just this once, she was thankful for it.

The other woman switched her focus from Darius to Isobel. Jade eyes so like her brother's met hers, the warmth that had greeted Darius replaced with ice. Isobel fought not to shiver under the chill. *She can't hurt you. No one in this house can hurt you,* Isobel reminded herself, repeating the mantra. Hoping it was true.

"Of course," Gabriella said, her tone even, polite.

"Hello, Isobel." She shifted her gaze to Aiden, who hugged Isobel's neck, his face buried against her coat. Unsurprisingly, he had a thumb stuck firmly in his mouth. Isobel didn't blame him or remove it. Hell, she suddenly wanted to do the same. "And this must be Aiden."

"Yes, it is." Darius removed his hand from Isobel's back and reached around to stroke a hand down her son's curls. Curls that were the same nearly black shade as Gabriella's. "Aiden, can you say hi?"

Shyly, Aiden lifted his head and whispered, "Hi," giving Gabriella a small wave.

The other woman stared at the toddler, her lips forming a small O-shape. Moisture brightened her gaze, and she blinked rapidly. "Hi, Aiden," she whispered back. Drawing in an audible breath, she looked at Darius. "He looks like Gage."

Anger flared to life in Isobel's chest. She wanted to snap, *Of course he does*, but she swallowed it down. Yet she could do nothing about the flames still flickering inside her.

Part of her wanted to say screw this and demand Darius drive them home. But the other half—the half that wanted the Wells family's derision toward her regarding Aiden's paternity laid to rest—convinced her to remain in place. She still resented their rejection of her son, but if they were willing to meet her halfway so Aiden could know them, then she could try to let it go.

Try.

"Come in." Gabriella stepped backwards, waving them inside, her regard still fixed on Aiden.

Minutes later, with their coats turned over to a waiting maid, they all strode toward the back of the house and entered a small parlor. Helena, lovely and regal, was perched upon the champagne-colored settee like a queen surveying her subjects from her throne. And Baron occupied the largest armchair, his salt-and-pepper hair—more salt now than the last time she'd seen him—gleaming under the light thrown by a chandelier.

Their conversation ended when Gabriella appeared with Darius, Aiden and Isobel in tow. Slowly, Baron stood, and Isobel just managed to refrain from frowning. Though still tall and handsome, his frame seemed thinner, even a little more…fragile. And perhaps the most shocking change was that the hard, condemning expression that had been his norm when forced to share the air with her was not in attendance. By no means was his gaze welcoming, but it definitely didn't carry the harshness it formerly had.

But the censure his demeanor lacked, Helena's more than made up for. She rose as well, her scrutiny as frigid and sharp as an icicle. Her mouth formed a flat, disapproving line, and for a moment Isobel almost believed she'd stumbled back in time. Gage's mother had disliked her on sight, and like a fine wine, the dislike had only aged. Into hatred.

Suddenly Isobel's arms tightened around Aiden, flooded with the need to shield him, protect him. And herself. He was her lodestone, reminding her that she was no longer that timid, impressionable girl from the past.

"Darius." Baron crossed the room, his hand extended. Darius clasped it, and they pulled each other close for a quick but loving embrace. Then the older man turned toward her, and even with his lack of animosity, she braced herself. "Isobel, welcome back to our home." He stretched his hand toward her, and after a brief hesitation, she accepted it, her heart pulsing in her throat. His grip squeezed around her fingers, rendering her speechless, the gesture the most warmth he'd ever shown her. "And this is Aiden."

Awe saturated his deep baritone, the same wonder that had filtered through his daughter's in the foyer. His nostrils flared, his fingers curling into his palms as if he fought the need to reach out and touch her son. Clearing his throat, Baron switched his gaze back to Isobel.

"He has your eyes, but his features… It's like looking at a baby picture of my son," he rasped. "May I…?" He held his arms out toward Aiden.

Nerves jingled in her belly, but the plea in the man's eyes trumped them. "Aiden? Do you want to go to Mr. Baron?" She loosened her grip on her son and tried to hand him, but the child clung harder to her as he shook his head. "I'm sorry," she murmured, feeling regret at the flash of disappointment and hurt in the man's gaze. "He's a little shy around new people."

"A shame," Gabriella murmured behind her.

Isobel stiffened, a stinging retort dancing on the tip of her tongue. But Darius interceded, tossing a quelling glance toward Gage's sister over his shoulder. With an arched eyebrow and open hands, he silently requested to take Aiden. Dipping her chin, she passed her son to Darius, who practically launched himself into the man's arms. Aiden popped his thumb back into his mouth, grinning at Darius around it.

"Well, how about that," Baron whispered. "He certainly seems to have taken to you."

Darius shrugged, sweeping a hand down Aiden's small back. "It doesn't take long for him to warm up. And once he does, he'll talk your ear off." He poked Aiden's rounded tummy, and the boy giggled.

The cheerful, innocent sound stole into Isobel's heart, as it'd had done from the very first time she'd heard it.

"I have to admit, he does resemble Gage," Helena said, appearing at her husband's side, studying Aiden. "Isobel." She nodded, before dismissing her and turning to Darius, an affectionate smile thawing her expression. "Darius." She tilted her head, and he brushed a kiss on her cheek. "I haven't seen you in days. But it seems you have time for everyone else." She tapped him playfully on the chest. "Beverly Sheldon told me how she saw you at the Livingstons' dinner party. And how Shelly Livingston couldn't seem to keep her hands to herself." Helena chuckled as if immensely amused by Shelly Livingston's grabby hands.

Isobel fought not to react to the first shot fired across the bow. It hadn't taken long at all. She thought Helena or Gabriella would've at least waited until after drinks before they got in the first dig, but apparently the "you're an interloper and don't belong, darling" portion of the evening had begun.

Yet her purpose—letting Isobel know that Darius had attended a social event without her on his arm, probably out of shame—had struck true. Which was as inane as that flash of jealousy with Gabriella. Pretending to be the newly engaged, loving couple hadn't been a part of their bargain. He could do as he wanted, escort whom he wanted, flirt with whom he wanted… sleep with whom he wanted. It didn't matter to her.

Liar.

Flipping her once again intrusive, know-it-all subconscious the middle finger, she shored up the walls surrounding her heart.

"Beverly Sheldon gossips too much and needs to find a hobby," Darius replied, frowning. "It was an impromptu business dinner, not a party, and I'm sure Shelly's fiancé, who also attended with her father, would've had some objections if she 'couldn't seem to keep her hands to herself.'"

Helena waved his explanation off with a flick of her fingers and another laugh. "Well, you're a handsome man, Darius. It's not surprising women flock to you."

"Helena," Baron said, a warning heavy in her name.

"Now, don't 'Helena' me, Baron." She tsked, brushing her husband's arm before strolling off toward the bar across the room. "Would anyone like a drink?"

Good God. This was going to be a really long evening.

"Have you decided on whether or not you'll acquire SouthernCare Insurance?" Baron asked Darius, reclining in his chair as one of the servants placed an entrée plate in front of him.

Isobel let the business talk float over her, as she had most of the discussions around the dinner table. If the topics weren't about business, then it was Helena and Gabriella speaking about people and events Isobel didn't know anything about, and neither woman had made the attempt to draw her into the conversation. Not that she minded. The less they said to each other, the better the chance of Isobel making it through this dinner without emotional injuries from their sly innuendoes.

Still, right now she envied her son. By the time dinner was ready to be served, Aiden had been nodding off in Darius's arms. He'd taken Aiden to one of the bedrooms and settled him in. Aiden had escaped this farce of a family dinner, but she hadn't been as lucky.

Mimicking Baron, Isobel shifted backward, granting the servant plenty of room to set down her plate of food. When she saw the food, she barely managed not to flinch. Prime rib, buttered asparagus and acorn squash.

Gage's favorite meal.

She lifted her head and met Helena's arctic gaze. So the choice hadn't been a coincidence. No, it'd been deliberate, and just another way to let Isobel know she hadn't been forgiven.

Nothing had been forgotten.

Message received.

Picking up her fork—the correct fork—and knife, Isobel prepared to eat the perfectly cooked meat that would undoubtedly taste like ash on her tongue.

"I was leaning toward yes before the trouble with their vice president leaked." Darius paused, murmuring a "thank you" as a plate was set in front of him. "One of their employees came forward about long-time, systematic sexual harassment within the company, and their senior vice president of operations is one of the key perpetrators. No," he said, shaking his head, tone grim. "I won't have King Industries Unlimited tainted with that kind of behavior."

Unlike the rest of the conversation surrounding business, Darius's comment snagged her attention, surprising her so much, she blurted out, "You would really base your decision on that?"

Silence crackled in the room. In the quiet, her question seemed to bounce off the walls. Everyone stared at her, but she refused to cringe.

It was Darius's scrutiny she resolutely met, ignoring the others'. And in his eyes, she didn't spy irritation at her interruption. No, just the usual intensity that rendered her breathless.

"Of course. I don't condone it, and I won't be associated with any business or person who does. Every person under my employ or the umbrella of my company should have the expectation of safety and an environment free of intimidation."

"Your employees are lucky to work for you then," she murmured.

More and more companies were trying to change their policies and eliminate sexual harassment—or at least indulge in lip service about removing it. But the truth couldn't be denied—not everyone enjoyed that sense of fairness or security. Even at the supermarket, the supervisor didn't think anything of calling her honey or flirting with her, going so far as to occasionally say how "lucky" her man was. She'd never bothered to correct him, assuming if he knew she didn't have a "man" at home, the inappropriate behavior would only worsen.

That Darius would turn down what was most likely a multimillion-dollar deal because of his beliefs and out of consideration for those under him… It was admirable. Heroic.

"I like to hope so," he replied just as softly.

A sense of intimacy seemed to envelop them, and

she couldn't tear her gaze away from his. Her breath stuttered in her lungs, her heart tap-dancing a quick tattoo at the heat in those golden depths.

"Of course his employees are fortunate," Gabriella interjected, shattering the illusion of connection. "Darius is a good man. He doesn't brag about it, but he's founded—and often single-handedly funded—several foundations that provide scholarships for foster children, housing for abused women coming out of shelters, and literacy and job-placement programs for under-privileged youth. And those are just some of his…projects."

The strategic pause before "projects" let Isobel know Gabriella considered *her* to be one of those charity cases. If passive-aggressiveness was a weapon, Gabriella and Helena would own codes and security clearances.

"It's wonderful to know Aiden will have an admirable role model in Darius," Isobel said, voice neutral. Silence once more descended in the room, but Isobel didn't shrink from it. The scared, quiet girl they had known no longer existed; the woman she was now wouldn't stand mutely like a living target for their verbal darts.

Darius glanced at her, and once more she found herself trapped in his gaze. Something flickered in the golden depths. Something that had her lifting her glass of wine to her lips for a deep sip.

"If Gage couldn't be here to raise him, he would've wanted family to do it," Darius finally said to the room, but his eyes… His eyes never wavered from her.

"Still," Helena pressed, not looking at Darius but keeping her attention firmly locked on Isobel. "A boy should know his father. Tell me, Isobel, since you claim Aiden is Gage's, have you showed him pictures? Does he know who his real father is?"

"Helena," Darius growled a warning.

"Darius, darling," Helena replied, tilting her head to the side. "We all commend you for your sacrifice in this difficult situation, but I think you'd agree that a child deserves to know who his true parents are, right?"

A muscle jumped along Darius's jaw, but Isobel set her glass down on the table, meeting Helena's scrutiny.

"I've always shown Aiden pictures of Gage, since he is Aiden's father, as well as talked to him about Gage. And he understands who his *real father* is, as much as a two-year-old can."

"Hmm," came Helena's noncommittal, *condescending* answer.

"Aiden looks so much like Gage when he was that age," Baron added from the head of the table, aiming a quelling glance at his wife.

But Helena didn't respond, instead turning to Gabriella and asking about a function she was supposed to attend that week.

Pain and humiliation slashed at Isobel, but she fought not to reveal it. Not only did she refuse to grant them that pleasure, but she didn't have anything to be ashamed of. They accused *her* of cheating, when the opposite had been true.

But what would be the point in trying to explain the truth to his family? They would never believe her. Not after they'd always accepted every utterance from Gage as the gospel.

And with him dead, he was even more of a saint.

And she would always be a sinner.

Chapter 8

Darius poured himself another glass of bourbon. This would be his third. Or maybe fourth. Didn't matter. He wasn't drunk yet; he could still think. So whatever number he was on, it wouldn't be his last. He'd keep tossing it back until the unease and anger no longer crawled inside him like ants in a colony.

Tonight had been a clusterfuck. Oh, it'd been frigidly polite, but still… Clusterfuck.

After crossing the study, he sank down onto the couch and took a sip of the bourbon. Clasping the squat glass, he slid down, resting his head on the couch's back, his legs sprawled wide.

Jesus, when would the forgetful part of this begin?

He hated this sense of…betrayal that clung to him like a filthy film of dirt. And no matter how hard he tried to scrub it clean with excuses, it remained, stubborn and just as grimy.

When he'd asked Isobel to the Wellses' house that night, he'd promised her they would be civil, and she would be in a safe space, be welcomed. Baron had, but Helena and Gabriella, they'd made a liar of him. He understood their resentment—even now, when he thought of Gage, that mixture of anger and grief still churned in his chest, his gut. But tonight had been about Aiden, about them connecting with the boy, and that meant forging a fragile truce with his mother. Showing her respect, at least.

Hours later, the disappointment, the disquiet continued to pulse within him like a wound, one that refused to heal.

Isobel had definitely been enemy number one when she'd been married to Gage. All of them believed Gage had moved too fast, married too young. Darius had been equally confused when he'd cut them all off for almost a year. None of them could understand why Gage hadn't divorced her, especially when he started confiding in them about her infidelity. As far as Darius could tell, his friend had genuinely been in love with his wife, and her betrayals had destroyed him.

Still. Remembering the woman he'd shared a hallway with in the dark… The woman who loved her son so selflessly… The woman whose family rallied around her, supported her and her son unconditionally… That Isobel didn't really coincide with the one the Wellses detested.

But if he were brutally honest—and alcohol had a way of dragging that kind of truth forth—it hadn't only been this evening that had unnerved him.

She did.

Everything about her unsettled him.

From the thick dark hair with the hints of fire to the delectable, curvaceous body that tempted him like a red flag snapping in front of a bull.

Earlier, when she'd thrust her chin up in that defiant angle, he'd had to force himself to remain in his seat instead of marching around the table and shocking the hell out of everyone by tugging her head back and claiming that beautiful, created-for-sin mouth.

Another truth he could admit in the dark with only bourbon for company.

He wanted her.

Fuck, did he want her.

Maybe if the past had stayed in the past, he could have convinced himself their space of time in the hallway had been just that—a blip, an anomaly. But once he'd kissed her again, once he'd swallowed her moans, once he'd felt her slick, satiny flesh spasm around his fingers as she came… No, he craved this woman with a need that was usually reserved for oxygen and water.

Even knowing that she'd betrayed Gage just as Faith had cheated on Darius, he still couldn't expunge this insane, insatiable desire.

So, what did that say about him? About his dignity? His fucking intelligence?

He snorted, raising his glass to his lips for a deep sip.

It said that, as much as he'd claimed to the contrary, his dick had equal partnership with his brain.

Yet…he frowned into the golden depths of the bourbon. The more time he spent with Isobel, the more doubt crept into his head, infiltrating his long-held ideas about her, about the woman he'd believed her to be. But for him to accept that she was not the woman who'd betrayed her husband in the past, it would mean that Gage had consciously—and maliciously—lied to Darius's face. And to his family. And to all of their friends. It would mean Darius's best friend, the man who'd been closer to him than a brother, had intentionally destroyed Isobel's reputation.

And that he couldn't believe.

Could Gage have somehow misinterpreted her actions? Or maybe there was more to the story that Gage hadn't shared with his family before his death?

"Darius?"

He glanced in the direction of the study's entrance, where the sound of his name in *her* voice had originated.

And immediately wished he hadn't.

Now the image of her standing in the doorway, barefoot, her long, toned legs exposed by some kind of T-shirt that hit her midthigh, and hair a sexy tumble around her beautiful face would be permanently branded onto his retinas.

"What are you wearing?" he growled.

Hell, he hadn't intended to vocalize that question. And with his bourbon-weakened control, no way in hell could he prevent the lust careering through him.

She peeked down at herself, then returned her fairy eyes to him. "What?" she asked. "This is what I sleep in. Excuse me if it's not La Perla enough for you, but I didn't exactly expect to bump into anyone."

La Perla. Fox and Rose. Agent Provocateur.

His ex-wife had insisted on only purchasing the expensive, luxury lingerie for herself, and they'd shown up regularly on his credit card statements, which was the only reason he recognized the brands.

But damn. Now, staring at her body with those lethal curves, he would love to put that useless-until-now information to work. To drape her in the softest silk and the most delicate lace. To personally choose corsets, bras and panties to adorn a woman who didn't need anything to enhance her ethereal beauty and earthy sensuality. And still he wanted to give them to her. To see her in them.

To peel them from her.

Taking another sip, he wrenched his gaze from the temptation in cotton.

"What do you want, Isobel?" he rasped.

She stepped into the room, the movement hesitant. It should be. If she had any idea of the need grinding inside him like a relentlessly turning screw, she'd leave.

"I was headed toward the kitchen and saw the light on in here. I thought you'd gone to bed." A pause. "Are you okay?"

"I'm fine," he said automatically. *Lie.*

"I'm sorry for you," she said, gliding farther into the room and halting a small distance from him. As if unsure whether or not she should chance come any closer.

Smart woman.

The way the alcohol and lust coursed through him like rain-swollen rapids, he should warn her away, bark an order to get out of the study. Instead he watched her, a predator silently waiting for his prey to approach just near enough for him to pounce.

"Sorry for me," he repeated on a serrated huff of laughter. "Why?"

"Because I went there tonight knowing I wouldn't be welcome. I wasn't surprised by anything that happened. But you were shocked…and hurt. And for that, I'm sorry."

He lifted his head, stared at her, astonishment momentarily robbing him of speech.

Discomfort flickered across her features, and she shrugged a shoulder. "Anyway… Your relationship with them isn't my business…"

"You weren't hurt?" He ground his teeth around a curse. He hadn't intended to snap at her. Dragging in a deep breath, he held it, then exhaled. "You weren't hurt by what they said, how they acted?"

She studied him for a long second, then slowly shook her head. "No, Darius. For me, it was business as usual. For the two years I was married, I was never good enough. Smart enough. Sophisticated enough. Just never…enough."

"I can't believe that," he snapped, banging his glass on the table and surging to his feet. Tunneling his fingers through his hair, he paced away from her. He *couldn't*. Because then what did that say about the past, about what he'd believed?

What would it say about the family he idolized?

"It's not that you can't believe it. You won't," she contradicted, her voice low, laced with an unmistakable thread of resignation. As if she hadn't expected much from him. Certainly not for him to accept her truth. "And you never will. You won't allow yourself to even consider that the brave man who saved you from a burning building, the honorable man who became your brother when you lost your parents could've changed. Or at the very least, had one side with you and another with his wife, who he grew to resent almost from the moment he said 'I do.'"

"No," Darius rasped, stalking closer and eliminating the small space between them. "He went against his family's wishes to have you, risking everything for you…"

"And he came to hate me for it," she whispered, tilting her head back to meet his gaze. "Just like you eventually will. You said you're going through with this engagement and marriage for Baron, Helena and Gabriella. What happens when they force you to choose between your pretend wife and them? Because it'll happen. They've earned your love, your loyalty, but you've given your word to me. Oh, yes." She nodded, shadows swirling in her lovely, haunted eyes. "In the end, you'll resent me, too."

He squeezed his eyes closed, his jaw so hardened, so tense, the muscles along it twinged. Emotion. So much emotion howled and whistled inside him, he feared one misstep, one wrong-placed touch, and he would shred under the power of it.

"I already resent you, Isobel," he ground out, forcing himself to meet her gaze. Her scent—delicate like newly opened rose petals and intoxicating like the bourbon he'd been drinking—wrapped around him with phantom arms. Heat emanated from her petite body, and he wanted to curl against it. "And it has nothing to do with tonight or a future emotional tug-of-war. I hate that I can't get you out of my head. Can't stop replaying a night that should've never happened. I can still *feel* you. Your lips parting for mine. Your skin under my hands. Your tight, soaking-wet flesh gripping my fingers so hard, it almost bruised me. You just won't get out of my goddamn head."

Lust churned his voice to the consistency of gravel. "I hate that I know who you are, and I still want to fuck you. I hate that I can't tell if you're the sweet, giving woman from that dark hallway or the conniving one who was married to my best friend." He shifted that scant inch forward and brought his chest to hers, his thighs to hers. His breath to hers. "I hate that I want to find out."

Her labored pants broke across his mouth, and he slicked his tongue across his lips, seeking to taste that hard puff of breath. Her scrutiny followed the movement, and like clouds moving in over a blue sky, lust darkened her gaze. God, why didn't she close those beautiful eyes? Shield both of them from the knowledge that she craved him as he did her? He placed the responsibility on her, because he was the weaker one. She had to be the strong one and save them both.

"Turn around and walk out of here, Isobel," he warned her, his voice so guttural, he almost winced. "I'll break your condition. I'll put my hands and mouth on you. I'll finish what we started in the dark if you don't."

A small, muted whimper escaped her. Almost as if she'd tried to trap the needy sound but hadn't been fast enough.

"You're not running, sweetheart." He lifted his hand, let it hover over her cheek for a weighty moment, granting her time to evade it. But she remained still, and he swept the pad of his thumb over her cheekbone, then lower, across the lush curve of her bottom lip.

"No," she whispered. "I'm not."

"Your rule," he whispered back.

"Break it… Break me."

The request, uttered on a trembling breath, snapped the already tattered ropes on his control, and with a groan, he crushed his mouth to hers. When her heady taste hit his tongue, that groan morphed into a growl. Delicious. Addictive. He drove his fingers into her hair, tipping her head back so he could gorge on her. Yeah, he was committing the sin of gluttony, and resigned himself to hell for it.

Her palms slid over his sides and up his back, curling into the backs of his shoulders. The bite of her nails sent pleasure sizzling through him like an electrical charge, arrowing straight for his cock. He shifted, pressing harder against her, giving her full, undeniable disclosure to what she did to him.

Abandoning her hair, he dropped his arms, molding his hands to her ass, cupping the curves. He bent his knees, then abruptly straightened, hiking her into his arms. A bolt of carnal satisfaction struck him when her legs wrapped around his waist and her arms encircled his neck, holding on to him. Her mouth clung to his, that wicked tongue twisting and tangling, dancing and dueling. Damn, he wanted that talented mouth on his skin, on every part of him.

After quickly striding back to the couch, he sank down to the cushions, arranging her so she straddled his thighs. He broke their kiss long enough to fist the hem of her shirt and yank it over her head. All that hair tumbled down around her shoulders, back and chest, transforming her into a seductive siren. He wanted to crash himself against her and drown in pleasure.

"You're going to take me under, aren't you?" he murmured, voicing his thoughts.

"Are you afraid?" she asked.

He shifted his enraptured gaze from her hair to her eyes.

Yes.

The reply erupted inside him, ringing with certainty, but he didn't vocalize it. Instead he cradled the nape of her neck and drew her forward until their lips brushed, pressed, mated.

Impatient, he stroked a caress over her shoulders, down her chest and finally reacquainted himself with the flesh he'd dreamed about before waking up, hard and hurting. He cupped her, squeezed...and it wasn't enough. Ripping his mouth free of hers, he bent his head, trailed his lips over the soft swell of her breast, then circled his tongue around the taut, dusky peak.

Her cry rebounded off the walls and windows, and her arms clasped him to her. Her scent, rich and deep, filled his nostrils, and he licked it off her skin. In response, her hips rolled, rocking her lace-covered folds over him. The pressure against his erection had him hauling in a breath and bracing himself against the stunning pleasure barreling through him. He shifted beneath her, sliding down a fraction so his length notched firmly against her. He dropped a hand to her hip, encouraging her to continue riding him. Continue stoking the fire between them until it consumed them.

"You're so sweet." He lapped at her nipple, then drew it into his mouth, suckling on her, tormenting her as she was doing to him. "Dangerous," he admitted.

Her only response was to buck those slim hips. It was the only response he needed. Switching to her neglected breast, he worshipped it, losing himself in the taste, texture and wonder of her.

"Let me," she panted, gripping his hair and tugging his head up. He resisted, but spying her flushed cheeks, swollen lips and glazed eyes, he relented. "I want to…need to…"

She didn't finish the thought, but with trembling fingers, plucked at his shirt buttons. Too impatient, he replaced her attempt with a hard yank. The buttons flew, scattered, and he tore off the offensive material.

"God," she breathed, flattening her palms to his chest. He shuddered, the sensation of being skin to skin almost too sharp. "You're beautiful. So…beautiful."

Another shiver rippled through him, just as intense, but it was the result of her words rather than her touch. Or rather the stark truth in her words. When they were clothed, minds and bodies not warped by passion, he didn't trust her. But here…with their bodies stripped… honesty existed between them. The honesty of lust and pleasure. She couldn't hide from him, couldn't lie to him. Not when the evidence of her desire soaked her underwear and his pants.

He loosened a hand from the soft ropes of her hair and slid it down her back, over her hip and between her legs. She stiffened a second, and he paused, imprisoning a groan as her wet heat singed him. But only when she melted against him, her whispered, "Please" granting him permission to continue, did he slip underneath the plain but sexy-as-hell underwear to the soft, plush flesh beneath.

She jerked, whimpered as he glided through the path created by her folds, ending his journey with a firm circle over her clit. The little bundle of nerves contracted and pulsed under his fingertip, and he teased it. She straightened, her hands clutching at his shoulders, her back arched, surrendering to his touch.

She was the most goddamn beautiful thing he'd ever seen.

"I love how wet you get for me," he rasped, stroking her hair away from her face, studying her pleasure-stricken expression. Dipping his hand lower, he rimmed her tiny, fluttering entrance. "You have more for me, sweetheart?"

He didn't wait for a reply but drove a finger inside her. Her cry caressed his ears even as her silken sex clutched at him, convulsed around him. He growled, loving her response to him. Hungry for more. Withdrawing, he slid in another finger, stretching her, preparing her to take him so he wouldn't inadvertently hurt her. And the selfish side of him reveled in the tight clasp of her body, in the soft undulations of her flesh that relayed her pleasure and impatience. Impatience for him, for what he was giving her. For what he was promising her.

"Can you take another?" he murmured, pulling free again.

"Yes." Her fingernails denting his skin. "Please, yes."

Leaning forward, he opened his mouth over the pulse throbbing like a snare drum at the base of her throat as he slowly buried three fingers inside her. She bucked her hips, twisting like a wild thing on his lap. Jesus, she was gorgeous in passion—sexy, uninhibited and burning like a blue flame. Her desire scorched him.

Grinding out a curse, he lifted her off his thighs

and set her beside him. Ignoring her disappointed cry, he shed her of the underwear, leaving her bare before him. With his gaze fixed on her lovely nakedness, he removed his wallet from his pants. Then he snatched out a condom and shoved his pants down his legs, too desperate to be inside her to completely strip them off.

With hands he prayed were gentler than the maelstrom of greed tearing at him, he repositioned her over him. He couldn't prevent the shiver that worked its way through him as he fisted the base of his cock, notching the tip at the entrance to her body. Perspiration trickled down his skin as he slowly—so damn slowly—lowered her over him.

God. Every muscle in his body tightened, with the control it required not to plunge himself inside exacting its toll.

Hot.

Tight.

Ecstasy.

Fire raced up and down his spine, snapping and crackling. It rolled and thundered through his veins, transforming his blood to pure, undiluted pleasure. Already she consumed him, and he hadn't even seated himself fully inside her. And though razor-sharp need sliced at him, he didn't rush it. He'd rather suffer before hurting Isobel. Even now those tiny muscles rippled and fluttered over his flesh, adjusting to his penetration. Tremors quaked through her petite frame, and whimpers slipped past her lips.

"Shh," he soothed, pausing. Keeping one hand braced on her hip, he cupped her cheek with the other, tipping her head down. "Your pace, sweetheart. Tell me what you need, and it's yours," he said against her lips.

"Kiss me."

She tilted her head, opening for him, and he twisted his tongue with hers, sucking on it. She joined in the duel, thrusting and parrying. Pursuing and eluding. It turned wild, raw.

Before the kiss ended, she sat fully and firmly on his cock.

With a snarl, he tore away from her, tipping his head back against the couch. She was...perfect.

"Isobel," he growled, raising his head again, unable to *not* see what she did to him. How she took him.

Cradling her hips, he lifted her, stared in rapt fascination as she unsheathed him, leaving his length glistening with the evidence of her desire. Then when just the head remained inside her, he eased her back down, still watching as she parted for him, claiming him.

Branding him.

"After that night in the hallway," he gritted out, pulling free again. "I regretted not taking you. Not knowing how it felt to bury myself inside you. But now," he rasped, lowering her. "Now I'm glad I didn't. Because then I would've missing seeing how you so sweetly spread for me. And that, sweetheart...that would've been a crime."

"Darius," she whispered, and the sound of his name on her lips tattered the remnants of his control.

He drove inside her, snatching her down to him. Not that he needed to. She rode him, fierce and powerful, and in that moment, she was the one doing the claiming. And he surrendered, letting her incinerate him. And he held on, thrusting, giving, willingly being rendered to ash.

"Please," she begged, her body quaking. She clung to him even as she surged and writhed against him. "Please, Darius."

He didn't need her to complete the thought; he already knew what she wanted. Reaching between them, he stroked a path down her belly and between her legs. Murmuring, he rubbed the pad of his thumb over her swollen clit. Once. Twice...

Before he could reach three, her sex clamped down on him, a strangling, muscular vise that dragged a grunt out of him. She exploded, seizing his cock, spasming and pulsing around him as she flew apart in his arms.

He rode her through it, thrusting hard and quick, ensuring she received every measure of the release that gripped her. Only when the quakes eased into shivering did he let go.

Pleasure—powerful, intense and brutal—plowed into him. His brain shorted, his vision grayed as he threw himself into an orgasm like a willing sacrifice, wanting to be consumed, obliterated, reshaped.

But into what? The unknown terrified him.

Then, as the darkness submerged and swamped him, he didn't think.

Couldn't think.

Could only feel.

And then, not even that.

Chapter 9

Isobel released a weary sigh as she pulled into an empty spot in the four-car garage.

Darius had moved one of his luxury vehicles so she could have a parking space, and had invited her to drive one of them. But she had yet to take him up on the offer. She'd already invaded his house, and she and Aiden were living off his money. Taking one of the cars as if she owned it edged her one step closer to being the gold-digging creature she'd been called. So no, she'd continued driving her beat-up but trusty Honda Civic. Even if parking it next to his Bugatti Chiron seemed like blasphemy.

Climbing out of her car, she inhaled the early evening air. Though she'd left work at the grocery store without wearing her jacket, she now drew it around her, the black collared shirt and khakis of her uniform not fighting off the nippy breeze.

Glancing down at her watch, she picked up her pace and strode toward the front door of Darius's home. It was just nearing five o'clock, and like the previous days, she was hoping she'd beat him home from work. Since she no longer had to work a second shift with her mother to make ends meet, she'd switched her hours at the store. Four days a week, she left the house at eight to arrive for her nine-to-four shift. Isobel liked the nanny, Ms. Jacobs, just fine. She was grateful for her, because her presence allowed Isobel to continue working even when she couldn't ask her mom to watch Aiden. Still, she missed her son fiercely when she left.

And yet over the last few days, she'd been thankful for her job. Concentrating on customers, price checks and sales prevented her from obsessively dwelling on…other things.

Other things being the cataclysmic event of sex with Darius.

A flush rushed up from her chest and throat, pouring into her face. She loosened her collar as the memories surged forth, as if they'd been hovering on the edges of her subconscious, waiting for the opportunity to flood her.

Her step faltered, and she stumbled. "Damn," she muttered.

No matter how many times those mental images flashed across her brain, they never failed to trip her up—literally and figuratively. She vacillated between cringing and combusting. Cringing at the thought of her completely abandoned and wild reaction to him.

Combusting as she easily—too easily—recalled

how his mouth and hands had pleasured her, marked her. How he'd triggered a need in her that eclipsed any previous sexual experience, rendering all other men inconsequential and mediocre.

He'd spoiled her for anyone else.

And she'd committed a fatal error in letting him know just how much she craved him.

So yes, she'd been avoiding him, trying to reinforce her emotional battlements. And surprisingly he'd allowed her to evade him. The few times they'd been in the same room since That Night, he'd treated her with a distant politeness that both relieved and irritated her. Pretending as if they'd never shook in each other's arms, him buried inside her to the hilt.

Pinching the bridge of her nose as she entered the house, she deliberately slammed the door on those memories, and not just locked it but threw three dead bolts just for good measure.

"Where have you been?"

She skidded to a halt in the foyer at the furious demand, her head jerking up. Shock doused her in a frigid wave, and she stared at Darius. Anger glittered in his amber gaze, tightened the skin over his sharp cheekbones and firmed the full curve of his mouth into a flat line.

"Hello to you, too, Darius," she drawled with acid sweetness.

"Where. Have. You. Been?" he ground out, his big body vibrating with emotion. It flared so bright in his eyes, they appeared like molten gold.

"At work, although I don't see how that's any of your business," she snapped. "Which is becoming a common refrain between us. I might be in your home, but no clause in that contract mandated me having to run my every movement by you."

A snarl curled the corner of his lips, and he shifted a step forward but stopped himself. "I beg to disagree with you on that, Isobel. When it has to do with Aiden's care and no one knows where the hell you've been for hours, and you don't answer your cell phone, then it most definitely. Is. My. Business." He pivoted away from her, the action sharp, full of anger. His fingers plowed through his hair, fisting it, before he turned back to her. "Aiden started coughing and became irritable, and when Ms. Jacobs took his temperature, he had a low-grade fever. She tried to call you to see if you wanted her to make a doctor's appointment for him. When she couldn't reach you, she called me. Damn it, Isobel," he growled. "I didn't know if something had happened to you or if you were in trouble or hurt…" Again, he glanced away from her, a muscle ticking along his clenched jaw. "No one could find you," he finally growled.

Worry for her son washed away her annoyance and propelled her forward. "Is he okay? I can take him to an after-hours clinic…"

"He's fine. I had a doctor come out and examine him. He has a virus, probably a twenty-four-hour bug, but nothing serious. I've just looked in on him, and he's sleeping."

Relief threaded through her concern, but didn't get rid of it. As a cashier, she wasn't allowed to have a cell phone on the floor. When her mother had been watching Aiden, this hadn't been a problem, as she'd trusted her mother to handle anything that came up. Not to mention that the store had been minutes from her mom's place. Maybe she should've given Darius her work schedule, or told him she was continuing to work at the store, period. And she'd just told Ms. Jacobs she was going to be out.

Damn. She turned toward the staircase, her thoughts already on her baby. But Darius's voice stopped her.

"I'll be in the library, Isobel. After you look in on him, come find me. This conversation isn't finished." The "don't make me come find you" was implicit in the order, but she ignored it, instead rushing up the stairs to her son.

Fifteen minutes later, after she'd satisfied herself that he was resting and breathing easily, she headed toward the library. Her heart thudded against her chest, her blood humming in her veins. Returning to the scene of the crime. She'd barely glanced at the entrance to the room since she'd last left it, and now she had to reenter it. Maybe sit on the same couch where she'd lost her control, her pride and possibly her mind.

She hated having to enter this room again and be reminded of how she'd come apart. Of how she'd cemented his belief that she was an immoral whore who would screw anyone. After all, she'd claimed not to want him, but at his first touch, she'd surrendered.

Break it... Break me.

Hadn't those been the words she'd uttered as she begged him? *Break the no-sex rule she'd instituted. Break her with his passion.*

Briefly, she closed her eyes, attempting to smother the humiliation crawling into her throat, squatting there and strangling her.

Deliberately keeping her gaze off the couch, she strode into the room and located Darius, who was in front of his desk, with his arms crossed and his eagle-eyed scrutiny fixed on her.

"Isobel."

"Can we get this over with so I can return to Aiden?"

He didn't move, but she could practically *see* him bristle. "How is he?" he asked, surprising her once more with his concern for her son.

"Sleeping, as you said," she murmured. "He's still warm, but he seems to be resting okay." Drawing in a breath, she mimicked his pose, crossing her arms over her chest. "I'm sorry you couldn't reach me. That was my fault. I was at work, and management doesn't allow us to have our cells on us. And I didn't even notice I had missed calls when I left. So I apologize for worrying...everyone."

"Work?" he asked, his voice dropping to a low rumble. "What 'work'?"

"I'm sure the private investigator you hired included my job in his or her report," she said, sarcasm dripping from her tone. "If not, you might want to request a refund for his shoddy performance."

He shook his head, dropping his arms to slash a hand through the air. "Don't tell me you're still going to that supermarket?"

"Of course I am," she replied. "That contract didn't require me to give up my job."

"Why?" he demanded. "You don't need the job, especially when it pays basically pennies. And yes, I do know how much you make, since my investigator's report included not only where you work but how much you're paid," he added.

"There's nothing wrong with ringing up groceries. It's good, honest work." She thrust her chin up. "Maybe you're so far removed from that time in the mail room, you don't remember what that's like."

"No, there's nothing wrong with your job." He frowned, cocking his head to the side. "But what do you need it for, Isobel? If there's something you want, why don't you just come to me and ask?"

His obvious confusion and—hurt?—smoothed out the ragged edges of her anger. How could she make him understand?

After his parents had died, he might've lived with the Wellses, but he'd never been totally dependent on them. Not with a multibillion-dollar empire waiting on him. Not with homes scattered around the country and money in bank accounts. He didn't know the powerlessness, the helplessness of being totally reliant on someone else's generosity…or lack of it.

She'd learned that particular lesson the hard way with Gage. Yes, she might've held down the job when she'd been married, but Gage had considered his role to be manager of their finances. And he'd been horribly irresponsible with them. And later, when his parents had parceled out sympathy money to him, he'd stingily doled that out to her, holding money for things like groceries and diapers over her head.

Never again would she be at the mercy of a man.

And if that meant keeping a low-paying job with good hours so she could maintain a measure of independence, then she would do what was necessary. If it meant losing some time with Aiden while she squirreled away her wages, well, then sacrifices needed to be made. She needed to be able to provide for them when Darius's charity finally reached its limits.

She was a mother first. And any good mother did what needed to be done.

"Then enlighten me, Isobel. Because I don't understand. You have a home. You don't have to pay any bills. You even have cars at your disposal if you'd stop being so damn prideful and use them—"

"No, you're wrong," she interrupted, her voice quiet but heavy with the emotion pressing against her sternum. Frustration, irritation and sadness. "*You* have a home. *You* have cars at your disposal. *Your* money pays the bills. None of this is mine. Even after we sign that marriage certificate and exchange vows, it still won't be. If you put me out, I couldn't leave with any of it. Couldn't lay claim to it. And you could put me out at any time, on any whim, because of any conceived sin on my part. And I would be on the street, homeless, with no money or resources for me and my son. No." She shook her head. "I won't allow that to happen."

He stared at her, shock darkening his eyes. His lips parted, head jerking as if her words had delivered a verbal punch.

"I would never abandon you or Aiden like that," he said, the words uttered like a vow.

She knew only too well how vows could be broken.

"I know you believe you wouldn't. But minds change, feelings change," she murmured. Then, suddenly feeling so tired that her limbs seemed to weigh a hundred pounds, she sighed, pinching the bridge of her nose. "Are we done here? I need to get back to Aiden."

"No," he said, the denial firm, adamant. As if it'd pushed through a throat coated in broken glass. "You don't believe me."

"I wanted to return to college. Did you know that?"

she asked softly. Without waiting for him to reply, she continued, "One of my regrets is that I quit school. I would've been the first one in my family to earn a degree if I'd stayed. So graduating from college was a dream of mine, but when I broached it with Gage, he convinced me to wait until after the baby was born. At the time, I thought him wanting that time for the two of us was sweet. So I agreed. But after Aiden came, I couldn't go back. Working a full-time job, being a mom..." She shrugged. "College would've been too much, so I had to place it on the back burner. But I've always wanted to go back. To obtain that degree. To have a career that I love. And when Aiden is older, I'll show him that no matter how you struggle, you can do anything you desire."

Scrubbing her hands up and down her arms, she paced to the wide floor-to-ceiling window and stared sightlessly at the view of his Olympic-size pool, deck and firepit. Her admission made her feel vulnerable, exposed.

"Did Gage support your dream?" Darius asked quietly.

She didn't turn around and face him. Didn't let him see the pain and anger she couldn't hide. Darius didn't want to hear the truth. Wasn't ready to hear it. And he wouldn't believe her anyway. College, money for tuition—those had been givens in his and Gage's worlds. He wouldn't understand or see how his friend would begrudge his wife that same experience.

"Gage had specific ideas about the wife he wanted," she whispered instead. "A wife like his mother." One to cater to him. Be at his beck and call. Place him as the center of her universe, at the exclusion of everyone else.

Images from that time flashed across her mind, and she deliberately shut them down, refusing to tumble back into that dark time when she'd been so helpless and powerless.

Silence descended on the room, and she swore she could feel Darius's confusion and disbelief pushing against her.

"If what you say is true, how——"

She'd expected him not to believe her. But she *hadn't* expected the dagger-sharp pain to slice into her heart. Uttering a sound that was somewhere between a scoff and a whimper, she turned, unable to stand there while he doubted every word that came out of her mouth. This is what she got for opening up and letting him in even a little.

Lesson learned.

"Wait. *Damn it, Isobel*," he growled, his arms wrapping around her, his chest pressing to her spine. His hold, while firm, wasn't constrictive, and it was this fact that halted her midescape. "That came out wrong. Just give me a minute. Don't I have the right to ask questions? To try to understand?"

A pause—where the only sound in the room was the echo of their harsh breaths. He loosened his arms, releasing her and taking his warmth with him. Turbulent emotions surged up from the place deep inside her that remained wounded and bruised. The place that cried out like a heartsore child for satisfaction, for someone to hear her, for acceptance. That place urged her to lash out, to hurt as she'd been hurt.

But flashes of Darius being so affectionate with

Aiden, of him upset on her behalf after the dinner with the Wellses, of him kissing and touching her—those flashes filled her head. And it was those flashes that tempered her reply.

"Love blinds us all."

Unable to say any more, unable to hear him defend his friend and family, she left the study and climbed the stairs to return to Aiden.

How they could ever forge a peaceful, if not loving, marriage when the past continued to intrude?

And to that question, she didn't have an answer.

Chapter 10

"No, Mommy!"

Darius heard Aiden's strident, high-pitched objection before he stepped into the doorway of the boy's room. Isobel sat on one of the large beanbag chairs, Aiden curled on her lap, reading a book. Well, Isobel was reading anyway, Darius mused, humor bubbling inside him.

"No," Aiden yelled again, stabbing a chubby finger at one of the pages. "Nose." He twisted around and declared, "Eye," nearly taking out hers with his enthusiastic poke. "Nose," he repeated, squishing his with the same finger.

Isobel laughed, dropping a kiss on his abused nose. "You're right, baby. Nose. Good job!"

"Good job," he mimicked, clapping.

Warmth slid through Darius's veins like liquid sun.

The previous evening had left him confused, and the maddening cacophony of questions lingered.

Gage had specific ideas about the wife he wanted.

She'd made it sound like she hadn't met Gage's standard. If so, had there been consequences? What had those consequences been? Had he and Gage's family been so fixated on Gage's side that they'd missed clues about the truth of Gage's marriage?

Darius closed his eyes, but when the image of Isobel's face, filled with sadness, hurt and resignation, just before she left the study, flashed across the back of his lids, he opened them again.

Nothing could excuse breaking one's marriage vows. But if her dreams had been crushed, if her marriage had been less than what she'd expected, if her husband had changed, was that why she'd turned to other men? Had she been seeking the affection and kindness she believed her husband hadn't given her?

Darius longed to ask her, because these questions tortured him.

"Darry!" Aiden shrieked, jerking Darius from his dark jumble of thoughts. Catching sight of him, Aiden scrambled out of Isobel's lap and dashed on his little legs toward him.

Joy unlike anything he'd ever experienced burst in his chest as he scooped the boy up and held him close. His heart constricted so hard, so tight, his sternum ached. But it was a good hurt. And not just because Aiden had thrown himself at Darius with the kind of confidence that showed he knew he would be caught. But also because, for a moment, Aiden's garbled version of his name sounded entirely too close to *Daddy*. And as selfish as it might be, he yearned to be Aiden's father. Already he fiercely loved this boy as if they shared the same blood and DNA.

He kissed Aiden's still-warm forehead. "How's he feeling this morning?" he asked Isobel.

For the first time since he'd entered the room, she met his gaze. He noted the wariness reflected in her eyes. Noted and shared it. He might have been knocked on his ass by her confession the previous night, but he still didn't—couldn't—trust her. No matter how much his body craved hers. Actually, that grinding need only cemented why he had to be cautious with her. He'd shown in the past he could be led around by his dick, and he would never be that foolish again. Especially with a woman who had already betrayed her vows of fidelity.

And that was the crux of the war waging inside him.

Though it was difficult to reconcile the materialistic gold digger with the woman he was living with—the doting, sacrificing mother, the proud fighter—loyalty came down to family.

They'd earned it.

Isobel hadn't.

"He's still running a small fever, but it's lower than yesterday, and he has more energy. As you can tell," she added dryly.

He nodded, poking Aiden in his rounded stomach and chuckling at the child's giggling and squirming. Setting the boy on his feet, Darius straightened, finding Isobel's stare again.

"Can I see you downstairs for a moment?"

"Fine," she said after a brief hesitation, rising from the floor and setting Aiden's book on his bed.

"I'll wait for you in the living room." Not waiting

for her response, he retraced his earlier path down the hallway and staircase. He'd purposefully chosen the living room. Right now the study contained too many memories.

Minutes later, Isobel entered the room, and though he resented his reaction to her, his blood sang and his pulse drummed, the throb echoing in his cock. This was what she did to him by simply breathing. How did he armor himself against her?

God forbid she discovered his weakness.

"You wanted to see me," she said.

"Yes." He picked up a manila envelope from the mantel over the fireplace and offered it to her.

Frowning, she strode forward and gingerly accepted it. "What is this?"

"Open it, Isobel."

Flicking him a glance, she reluctantly acquiesced. He studied her as she withdrew the thin sheaf of papers and scanned the contract and bank documents. Bewilderment, shock and finally anger flitted across her face in rapid-fire succession. Her head snapped up, and her eyes narrowed. She pinned him with a glare.

"What. Is. This?" she repeated, her tone as hard as stone.

"Exactly what it looks like," he replied evenly, unsurprised by her response. "An addendum to our original contract. For entering our agreement, you receive one million dollars that will be deposited in an account under your name alone, as the bank documents reflect. It's yours free and clear. Even if you seek a divorce, it will still be yours."

"Like a signing bonus?" she drawled, the words acerbic.

He dipped his head. "If that's what you want to call it."

"No." She dropped the papers and the envelope on the glass table next to them as if they burned her fingers. "Hell no."

"Isobel—"

But she slashed a hand through the air, cutting off his explanation. "Is this about last night?" She shook her head so hard, her hair swung over her shoulders. "I didn't tell you that to make you feel guilty. If you hadn't pushed me, I wouldn't have said anything. At. All. But I damn sure won't take pity money from you now. If you wanted me to have that money—" she jabbed a finger in the direction of the papers "—then you would've included it during our original *negotiations*."

"You're right," he growled, and from her silence, he surmised his admission shocked her. "But at the time, I didn't want to hear anything except a yes. But now I want you to have it. And I can't unhear your fears or your dreams." Or the other things hinted at but left unsaid. "Maybe I need to give you what you missed. Your education. A father for your son. Help raising him. Time with him. Let me try to give it back to you, Isobel."

The only time in his life that he'd ever begged anyone for anything was when he'd pleaded with God to return his parents to him. But here, he came damn close.

She stared at him, and he battled the urge to turn away and evade that fey gaze that cut too deep and saw too much.

"Okay," she murmured.

He paused, her capitulation rendering him momentarily speechless. "Okay," he repeated. "And I'm not asking you to quit the supermarket or not replace it with something else. You can return to college, or I can arrange an entry-level position in a company or field of your choice that will allow you to get your foot in the door of your career. Or both college and the job. I don't want to steal your independence, Isobel. I don't want to be your jailor."

"Well, I really didn't want to ask my current manager for a reference anyway." A small smile flirted with her mouth. "Thank you, Darius."

"You're welcome," he said, his fingers suddenly tingling with the need to brush a caress over those sensual lips and feel that smile instead of just seeing it.

Silently, they stood there, snared in each other's gazes. She was the first to break the connection, and he bit back a demand for her to return to him, to give him her thoughts.

"I was going to bundle Aiden up and take him to see my mom. She's been calling nonstop since yesterday. I think she just needs to lay eyes on him." She halted, her eyes again meeting his. "Did you… I don't know if you'd like to…" Her voice tapered off, red staining the slashes of her cheekbones.

She was inviting him to come with her to visit her mother. Considering they didn't have a traditional relationship, introducing him to her family hadn't occurred. But she was offering that to him. It…humbled him.

"Why don't you invite her here instead since his fever isn't completely gone? I can send a car for her.

Or go get her myself. Whichever she prefers. If you'd like, she can spend the day here with you and Aiden."

She blinked. "A-are you sure?" she stammered. "This is your home. You don't have to…"

"No, Isobel," he contradicted, injecting a thread of steel in the words. "This is our home. And it is always open to your mother, to your family."

She didn't agree with him—but she didn't refute him either.

And for today at least, it was a start.

Chapter 11

Isobel removed her earrings and dropped them into the old wooden jewelry box that had been a gift from her mom for her thirteenth birthday. Closing the lid, she picked up her brush and dragged it through her hair, meeting her own gaze in the mirror of the vanity. A smile curved her lips, and she didn't try to suppress it. Even if she looked like a dope wearing a silly grin for no reason.

Well, that wasn't true. She had a reason.

A wonderful day with her mom, Aiden...and Darius.

She carefully set the brush down as if it were crafted out of fragile glass instead of durable plastic. When truthfully, she was the one who felt delicate... breakable.

Inhaling a deep breath, she splayed her fingers low on her belly in a vain attempt to stifle the chaotic flutter there.

Once the car bringing her mother had arrived, she'd expected Darius to retreat to his study or even head to his office. He'd done neither. Instead Darius had stayed with them, warmly welcoming her mother and melting her reserve toward him with his graciousness and obvious adoration of Aiden. They'd watched movies, played with Aiden, cooked, ate and laughed. She'd glimpsed another side of Darius that day. Charming. Relaxed.

Like his gift of the contract addendum and the bank account with more money than she'd ever see in five lifetimes. She shook her head. She still couldn't believe that. Not only had he handed it over to like it'd been change in a car ashtray, but he'd given it to *her*, the woman he considered a money-grubbing user. When she thought on it, the shock returned, and she had to stop herself from pinching her skin like some kid.

She could take care of Aiden.

She didn't have to work at the supermarket.

She could return to college.

She had no-strings-attached options.

A whirl of electric excitement crackled inside her. In the space of minutes, her world had expanded from the size of a cramped box to a space without walls, without ceilings.

He'd done that for her. For her son.

Isobel spun on her heel, charged out of the bedroom and marched down the hall before she could change her mind. Seconds later, she knocked on the door of Darius's room. Already cracked, it swung further open under her hand.

"I'm sorry," she apologized, wincing as she shifted into the opening. "I didn't…know…it…"

The words dried up on her tongue, along with all the moisture in her mouth.

Good. Lord.

Darius stood in the middle of the room, naked to the waist. Miles and miles of golden, taut skin stretched over muscle like barely leashed power. Wide, brawny shoulders, strong arms roped with tendon and veins that seemed to pulse with vitality and strength. A solid chest smattered with dark brown hair that her fingers knew was springy to the touch. It thinned into a silky, sexy line that bisected his rock-hard stomach. Her gaze trailed that line, following it with complete fascination as it disappeared beneath the loosened belt and unbuttoned jeans.

Face heating, she jerked her head up, her stare crashing into his whiskey-colored one. Whiskey. Yes. She'd always compared it to an eagle's gaze, but whiskey was more accurate. Especially considering the punch it delivered and the heat it left behind.

"I'm sorry," she apologized again, inwardly cringing at her hoarse tone. Like sandpaper smoothed with jagged rock. "I didn't mean to interrupt…" She waved a hand up and down, encompassing his towering frame. "I'll just go," she said, already whirling around.

"Isobel." Her name halted her escape. No, it was the swell of arousal low in her belly that froze her. "Come here."

No "I'll meet you downstairs." Not "it's fine. Let me get changed and we'll talk later." Not even "come back." But, *come here.*

It was a warning. An invitation.

A threat. A seduction.

"Come here," he repeated, and she surrendered, her feet shifting forward, carrying the rest of her with them until she stood in front of him.

His heat, his cedar-and-musk scent, his almost tangible sensuality called out to her, enticed her to eliminate those scant few inches and bury her face against his chest. Inhale him *and* feel him. Somehow she resisted. But just. And even now that resistance was pockmarked, and so thin one touch would shred it.

"What do you want?" he asked, the sharp blades of his cheekbones and the hewn line of his jaw only emphasizing the blaze in his eyes. "Why did you come in here?"

"To thank you for today," she murmured. "For... everything."

"You're welcome," he rumbled, and as if in slow motion, he lifted a hand and rubbed the back of his fingers down her cheek. "Now tell me why you really came to find me."

She parted her lips to deliver a stinging reply, but it didn't come. Before she could contain it, the truth that she hadn't even acknowledged burst free.

"For you. I want you."

Another blast of flames in his eyes, and then her world tipped upside down. In one breath, she stood trembling before him, and in the next her back met his mattress, and Darius loomed over her. Her world narrowed to his big body and starkly beautiful face.

He tunneled his fingers through her hair, the blunt tips pressing against her skull. His gaze burned into hers, capturing her. Not that she wanted to be anywhere but here—his breath tangling with hers, his chest and legs covering hers, his cock branding her stomach through their clothes.

"Take it back," he ordered. When she stared up at him, confused, he lowered more of his weight onto her. She felt claimed. His flesh ground into her, teasing her with the promise of the pleasure only he was capable of delivering. "Take back your condition. Tell me you don't want me to fuck anyone else," he growled. "Tell me the thought of me touching another woman would drive you insane. Tell me I'm allowed to have you and only you."

She dug her nails into his shoulders, the words he demanded to hear crowding the back of her throat.

"Isobel," he growled.

The sexy, primal rumble unlocked her voice. "You can't touch another woman except me. You're not allowed, because it would drive me crazy," she finished on a gasp, with the word *crazy* barely out of her mouth before he swallowed it, his tongue thrusting forward past her parted lips and taking her in a kiss so blatantly carnal, so wild and possessive, it propelled the breath from her lungs.

But that was okay, because he gave her his.

He devoured her. It was wild, a clash, an erotic battle where both seized and neither lost. An ache opened wide in her, like a deep chasm that could never be filled. And yet she would never stop trying.

Did it register somewhere underneath the turbulent, consuming need that he hadn't asked her to make the same request? Yes. Did it also occur to her that he didn't ask because he didn't believe she would honor his demand of faithfulness? Yes. Did it hurt like a nagging, old wound? God, yes.

But right now, with his mouth working hers like he owned it, she didn't dwell on the pain. She submerged it beneath the waves of passion crashing over her. Later, when his hands didn't tilt her head back to receive more of him, that's when she'd think on it. But not now.

Darius abruptly straightened, tugging her up with him. With hurried hands, he balled the hem of her sleep shirt and yanked it over her head, leaving her clad only in a plain pair of black boy-short panties. Definitely not the expensive, seductive lingerie he was probably used to, but as he stared down at her, unchecked desire lighting his amber gaze, it didn't matter. Not when, without uttering a word, he told her he wanted her with a hunger that rivaled the need grinding her to dust.

Slipping a hand behind his neck, she drew his head down to her as she arched up to meet him. This time their kiss was slower, wetter. Somehow hotter.

He eased her back to the bed, his chest pressed to hers, and she undulated under him, rubbing her breasts over him, dragging her nipples across the solid wall of muscle. Correctly interpreting her message, he tore his mouth away from hers and blazed a path down her neck to the flesh that tightened in anticipation of his wicked attention.

As he cupped one breast, he nuzzled the other. She cradled his head, silently demanding he stop toying with her. And with a rumble that vibrated against her abdomen, he obeyed, parting his lips over her and drawing her in. She cried out, bowing so hard, her back lifted off the mattress. The strong pull of his mouth set off sparks behind her closed eyelids and matching spasms deep inside her. *God*, the ache. She wrapped her legs around his hips and ground against his cock, shuddering at the swell of pain-tinged pleasure. Whimpering, she repeated the action. Coupled with the mind-twisting things his mouth was doing to her breasts, she teetered close to the edge of release. So close...

"Not yet, sweetheart," he rasped against her skin.

Treating her nipple to one last kiss, he trailed his lips down her stomach, pausing to lap at her navel before continuing to the drenched center of her body. With an abrupt tug, he had her panties down her legs and tossed behind him.

Mortification didn't have time to sink its sharp nails in her as he lodged himself between her thighs, which were perched on his shoulders. She didn't have the opportunity to inform him that she'd never cared for oral sex, had never understood the allure of it. Didn't have a chance to tell him she'd just rather have him inside her because she didn't want to disappoint him.

No, she didn't say any of that because the second his mouth opened over her sex, shock and searing pleasure robbed her of the ability to think, to form coherent sentences.

"Oh, God," was all she could squeeze out of her constricted throat. He stroked a path through her folds, lapping at her, his growl humming against her. Grasping his head, she fisted his hair, to hold on and to keep him right there. He circled her clit, blowing on the pulsing knot of nerves, then he tortured her with short stabs and long sweeps. She writhed against his worshipping lips. Bucked into each stroke. Begged him to suck harder, faster, slower and gentler. She went wild.

And when release rushed forward in a flood so strong, so sharp, so potent, she didn't fight it. She surrendered to the undertow with a loud, piercing cry, chanting his name like an invocation.

Dimly, she registered the mattress dipping. Heard the soft shush of clothing over skin. Caught the crinkle of foil. Didn't have enough energy to turn her head and investigate. But when Darius reappeared over her, his big, beautiful body crouched over her like the gorgeous animal he was, desire rekindled in her veins, burning away the post-orgasm lassitude. It was unbelievable. She'd just come hard enough to see stars, and now, when it should've been impossible, her sex trembled and clenched, an emptiness deep inside her begging to be filled.

She lifted her arms to him, and without hesitation, he came down over her, one hand curving behind her head and the other cupping the back of her thigh, holding her open. With her eyes locked on to his, she waited, her breath trapped in her throat. Even when he pushed forward, penetrating her, stretching her, she didn't look away. The inexplicable but no less desperate need to see his face, his eyes, gripped her. She longed to see if they reflected the same awe, rapture and relief that surged within her. To determine if she was alone on this tumultuous ride.

His full, sensual lips firmed into a line. His nostrils flared, the skin across his cheekbones tightened and in the golden brown depths of his eyes…there, she saw it. The flare of surprise, then the blazing hungry heat and something shadowed, something…more.

No, she wasn't alone. Not in the least.

Wrapping her arms tighter around his neck, she burrowed her face in the strong column, throwing herself into the ecstasy, the burn, the passion—into him. Opening her mouth over his skin, she tasted his tangy, musky flavor, mewling as he burrowed so deep inside her, she wondered how far he would go, how much he would take.

Not enough. The answer quivered in her mind. *It won't ever be enough.*

A trill of alarm sliced through her, but it was almost immediately drowned out by the carnal havoc he created within her body. After sliding his hands down her back, he palmed her behind and held her for his long strokes. He forged a path that only he could travel, dragging his thick length in and out of her and igniting tremors with each thrust. She savored each one, rolling up to meet each plunge.

"With me, sweetheart," he murmured in her ear. Tunneling his fingers into her hair, he gripped the strands and tugged her head back. His eyes so dark with lust that only flickers of gold remained, he grated through clenched teeth, "I'm not going alone. Get there and come with me."

The words, so arrogant and commanding, but strained with lust and drenched in need, were like a caress over her flesh. Clawing at his back, she slammed her hips against his, and his cock rubbed against a place high inside her, forming a catalyst, a detonator to her pleasure.

She shattered.

Screaming, she threw her head back against the pillows, propelling herself into the orgasm that claimed her like a ravenous beast, devouring her, leaving nothing. Above her, Darius rode her through it, until he stiffened and quaked. The throbbing of his flesh triggered another orgasm, rolling into the previous one like an unending explosion of ecstasy.

Darkness swept over her, pulling her under, but not before a seed of worry sprouted deep in her head. In the heat of passion, they'd become something new tonight.

But what? *Who?*

And would they survive it?

Chapter 12

Darius stared at his computer monitor, but he didn't see the report on the possible acquisition. Too many other thoughts crowded his mind. No, he had to be honest with himself.

Isobel.

Isobel crowded his mind, not leaving room for anything else.

Who was this woman? The selfish, devious conniver he'd believed her to be these past years? Or the woman he'd come to know since the night of the blackout? Just a week ago, he would've said both. That maybe single motherhood and being on her own had matured her from the person she'd been. But now…

Now doubts niggled at the back of his mind; perhaps he'd been wrong all along.

The things Isobel had hinted at—the controlling

nature of her marriage, the lack of independence, the chameleon nature of the man Darius had called friend and she'd called husband—as well as the things she'd left unsaid. Working at a neighborhood grocery store even though she resided in one of the wealthiest zip codes in the state.

But if he believed Isobel—and God help him, he was starting to—then that meant Gage had concealed a side of himself from his family. What else had he hidden? Was it possible that Darius's best friend could've lied to them, to him? And if so, how could he have been so blind? He couldn't have been...right?

The urge to unearth the truth swelled within him, and he reached for the phone. He could have the company PI investigate for him. Contact Gage and Isobel's old neighbors or employees that had worked with Isobel at the time. It'd been years, but maybe they could give him some insight...

Just as his fingers curled around the receiver, the desk speaker crackled, and his executive assistant's voice addressed him.

"Mr. King, Mrs. Wells is here to see you."

Darius pressed the intercom button. "Thank you, Charlene," he replied. "Please let the marketing team know we're going to move our one o'clock meeting to one thirty."

"Yes, sir."

Darius rose from his chair and was already halfway across his spacious office when Helena opened his door and strode in. In spite of his unsettled thoughts, pleasure bloomed inside him at the unexpected but welcome visit. Several weeks had passed since the disastrous dinner at her home. Since then, he'd visited them several times, but without Isobel and Aiden. Though they'd asked about the boy and when they could spend time with him, Darius hesitated. First, he'd promised from the beginning that he wouldn't make arbitrary decisions about Aiden without consulting Isobel. And that included taking him to see his grandparents without her permission, even if he longed for them all to build a loving relationship.

Helena, regal in a black dress that wrapped around her still-slender figure, met him with outstretched arms.

"What brings you here today?" He led her to his office sitting area, lightly clasping her elbow.

She arched a dark, elegant eyebrow. "Do I need a reason to come see family? Especially when he's been a bit of a stranger lately?"

Darius laughed as he helped her settle on the black leather couch and then took a seat beside her. "That was subtle," he drawled. "Like a claw hammer to the head."

She smiled, but her point was well-taken. True, he hadn't been by the Wellses' home as often as he'd visited in the past. In the past weeks, he, Isobel and Aiden had settled into a cautious but peaceful routine. A truce that included Isobel in his bed, where they fucked until neither could move. God, she stripped him of his control, and that both terrified and thrilled him. Intimidated him and freed him.

It was the terror and intimidation that kept his mouth sealed shut when she slipped out of his bed in the dark, early mornings, returning to her room and leaving him alone. She never slept the night through with him. That bothered and relieved him.

Relieved him because the intimacy of sharing a bed smacked of a relationship, a vulnerability he wasn't ready to reveal to her. He'd given that trust to one woman, and she'd screwed him, literally and figuratively.

Bothered him because her sneaking out like he was her dirty secret didn't sit well with him.

"So you're here because you miss me?" he teased, deliberately dismissing his disquieting thoughts.

Helena's smile dimmed just a fraction, taking on a faintly rueful tinge. "Of course I do, darling. We all do. But I have another reason for coming to you. Next week is Thanksgiving. What are your plans?"

He stifled a sigh. Him joining them for the holidays was a tradition. But this year, it wasn't only him.

"I haven't discussed it with Isobel yet. She might want to spend the holiday with her family. And if that's her choice, I can come by the house afterward."

Anger flashed in her eyes, and she thinned her lips. "I see," she finally said. "You have a new family, whose wishes come first."

"Helena—"

"No." She sliced a hand through the air. "I'm glad you said that, it makes my next reason for being here easier to say." Her chin hiked up. "I want a DNA test for Aiden."

Shock whipped through him, and he stiffened under the blow of it. "What?"

"We want a DNA test," she repeated. "Yes, Aiden does resemble Gage, but that's not enough. In order for us to erase any doubt, we need to know he's Gage's son. And that can only be answered with a paternity test." Her features softened, and she settled a hand over his knee, squeezing lightly. "I need this, Darius."

His first reaction had been to flat-out refuse, but then reason crept in. Would having a DNA test done be so wrong? It would cement that Aiden was indeed Gage's son, and once the Wellses had the truth, they could finally lay this issue to rest and move on. He could give them that; he owed them that.

Isobel. He briefly closed his eyes.

Isobel wouldn't agree, just as she hadn't years ago. She would view it as an insult, but if it could facilitate healing... Yes, she would be angry about him going behind her back, but the results...how could she argue with the results when it meant the Wellses laying down their swords and Aiden having all of his family in his life, without doubts?

Meeting Helena's gaze, Darius nodded. "I'll arrange it."

Satisfaction flared in the blue depths. "Thank you, Darius. Another thing? Let's keep this between us for now. Baron doesn't know I'm here, and I don't want this impacting his health. So when you have the results, please contact me."

Unease over the further request for secrecy ate at him, but again he nodded.

"I should go," she murmured, standing. But then she hesitated, staring at him. "You're like a son to me, Darius," she said, steel entering her tone, belying the sentimental words. "And I love you, which is why I believe I have the right to say this to you. Gage fell for Isobel's sweet, innocent act, and look how he ended up. Betrayed, broken, angry...and dead. I would want to die myself if she did the same to you. So please,

Darius, be careful, and don't succumb to the same game. Just…be aware, because Isobel is not who she pretends to be."

Darius didn't stop Helena as she left his office. After the door shut with a soft click, he slowly rose, her words of caution whirling inside his head.

Please be careful, and don't succumb to the same game… Isobel is not who she pretends to be.

He shook his head as if he could dislodge them, but they clung to him like burrs. Anger continued to dog him the rest of the day, nipping at him. He'd refused to play the fool again. But with Helena's warning ringing in his head, he couldn't shake the thought that her words had come a little too late.

Darius shoved open the front door to his house, the usual peace it brought him as he stepped into the foyer absent. His day had gone from hell to shit. By the time he left, hours earlier than his usual time, his employees had probably tossed confetti in the air as the elevator doors closed behind him. And if he were honest, he wouldn't blame them. His mood had been dark ever since Helena's impromptu visit, and even now, shutting the door behind him, he couldn't shake it loose.

He needed a drink. And time alone. Then, he mused, heading toward his study, he'd go find Aiden and Isobel. It wouldn't be fair to inflict his attitude on them.

What the fuck?

He slammed to a halt in the doorway of the study, shock winding through him like frigid sleet.

Gage fell for her sweet, innocent act, and look how he ended up. Betrayed, broken, angry… Please be careful, and don't succumb to the same game... Isobel is not who she pretends to be.

As they had all day, Helena's words tripped through his brain, growing louder and louder with each pass.

Isobel sat on the couch in his study, with her head bent close to the man perched next to her.

On the same couch where she'd straddled him, and he'd pushed into her body for the first time.

Jealousy, ripe and blistering, ripped through him. The power of it rocked him, and it was only the unprecedented intensity that unlocked its grip on him. Dragging in a breath, he forced the destructive emotion under a sheet of ice.

As if she'd heard his deep inhale, her head lifted, and their eyes met.

Surprise rounded her eyes, and an instant later, a smile started to curve her mouth, but that stopped as she scanned Darius's face. It shifted into a frown, before smoothing into a carefully blank expression.

"Darius, I didn't hear you arrive," she finally said, voice neutral as she rose to her feet.

What did that expression hide?

Isobel is not who she pretends to be.

"Obviously," he drawled, then shifted his attention to the tall man who now stood beside her. Handsome, wearing an expensive gray suit and about Darius's age. Green-tinged acid ate at his gut.

Faith used to wait until he'd left for the office, then sneak men into their house. Their bed had been a favorite location for her trysts. She'd gleefully thrown that information at him. Part of her pleasure had been in knowing that, at night, Darius would lie in the same bed where she'd fucked other men.

And here Isobel stood with some stranger. Playing the same game? After all, she hadn't expected him home from work this early. He studied her. Seeking signs of deceit, of guilt, but not expecting to find any. She was more of an expert than that.

"Where's Aiden?" he asked.

Translation: *Where is Aiden while you're down here...entertaining?*

From the narrowing of her eyes, she didn't require a translator. "He's upstairs, taking a nap. Ms. Jacobs is with him," she replied, tone flat. Turning to the man beside her, she waved a hand in Darius's direction. "Ken, let me introduce you to Darius King. Darius, Ken Warren."

"Nice to meet you, Mr. King," the other man greeted, striding forward with his hand outstretched. "Ms. Hughes speaks highly of you."

"Does she now?" he murmured, and after a pause in which he stared down at the extended palm, he clasped it. "A shame I can't say the same."

"Thank you, Ken," Isobel said, walking forward and shooting Darius a look that possessed a wealth of *fuck you*. "I appreciate you coming all the way out here. I bet house calls are rare in your profession."

"Not as much as you'd think." He chuckled. "Call me if you have any questions." Nodding at Darius, he said, "Again, nice to meet you."

She ushered him out of the room, and Darius moved into the study, stalking toward the bar. He poured Scotch into a glass and then downed it, welcoming the burn.

With his back to the door, he didn't see her reenter the room, but he felt it. The air seemed to shift, to shimmer like steam undulating off a hot sidewalk after a summer shower. That's how aware he was of her. He could sense the moment she entered a damn room.

Pivoting, he leaned a hip against the edge of the bar, taking another sip of the alcohol as he watched her approach.

"You are an asshole," she hissed, the anger she'd concealed in front of Ken Warren now on vivid display. It flushed her cheeks and glittered in her eyes like stars as she stalked to within inches of him. "I don't know what happened at the office, but you had no right to be so rude to him and to me. What the hell is wrong with you?"

"What's wrong is that I came home to find a strange man in my house, with my soon-to-be-wife, sitting on the same couch where I've fucked her," he drawled. "So forgive me if my mood is a little…off."

"I knew it," she murmured. For a long moment, she studied him as if trying to decipher a code that baffled her. "I *knew it*," she repeated, a soft scoff accompanying it. "I took one look at your face and could've written a transcript of your thoughts. *I caught her with her latest screw. In* my *house. I knew she wouldn't be able to keep her legs closed for long.* Am I close?" The sound that escaped her lips was a perversion of laughter. "You're so predictable, Darius."

She whipped around and stalked to the couch. Leaning over the arm, she picked up a small, dark brown box and marched back to him.

"Here." She thrust the case at him. "Ken is the husband of one of the moms I met at the Mommy Center Aiden and I go to on Tuesdays and Thursdays. When I found out he was a jeweler, I thought of you. Take it," she ordered, shoving the item at him again.

A slick, oily stain spread across his chest and crept up his throat as he accepted the box. As soon as he did, she moved backward, inserting space between them that yawned as wide as a chasm.

He clenched his jaw, locking down the need to reach for her and pull her back across that space. Instead he shifted his attention to the case. It sat in the middle of his palm. A jeweler. She'd said Ken Warren was a jeweler.

With his heart thudding dully against his sternum, he pried the top off. And it ceased beating at all as he stared down at the gold pocket watch nestled on a bed of black silk. A detailed rendering of a lion was etched on the face of it, the amber jewels of its eyes gleaming, its mouth stretched wide as if in midroar. Awed, he stroked a fingertip over the excellent craftsmanship and artistry.

It was…beautiful.

"When I saw it, I knew it was yours. A lion for both your first and last names. *Darius*, which means royalty, and then *King*," she murmured. "I thought it would be a perfect addition to your and your father's collection."

He tore his gaze away from the magnificent piece and met her eyes. Awe, gratefulness, regret and sadness—they all coalesced into a jumbled, thick mass that lodged in his throat, choking him.

She'd bought a gift for him, had chosen it with care and thoughtfulness.

And he'd returned that kindness with suspicion and scorn.

He'd fucked up.

"Thank you," he rasped. "Isobel…"

"Save it." She took another step back. "You're sorry now. Until the next time when I fail some test or, worse, pass it. Is this what I have to look forward to for however long this *agreement* lasts? I spent two years walking on eggshells. At least give me a handbook, Darius. Tell me now so I can avoid the condescending comments, the scathing glares and condemning silences."

"I'm sorry," he said, trying again to apologize. "You didn't deserve that."

"I know I didn't," she snapped. "But the truth is, you can say those two words, but you obviously believed I did. You convicted me without even offering me the benefit of the doubt. Of course, me sitting with a man couldn't be innocent. Not Isobel 'The Gold Digger' Hughes."

Suddenly the anger leaked from her face, from her body. Her shoulders sagged, and a heavy sadness shadowed her eyes. The sight of it squeezed his heart so hard, an ache bloomed across his chest.

"I just wanted to do something nice for you. To show you how much I appreciate all you've done for Aiden, show you all that you…" She trailed off, ducking her head briefly before lifting it. *Finish it*, he silently yelled. *Finish that sentence.* "I'm fighting a losing battle here, and Darius, I'm tired. Tired of trying to change your mind, of proving myself, of paying the price for a sin I never committed. I'm…" She shrugged, lifting her hands with the palms up in surrender. "Tired."

Slowly, she turned and headed toward the study entrance.

"Isobel," he called after her, her name scoring his throat. But she didn't pause, and desperation scratched him bloody, demanding he *stop her*. Give her the truth he'd kept from her. Pride and honesty waged a battle inside him. Self-preservation and vulnerability. "Stop. Please."

She'd jerked to a halt at his "please." Probably because she'd never heard him utter the word before. Still, her back remained to him, as if he had mere seconds before she bolted again.

Shoving a hand through his hair, he thrust the other in his pants pocket and paced to one of the walls of windows. "I don't remember you at the wedding, but you might recall that I married. Her name was Faith." He emitted a soft scoff. "When we first met, her name had seemed like a sign. Like fate or God sending me a message that she was the one. I'd wanted what my parents had, and I thought I'd found that with Faith.

"She'd reminded me of my mother. Not just beautiful and elegant, but full of life and laughter. Faith had a way of dragging a smile out of you even when everything had gone to hell. Dad used to call it the ability to 'charm the birds right out of the trees.'" In spite of the ugly tale he was about to divulge, a faint smile quirked a corner of his mouth. He couldn't count how many times his father had lovingly said that about his mom, usually after she'd used said charm to finagle something out of him. "Faith and I only dated several months, but the Wellses loved and approved of her, and I believed we would have a long, happy marriage... I was wrong."

Isobel's scent, delicate and feminine, drifted to him seconds before she appeared at his side. She didn't touch him but stood close enough that he could feel her.

"Within six months, I realized I'd made a mistake. The affectionate, witty woman I'd known turned catty, cold and spiteful. Especially if I said no to something she wanted. I discovered a little too late that she didn't love me as much as she loved what I could afford to give her. As much as the lifestyle I offered her." He clenched his jaw. The despair, disillusion and anger that had been his faithful companions back then returned, reminding him how foolish he'd been. "But even then, I'd still been determined to salvage our relationship. Hoping she'd change back into the woman I'd married. Then..." He paused, fisting his fingers inside his pants pockets. "Then I came home a day early from a business trip. Since it'd been late, I hadn't called to let her know I was arriving. I walked into our bedroom and found her. And one of my vice presidents. I froze. Stunned. And in so much goddamn pain, I couldn't breathe. By this time, our marriage was hanging on by a thread, but I was still hopeful. Of all the things she could do—had done—I hadn't expected this betrayal. Didn't think she was capable of it."

Again, he paused, his chest constricting as the memories of that night bombarded him, the utter helplessness and grief that had grounded his feet in that bedroom doorway, rendering him an unwilling voyeur to his wife's infidelity.

A delicate hand slipped into his pants pocket and closed over his fist. He tore his sightless gaze away from the window and glanced at Isobel. She didn't face him, keeping her own stare focused ahead, but the late afternoon light reflected off the shiny track of tears sliding down her cheek.

She was crying.

For him.

Clearing his throat, he looked away, that tightness in his chest now a noose around his neck. He forced himself to continue. To lance the wound.

"I filed for divorce the next morning. We'd only been married a year and a half. A year and a half," he repeated. "I felt like a failure. Still do. I was so ashamed, I hid the truth from Baron, Helena and Gabriella. They still don't know why Faith and I divorced."

His admission echoed inside him like a clanging church bell. He'd never voiced those words aloud. Didn't want to admit that his disastrous marriage continued to affect his life years after it had ended. Thank God he hadn't been so lovestruck that he'd forgone a prenup. He wouldn't have put it past Faith to try to clean him out just from spitefulness.

"Why?" Isobel asked, her voice gentle but strong. "You made a mistake. It doesn't make you a failure. Just human. Like all of us mortals. Wanting to believe in a person, wanting to believe in love, doesn't reflect on your intelligence or lack of it. It speaks volumes about your integrity, your honor, your heart. Just because that other person didn't have the character or dignity to respect their vows, to cherish and protect your heart, doesn't mean you're a fool or a disappointment. She didn't respect your relationship, you or herself. That's her sin, not yours. But, Darius," she turned to him, and he shifted his gaze back to her. "It's your decision, but you should forgive her, let it go."

He frowned. "I have forgiven her, and obviously I've moved on. I'm not pining for her." Hell no. That bridge had not only been burned, but the ashes spread.

"No, you haven't," she objected. "Forgiveness isn't just about cutting someone off or entering new relationships. It's deciding not to allow that person or that experience to shape your decisions, your life. It's not giving that person power over you even though they're long gone. And when your choices, your views, are influenced by past hurt, then those betrayals do have power over you." Her mouth twisted into a rueful smile. "I should know. I've fought this battle for two years. But understand—this is what I've had to come to grips with—forgiveness isn't saying what that person did was okay. It's just choosing to no longer let that poison kill you."

"Who have you forgiven, Isobel?" he murmured, but his mind already whispered the answer to him.

She didn't immediately answer, but seconds later she sighed and dipped her head in a small nod.

"Every day when I get up, I make the choice to forgive Gage. It's a daily process of letting go of the pain and anger. Especially since he's Aiden's father. I refuse to taint that for him with my own bitterness. And I refuse to be held hostage by it. Gage isn't here any longer. I'm never going to hear 'I'm sorry' from him. And even though Faith is very much alive, you most likely won't receive an apology from her either. So, what do we do? Forgive ourselves for the guilt and blame that isn't ours. But as long as we hold on to the past, we can never grab ahold of the future and all it has for us."

He stood still, her words sowing into his mind, his

heart. By her definition, had he really released Faith, the past? He bowed his head, pinching the bridge of his nose.

"What about wisdom, Isobel? Only a fool or a masochist doesn't learn from his mistakes."

She slowly removed her hand from his and stepped back. He checked the urge to reach for her, to claim her touch again.

"Wisdom is applying those lessons, Darius. It isn't judging someone based on your own experiences. It isn't allowing the past to blind you to the reality even when it's staring you in the face." She lifted her hands, palms up. "Today you walked in here and jumped to the conclusion that I was sneaking behind your back with another man. That I had brought him into your home like your ex-wife. It's easier for you to be suspicious than to believe that maybe I'm not like her."

She inhaled and tilted her chin up, with defiance in the gesture, in the drawing back of her shoulders.

"I did not cheat on Gage, Darius. I never betrayed him—he betrayed me. He was the cheater, not me."

Before he could object, question her accusation or deny it—maybe all three—she pivoted on her heel and exited the room. Minutes passed, and when she returned, he remained standing where she'd left him, too stunned by her revelation. *Gage cheated? No. Impossible.* He'd loved Isobel. Hell, sometimes it'd seemed he'd loved her to the point of obsession. He couldn't, *wouldn't have*, taken another woman to his bed. Not the man Darius had known.

Did you really know him?

The insidious question crept into his brain, leaving behind an oily trail of dread and doubt.

"Here." She extended a cell phone to him. He reached for it before his brain sent the message to ask why. "It's my old phone, the one I had when I was married to Gage. I saved it for the pictures I'd taken of him for Aiden when he was older. But I want you to read this."

She pressed the screen and a stream of text messages filled the screen.

From Gage.

He tore his attention away from her solemn face to the phone.

I should divorce you. Where would you be then? Back in that dirty hole I found you. It's where you belong.

You'll never find someone better than me. No one would want you, anyway. I don't even know why I bother with you either. You're not good enough for me.

Don't bother waiting up for me. I'm fucking her tonight.

And below that message, a picture of Gage maliciously smiling into the camera, his arm wrapped around a woman.

Bile raced up from the pit of Darius's stomach, scorching a path to his throat. He choked on it, and on the rage surging through him like a tidal wave. Swamping him. Dragging him under.

She hadn't deserved the kind of malevolent vitriol contained in those texts. No woman did. And that his friend, one of the most honorable, kindest men he'd ever known, had sent them to his *wife*… The woman he'd proclaimed to love beyond reason…

Had Gage been that great of an actor? And to what end? The questions plagued him, drumming against his skull, not letting up. Because he needed answers. He needed to understand. His heart yearned to reject the idea that Gage could've been that spiteful… an abuser.

"Tell me," he rasped. "All of it."

After a long moment, her soft voice reached him.

"I was twenty when we met. And he was handsome, charming, funny and, yes, wealthy. I didn't—still don't—understand why he chose me. And I didn't care—I loved him. Becoming pregnant so soon after we married was a little scary, but seemed right. He'd started becoming a little moody and irritable a few months after we married, but soon after the baby arrived, and I refused the paternity test, he completely changed. I didn't understand then, but now I see he hated being poor, regretted being cut off from his family and blamed me for it. Resented me. That's when the isolation started. He needed to know where I went, who I was with. He decided my every move, from who I could spend time with to what I wore. Since I just wanted to please him, I gave in. But then I couldn't see my family because they were a 'bad influence.' And if I spoke to a man for too long, or smiled at one, I was cheating. The little money I earned, and the money his parents started giving him, he controlled that, as well. If I needed anything—from personal hygiene items to new clothes for Aiden—he bought them, because he couldn't trust me to spend wisely. I was trapped. A prisoner. And my husband was my warden."

"Why did you stay?" Darius asked, desperate to

understand. To punch something. "Why didn't you leave?"

"Love," she murmured. "At first, love kept me there. I foolishly believed it could conquer all. But then that fairy tale ended, and fear and insecurity stepped in. I'd left school, had no degree. A minimum wage job. At that point, the unknown seemed far more terrifying than the known. And I never stopped believing that if I learned the proper way to act and speak, if I could get Gage to love me again like he used to, everything would be okay. His family would love and accept me, too." She shook her head, letting loose a hollow chuckle that bottomed out Darius's stomach. "And I wanted our child to have a two-parent home like I didn't. So I stayed longer than I should've. The night I told Gage I wanted a divorce is the night he…"

Grief tore through Darius. And, still clutching the phone with its offensive messages, he turned and stalked away from Isobel. His thigh clipped the edge of his desk, and he slammed his palms on the top of it, leaning all of his weight on his arms.

It was a death.

A death of his belief in a man he'd called brother. The demise of his view of him. Whom had Darius been defending all these years? How could he still love Gage…?

Her arms slid around him. Her cheek pressed to his back.

The comfort—the selfless comfort—nearly buckled his knees.

"It's okay to love him," she murmured, damn near reading his mind. Her voice vibrated through him, and he shivered in her embrace. "A part of me still does. For the memory of the man I initially fell in love with, for the father of my son. With time and distance, and loving Aiden, who is a part of Gage, I can't hate him. He was a man with faults, with issues and weaknesses. But he was also everything you remember him to be. A great, loyal friend. A loving son. A brother who would literally lay down his life for you. You can love those parts of him and dislike the parts that made him a horrible husband. There's no guilt or betrayal in that, Darius."

He pushed off the desk, spun around and grabbed her close, closing his arms around her. Crushing her to him. As if she were his lifeline. His absolution.

She clung to him just as tightly.

"I have a confession," she whispered against his chest.

"Yes?" he asked, the word scratching his raw throat.

"I never betrayed Gage, but…" She hesitated, tilted her head back. He lifted his gaze, meeting hers. She studied him for several long moments before dipping her head in a slight nod. "I noticed you, admired you. Somehow I instinctively knew you would never mistreat a woman. You were too honorable. And you've always been beautiful to me."

The soft admission reverberated in the room like a shout. He stared into her eyes—eyes that had captured his imagination and attention from the first glance.

"Sweetheart," he growled. It was all he got out before he cupped her face and crashed his mouth to hers. He couldn't stop, couldn't rein himself in if he'd wanted to.

And he didn't want to.

The avalanche of emotion that had eddied inside

him burst free in a storm of passion and need so sharp, so hungry that fighting it would've been futile.

Her fingers curled around his wrists, holding on to him. Maybe designating him as her anchor as she, too, dove into the tempest. She leaned her head back, angled it and opened wider for him. Granting him permission to conquer, to claim more. More. Always more with her.

He dragged his mouth from hers, and turning with Isobel clasped to him, swiped an arm across the surface of his desk, sending books, folders, the cell and his home phone tumbling to the floor. After grabbing her by the waist, he hiked her onto the desk, following her down. Covering her. Impatient, with a desperation he didn't want to acknowledge racing through him, he jerked her pants and underwear down her legs, baring her. Her trembling fingers already attacked his pants, undoing them while he removed his wallet and jerked a condom free. Within seconds, he sheathed himself and thrust inside her. His groan and her cry mingled, entwined together as tightly as their bodies.

And as they lost themselves in each other, as he buried himself in her over and over, he forgot about everything but the pleasure of this woman.

Of Isobel.

And for those moments, it was enough.

Chapter 13

Isobel leaned closer to the vanity mirror, applying mascara to her lashes. When the doorbell rang, echoing through the house, she almost stabbed herself in the eye.

"Damn," she whispered, replacing the makeup wand.

It was Thanksgiving Day. Who could that possibly be?

She glanced at the clock on her dresser. One o'clock. A loud holiday meal with her mother, brothers and plethora of aunts, uncles and cousins was set for three o'clock at her mom's house. They were supposed to leave as soon as Darius returned from the store after a last-minute errand. For someone to show up uninvited on their doorstep on a holiday, it must be important.

Quickly rushing down the hall to Aiden's room,

she leaned inside the doorway. "Ms. Jacobs, I'm going to get the door. But we should be ready to go in just a few."

The older woman smiled from where she played blocks with Aiden. "We're fine until then, Ms. Hughes."

"Isobel," she corrected, but the nanny just smiled and returned her attention to Aiden. Shaking her head and chuckling, she descended the steps. She'd been waging the war of getting Ms. Jacobs to call her Isobel, but to no avail. In the short time she'd known the woman, they had grown fond of each other. So much so, Ms. Jacobs was spending Thanksgiving with them since she didn't have children of her own.

It'd been Darius who had thought of that kindness. Darius.

A spiral of warmth swirled through Isobel's chest, landing in her belly.

Ever since that evening a week ago, when he'd come home to find her with Ken and heard her full admission about Gage, a…connection had forged between them. One that, while tenuous, had her heart trembling with a cautious hope that what had started out as a marriage bargain between them might evolve into a real relationship. A relationship based on respect, admiration…trust.

Love.

The nervous snarls in her stomach loosened, bursting into flutters.

There'd been a time—not too long ago—when she wouldn't have believed herself capable of falling for another person. She hadn't thought she could ever take the risk of trusting someone with not just her heart, but with Aiden's.

But here, only weeks later, she stood on the crumbling precipice of a plunge into something powerful and dangerous—love.

And it was a beautiful, strong, loyal and fierce man who had her heart whispering with the need to take the fall.

She was afraid. Even as a fragile hope beat its wings inside her, she was *afraid*.

She reached the foyer and glanced out the window next to the door. Shock rocked through her.

Helena and Gabriella.

What…?

As if on autopilot, Isobel unlocked the door and opened it.

"Hello," she greeted, surprised at the calmness in her voice. "Please come in." As they passed by her and entered the house, she shut the door behind them. "Darius isn't here at the moment…"

"That's fine. We can wait," Helena said, turning to face Isobel with a coldly polite smile. "We apologize for showing up unannounced, but he told us you were having Thanksgiving dinner with your family. We wanted to catch him before you left."

Unease sidled through her veins, but she pasted a smile on her lips and waved a hand toward the living room. "He should be back shortly, if you'd like to wait for him in here."

Part of her wanted to run up the stairs and let Darius deal with his visitors when he returned, but at some point she had to become accustomed to being around them without Darius as a buffer. She could handle a few minutes.

"You and Darius seem to be getting along well," Helena commented as she moved into the room and settled on the couch.

Isobel nodded, stalling as she considered how to answer. As if a physical trap waited to be sprung at the end of her reply. "Darius is a kind man."

Gabriella strode over to the mantel and studied the array of pictures there. "Yes, he is. It's both a blessing and a curse," she said. "Have you two set a wedding date yet?"

Unease knotted Isobel's stomach, at both the cryptic comment and the switch in topic. "Not a definite date," she replied. But remembering the stipulations Darius had set in their contract, she added, "Sometime in January, I believe."

"You believe," Helena echoed, and Isobel couldn't miss the sneer in her words as her gaze flicked to Isobel's left hand. "No ring yet, I see. Doesn't that tell you something, Isobel?"

"No," Isobel murmured, sensing the shift in the other woman's demeanor and steeling herself. "But I suppose you have an idea about that."

"He hasn't set a wedding date and hasn't even bothered buying you a ring." Helena cocked her head, her steady contemplation condescending, pitying. "What you said earlier is very true. Darius is a good man. The kind who would sacrifice his own happiness for those he loves. Yet he's obviously reluctant to shackle himself to you. A man who is looking forward to marriage publicly claims his fiancée."

"I'm afraid she's correct, Isobel," Gabriella agreed,

strolling the few feet to stand next to the couch her mother perched on.

A smirk curved the younger woman's lips, and a sinking, dread-filled pit yawned wide in Isobel's chest. Was insulting her the purpose behind their visit? Or just a bonus since Darius wasn't home yet? She glanced toward the bottom of the staircase. *Please, God, let Ms. Jacobs keep Aiden upstairs.*

Briefly, she considered exiting the room. But that smacked too much of running, and she'd quit doing that when she returned to Chicago.

"You don't know anything about my relationship with Darius," she said, tone cool. "But why don't you go ahead and have your say so we can get all this out in the open? That way we no longer have to indulge in this pretense. You don't want me with Darius."

Helena's lips firmed into a flat, ugly line, anger glittering in her eyes. "I thought we were rid of you for good. But you found a way to sneak back in, didn't you? It wasn't enough that you used my son and took him away from us, but now you've latched onto my other son. And if we don't want to lose him or our grandson, we have to deal with *you*," she spat out.

"I would never come between you and Darius," Isobel objected.

"As if you could," Gabriella snapped. "We have a real relationship. We love each other. You don't know anything about that."

Dragging in a breath and struggling to contain her temper in the face of their venom, Isobel straightened her shoulders and tipped up her chin.

"As I was saying," Isobel gritted out. "I would never come between you and Darius. His relationship with you is yours. And if it's as strong as you say, then there's nothing I could do to harm it," she pointed out. Ignoring Helena's outraged gasp, Isobel continued, "But while you might revise history with Darius, don't look me in the eye and speak it to me. We both know I've never tried to keep you from your grandson. You were the ones who didn't believe he was a prestigious *Wells*." She uttered that name as if it were sour. "You decided he wasn't worthy of your time and attention. Your love. As for me, I don't need your approval or acceptance. I don't even want it. But now, for some reason, you've changed your mind, and I won't deprive Aiden of knowing his father's family. But if you believe for one second that I'll let you twist and poison him, then you're absolutely correct. You won't see him."

I won't allow you to turn him into his father.

"Twist him? Poison him?" Gabriella bit, her lips curling in a snarl. "That is rich coming from you of all people. You, a gold-digging wh—"

"What's going on here?"

All of them turned toward the living room entrance at the sound of Darius's voice. A steadily darkening frown creased his brow as he scanned Isobel's features before moving to Helena and Gabriella.

Relief coursed through her, but she locked her knees, refusing to betray any sign of weakness in front of the two women.

"Helena? Gabriella?" he pressed. "What are you doing here?"

Isobel desperately needed to retreat and regroup. Shore up her battered shields.

"They came by to see you. I'm just going to check

on Aiden. I'll be right back." Forcing a smile that felt fake and brittle on her lips, she left without a backward glance at Helena and Gabriella.

"Isobel," Darius murmured, catching her arm in a gentle grasp as she passed him. "Sweetheart…"

"No, Darius," she said, slipping free of his hold. "Just give me a minute."

She left the room and prayed that when she returned, the two women he considered a surrogate mother and sister were gone. If not, she might not be responsible for her actions.

Chapter 14

"What happened?" Darius demanded as soon as Isobel disappeared from sight. "And can one of you explain to me why I received a phone call from my nanny to return home as soon as possible because two women were attacking Isobel?"

Fury simmered beneath his skin. They both stared at him, their faces set in identical mutinous lines. Helena rose from the couch, turning fully to face him.

"Helena? Gabriella?" He strode farther into the room, halting across from them. "What. Happened? And don't tell me 'nothing' or 'everything is fine,' because both would be lies."

He'd glimpsed Isobel's face when he'd first entered the room. That cold, shuttered mask had relayed all he needed to know. She only wore that blank expression when hurt or angry. And from the shadows that had swirled in her eyes before she'd pulled away from him, both emotions had applied.

"I love you, Darius," Helena said, approaching him with her hands outstretched toward him. "You know I do. But how much longer is this supposed to go on? How much longer are we supposed to pretend that that...*woman* is welcome in our family?"

"Helena," he warned, his muscles tensing when she clutched his forearms.

He'd never pulled away from her touch before, but with those vicious words ringing in the room—no matter the pain they originated from—he couldn't take it. He stepped back, her arms dropping away. Hurt flashed across her face, her lips parting in surprise.

"Darius," Gabriella murmured, glancing at her mother, then back at him. A plea filled her gaze. "That's why we came here today. To tell you that we know you went through this farce of a relationship so we could have Aiden in our lives. You've sacrificed for us, but you don't have to anymore. Mother told me about the DNA test. And now that we have the results back—"

He slashed his hand through the air, dread spiking in his chest. "Did you tell Isobel about the DNA test?" he growled. Driving his fingers through his hair, he glanced away from the women. His motives—bringing closure to the family—had been pure, but Isobel would see it as a betrayal. He needed to talk to her first, to explain. "Gabriella, did you say anything to Isobel about the test?"

"No, I didn't say anything to your precious Isobel," she snapped, whipping around and pacing away from him. "But you should know that we've been talking and have come to some decisions."

The unease that had coiled inside him slowly unfurled. "What are you talking about?"

For a heartbeat, Helena and Gabriella didn't respond, just stared at him. The tension thickened until it seemed to suck all the air out of the room.

"Answer me," he grated out.

"Now that we know for certain that Aiden is Gage's son, we intend to go forward with the suit for sole custody," Helena announced. "We've already contacted our attorney."

"You. Did. Not," he snarled. Betrayal, rage and despair churned in his chest, and he fought not to hurl curses and accusations that would irrevocably damage his relationships with these people. "That wasn't my plan or my agreement with Isobel. The terms of which I expressly discussed with you."

Helena scoffed, waving a hand. "That was before we knew that Aiden was our grandson. *Ours*," she stressed, pressing a fist to her heart. "Gage would've wanted him raised with us. By *us* and not that...that deceiver, that liar. And no judge on this earth wouldn't see that we're much more fit parents than her."

"Darius, don't you see?" Gabriella implored, moving closer to him. She clutched his upper arm, and he curbed his automatic reaction to shake her off. And that reaction sent a blast of pain through him. "This is for you, too. Now you can break off this joke of an engagement. You did all this for us, and we love you for it. But now, with us suing for custody, you don't have to chain yourself to a woman you hate. We know you might not agree with this, but we believe it is for the best."

"For the best," he repeated. "Do you know all Isobel has been through with her marriage to Gage? He wasn't a loving, faithful husband. He emotionally beat her down, cheated on her. He mentally abused her. Now, after she survived that, you want to rip her child away from her."

"How dare you?" Helena hissed, anger mottling her skin. She advanced on him, eyes narrowed and glittering. "I love you like a son, Darius, but I won't allow you to speak ill of my son in this house. Who told you these lies that you're so willing to swallow? Isobel?" She spit the name, her mouth twisting into an ugly sneer. "So, you believe her over a man who you loved as a brother? Did she warp your mind? Is that it, Darius? Do you think you're in love with her?"

He parted his lips, but no words emerged. His pulse pounded in his ears, and his tongue suddenly seemed too thick for his mouth. Helena's question ricocheted off the walls of his skull.

Do you think you're in love with her? Do you think you're in love with her?

Over and over. *No*, his mind objected. *Not possible.*

He pivoted sharply on his heel and strode to the bank of windows. After Faith, he hadn't believed himself capable of having deep feelings for another woman. Just the idea of opening himself and risking that kind of pain once more... He'd vowed never to make himself vulnerable—*weak*—again. And Isobel...

She had the power to hurt him like Faith never did.

If he gave her the chance, and she betrayed him, she could wreck him.

The knowledge had fear and anger cascading through him. Could he take a chance? Could he crack himself open and lose not just his family—because the Wellses would view him as choosing her as the biggest betrayal—but also risk losing himself?

No.

Coward that he was, no, he couldn't risk it.

"Darius."

He jerked his head up, spinning around.

Isobel stood in the doorway. *How long had she been standing there? How much had she overheard?* He moved towards her, but she shifted backward.

And that one movement supplied the answers.

"Isobel, please let me explain."

She stared at him, numb. The blessed nothingness had assailed her from the moment she'd returned to the living room and overheard his conversation with Helena and Gabriella.

Did you tell Isobel about the DNA test?

We intend to go forth with the suit for sole custody.

No judge on this earth wouldn't see that we're much more fit parents than her.

Do you think you're in love with her?

That awful, damning silence.

The two women had left soon after she'd appeared in the room, but she hadn't moved. Hadn't been able to. And now, as pain invaded her body, she prayed for the return of the numbness.

"Yes," she agreed, voice hoarse. "You're right. Which should we talk about first? The violation of running a DNA test on my son behind my back? Or how *your family* intends to take my son away from me?"

He closed his eyes, and a spasm of emotion passed over his face. But it disappeared in the next instant.

"I'm sorry for not telling you about the DNA test, Isobel," he murmured.

"You're sorry for not telling me, but not for doing it," she clarified. A sarcastic chuckle escaped her. "You promised me we would make decisions regarding Aiden *together*. Without interference from the Wellses. You betrayed my trust."

"I didn't..." He broke off his sentence, briefly glancing away. "Yes, I did break that promise. And I'm sorry," he said, returning his gaze to her. "I am, Isobel. But my motives weren't to hurt or betray you. I thought if Baron, Helena and Gabriella knew for certain that Aiden was their grandson and nephew, he could bring healing to them. To this family. I wanted to give them that. But also, knowing you told the truth about him being Gage's would start to change their view of you, as well. Not only do they need to know their grandson and nephew—they need to begin to know you."

"No, Darius. Now they just think it was luck that Gage fathered him, out of all the other men I supposedly screwed." She shook her head. "But this isn't about them. It's about how you lied to me. It's about how you put them—their feelings, their welfare— above Aiden." *Above me.* "And you handed them cause to take him away from me."

"I won't allow that to happen," he growled, moving toward her, his arms outstretched. As if to touch her.

No. No way could she allow that. Not when she was

so close to crumbling. She shifted backward, steeling herself against the glint of pain in his eyes.

"Agreeing to marry you, to move in here, to put my son under your protection was supposed to stop it from occurring. But it didn't. I still find myself at their mercy. A place I vowed two years ago I would never be again. And all because I trusted you."

"Do you really believe I would throw you to the wolves? That I would abandon you to face this alone? Do you think I'm capable of that?" he demanded, stalking forward, but he drew up several feet shy of her.

"Would you want to? No," she whispered. "But would you do it all the same? Yes. If Baron, Helena and Gabriella made you choose between them and me, I have no illusions about whose side you would come down on. And I'm so tired of waging a losing battle between the past, your mistrust and Gage's family. *Your family*. Because I'll never be considered a member of that perfect unit."

"That's bullshit," he snapped, his features darkening in anger. "We've been building something here. Something good. Our own place, our own family. You can't deny that."

She shook her head once more. Desperately needing space, she backpedaled, then caught herself midstep. She was through running. Through letting others dictate her life, her truth.

"What we've 'been building' was founded on blackmail, lies and mistrust. It'll never be 'something good.'"

Raising her head, she committed every one of his features to memory. Though she might wish she could evict him from her heart, she never would.

That didn't mean she wouldn't try. She had to. For her peace. For her sanity. For her future.

"I love you, Darius," she admitted quietly.

His body stiffened, and lightning flashed in his eyes, brightening them so the gold almost eclipsed the dark brown. "Isobel," he rumbled.

"No." She slammed a hand up, though he hadn't moved toward her. "Let me finish. I didn't think I would ever be able to open my heart to another man. But you did the impossible. You made me trust again. Love again. Made me believe in second chances. And I thank you for that. And I might hate you for that," she whispered. "Because you showed me what happily-ever-after could be, then snatched it from me."

"Isobel," Darius rasped again, erasing the distance between them and cradling her cheek.

And for a moment, she cupped her hand over his, pressing his palm to her face and savoring his touch. But then she dragged his hand away from her.

"Do you love me?" she asked, staring into his eyes. Glimpsing the surprise flicker and then the shadows gather in them.

Darius stepped backward, a dark frown creasing his brow. But he said nothing. And it was all the answer she needed.

"You awakened something in me," she said softly. "Something I wish would fall back asleep, because now that it's alive, I hurt. I...hope. The Isobel from two years ago would believe she could change you, make you accept her. Fight for her, if she just loved you hard enough. That Isobel would be happy with the parts of yourself you were willing to give her. But I'm not that woman anymore. I deserve to be a man's number one and to be loved and cherished and valued and protected. I deserve a man who will love me beyond reason, and though I'm not perfect, he will love me perfectly."

"What you want, I…" he trailed off.

The raw scrape of his voice and the sorrow in his gaze should've been a balm to her battered soul, but it did nothing.

"I'm not telling you this to emotionally blackmail you, Darius. I'm admitting this for *me*, not you. So when I walk out of here, I won't have regrets."

"Walk out of here?" he repeated on a low growl. His arms lifted again, but once more he dropped them, his fingers curling into fists. "We had an agreement. A contract. You can't just break it."

"We've been breaking the contract from the beginning. Becoming lovers. The DNA test. Falling in love with you." The contract was supposed to have been a defense against that. A reminder of who she was marrying and why. But it hadn't shielded her heart, just as Darius hadn't protected her and Aiden. "Do what you feel you need to do regarding the consequences. But I won't remain in this home, in this…arrangement knowing I can't trust you. That I will continue to pay the price for Gage's lies and the Wellses' grudges. I refuse to be someone's emotional and mental punching bag again. And every time you side with Gage's memory and his family, you deliver another blow. No, Aiden and I will be leaving today. But I won't keep him from you. He loves you, and I know you feel the same. We'll set up a schedule after we're settled…"

Her arms tingled with the need to throw themselves around him. Her throat ached with the longing to ask him to say something, to beg her not to go. To declare his love and loyalty.

But nothing came from him.

She straightened her shoulders and inhaled past the pain. Then she turned, exited the room and climbed the stairs. Once she entered her bedroom and shut the door, her back hit the wall and she slowly slid to the floor. The tears she'd been reining in fell unchecked down her cheeks. How long she sat there, quietly sobbing and hugging herself, she didn't know. But during that time, her resolve to do right by Aiden, and by herself, firmed until it resembled a thick, impenetrable wall.

She might be losing Darius, losing the future she'd so foolishly allowed herself to imagine for her and Aiden, but she was gaining more.

Her self-respect.

Her dignity.

Her.

And it was more than enough.

Chapter 15

Darius stared down into the squat glass tumbler and the amber-colored bourbon filling it.

At what point would the alcohol send him tumbling into oblivion, where the memories from Thanksgiving couldn't follow? He'd been seeking the answer to this for four days now. But while he'd been fucked up, that sweet abyss of forgetfulness had eluded him. No matter how many bottles he'd gone through, he could still see Isobel's beautiful face etched with pain and fierce determination as she confessed she loved him—and then left him. Could still hear the catch in her voice as she accused him of betraying her trust. Could still hear the sound of the front door closing behind her and Aiden that afternoon.

Closing his eyes, he raised the glass to his lips and gulped a mouthful of the expensive but completely useless liquid. But he was desperate to not just escape the mental torture of his last, devastating conversation with Isobel, but the terrible, deafening silence of his house. It'd chased him into his study, where he'd shut himself away. But there was no refuge from the emptiness, from the *nothing* that pervaded his home.

I deserve a man who will love me beyond reason, and though I'm not perfect, he will love me perfectly.

If Baron, Helena and Gabriella made you choose between them and me, I have no illusions about whose side you would come down on.

You betrayed my trust.

Do you love me?

Her words haunted him, lacerated him…indicted him.

But goddamn, he'd been crystal clear that he hadn't gone into this arrangement for love. He'd been more than upfront that he'd wanted to save the Wellses and her from an ugly custody battle. To protect Baron from any future health risks that a custody suit could inflict. To provide for Aiden. To unite the boy with his father's family. And everything he'd done—the engagement, the dinner with the Wellses, the DNA test—had been to work toward those ends.

He'd never lied. Never had a secret agenda.

He'd never asked for her love. Her trust.

When you let people in, they leave. He'd learned this lesson over and over again.

Isobel had left him.

Like his parents.

Like Faith.

Like Gage.

Anguish rose, and he bent under it like a tree conceding to the winds of a storm.

She'd begun to hope. Well, so had he.

In this dark, closed-off room, he could admit that to himself. Yes, he'd begun to hope that Isobel and Aiden could be his second chance at a family. But just when he'd had it within his grasp, he'd lost it. Again. Only this time… This time didn't compare to the pain of his marriage ending. As he'd suspected, Isobel had left a gaping, bleeding hole in his world. One that blotted out the past and only left his lonely, aching present.

A knock reverberated on his study door, and Darius jerked his head up. Before he could call out, the door opened, and Baron appeared. Surprise winged through Darius, and he frowned as the older man scanned the room, his gaze finally alighting on Darius behind his desk.

With a small nod, Baron entered, shutting the door behind him. Darius didn't rise from his seat as Baron crossed the room and lowered himself into the armchair in front of the desk.

"Darius," Baron quietly said, studying him. "We've been trying to contact you for the past few days, but you haven't answered or returned any of our calls. We've been worried, son."

The apologies and excuses tap-danced on his tongue, but after taking another sip of bourbon, "Isobel left. Her and Aiden. They left me," came out instead.

Baron grimaced, sympathy flickering in his eyes. "I'm sorry, son. I truly am."

"Really?" Darius demanded, emitting a razor-edged chuckle. "Isn't this what the plan was from the moment I announced my intentions to marry her? Trick her into complying with my proposal long enough to order a DNA test. And once the results were in, take her son and free me from her conniving clutches?" he drawled. "Well, you can tell Helena and Gabriella it worked. Congratulations."

He tipped his glass toward Baron in a mock salute before downing the remainder of the alcohol.

"I'm sorry we've hurt you, Darius. I truly am," Baron murmured. "Their actions might have been... heavy-handed, but their motives were good."

"Why are you here, Baron?" Darius asked, suddenly so weary he could barely keep his body from slumping in the chair. He didn't have the energy to defend Helena and Gabriella or listen to Baron do it.

Baron heaved a sigh that carried so much weight, Darius's attention sharpened. For the first time since the other man had entered the room, Darius took in the heavier lines that etched his handsome features, noted the tired slope of his shoulders.

Straightening in his chair, Darius battled back a surge of panic. "What's wrong? Are you feeling okay? Is it Helena? Gabrie—"

"No, no, we're fine." Baron waved off his concern with an abrupt shake of his head. "It's nothing like that. But I..." He faltered, rubbing his forehead. "Darius, I..."

"Baron," Darius pressed, leaning forward, bourbon forgotten. Though his initial alarm had receded, concern still clogged his chest. "Tell me why you're here."

"This isn't easy for me to say because I'm afraid to lose you. But..." He briefly closed his eyes, and when he opened them, a plea darkened the brown depths. "I can't keep this secret any longer. Not when the reasons for keeping it are outweighed by the hurt it's inflicting."

The patience required not to grab Baron and shake the story from him taxed his control. Darius curled his fingers around the arm of his chair and waited.

"On Thanksgiving, you told Helena and Gabriella about Gage and Isobel's marriage. That he'd been cruel, abusive and faithless. Everything you said..." He dragged in an audible breath. "It was true. All of it. Their marriage was horrible, and Gage's jealousy, insecurity and weakness were to blame."

Shock slammed into Darius with an icy fist, rendering him frozen. He stared at Baron, speechless. But his mind whirred with questions.

How do you know? Why didn't you say anything to your wife and daughter?

How could you not say anything to me?

"How?" he rasped. "How do you know?"

Another of those heavy sighs, and Baron turned away, staring out the side window. As if unable to meet Darius's gaze.

"Gage told me," Baron whispered. "The night he died, he told me the truth."

"What?" Darius clenched the arms of his chair tighter. If they snapped off under the pressure, he wouldn't have been surprised.

Baron nodded, still not looking at him. "Yes, he found me in the library that evening and broke down, confessing everything to me. Isobel had demanded a divorce, and he'd been distraught. I'd barely understood him at first. But as he faced losing Isobel and Aiden, he'd come to me, horrified and ashamed."

Baron finally returned his attention to Darius, but

the agony on the older man's face was almost too much to bear.

"My son... He was spoiled. Yes, he had a big heart, but Gage was entitled, and the blame for that rests on Helena's and my shoulders. He'd defied us by marrying Isobel but hadn't been prepared for the separation and disapproval from his family. Hadn't been ready to live on his own without our financial resources. But instead of faulting himself, he blamed Isobel. Yet he loved her and didn't want to let her go. So he'd alienated her from us physically and with his lies of mistreatment and infidelity. He admitted he lied about the cheating, but at some point he'd started to believe his own lies. Became bitter, resentful, jealous and controlling. It transformed him into someone he didn't know, someone he knew I wouldn't be proud of. Who he'd become wasn't the man I'd raised him to be. And I think that's why he confessed to me. His shame and guilt tore at him, and in the end it drove him out into the night, where he crashed his car and died." Baron swallowed, his voice hoarse, and moisture dampening his eyes. "Do I think Gage killed himself that night? No. I don't think it was intentional. But I also believe he was reckless and didn't care. He just wanted the pain to stop."

Air whistled in and out of Darius's rapidly rising and falling chest. A scream scored his throat, but he didn't have enough breath to release it. He squeezed his eyes shut, battling the sting that heralded tears. Tears for Isobel's senseless suffering at her husband's and family's hands. Tears for the man he'd loved and obviously hadn't known as well as he'd thought. Tears for the agony of conscience Gage succumbed to at the end.

"I'm sorry, Darius," Baron continued. "Sorry I lied to you, to Helena and Gabriella. Gage didn't ask me to keep the truth a secret, but I did because I couldn't bear causing them more pain on top of losing him. Even if keeping the secret meant standing by while Isobel was villainized. I made a choice between protecting his memory and protecting her, and now I realize my lie by omission is hurting not just my wife, daughter and Isobel, but *you*, a man I love as a second son. I can't continue to be silent. I can't allow her to be crucified when she's been guilty of nothing but falling in love with my son. Both of my sons."

Trembling, Darius shoved to his feet, his desk chair rolling back across the hardwood floor. He pressed his fists to the desktop, wrestling against the need to lash out, to rail over the injustice and torment they'd all inflicted on Isobel.

Stalking across the room, he tunneled his fingers through his hair, gripping the strands and pulling until tiny pinpricks of pain stung his scalp.

"You're going to tell Helena and Gabriella the truth," he demanded of Baron, who'd also stood, silently watching him.

"Yes," he murmured. "I planned on doing it today, but I felt you deserved to hear it first. Darius." Baron lifted his hands and spread them out in a plea of mercy, of surrender. "I'm so sorry."

"Sorry?" Darius laughed, the sound crackling and brittle with cold fury. "Sorry doesn't give her back the years where she was abandoned, left to raise a child on her own. If you knew Aiden was Gage's, why didn't you help her?"

"Gage said he believed Aiden was his, but I didn't

know for sure. And she'd refused the paternity test, which deepened my doubts. And honestly, I hated her after Gage's death. I wanted her to suffer because I no longer had my son. I didn't want any reminders of him around—and that included her and a baby that might or might not have been Gage's. It was selfish, spiteful. Yes, I know that now, and I don't know if I can forgive myself for it. Gage told me I'd raised him to be a better man. But I don't know if I did."

Darius clenched his jaw, choking on his vitriolic response.

Helena and Gabriella might not have known the truth, but their behavior toward Isobel since she'd re-entered their lives had been spiteful, hurtful. So unlike the gracious, kind, affectionate women he'd known for over a decade.

And he'd excused it.

Which meant he'd condoned it, just as Baron had.

Grief and searing pain shredded him.

He'd told Isobel he would never leave her out to dry. Throw her to the wolves. But he'd done it. He'd broken more than a contract. He'd shattered her trust, his word.

His concern had been about betraying the Wellses, when he'd ended up betraying and tearing apart the family he'd created, the family he'd longed for—with Isobel and Aiden. The roar he'd been trying to dam up rolled out of him on a rough, raw growl. Every moment they'd shared since the night of the blackout bombarded him.

Laughing together in the hallway.

Sharing the stories of his parents' death and Gage in the dark.

Touching her.

Her fiery defiance in her apartment.

Her surrendering to the incredible passion between them.

Her quiet dignity as she confessed about her marriage.

Her resolute pride as she admitted she loved him, but could, and would, live without him.

Jesus.

He slammed a fist against the wall, the impact singing up his arm and reverberating in his chest. He'd marched into her apartment, self-righteous and commanding, accusing her of being deceptive and manipulative, when he'd been guilty of both to maneuver her into doing what he wanted. He'd entered their agreement acting the martyr. When in truth she'd been unjustly persecuted. It'd been he who'd entered their relationship without clean hands or a pure heart.

She was the only one—out of all of them—who could claim both.

And he loved that purity of heart. Loved that spirit and bravery that had looked at all the odds stacked against her and plowed through them one by one. Loved the passion that had stealthily, without his knowledge, thawed and then healed the heart he'd believed frozen beyond redemption.

He loved her.

The admission should've knocked him on his ass. But it didn't. Instead it slid through him, warm and strong, like a spring nourishing a barren field.

He loved her.

Maybe he'd started falling from the moment she'd coaxed him out of his panic attack with talk of movies and Ryan Reynolds. No doubt he'd fought his feelings for her, but if he were brutally honest with himself, the inevitable had occurred when she'd embraced him and assured him his love for his friend—her abusive husband—wasn't wrong.

A weight that had been pressing down on his shoulders lifted, and he could breathe. He could suck in his first lungful of air unencumbered by the past. Turning, he faced Baron. Darius loved him. But if it came down to a choice between him, Helena and Gabrielle, and Isobel and her son—*their son*—then Isobel and Aiden would win every time.

"I'm going to go find my family," Darius said.

His family. Isobel and Aiden.

From the slight flinch of Baron's broad shoulders, the emphasis hadn't been lost on him.

"I don't know what this means with you, Helena and Gabriella in the future. Maybe after you tell them the truth, they can find it in their hearts to forgive Gage and let the past go, including their hate of Isobel. But right now, that's not my issue—it's theirs and yours. If they can't, then we won't be a part of your lives. And that includes Aiden. I won't allow them to poison him, and you can inform them that if you continue in the pursuit of custody, I'll stand beside Isobel and fight you."

Darius pivoted and strode out of the study without a backward glance, steady and determined for the first time since Isobel and Aiden had left.

He had his family to win back.

If they'd have him.

Chapter 16

Isobel pushed open the front entrance to her mother's apartment building, shivering as she stepped out into the cold December air. Her arms tightened around Aiden for a second before she set him on the ground.

"You're okay?" she asked, kneeling next to him and making sure his jacket was zipped to the top. "Warm?"

Aiden nodded as she tugged his hat lower. "See Darry?" he asked, his eyes wide, hopeful.

A dagger of pain slipped between her ribs at his expectant question. Just as it did every time he asked about Darius. Which was at least five times a day since they'd moved out of the house. At least. Aiden missed Darius, and to be honest, so did she. It'd been a long week. One where she forced herself not to dwell on him every minute of the day. She only succeeded a quarter of the time.

She smothered a sigh, shaking her head. "No, baby," she said, crying inside as his little face fell, the sparkle of excitement in his eyes dimming.

He didn't understand that they were no longer living with Darius, that he would no longer be a permanent part of their lives. And it crushed her to hurt and disappoint her son. Darius had called a few times, but as soon as she saw his number, she'd passed the phone to Aiden.

Hearing his voice, talking to him—she wasn't ready for it yet. Didn't believe she would still have the courage and determination to say no if he asked her to return home.

Home.

She'd constantly told Darius his house wasn't hers, but somewhere along the way, she'd started thinking of it as home. And she missed it. Missed Ms. Jacobs.

Missed him.

"See Darry," Aiden whined, tears pooling in his eyes. His bottom lip trembled.

She hugged her son tight, as if she could somehow squeeze his hurt and confusion away. "I know, baby. But right now we're going to see the lights and animals at the zoo, okay?"

She'd kept Aiden—and herself—busy with outings. They'd visited the Children's Museum at Navy Pier, the Christmas tree at Millennium Park and the model trains at Lincoln Park Conservatory. And now they were headed to Zoolights at Lincoln Park Zoo. Yet, during all the trips, she couldn't help but imagine how different they would be if Darius had been by her side. As a family.

Standing, she forced the thoughts away. Yes, she

loved Darius. Maybe she always would. But he didn't return the feeling, and there was no getting past that.

They weren't a family.

"Good," she said, injecting cheer into her voice for Aiden's benefit. "Let's go—"

"Darry!" Aiden's scream burst in the air seconds before he yanked his hand out of hers and took off across the tiny courtyard.

"Aiden!" she yelled, but her footsteps faltered, then jerked to a complete stop as she took in the man stooping low to catch her son and toss him in the air before pulling him close for a hug.

And the love on that face as he cuddled Aiden... It stole what little breath her baby's mad dash away from her hadn't.

Darius.

Oh, God. Darius. *Here.*

Stunned, she watched as he kissed Aiden's cheek, grinning at whatever Aiden chattered about. Joy, sadness and anger filled her, and heat pulsed in her body at the sight of him. The wind flirted with his hair, and her fingers itched to take its place. Hair that just passed the five-o'clock shadow covered his jaw and emphasized the sensual fullness of his mouth. A long black, wool coat covered his powerful body. But she remembered in vivid and devastating detail what was beneath it. She craved the strength of it at night.

Darius shifted his attention away from Aiden and pinned her with that golden gaze. The intensity of it snapped her out of her paralysis. Still, her feet wouldn't move, and she stood, immobile, as he approached her, carrying her son in his arms.

"Isobel," he said, and she worked not to reveal the

shudder that coursed through her at the velvet sound of her name.

"What are you doing here?" she whispered. Damn it. Clearing her throat, she tried again. "What are you doing here, Darius?"

Sighing, he lowered Aiden to the ground, and turning, pointed in the direction of the curb where his town car idled. "Aiden, look who came to see you."

The window lowered, and Ms. Jacobs popped her head out, waving to him. Shrieking, he ran to the car, and the older woman opened the door, scooping him up. In spite of the emotional maelstrom whirling inside her, Isobel smiled. Aiden had asked about her only slightly less than he had asked about Darius.

Rising, Darius slid his hands into his coat pockets. "I hope you don't mind. I didn't want him to overhear our conversation."

"No. He's missed her," she admitted softly. Shifting her gaze from the ecstatic pair back to him, she murmured. "You, too."

Darius nodded, studying her face as if he, too, were cataloging any changes that had taken place in the last week. "You look tired," he observed in a gentle tone.

She hardened her heart against his concern, shielding herself against the tenderness that immediately sprang to life. "What are you doing here, Darius?" she repeated her question.

"To see Aiden. And you," he said, his eyes gleaming. "I've missed you both. I just needed to lay eyes on you." Then he loosed a short bark of laughter that fell somewhere between self-deprecating and rueful. "That's not quite the truth. I came to find you and beg you to come back home. To give me—give us—a second chance."

Beg you to come back home.

The words echoed in her head and her chest, and swirled in her belly. A yearning swelled so high, so strong, that it nearly drowned out the steely resolve to not give in. She wanted to—God, she wanted to just walk into his arms and have him hold her.

But she couldn't live a life without love, acceptance, trust and loyalty.

She refused to settle anymore.

"Darius, we can't," she murmured, but he clasped her hand, and the *goodness* of his touch cut her off. But just as quickly as he'd reached for her, he released her.

"Please, sweetheart. I know I don't have the right—don't deserve the right—to ask you to hear me out. But I am." He paused, as if gathering his thoughts, then continued. "Everything you said to me was true. I betrayed your trust. I betrayed you. Our family. And I do mean *our family*, Isobel. Because that's who you and Aiden are to me. You two are who I look forward to coming home to when I leave the office. And that's who you are for me, Isobel—home. All these years I believed the memories of my time there with my parents made it that. But I forgot the reason I love the house so much is because it means family. It means love. And I didn't realize what was missing until you and Aiden came to live with me. The moment you left, it was empty, a shell. And I need you to come back, to return it to my haven, my sanctuary."

Her heart thudded against her chest, her pulse deafening in her ears. Hope—that stubborn, foolish hope—tried to grow. But she shut it down. Only more pain led down any road hope traveled.

"I can't…" She shook her head. "Darius, I know you love Aiden. And we…we…" God, she couldn't get it out.

"We burned together, Isobel," he supplied, and her breath snagged in her throat. "But that's not all that was between us. Is still between us. Before I knew who you were, I trusted you with things I hadn't spoken to another living soul in years. I didn't need to see your face to tell you were special, loving, kind and compassionate. You didn't change, Isobel. I did. I turned on you. I allowed the past with Faith and Gage to warp what my heart acknowledged all along."

He shifted closer, but still didn't reach for her. But his gaze… It roamed her face, and she shivered as if his fingertips had brushed her skin.

And inside…oh, inside she couldn't battle hope anymore. It broke through her shields and flowed into her chest, filling her.

"I love you, Isobel." He raised his arms, and after a moment's hesitation, he cupped her face between his palms. "I love you," he whispered. "Remember when I told you about my fear of the dark and falling asleep in our burning building?" She nodded, his tender clasp, his soft words rendering her speechless. "I didn't tell you everything. I believe I heard my mother and father shout my name, and that's what woke me up. I know how insane it sounds, but even from where they were, they saved me. And now I think it's not just because they loved me, but because they knew what waited for me. You and Aiden.

"I've waited for you. And I hate that I almost threw

away our future, *us*. Sweetheart," he murmured, sweeping his thumb over her cheekbone. "I promise I'll never place anyone else above you and our son and any more children we have together. But if I've hurt you too badly and you can't give me your heart and trust right now, I understand. Know this—I'll still provide for you and Aiden until I can convince you to forgive me. Because, sweetheart, my heart *is* yours. And I refuse to give up on us ever again. I'll love you perfectly."

He'd gifted her with her own words. She blinked, trying to hold back the tears, but they slipped free. And he pressed his lips to her cheek, kissing them away.

"Talk to me, sweetheart. I need to hear your beautiful voice. You're the only thing keeping me sane," he whispered, his voice carrying her back to that dark hallway where they'd first connected. Where she'd started to fall for him.

Where they'd begun.

"I love you." She circled his wrists and held on to him. "I love you so much."

He crushed his mouth to hers, taking and giving. Savoring and feasting. Loving and worshipping. And she surrendered it all to him, while claiming him.

"Sweetheart," he said against her lips, scattering kisses to her mouth, her jaw, her chin. "Tell me again. Please."

"I love you." Throwing her arms around his neck, she jumped, and he caught her, his hands cradling her thighs. Laughing, she tipped her head back, happiness a bird catching the wind and soaring free. "Now take us home."

Epilogue

Six months later

Isobel groaned through a smile. "This is your fault. And you're going to deal with the fallout."

Beside her, Darius snorted, laughter gathering in his chest and rolling up his throat. "Do you want to go over there and tell him to leave the bouncy castle?"

She scoffed. "And face World War Three *and* Four? God, no." She elbowed him in the side. "I thought we had a conversation about this party, though. Low-key. Nothing too big or grand."

Darius scanned their backyard, where they were holding Aiden's third birthday party. The aforementioned bouncy castle claimed a place of honor right in the middle of the lawn, surrounded by a petting farm, a huge slide, games, face painting, clowns… Their place could double for a carnival.

He shrugged. What could he say? Having missed Aiden's previous two birthdays, he'd really wanted to handle this one. So, he might have gone a little…overboard. Still, as Aiden's high-pitched laughter reached Darius, he had zero regrets.

"Well, he is having a blast," Darius noted, watching their son slide down the "drawbridge" of the castle. "And look on the bright side. At least the party is out here, so in case of a blackout, no one can get trapped inside. With all these animals."

She laughed. "True." Smiling, she slid an arm around his waist and leaned her head against his shoulder. "He'll never forget this. All of his family here to celebrate him." Including Isobel's mother and brothers. They mingled with the children and parents with ease, laughing and talking.

Well, not with Darius's family. Since Baron had confessed the truth to Helena and Gabriella, they'd dropped the custody suit. Discovering Gage's faults hadn't been easy on them, and even now, months later, they still struggled with the magnitude of his lies. And his death. Though he knew Isobel held sympathy for them, relations between her and the Wellses had been put on hold. It would take a while to heal years' worth of pain, and Darius refused to push that reconciliation. Isobel had to move forward when she was ready, and until then Darius had her back. At least she'd allowed Aiden to see them, but only if Darius was there to supervise. And he would never betray her trust again.

It'd been six months since he'd gone to Isobel to plead for her forgiveness and love. Six months since she'd given him both, plus her trust, her heart and her body. She'd given him his family back. That had been the happiest day of his life. And the days that followed were just as wonderful, filled with laughter and joy.

She'd been accepted into the University of Illinois and was majoring in psychology to become a domestic-violence counselor. He wholeheartedly supported her. Isobel was living proof that a person could emerge from a destructive situation stronger, whole, and with the ability to find happiness and peace.

"And just think," Darius said, sliding behind her and settling his hands over the small bump under her tank top. "In another five months, we'll have another one to spoil. A girl. Just imagine the princesses and unicorns that will be prancing around here in another two years."

Isobel groaned, but it ended on a full-out laugh. The joy in it flowed over him.

"Thank you," he murmured, pressing a kiss under her ear. And when she tipped her head back, he placed another kiss on her generous, lovely mouth. "Thank you for filling my life with love and family. I love you."

Her grin softened, and she lifted an arm, cupping the back of his neck. "I love you, too. Always and forever."

"Always and forever."

* * * * *